By Troy Denning

APOCALYPSE

STAR WARS

Fate of the Jedi

APOCALYPSE

TROY DENNING

Ballantine Books • New York

Excerpts from *Star Wars*®: *X-Wing: Mercy Kill* and *Star Wars*®: *Scourge*
copyright © 2012 by Lucasfilm Ltd. & ® or ™ where indicated.
All Rights Reserved. Used Under Authorization.

Published in the United States by Del Rey,
an imprint of The Random House Publishing Group,
a division of Random House, Inc., New York.

DEL REY is a registered trademark and the Del Rey colophon
is a trademark of Random House, Inc.

This book contains excerpts from *Star Wars*®: *X-Wing: Mercy Kill*
by Aaron Allston and *Star Wars*®: *Scourge* by Jeff Grubb.
These excerpts have been set for this edition only and may not
reflect the final content of the forthcoming editions.

ISBN 978-0-345-50922-2
eISBN 978-0-345-51960-3

Printed in the United States of America on acid-free paper

www.starwars.com
www.fateofthejedi.com
www.delreybooks.com
facebook.com/starwarsbooks

3 5 7 9 8 6 4 2

Book design by Elizabeth A. D. Eno

To Sue Rostoni

It's been a joy and a privilege working with you in the *Star Wars* Expanded Universe. Have a blast on your next adventure!

Acknowledgments

Many people contributed to this book in ways large and small. I would like to thank them all, especially the following: Andria Hayday, for her invaluable suggestions and creative support; James Luceno, Leland Chee, Pablo Hidalgo, Keith Clayton, Erich Schoeneweiss, Scott Shannon, Frank Parisi, and Carol Roeder for their fine contributions during our brainstorming sessions; Shelly Shapiro and Sue Rostoni, for *everything,* from their remarkable patience to their insightful markups to their great ideas; Jennifer Heddle, for her contributions to *Apocalypse* and her graceful arrival in the final stages of a long and exciting series; Jason Fry, for our email brainstorming regarding the "Celestial overlap" in our two projects—I really wish that chapter had made it into the *Essential Guide to Warfare*!; my fellow *Fate of the Jedi* writers, Aaron Allston and Christie Golden, for being such a blast to work with; Laura Jorstad, for her usual attention to fine detail; all of the people at Lucasfilm and Del Rey who make writing *Star Wars* so much fun; and, finally, to George Lucas for sharing the galaxy far, far away with us all.

THE **STAR WARS** NOVELS TIMELINE

OLD REPUBLIC
5000–67 YEARS BEFORE
STAR WARS: A New Hope

Lost Tribe of the Sith†
Precipice
Skyborn
Paragon
Savior
Purgatory
Sentinel

3954 *YEARS BEFORE STAR WARS: A New Hope*

The Old Republic: Revan

3650 *YEARS BEFORE STAR WARS: A New Hope*

The Old Republic: Deceived

Lost Tribe of the Sith†
Pantheon
Secrets

Red Harvest

The Old Republic: Fatal Alliance

2975 *YEARS BEFORE STAR WARS: A New Hope*

Lost Tribe of the Sith†
Pandemonium

1032 *YEARS BEFORE STAR WARS: A New Hope*

Knight Errant

Darth Bane: Path of Destruction
Darth Bane: Rule of Two
Darth Bane: Dynasty of Evil

RISE OF THE EMPIRE
67–0 YEARS BEFORE
STAR WARS: A New Hope

67 *YEARS BEFORE STAR WARS: A New Hope*

Darth Plagueis

33 *YEARS BEFORE STAR WARS: A New Hope*

Darth Maul: Saboteur*
Cloak of Deception
Darth Maul: Shadow Hunter

32 *YEARS BEFORE STAR WARS: A New Hope*

> **STAR WARS: EPISODE I**
> **THE PHANTOM MENACE**

Rogue Planet
Outbound Flight
The Approaching Storm

22 *YEARS BEFORE STAR WARS: A New Hope*

> **STAR WARS: EPISODE II**
> **ATTACK OF THE CLONES**

22–19 *YEARS BEFORE STAR WARS: A New Hope*

The Clone Wars
The Clone Wars: Wild Space
The Clone Wars: No Prisoners

Clone Wars Gambit
Stealth
Siege

Republic Commando
Hard Contact
Triple Zero
True Colors
Order 66

Shatterpoint
The Cestus Deception
The Hive*
MedStar I: Battle Surgeons
MedStar II: Jedi Healer
Jedi Trial
Yoda: Dark Rendezvous
Labyrinth of Evil

19 *YEARS BEFORE STAR WARS: A New Hope*

> **STAR WARS: EPISODE III**
> **REVENGE OF THE SITH**

Dark Lord: The Rise of Darth Vader

Imperial Commando
501st

Coruscant Nights
Jedi Twilight
Street of Shadows
Patterns of Force

The Han Solo Trilogy
The Paradise Snare
The Hutt Gambit
Rebel Dawn

The Adventures of Lando Calrissian
The Force Unleashed
The Han Solo Adventures
Death Troopers
The Force Unleashed II

*An eBook novella
**Forthcoming
† Lost Tribe of the Sith: The
  Collected Stories**

REBELLION
0–5 YEARS AFTER
STAR WARS: A New Hope

NEW REPUBLIC
5–25 YEARS AFTER
STAR WARS: A New Hope

The STAR WARS Novels Timeline

NEW JEDI ORDER
25–40 YEARS AFTER
STAR WARS: A New Hope

Boba Fett: A Practical Man*

The New Jedi Order
Vector Prime
Dark Tide I: Onslaught
Dark Tide II: Ruin
Agents of Chaos I: Hero's Trial
Agents of Chaos II: Jedi Eclipse
Balance Point
Recovery*
Edge of Victory I: Conquest
Edge of Victory II: Rebirth
Star by Star
Dark Journey
Enemy Lines I: Rebel Dream
Enemy Lines II: Rebel Stand
Traitor
Destiny's Way
Ylesia*
Force Heretic I: Remnant
Force Heretic II: Refugee
Force Heretic III: Reunion
The Final Prophecy
The Unifying Force

35 *YEARS AFTER STAR WARS: A New Hope*

The Dark Nest Trilogy
The Joiner King
The Unseen Queen
The Swarm War

LEGACY
40+ YEARS AFTER
STAR WARS: A New Hope

Legacy of the Force
Betrayal
Bloodlines
Tempest
Exile
Sacrifice
Inferno
Fury
Revelation
Invincible

Crosscurrent
Riptide

Millennium Falcon

43 *YEARS AFTER STAR WARS: A New Hope*

Fate of the Jedi
Outcast
Omen
Abyss
Backlash
Allies
Vortex
Conviction
Ascension
Apocalypse

X-Wing: Mercy Kill**

*An eBook novella
**Forthcoming

Dramatis Personae

Abeloth; female entity
Allana Solo; child (female human)
Ben Skywalker; Jedi Knight (human male)
C-3PO; protocol droid
Corran Horn; Jedi Master (human male)
Han Solo; captain, *Millennium Falcon* (human male)
Jagged Fel; Head of State, Galactic Empire (human male)
Jaina Solo; Jedi Knight (human female)
Leia Organa Solo; Jedi Knight (human female)
Luke Skywalker; Jedi Grand Master (human male)
R2-D2; astromech droid
Raynar Thul; Jedi Knight (human male)
Saba Sebatyne; Jedi Master (Barabel female)
Tahiri Veila; former Jedi Knight (human female)
Vestara Khai; former Sith apprentice (human female)
Wynn Dorvan; acting Chief of State, Galactic Alliance (human male)

A long time ago in a galaxy far, far away. . . .

Fate of the Jedi

APOCALYPSE

Chapter One

THE STARLINER SWUNG INTO ORBIT AROUND THE PLANET CORUSCANT, and beyond the observation bubble appeared the glittering expanse of a billion golden lights. Through a thousand centuries of strife, those lights had continued to shine. Nothing had dimmed their brilliance—not the Rakatan enslavement, not the tyranny of the Empire, not the chaos of civil war. And they continued to shine now, in this new age of creeping shadow, when enemy impostors ruled the Galactic Alliance and Sith Lords slept in the Jedi Temple itself. But all those gleaming lights made Jaina Solo wonder whether Coruscant's trillion residents actually cared who won the coming war—whether it mattered that they were living under Sith rule, so long as those billion lights continued to shine.

The answer came to her almost instantly, in the form of a dark tinge in the Force that could only mean *Sith*. Jaina shifted her gaze to the interior of the starliner, where a teeming mass of passengers hung floating in their transit harnesses, tethered to the walls of the EconoClass hold. Floating down the central access aisle was a Coruscanti Immigration inspector, his zero-g motility pack emitting small hisses as he twirled in slow-motion cartwheels, demanding identichips and ten-credit "expediting fees." Behind him followed a pair of Bothan escorts, their snouts wrinkling in disdain each time their superior solicited another bribe.

Jaina would have liked to believe the inspector was merely a greedy Sith Saber trying to line his pockets, but she knew better. Vestara Khai, newly defected from the Lost Tribe of Sith, had warned the assault teams to take nothing for granted. In her briefings, Vestara had emphasized that the Sith were not stupid. After insinuating themselves in the Galactic Alliance Senate, they would have moved quickly to take control of the Coruscanti Immigration Service and other key bureaucracies. They would expect the Jedi to be coming, and they would be on the lookout for infiltrators—and petty extortion was an ideal cover for someone trying to identify enemy agents.

The inspector stopped near a pair of human siblings in their late twenties. Both were slender and good-looking, with wary eyes and small expressive mouths. The sister's hair was reddish brown, the brother's merely brown. Their fierce loyalty to each other showed in the way they remained shoulder-to-shoulder when they turned to face the immigration team.

The inspector oriented himself to the same attitude as the siblings—head-down relative to Jaina—and studied the pair without speaking or reaching for their travel documents. The unexpected change of routine sent a cold ripple through Jaina, but she quickly let out a calming breath and forced herself to relax. Allowing her alarm to permeate the Force would only confirm to the inspector that he had found something worth investigating.

The siblings, Jedi Knights Valin and Jysella Horn, continued to hold their documents, doing a good job of looking like ordinary passengers who were a little bit nervous. The inspector narrowed his eyes and waited, giving them a chance to betray themselves by doing something foolish. Jaina would probably never learn exactly what had caught the Sith's attention, but she *did* know that it pointed to the one weakness of the Jedi Masters' attack plan. These Sith were both careful and capable, and they outnumbered the Jedi ten to one.

Finally, the inspector said, "Documents."

Valin and Jysella extended their hands, each holding a small packet containing a fare receipt, a forged identichip, and the expediting fee. The inspector took Jysella's packet, then slid her chip into a handheld reader and compared it with the point of origin listed on the fare receipt.

"You were born on Kalla Seven?" the inspector asked.

"That's right," Jysella lied. "My brother and I both."

The inspector glanced at Valin, then asked him, "Is this a family trip?"

Valin shook his head. "No, my sister and I are traveling alone."

"Is that so?" The questions were the mundane sort that customs officers all over the galaxy used to probe for story discrepancies. But the real test would be taking place on another level, Jaina knew, with the inspector searching their Force auras for the sour hint of a lie. "Then you've come to *visit* family?"

"No," Jysella replied confidently. Like every Jedi on the assault force, she had spent weeks perfecting her ability to lie without betraying herself in the Force. "We're tourists."

"I see." The inspector glanced at her fare receipt again, then spoke to Valin in a casual voice. "Four thousand credits is a lot of money to visit a few monuments and museums. You should have used the HoloNet instead."

"And spend our lives stuck in lower management?" Valin retorted. "I think not."

"If you haven't been to Coruscant," Jysella added, "you go *nowhere* at UHI."

"UHI?" the inspector asked.

"Unlimited Horizons Incorporated," she explained, managing to sound just astonished enough to imply that she thought *everyone* knew what the acronym stood for. "You know—the UHI that controls most of the pallodenite reserves in the Corporate Sector?"

"Ah . . . *that* UHI." The inspector had clearly been put off balance by the tactic—just as Vestara had predicted. The Lost Tribe's greatest weakness lay in their inexperience with the greater galaxy. Vestara had said that the quickest way to put a Lost Tribe impostor on the defensive would be to play on that ignorance. "There are so many."

When the inspector pocketed the bribe and returned Jysella's documents, Jaina finally began to breathe easier. She turned her gaze back to the observation bubble and saw that the *Plain Lady* was crossing the terminator line into Coruscant's daylight side. It would not be long now, she knew, before she was on the surface, fighting to save her homeworld . . . again.

Bazel Warv was "Jade Masher," a celebrated Ramoan float wrestler. Seff Hellin was his human manager, and Vaala Razelle was Seff's Arcona assistant. The three had just arrived from a series of grudge matches in the Bothan system, and they were passing through the Galactic Center Spaceport on their way to a championship match at the Iblis Globe. All Bazel had to do was remember all that—and *believe* it. Belief was the key to defeating a Force-user's ability to detect lies. As long as Bazel truly *felt* like Jade Masher—the newest, greatest rising star in the Pan-Galactic Float Wrestling Syndicate—he would have no trouble fooling Coruscant's new immigration inspectors. His friend Yaqeel Saav'etu had assured him of that.

Bazel glanced across the sea of heads that were in Arrival Lobby 757 and found Yaqeel three lines over. She was already at her inspection station, standing alongside another Bothan Jedi, Yantahar Bwua'tu. Wearing the ash-gray tabards of businessbeings, the two Jedi Knights were at the front of a long line of passengers waiting to be formally admitted onto a planet that had once greeted visitors with open arms. So far, the Coruscanti populace seemed willing to believe that these new precautions were due to an influx of spice lords, and Bazel was glad. There was no need for the citizens of Coruscant to get hurt—not when the Jedi were coming to save them.

But first the Jedi had to get past the inspection stations, and that part of the plan wasn't going well for Yaqeel and Yantahar. Their Duros immigration inspector had been joined by his captain, a narrow-eyed blond whom Bazel judged to be fairly beautiful for a human. She was firing questions at the Bothans faster than they could answer. Meanwhile, a squad of body-armored Galactic Alliance Security guards were standing ready at a nearby security post. Clearly, something was wrong.

Bazel cocked an ear in Yaqeel's direction, consciously tuning out the general din of the lobby and opening himself to the Force. A cool haze of fear permeated the line a few meters behind him, but he had been sensing that off and on since debarking the starliner. There did not seem to be anything menacing in the aura, so he ignored it and focused on the conversation between his friends and the blond immigration captain. His thick hide began to prickle with the bitter margin of a dark side Force aura. Suddenly he understood why his Bothan friends were having trouble.

Sith.

Ignoring the growing press of the crowd behind him, Bazel extended his Force awareness toward the security post. To his relief, he felt only the weak auras of non-Force-sensitive guards. The immigration captain was the only Sith in the area—probably just a Saber, assigned to keep watch on the arrival lobby.

". . . all the way to Coruscant to place an order you could have filled anywhere in the galaxy?" the impostor-captain was asking. "United Hydrologic Institute is hardly the only Tibanna gas supplier in the Mid Rim."

"But it *is* the only one with access to Hutt space," Yantahar replied in his gravelly Bothan voice. "And since Nar Kagga will be the closest inhabited system to our operation, naturally we want to be certain of our supply chain."

"And your operation will be . . . *what*, exactly?" the blond impostor asked.

"A trade secret, I'm afraid." Yaqeel glanced around the inspection station, then added, "There are spies everywhere, Captain. I'm sure you understand."

The Sith's reply grew inaudible when Bazel's human "manager" grabbed the huge Ramoan's wrist and asked, "Masher, you awake up there?" Seff Hellin started forward, trying to pull Bazel into the gap that had opened in the line ahead of them. "We're holding things up."

Bazel paid no attention, for over at the station where his friends were being questioned, the impostor-captain was looking over Yaqeel's shoulder toward the security post. When the Sith gave a slight nod, the guards drew their stubby Merr-Sonn Urban blaster rifles and started toward the inspection station.

Vaala grabbed Bazel by the other wrist. "Mighty Masher, sir." The Arcona's voice was soft and bubbly. "We *really* should keep moving."

Bazel shook his head, then stepped through the cordon-beams that marked the edge of the queuing area. With matching sighs, Seff and Vaala stepped out of line behind him, each pulling a pair of expensive Levalug travel cases that were large enough for Vaala to sleep inside.

"Masher!" Seff growled, putting just enough frustration into his voice to sound like a weary manager at the end of his wits. "There's no time for your temper right now. We have only two hours before the weigh-in."

They wouldn't be making the weigh-in, Bazel rumbled in his native Ramoan. He could speak Basic when necessary, but his large mouth had trouble shaping the common language's delicate vowels and subtle consonants, and he needed to make himself clearly understood. Yaqeel was in trouble, he explained, and he was *not* going to leave until she was safe.

Seff groaned and carefully avoided looking toward Yaqeel and Yantahar. "Drawing attention to ourselves won't help *anyone*, Masher," he said. "Our friends can take care of their own problems."

As Seff spoke, the GAS guards shouldered their blaster rifles and fanned out behind Yaqeel and Yantahar. The two Bothans reluctantly opened their tabards, and the Sith impostor-captain stepped forward to frisk them. Bazel knew the woman wouldn't find a lightsaber or anything else to identify his two friends as Jedi Knights. The assault team's equipment had been shipped ahead, and it would be returned to them later, by an operative from the Club Bwua'tu resistance society. But Bazel also knew the impostor wouldn't be searching his friends at all if she hadn't sensed that something was amiss. He had to find a way to distract her before she confirmed her suspicions . . . a way that wouldn't *seem* like it was a distraction.

Vaala clamped a three-fingered hand around one of Bazel's stubby fingers and quietly bent it back against the joint. "Mighty Masher, sir, we need to focus on our match." She tried to lead him through the cordon-beams back into the processing line. "The, uh, championship is still on, even if a couple of competitors can't make it to the arena."

Balling his hand into a fist to stop Vaala from hurting his finger,

Bazel remained where he was. If a pair of clever Bothans couldn't make it past the immigration inspectors, he replied quietly, there was no reason to think *he* could. Besides, they didn't know how many of their peers had *already* been captured, and if the Sith caught even two teams of infiltrators trying to sneak onto the planet, the Jedi would find themselves attacking without the advantage of surprise, and the battle would grow very big very fast. A lot of innocent civilians would get caught in the crossfire, maybe a *million* of them, and Bazel wasn't going to allow that. He was going to find another way.

Seff exhaled in exasperation. "*What* other way?"

Bazel wasn't sure. Maybe he could go on a rampage. *That* would draw attention away from Yaqeel and Yantahar.

"Don't you think that would be a bit obvious, Mighty Masher, sir?" asked Vaala.

Bazel nodded. Tactical planning wasn't his strong point, he reminded them, but he could tell that Seff and Vaala just wanted to follow orders, and that meant he had to develop his own idea. Maybe he could just bull ahead to the front of the line and try to push past the processing station.

"And get *yourself* arrested instead?" Seff lowered his voice to a whisper. "Do you really think you can outwit an interrogator better than a pair of Bothans?"

Bazel had to admit that was unlikely. What he needed was to present the impostor-captain with another reason for the anxiety she seemed to be sensing in Yaqeel's and Yantahar's Force auras. He thought for a moment, then turned back toward the line he had just left and opened himself to the Force.

Soon he felt the same cool haze of fear he had noticed earlier, a cloud of uncertainty and dismay centered on a small cluster of amphibious Ishi Tib who had clearly not been informed of the new security procedures on Coruscant. The three females were shuffling forward reluctantly, propelled by the pressure of the crowd at their backs, while their male escort was slowly swiveling his eyestalks about, trying to appear casual as he searched for a way to bypass the inspection station. All four carried identical luggage—large kaadu-hide traveling cases with matching satchels slung over their shoulders—and it was obvious by their reluctance to set their baggage on the floor that they were as worried about losing it as they were about being caught with the contents.

Spice.

Bazel stepped back through the cordon-beam. Using the Force, he gently opened a path in front of him, then began to work his way toward the pod of smugglers. Seff and Vaala followed close on his heels, Seff grabbing for his sleeve.

"Masher, the inspection station is the *other* way."

Bazel growled that Seff and Vaala should go on. He had a better plan.

"I'm not sure changing plans is a good idea at the moment," Vaala objected. "The promoters are counting on you."

The promoters were counting on them *all*, Bazel reminded her, and if he saw a way to save Yaqeel and Yantahar, he was going to try it. He came to an Aqualish couple who had taken advantage of the path he had opened to sneak forward. The pair glared at him defiantly, daring him to object. He merely shouldered them aside and stepped over to the Ishi Tib, who instinctively shied away and looked as though they were going to flee.

Bazel distracted them by raising his stubby-fingered hand in a calming gesture, then spoke in Basic, warning them about the security check ahead.

The male curled his eyestalks forward in confusion. *"What?"* he asked. "Check your head?"

"There's a security check ahead," Vaala clarified, stepping to Bazel's side. She glanced up at him, silently signaling her reluctant acceptance of his new plan. Then she turned back to the smugglers and put a little Force energy into her voice. "You should allow our friend to take those packages across for you."

The Ishi Tib let their beaks gape in surprise. "You're with . . . *them?*"

"Did you think *they* would leave a shipment this big to chance?" Seff asked, also joining them. As the line continued to shuffle past, he lowered his voice and pointed at Bazel. "You need to hand over the cases *now.*"

The male's eyestalks quivered slightly, and he turned to his three companions. "We need to hand our cases over." He gave his traveling case to Bazel, then took the satchel off his shoulder and passed it over, as well. *"Now."*

The three females were all too happy to obey, and within moments Bazel had four satchels slung over his head and four heavy cases tucked beneath his arms. Seff watched as the much-relieved Ishi Tib melted back into the processing line, then looked up at Bazel.

"You're sure about this?"

Bazel glanced across the lobby toward Yaqeel and Yantahar. They had already removed their outer tabards, and now they stood with their fingers interlaced behind their heads while the imposter-captain searched their pockets. As soon as the Sith found something to use as an excuse for an arrest, she would turn his friends over to her superiors for "questioning." Yaqeel and Yantahar could withstand any kind of normal interrogation, Bazel knew, but nobody could withstand Force torture. Under that kind of pressure, even Yaqeel would start to reveal important details about the Jedi plan—how Nek and Eramuth Bwua'tu had been running a secret intelligence network, for instance, or how many Jedi Knights had landed on Coruscant. She might even reveal how much the Jedi truly knew about what was happening on the planet.

Bazel nodded. He assured his companions that he would meet them at the original rendezvous point, and then he began to work his way across the lobby toward his friends. Although it was impossible for a being his size to cut across so many processing lines without drawing attention, Bazel attempted to do exactly that, sliding into each line from the side and shooting a menacing glower at anyone who appeared to object. By the time he reached the target line, the impostor-captain and her GA Security guards were frowning in his direction.

Continuing to hold the Ishi Tib's traveling cases beneath his long arms, Bazel looked away and pretended not to notice that he was being watched. Of course, the act didn't fool anyone.

"You there!" the Sith barked. "Step forward."

Bazel continued to look at the ceiling, pretending to study one of the giant sparkle balls that provided illumination for the lobby.

"You, the big green one!" the Sith called again. "Come forward."

Bazel turned his head away, then heard the clatter of two GAS guards shoving through the crowd. He started to move away, the line now parting before him to avoid getting caught in a fight.

A reedy Rodian voice ordered, "Halt!"

"Don't make us use the shock net, big fella," added the second guard, a human male. "There's nowhere for you to go."

Bazel dropped his chin and let out a long, lip-flapping moan, then slowly turned to face the two guards. The human was aiming a big-barreled netgun at him. The Rodian had shouldered his blaster rifle.

"You are talking to *me*?" Bazel asked in his rumbling Basic. "Sorry—I didn't know."

The guards scowled at his thick accent, then the Rodian motioned him toward the inspection station. "Captain Suhale wants to see you."

"You are taking me to the front of the line?" Bazel forced a nervous grin. "Thank you."

He walked a dozen paces to the front of the line, taking pains to be obvious about trying to avoid the eyes of both the Sith female—Captain Suhale—and the two Bothans she was questioning. Suhale let him continue until he was almost past the station, then spoke in a voice so cold it sent a shiver down his back.

"I *will* have them open fire, you know."

Bazel stopped and slowly turned to face her. This close up, the Sith was more intimidating than beautiful, with cold lavender eyes and cheekbones so prominent they looked like stone. He glanced toward Yaqeel and Yantahar, who were doing a good job of concealing any alarm they might be feeling, then looked away so quickly he could almost feel Yaqeel cringing at his ineptitude.

Perfect.

"*Thank* you," Suhale said. "Now, why are you keeping a watch on these two Bothans?"

"*Bothans?*" Bazel made a point of *not* looking in Yaqeel's direction. "I don't know any Bothans."

Suhale's eyes flared. "You're lying," she said. "And I want to know why. Shall we have a look inside those traveling cases you're carrying?"

Bazel shook his head and clamped the cases more tightly beneath his arms.

"I *wasn't* asking." Suhale nodded at one of the guards, and the Rodian pressed a blaster muzzle into the small of Bazel's back. "Place them on the table."

Bazel exhaled loudly, then glanced toward Yaqeel as though looking for permission.

Yaqeel frowned in obvious confusion, then demanded, "Why are you looking at me, Green Thing?"

"I was just wondering the same thing," Suhale replied. She crooked a finger and motioned Bazel forward. "Come now. Matters will go very hard on you if I am forced to tell you again."

Bazel reluctantly placed the traveling cases on the inspection table, then removed the matching shoulder satchels from around his neck and placed them on the table, as well.

"That wasn't so hard, was it?" Suhale motioned to the first case. "Open it."

Bazel stood the case upright, then leaned over the latch . . . and saw the weakness in his plan.

Locks.

Confident that *his* thumbprint wasn't going to deactivate the security mechanism, Bazel thought for a moment, trying to recall his lectures on spice smuggling. Finally, he held his huge thumb above the tiny scanning pad and shrugged.

"I can't."

Suhale scowled. "What do you mean you *can't?*" she demanded. "They're your cases, aren't they?"

Bazel turned to Yaqeel. Her narrowed eyes suggested that she had finally begun to understand his plan, but she merely curled her lip and snarled, "Like I said, why are you looking at *me?*"

"Because the cases are yours, obviously," Suhale said. "Open them. *Now.*"

"*You* open them," Yaqeel retorted. "They're not mine."

"Or mine," Yantahar added before Suhale could look in his direction. "I've never seen them before. Not the big green thing, either."

"Very well," Suhale said, pulling a vibroknife from her equipment belt. "*I'll* open them."

Before she could activate the blade, the original inspector's blue hand shot out to catch her by the wrist. "Captain, you might want to reconsider that."

Suhale shot the Duros a scowl that suggested she was considering using the tool on him instead. "And why would that be, Inspector?"

The Duros seemed genuinely surprised. "Spice smuggling, ma'am. The containers may be rigged to keep the couriers from stealing the cargo."

"Spice?" Suhale turned back to Bazel, the disappointment in her voice a clear suggestion that she was there to catch Jedi, not smugglers. "Is that what you're carrying?"

Bazel dropped his gaze and tipped his head toward Yaqeel. "Ask *her.*"

"You're dead, Ramoan," Yaqeel rasped, taking her cue from Bazel. "You know that, right?"

Suhale smirked, though without enthusiasm. "I do believe that sounds like a *yes.*"

She placed her thumbs over the scanning pads. Bazel felt a slight stirring in the Force, and the latches popped. The Duros inspector cringed openly—then drew a look of open disdain from Suhale.

"There's nothing to be afraid of, Inspector Modt," she said. "It wasn't locked, after all."

The Duros—Inspector Modt—stepped back anyway. Confident that Suhale had used the Force to disable the explosives before she unlocked the case, Bazel remained next to the inspection table as she spread it open. The interior was filled with clothes in the glistening materials favored by sea species—sleeveless zhoopsuits in teal scalara, shimmersilk blouses in every color beneath the water.

Suhale pulled out a short orange dress and held it up between her and Yaqeel, then frowned. "Not really your style."

"Do I *look* Ishi?" Yaqeel replied quickly.

"That's hardly relevant," Modt said.

"Why not?" Suhale asked.

Modt studied her for a long time, his raised chin betraying the contempt he felt for a "superior" who obviously did not have the slightest experience catching smugglers. This ignorance of galactic culture was, Bazel knew, a great part of the reason the Jedi were going to defeat the Lost Tribe.

Finally, Modt said, "It's a common technique." He reached over and pulled the Ishi Tib clothes out of the case. "Smugglers establish inconsistencies so that if they're caught carrying contraband, they can claim the luggage belongs to someone else."

Modt ran his long Duros fingers along the inner edge of the case, then tore the lining away from the top, near the latches, and pulled out a detonator wire. He removed a detonite charge large enough to blast the entire inspection area back to protons and electrons, then used a laser scalpel to carefully cut away the travel case's interior panel. Packed into the space between the panel and the outer shell was a thin layer of blue paste, its surface sparkling with millions of microscopic yellow crystals.

The Duros touched the tip of his smallest finger to the paste, then shuddered and jerked his hand away. *"Neutron pixie,"* he gasped. "Pure!"

"Pure?" Suhale glanced at the other three cases, though she still seemed disappointed at having caught nothing more than a few spice smugglers. "It seems we have made quite a haul, then."

"You could say that," the Duros confirmed. "After it's cut, this much pixie would have to be worth ten, maybe twenty million credits."

"That much?" Suhale grew thoughtful, then said, "You seem to have caught a team of smugglers. Perhaps you should take them into custody."

"My pleasure, Captain," responded the Duros.

He signaled for the GAS squad to make the arrests, then closed the traveling case and motioned a couple of agents forward to seize the evidence. Bazel was not surprised to see Suhale raise a restraining hand.

"The security team is going to have their hands full with the prisoners, I think," she said, eyeing Bazel's mountainous form. "I'll bring the spice along later."

The Duros' eyes narrowed in suspicion, but he did not attempt to object. There was a new order on Coruscant, and it did not like to be questioned.

A pair of GAS agents pulled Bazel's arms behind his back and slapped his wrists into a set of oversized stun cuffs. As they spun him toward their security post, Yaqeel caught his eye, then nodded and flashed a barely perceptible smile. Bazel almost winked. They both knew the hard part was behind them. All they had to do now was escape a security detail, and *that* was not going to be a problem.

*   *   *

The hologram of a human newscaster was floating above the boarding berth, a huge female face with pouty lips, amber eyes, and a radiant complexion. The few passengers still lingering in the area seemed transfixed by her silken voice, which rolled across the platform in a steady, hypnotic patter that Luke Skywalker recognized as a Force technique designed to lull listeners into a receptive state of mind.

"Citizens are advised to avoid confronting members of the Jedi Spice Cartel," the newscaster was saying. Intelligence reports from Eramuth Bwua'tu identified her as Kayala Fei, a Sith Saber who had been planted on the staff at the BAMR News Network. "All members are known to be trained assassins, and most have a documented history of violence."

Fei's image was replaced by one of Luke himself, and her lilting voice continued, "In other news, rumors persist that the overlord of the Jedi Spice Cartel, Luke Skywalker, has returned to Coruscant. Citizens are ordered to report all possible sightings of Skywalker—either to the nearest GAS agent, or through normal emergency channels."

The hologram switched again, this time to an image of a dark-haired male. As handsome as Fei was beautiful, he had a coppery complexion, violet eyes, and a thin face with sharp features.

"GAS Superintendent Vhool continues to investigate the full scope of the Jedi spicerunning operation," Fei's voice said. "Vhool believes the Jedi are running spice to finance their own covert operations, including attempts to subvert the abolitionist organization known as Freedom Flight. Senior officers have suggested that their intention is to destabilize the Galactic Alliance by overthrowing legitimate governments along the entire·galactic rim."

Luke looked away in disgust. The Jedi were no more attempting to subvert Freedom Flight than they were running spice, but BAMR was such a tool of the Sith that it did not even bother to pretend its propaganda had any basis in fact.

On the opposite side of the half-empty platform, Luke saw two members of his infiltration team, Doran Tainer and Seha Dorvald, trying to catch his eye. Dressed in the festive, rumpled clothes of vacationers returning home from a trip packed with more dancing and gambling than relaxation, the two Jedi Knights were almost indistinguishable from the handful of passengers between them and Luke. The one difference was how alert they seemed, how unaffected they were by the hypnotic lies rolling from Kayala Fei's shapely mouth.

Once it grew clear that they had caught Luke's eye, Seha's gaze slid away, as though her attention had shifted. Doran tipped his head toward the back of the platform, where a long pedramp descended from the arrival lobby of the Manarai Heights Spaceport.

For a moment Luke thought they were trying to draw his attention to the tall, broad-shouldered male just stepping onto the top of the pedramp. His face was decorated with a web of dark, awl-shaped lines radiating outward from an angry gaze. At first glance, the fellow appeared to be a member of the Lost Tribe attempting to follow Luke's assault team in full vor'shandi face markings. But as the man descended, it grew apparent that his chiseled features were much too weathered and rugged to be those of a Sith from Kesh, and that the face markings were, in fact, permanent tattoos. Still, there was a darkness in the man's Force aura that Luke found troubling, and he continued to think this was the object of Doran's attention until the tattooed man suddenly met Luke's gaze and nodded toward the other side of the pedramp.

Ascending the up-lane was a squad of GAS guards who had arrived on the last levtram. Their ill-fitting uniforms and bellicose demeanor identified them as new recruits, many of whom Chief of State Kem had rushed into service shortly after assuming office. Their sergeant was at the rear of the squad, his handsome face showing in profile as he scrutinized a teenage couple descending the other side of the pedramp.

Luke saw no reason for the scrutiny, no mistakes in disguise or behavior to suggest that Ben Skywalker and Vestara Khai were anything other than the two young lovers they were clearly becoming. Their arms were entwined around each other's waists so tightly they seemed joined at the hip, and the affection they felt for each other was a bright heat in the Force. Both were dressed in the latest teenage fashion—sparkling capes over black exercise suits. They had even dyed their hair the same shade of yellow, and they wore it in equally outrageous styles, Ben's gelled into double head-fins and Vestara's lacquered into a straight fall that just brushed her shoulders.

And yet the GAS sergeant continued to stare as the pedramp carried them closer, his attention locking on Vestara. She did a good job of pretending to be unnerved by the scrutiny, allowing her gaze to continually drift back in his direction to see if he was still watching her. Then, when they had drawn to within a few meters of each other, she finally turned on him with a withering teenage sneer.

The sergeant merely smirked and held her gaze.

She looked away almost instantly, and Luke cursed beneath his breath. The recognition had been as plain to see in Vestara's shock as it had been in the sergeant's smirk, and that could only mean they knew each other from her time as an apprentice in the Lost Tribe of the Sith.

Luke glanced back toward the tattoo-faced stranger and found the man's gaze resolutely locked on the BAMR news holo above the platform. Whoever he was—perhaps one of Club Bwua'tu's more sinister operatives—he clearly had no wish to involve himself any deeper than he already had.

And that was fine with Luke. He used his eyes to signal Doran and Seha back onto the pedramp, then began to drift toward the rear of the platform, feeling more frustrated by the turn of events than alarmed. All of the other teams had reported a flawless infiltration, and now an unlikely coincidence threatened to eliminate the advantage of surprise. It reminded him of one of Nek Bwua'tu's favorite maxims: *No battle plan survives the first ten minutes of battle.*

As Luke drew near the pedramp, he unleashed a powerful burst of Force energy. The hologram of Kayala Fei dissolved into static, and every comlink on the platform began to chime for attention. In the same instant the Sith sergeant whirled around with narrowed eyes, obviously searching for the source of the tempest he had just felt in the Force. Then the overhead illumination panels began to sizzle out, and the sergeant's gaze found Luke just as the entire waiting area was plunged into darkness.

Luke felt the sergeant—the impostor-sergeant—reaching for him in the Force. He allowed the Sith to grab hold—then *pulled,* jerking the man off the pedramp. The sergeant let out a muffled cry of surprise, then activated his lightsaber in mid-flight.

The lightsaber was a big mistake. Totally unaware of their

sergeant's true identity, one of the GAS recruits cried out in alarm, and another yelled, *"Jedi!"*

Blasterfire began to scream out from the pedramp, turning the darkened platform into a blinding storm of color and flashes. The impostor began to bat bolts back toward the GAS recruits, and shrieking passengers raced about in the dark, slamming into walls and one another.

Then the impostor landed less than two meters away from Luke. He whirled into a shoulder-high slash, simultaneously batting bolts aside and trying to behead Luke. With his own lightsaber still waiting for him at the rendezvous point, Luke could only drop to a crouch and spin into a sweeping heel kick, which the Sith avoided by leaping back out of range.

A gurgle of pain and astonishment suddenly spilled from the sergeant's mouth, then his lightsaber dropped to his side and deactivated. An instant later his body thumped to the platform, and he began to wail in agony.

"Everyone okay?" Vestara asked, using the wailing of her victim to mask her own voice.

"Yep," Ben answered. When he spoke again, his voice was moving closer to Vestara. "Are you?"

"I'm fine." Vestara's voice was warm. "How about you, old man?"

"Not a scratch," Luke said, more surprised at Vestara's quick reaction than he should have been. How many times had she saved his life? And Ben's? "Thanks . . . again."

"My pleasure," Vestara said.

More blasterfire sounded from high up the pedramp, followed by the snap of breaking bones and the thud of bodies being thrown into walls. In the flashing light, Luke caught a glimpse of two athletic shadows—Doran and Seha—leaping over the separation barrier onto the down side of the pedramp.

"A levtram should be arriving any second," Luke said. "You two go ahead and board."

"You coming?" Ben asked out of the darkness.

"Right behind you." Luke reached out in the Force and found the boiling cloud of anguish that was the wounded impostor's Force aura. He hated the idea of killing any enemy in cold blood—even a Sith. But he couldn't take Sith prisoners, and leaving the man alive was not an option. He had recognized Vestara Khai, and if he survived to report that to his superiors, the Lost Tribe would realize that the Jedi had arrived. "I need to take care of something."

A soft female hand touched his arm. "No, you don't," Vestara said. "He's not going to tell anyone what he saw."

The lights of a levtram appeared in the transit lane, and Luke felt Doran and Seha reaching out to him as they scurried past. They were pouring reassurance into the Force, letting him know that the fight had been obscured by darkness. And that meant it would be difficult to confirm that Jedi had been involved. After all, no matter what the GAS recruits thought they had seen, anyone the Sith sent to investigate would quickly realize that the only lightsaber involved belonged to a member of the Lost Tribe.

Luke breathed a sigh of relief, then glanced toward the levtram boarding berth. In the brightening glow of its headlamps, he could already see the silhouettes of dozens of passengers lining up to escape the chaos on the platform. He turned back toward Vestara's voice. The recruits might not have anything useful to tell their superiors, but their wounded leader *would*.

"Go," he ordered her. "I won't be a second."

"No," Vestara replied. "Trust me. He won't live long enough to tell anyone anything."

Something small and glassy shattered on the platform at her feet, and Luke realized why the impostor was still screaming in anguish. Vestara had attacked him with a shikkar, a glass stiletto used by members of the Lost Tribe to express disdain for the victim of the assault. After stabbing an enemy, they would snap off the hilt and leave the blade buried deep in a vital organ, condemning the victim to a death as certain as it was painful.

"I had to use his own shikkar against him, so the High Lords will assume this is a vendetta killing." Vestara tried to pull Luke toward the boarding berth. "But it won't work if we're still standing over the body when the lights come on."

"We won't be." Luke pulled his arm free. As much as he admired Vestara's quick thinking, there was a ruthlessness in her casual willingness to prolong the man's anguish—a *coldness*—that made him wonder if she would ever be capable of becoming a true Jedi Knight. She still didn't seem to understand that the *way* a person won a battle was far more important than *whether* she won it. "But there's no need to make him suffer. Dead is dead."

Luke reached out in the Force and found the sensation of burning cold that was the shikkar buried inside the Sith's torso. It seemed to be only a few millimeters below the throbbing fire of the man's heart, a placement likely to kill him a bit more slowly than Vestara believed. Luke touched the blade in the Force and tipped it upward just a millimeter—then heard the impostor gasp as it sliced into his heart.

Vestara's hand tightened on Luke's arm. "What happened? You didn't—"

"It will look like the blade shifted," Luke assured her. "Even the High Lords will never know why. Who was he?"

"An old friend of my father's," Vestara said, sounding a bit sad and disappointed. "Master Myal."

"I see," Luke replied.

The levtram arrived at the boarding berth and opened its doors, and panicked passengers from the platform began to push inside without giving anyone on board a chance to debark. Luke took a moment to look around, then—when he did not see any trace of the tattooed man from the pedramp—he and Vestara pushed into the panicked crowd.

As they entered the glow from the lights inside the car, Luke was surprised to see that there were tears welling in Vestara's eyes.

"What did he do to make you hate him so much?"

"*Hate* him?" Vestara looked up to meet Luke's gaze. "I didn't hate him. He was always very kind to me."

Luke frowned. "Then you used his own shikkar because . . ."

"Because I didn't have mine, and we have a war to win." Vestara rose onto her tiptoes and whispered into his ear. "I did it for the Jedi cause, Master Skywalker."

Chapter Two

SHE CAME TO HIM IN DARKNESS, AS HIS TORMENTORS ALWAYS DID, A cold malevolence waiting at the foot of his cot. Wynn Dorvan did not move, did not change his breathing, did not even test the restraints holding his limbs splayed and immobile. He merely closed his eyes and willed himself to escape into sleep.

"Come now, Wynn." The voice was female and familiar, a voice he had heard before. "You *know* you won't be rid of me that easily."

The cell grew bright as the illumination panels activated overhead, and Wynn squeezed his eyes shut against the brilliance. It was impossible to mark the passing of time in the ceaseless darkness between torture sessions, but the pain stabbing through his head suggested it had been many days since his last interrogation.

"Wynn, you mustn't keep me waiting," the voice said. Something cold and slimy slithered around his bare ankle. "Not your Beloved Queen of the Stars."

Wynn's eyes popped open, filling his head with an explosion of pain and light, and he raised his head. Standing at the foot of his cot he saw two silhouettes, one a female human and one . . . something else.

"That's better." The voice seemed to be coming from the silhouette on the left—a hideous, sinuate thing with tentacles instead of arms, with blazing white stars where there should have been eyes. *Abeloth.* "I was afraid you were going to make me summon Lady Korelei."

The memories of his recent Force torture only grew stronger as time passed, and the mere mention of Korelei's name sent an electric bolt of fear shooting through his body. He ignored it—just as he ignored the inner voice telling him to scream and beg for mercy. The slightest hint of weakness would only bring Korelei back all the sooner, to pry from him the few secrets he had not yet surrendered—his most important secrets, the ones he was determined to carry into oblivion with him.

And so Wynn said the only thing he *could* say, the one thing that just *might* get him killed before Korelei returned: "Are you real?" He let his head drop back to the cot. "You *can't* be real. You're too blasted ugly."

The silhouette remained silent for a moment, and had Wynn been a Jedi, he was fairly certain he would have felt her anger building in the Force. But when Abeloth spoke, her voice remained cool and in control, and Wynn knew he would not escape his torment so easily.

"I am very real, Wynn—more real than you can know," she said. "And I grow weary of your tricks, as do the Sith. Lady Korelei is ready to employ the necromantic option."

Wynn managed a sort of nod. "Let her." As he spoke, the light started to grow less painful, and when he glanced toward the silhouette it began to seem less hideous and sinuate—more substantial and . vaguely human. "If Lady Korelei could get truth from a dead man, she wouldn't be wasting time trying to extract it from a living one."

"So you *have* been lying to her?"

"No one can lie to a Sith Lord," he said. "That's what she keeps telling me."

"You might be an exception," the woman said. "You are certainly not telling her what the Sith wish to know."

Now that Wynn's vision was clearing, he could see that his visitor had changed from the hideous tentacle-armed Abeloth into an elegant, blue-skinned Jessar female. There was a slight bulge to her eyes, and her face looked as though it were starting to peel from a bad sunburn. But anyone with access to the HoloNet would have no trouble recognizing her as Rokari Kem, Chief of State of the Galactic Alliance.

"You might suggest that she ask nicely," Wynn said. "Really, who wants to cooperate with someone who keeps blasting Force probes through his mind?"

"Then perhaps we *should* try something else," Kem suggested. "How would you like to be released from this cell?"

Wynn raised his head as high as was possible. "You must know how very silly that question is."

Kem's only response was a series of soft *click*s as the cuffs around Wynn's wrists and ankles fell open. The tension vanished from his arms and legs, and when he tried to pull his pain-numbed limbs in toward his body, they actually moved.

More suspicious than surprised, Wynn struggled into an upright position and was finally able to get a good look at Kem's companion. Dressed in the gray jumpsuit of a GAS prisoner, the woman had blond hair, narrow eyes, and a hard, familiar face that Wynn knew he should have recognized, but could not quite place in his current condition.

He shifted his gaze back to Kem. "Well, that was easy," he said. "What's the catch?"

"*Catch?*" Kem asked. "Ah—what I want in return. That would be your help."

"My help?" Wynn echoed, still trying to work out the second woman's identity—and what she had to do with his own captivity. "To do what?"

"Help me rule," Kem replied simply.

Now Wynn *was* surprised. "You want me to help you rule the Galactic Alliance?"

"You would help me run the government, yes," Kem confirmed. "You would be saving lives, Wynn—a great many lives."

Keenly aware that there had to be a trap—with Abeloth and her Sith, there was *always* a trap—Wynn fell silent and did his best to sort through priorities with his torture-raddled brain. His most important goal was to protect the informal intelligence network he had been operating with Admiral and Eramuth Bwua'tu. By now, the two Bothans knew of his capture, and they had undoubtedly taken precautions to protect themselves. But the network itself would be vital to the Jedi when they returned to liberate the planet, and so far he had managed to avoid revealing its existence to Lady Korelei and her assistants.

But Wynn knew he could not put that off much longer. He had run out of unimportant details three sessions earlier and begun to feed his tormentors small scraps of more valuable information. Now they were beginning to put together a more complete picture of the secret workings of the Galactic Alliance government—a picture that was leading them closer to Club Bwua'tu all the time.

"Is it such a hard decision, Wynn?" Kem asked. "You can save lives and escape your torture. Or you can condemn thousands to die . . . and remain here to feed Lady Korelei's appetites."

Of course, it wasn't a hard decision at all—and that's what made Wynn hesitate. Rokari Kem—or Abeloth, or whatever she called herself—was not only the new leader of the Galactic Alliance. She was also the secret leader of the Sith, and Sith cared nothing about the lives they took or the harm they caused. They cared only about their own power. If Abeloth was willing to forgo the secrets that her torturers were slowly prying from his mind, then it could only mean she saw a more valuable way to use him—a way that would allow her to do even more damage to the Galactic Alliance.

But Abeloth didn't know everything, and one of the things she didn't know was that Wynn just needed to buy time—time for the Jedi to arrive *before* he broke. Finally, he looked up and met Kem's gaze.

"You'd move me out of this cell?" he asked. "And keep me away from Lady Korelei?"

"Of course," Kem assured him. "As long as you continue to serve me, you'll be safe from Lady Korelei."

"I won't be your mouthpiece," Wynn warned. His demands, he knew, would mean nothing to her—but he had to make them, or she would grow suspicious of his true motives. "And I won't feed you the names of beings who stand against you."

"I expect nothing of the sort," Kem assured him, smiling broadly and warmly. "I have enough names to last a standard year."

Wynn allowed his discomfort at the assertion to show in his face, but asked, "Well then, what *do* you expect from me?"

"Nothing but what you gave Chief Daala," Kem said. "By all accounts, you're an excellent administrator and a capable adviser."

"You want *my* advice?" Wynn began to think he was hallucinating—that he had finally broken under Korelei's attentions and lost his mind. "You can't be sincere."

"But I *am* . . . so very sincere." Kem reached for the arm of the woman she had brought along, then pulled her forward to stand next to the cot. "I'm sure you remember Lieutenant Lydea Pagorski?"

Pagorski—of course. She was the Imperial intelligence officer who had perjured herself at Tahiri Veila's murder trial. Wynn nodded and turned to the woman.

"I do," he said. "I'm sorry to see you here, too."

Pagorski's face grew even paler, and she cast a nervous glance toward Kem.

Kem merely rolled her eyes. "There's no need to feel *sorry* for the lieutenant," she said. "The Empire wants her returned, and I'd like to know whether to grant their request."

"You're asking me to make the decision?" Wynn asked, more suspicious than ever.

"To give me your opinion, yes," Kem said. "You won't be making any decisions yourself."

Wynn began to feel a little better about the arrangement. Kem and her Sith were, after all, practically strangers to the galaxy at large. It made sense that they might need someone like him to help sort through the thousands of diplomatic petitions that came through the Chief of State's office every day.

"What did the Empire offer in return for Lieutenant Pagorski's release?" he asked.

Kem frowned. "Nothing."

"Not even a task force port call?"

"Nothing at *all*," Kem said. "I'll deny the request."

Wynn shook his head. "You should grant it."

"I should grant it, when they offer nothing?" Now that the possibility of payment had been raised, Kem seemed offended that none had been offered. "And if they *had* offered something, what should I have done? Taken only half?"

"No," Wynn replied. "You should have refused to return the lieutenant at all, then moved her into a military interrogation facility before they could assassinate her."

Kem looked truly confused. "Because the offer was an insult?"

"Because it would have meant that Lieutenant Pagorski was valuable to them," Wynn explained. "And before you even considered releasing her, you would want to know the nature of that value."

"And because they offer nothing, she has no value?"

"That's right—the request is merely routine." Wynn turned to Pagorski. "You have family on Bastion, don't you? Someone important?"

Pagorski's eyes widened. "My father is an admiral in Fleet Provisions," she said. "How did you know?"

"He's putting pressure on the diplomatic corps," Wynn replied. "They made the request so they could tell him they're doing something."

"I can't grant such a request," Kem objected. "It will diminish my stature."

Wynn shook his head. "You're forgetting your public persona," he said, surprised that the leader of the Sith would make such a mistake. "You're supposed to be Rokari Kem, a wise and compassionate leader from B'nish—not Rokari Kem, a greedy and power-hungry Sith overlord."

"Yes, I see your point," Kem said, her eyes flaring at the terms he had used to describe her. She sighed and turned to Pagorski. "I cannot allow you to return to the Empire knowing my true—"

"I won't tell *anyone*!" Pagorski interrupted, clearly terrified. "I give you my word as—"

"If your word had any value, you wouldn't have been in a GAS detention center in the first place," Kem retorted. "But there's no need to kill you. I'm just going to use the Force to wipe away some of your memories."

Relief flooded Pagorski's face. "I understand," she said, visibly relieved. "Feel free."

"I wasn't asking, Lieutenant."

Kem placed her hands on the sides of Pagorski's head, then looked into the woman's eyes and locked gazes. For a moment, nothing seemed to happen, and Wynn thought the mindwipe might be as painless as it was mysterious.

Then the air between the two women began to shimmer. Pagorski's eyes opened wide, and her face twisted into a mask of horror. Rokari Kem's fingers grew long and thin, and suddenly her arms dissolved into gray slimy tentacles, and in the Sith's place stood the hideous thing that Wynn had glimpsed on waking, a slender sinuate form with coarse yellow hair and a mouth so broad that it reached from ear to ear.

Abeloth.

Pagorski's jaw fell open in a wordless scream. The tentacles shot down her throat, into her ears and nostrils, and began to pulse. Horrible gagging noises erupted from her mouth. Her entire body went limp and hung, convulsing, by the ropy tendrils that had been inserted into her head.

Finally, Pagorski's expression went blank. Her complexion grew so pale and translucent that Wynn could see the tentacles throbbing inside her face, pumping something dark and viscous into her sinuses and her ears and down into her trachea. He began to scramble back, pressing himself against the wall behind him so fiercely it seemed to yield. The cell reverberated with a loud, growling howl that he did not recognize as his own voice until he found himself crouching in the corner, gnawing at his knuckles and banging his skull against the durasteel.

The thing turned its gruesome head toward Wynn's corner, then fixed its blazing white eyes on him and smiled a grin as deep and dark as the Maw itself.

"Now that you'll be serving me, you should know this about your Beloved Queen of the Stars," Abeloth said. "She is *so* much more than a Sith."

Chapter Three

FOR THE TENTH TIME IN AS MANY MINUTES, BEN SKYWALKER GLANCED at the chrono hanging on the wurlwood panel across from him. The liberation of Coruscant was scheduled to begin . . . well, *now*, and he and Vestara were still sitting in the pages' closet outside Senator Suldar's office. Hovering before them was a float pallet bearing a large crate wrapped in glitterfilm, and in her hands Vestara held a silver tray bearing a small envelope addressed to MY DEAR FRIEND KAMERON.

"You have a hot date waiting?" Vestara asked in a taunting voice. Dressed in the dark blue robe of a Senate page, she was wearing a custom-built disguise that would convince even the most sophisticated facial recognition software in the galaxy that she was a Falleen adolescent. "The way you keep checking the chrono, she must be a real dazzler."

Ben smiled. The only date he had was after the battle . . . with Vestara herself. "She's quite beautiful—for a human." Also dressed in the robe of a Senate page, Ben was disguised as a male Twi'lek. "But the party we're going to, you can't be late for."

Vestara arched one brow. "Then maybe she should go alone. If you don't like human girls, she'd probably have more fun without you anyway."

"I don't think so," Ben said, still smirking. "She's fallen for me pretty hard. I think it's the head tails."

Vestara rolled her eyes. "Typical male—one little smile, and you think it's love." She turned her gaze toward the back of the closet, where a tall man in the red cape and golden armor of the Senate Security Force stood next to a wurlwood door leading to the Senator's inner sanctum. "In any case, watching the chrono isn't going to change the Senator's schedule. He's the chair of the Galactic Alliance Senate, after all. He'll see us as soon as he can."

"I hope so." Ben cast a meaningful glance at the crate. The battle for Coruscant would be won or lost in the next half hour, and the outcome could depend on getting that crate into Suldar's office before the Sith knew they were under attack. "If we're still here in five minutes, I'm going anyway."

Vestara exhaled in exasperation. "Hold this."

She passed the silver tray to Ben, then rose and walked to the security guard. The man was lean and good-looking, with a square jaw and the flawless grooming that Ben had learned to associate with the vanity of Lost Tribe Sith.

"Excuse me." It was impossible to see Vestara's expression because she was facing away from Ben, but he had heard that particular voice quiver often enough to know she would be flashing a smile that appeared more nervous than it really was. "Have you announced our presence?"

The guard glared at her for a moment; then his brows came together, and he glanced toward Ben. "I have."

The nervousness vanished from Vestara's voice. "And have you mentioned that the gift is a peace offering from Senator Wuul?"

The guard's eyes widened just enough to suggest that he knew more about the feud between the Senators Suldar and Wuul than any true security guard should have.

Vestara leaned a little closer. "I mean, I'd hate to think of the Senator in there, trying to line up support for a Tibanna tax increase, when Senator Wuul is ready to give in."

"You know this for a fact?" The guard's eyes narrowed. "How?"

Vestara shrugged. "Pages have ears, the same as security guards," she said. "We know a lot of things we shouldn't."

The guard considered this for a moment, then glanced back toward Ben. "Wait here."

He depressed a hidden latch, and a gap appeared in the boiserie behind him. Pulling one of the panels open just far enough to squeeze through, he slipped into a hidden corridor beyond, then closed the panel behind him.

Vestara glanced back and cocked a brow. Ben rolled his eyes, but he had to smile and give her a grudging nod of approval. Her knowledge of the Sith and their vulnerabilities had proven invaluable in planning the liberation of Coruscant, and now her presence was turning out to be just as crucial in executing the operation. Only a former Sith could truly understand how a mind steeped in the dark side worked, how to appeal to their greed and vanity without revealing the trap. Ben was glad she had persuaded the Masters that her presence on Coruscant, during the battle itself, would be crucial to the success of the initial assault.

But Ben also knew how difficult this particular operation had to be for Vestara. She loved him as much as he loved her, he was sure. But choosing him and the Jedi meant turning her back on her people and her home, never again breaking bread with childhood friends, and he would have been a fool to think she had made her choice with no regrets. There would always be a part of her that remained Sith, that longed to return to Kesh, and she had once confided to him that she hoped someday to do just that—to return home at the head of a Jedi peace delegation, so she could teach her people that there was no need to conquer the galaxy to live in it.

She was being atypically naïve, but she had given up so much already that Ben could not bear the thought of depriving her of this one dream—and that was why he had persuaded his father to stop pressing her for Kesh's coordinates. The hard truth was that redeeming an entire tribe of Sith was about as likely as stopping a nova, but this was a conclusion Vestara needed to reach herself. And when she did, Ben knew, she would be a true Jedi.

Vestara returned and held out her hands. "Get ready," she said. "We'll be inside in less than a minute."

Ben returned the plate and stood. "You seem pretty sure of your-self," he said. "So why did he scowl?"

"He scowled?" Vestara asked. "When?"

"Right after you approached him," Ben said. "When you asked if he had announced us yet."

"Oh, *that* scowl," Vestara said lightly. "I don't know—maybe he isn't accustomed to pretty pages smiling at him."

She flashed him a playful grin, and Ben had to admit that she could be pretty disarming.

"I can see how you might have unsettled him," he said. "But that doesn't mean your charm is going to work on the Senator—not from out here."

Vestara rolled her eyes. "Come on," she said. "What *politician* is going to put off accepting a surrender?"

By *politician*, Ben knew, Vestara meant *Sith*. Kameron Suldar, chair of the Galactic Alliance Senate, was actually High Lord Ivaar Workan of the Lost Tribe of the Sith. Ben and Vestara were there to set him up for a surprise attack. They had to be inside the office before the battle began, holding the High Lord's attention so he wouldn't sense the rest of the Skywalker team coming to capture or kill him. Ben didn't like being part of what would probably end up being a targeted killing. But there was a war under way, and he and his fellow team members were commandos sent to destroy the enemy's command-and-control structure. If they could do it quickly and quietly enough, the Sith in-vaders would be leaderless before they realized they were under attack. And *that* would save thousands of civilian lives—perhaps hundreds of thousands—by preventing the fight from spilling over into the general population.

The wurlwood panel swung open again, and the red-caped guard emerged. He was followed by a stunning redhead with the striking fea-tures of a HoloNet star and the calculating eyes of a seasoned political operative. She crossed the closet in a few quick steps and took the en-velope from Vestara's tray.

" 'My dear friend Kameron,' " the woman read drily. She returned the envelope to the tray, then looked to the float pallet. "What's all this?"

"A cafasho steamer," Vestara said. She leaned closer and spoke in a confiding tone. "Senator Wuul has observed that Senator Suldar has a certain fondness for the drink, and he thought Senator Suldar might enjoy having a steamer of his own."

The redhead studied the gift for a moment, then turned to the guard. "Has the package been screened?"

The guard sneered, obviously offended. "Of course. Them, too."

"There's no need for your concern," Vestara assured the redhead. "I have the impression that Senator Wuul is looking for a graceful way to capitulate."

The woman considered this for a moment, then looked to Ben. "And what about you, Twi'lek?" she asked. "Do you have the same impression?"

Ben nodded. "It's definitely a cafasho steamer," he replied. "We were instructed to set it up and teach Senator Suldar's staff how to use it."

The redhead narrowed her eyes, then suddenly turned toward the back of the closet. "Very well," she said. "The Senator will see you now."

"Thank you," Vestara replied. She looked over at Ben and cocked her brow, then followed the redhead into the secret passage. "I can't tell you how excited I am to be meeting the Senator in person."

All across Coruscant, Sith impostors began to receive their final warnings, a simple message that said:

> SURRENDER OR DIE. DECIDE NOW.
> —THE JEDI ORDER

Sitting in the backseat of his armored limousine, GAS Superintendent Jestat Vhool snorted at the arrogance of the Jedi fools and snapped his datapad shut . . . and then recalled the unexplained hesitation he had felt the last time his pilot had engaged the repulsorlift drive. A shiver of danger raced down his spine, and a single thought filled his mind: *Bomb!*

Vhool flung open the door and Force-leapt from the limo onto the nearest balcony. He landed in a diving roll and used the Force to counteract his momentum, then returned to his feet, lightsaber in hand. He ignited the crimson blade and slipped into a combat crouch, eyes sweeping left and right.

An instant later a fast-descending scaffold dropped from the floor above and crushed him flat.

The maintenance man who had been operating the scaffold—a green-eyed human whose chin sported a tuft of graying beard—stepped off the scaffold and found nothing but a blood-soaked arm protruding from beneath the heavy equipment. He took note of the GAS insignia on the sleeve cuff, then checked for a pulse and found none. When he glanced down the skylane and saw the GAS limo decelerating, he hurled himself over the balcony railing.

The maintenance man landed on the back of a two-seat swoop bike, piloted by a golden-eyed Arcona named Izal Waz.

"Welcome aboard, Master Horn," Izal called over his shoulder. "No surrender, I gather?"

"Scratch target one," Corran confirmed. "Let's try number two."

Izal swung the swoop bike down an access lane and accelerated hard. Behind them, the limo never did explode.

Kayala Fei was delivering BAMR's midday newscast, halfway through a kicker story about Jedi healers conducting medical experiments on Chandrilan younglings, when a peculiar message appeared on her holoprompter: SURRENDER OR DIE. DECIDE NOW.

Fei did not hesitate, did not even blink. She simply used the Force to send her chair rocketing away from the anchor desk, toward the holographic skyline being projected at the rear of the stage. The instant the chair began to tip, she was on her feet, her lightsaber flying into her hand from a holster concealed inside her stylish knee boots.

The space her head had just occupied now had a stage light swinging through it. Affixed to the bottom end of a broken support batten, it had crossed the anchor desk and was coming toward her. She ignited her lightsaber and pivoted to the side, cutting the batten at head height to keep the heavy lamp from catching her on the return trip.

But there was a broken cable snaking down behind her, and that Fei had no chance to avoid. By the time she identified the hot sizzle rushing through her body as electricity rather than her own danger sense, the cable was wrapping itself around her neck. Its bare end snapped down and caught her just above the heart, pouring so much current into her chest that a smoking hole appeared in her shimmersilk tunic.

Fortunately, the relief producer was up to the emergency. She had been called in after the normal production crew had been served a bowl of spoiled thakitillo, and she was the type who kept her head. She typed a new message into the holoprompter, then activated the studio's PA system and instructed Fei's co-anchor to move to the auxiliary anchor desk.

The new anchor, a jowly man with an oversized nose and a baritone voice, looked at the speaker above his head and asked, "You want me to go *on?*" He glanced toward the back of the stage, where Fei's body was still hanging from the cable and continuing to convulse. "What about Kayala?"

"The Emdee droid is on his way," the relief producer said. A tall, dark-haired woman with a commanding presence, Jedi Master Octa Ramis knew how to take control of a chaotic situation. "And we still have four minutes of newscast to fill. Move! Read!"

The anchor jumped up and raced ten paces to the auxiliary desk, then sat down and began to read from the holoprompter floating above the active cam.

"Uh, we apologize for the technical difficulties we have just experienced." His voice returned to its smooth baritone. "We are sorry to report that BAMR anchorwoman Kayala Fei has suffered an untimely death in a freak accident. The incident occurred only moments ago, during a live holocast in front of billions of viewers . . ."

Octa Ramis removed the sound bud from her ear and tossed it on the mixing console, then turned to her three Jedi assistants. "And that's a wrap," she said. "Let's move on to our next target."

When the alarm began to blare down from the coffered ceiling of the High Court Chamber, Grand Justice Tela Rovas did not reach for the lightsaber beneath her robes. She simply unfolded the flimsi that her clerk had just passed her, read the ominous note, and frowned at the signature line—THE JEDI ORDER—then turned to her

fellow High Justices, seated beside her along the elegant hamogoni-
wood bench.

"It seems the alarm is genuine," she announced calmly. "Court is
adjourned for evacuation."

The chamber erupted in panic, with spectators and litigants alike
boiling toward the exits. Rovas, in contrast, calmly rose from her seat
and started toward the justices' private exit, all the while shielding herself from attack by drawing her fellow judges into a tight knot of conversation around her. As they crossed the threshold, she took the arm
of Justice Robr Selvi and pulled him close, being careful to keep him .
between her and the sliding door.

Jaina cursed beneath her breath, then reluctantly released the hidden trigger that would have sent the heavy door shooting out to crush
the pair. Corrupt as he was, Selvi was no Sith—and that made him safe
from the Jedi. Jaina glanced across the broad central aisle to her two
companions and nodded toward the exit.

Valin returned her nod and rose instantly, but Jysella—carrying a
datapad and wearing her brown hair in a tight bun—scowled.

"We're just going to let her *go*?" Jysella asked. She was speaking in
a Force whisper so soft that her voice was a mere rustle in Jaina's ears.
"A *Sith Lord*?"

Jaina shrugged and nodded toward the exit more firmly. Their orders were clear: No attack until the target reaches for a weapon. And
no civilian casualties—even if it means letting a Sith Lord escape.

By the time Vestara and Ben were finally ushered in to meet High Lord
Ivaar Workan—better known to the Galactic Alliance as Senator
Kameron Suldar—there was no longer enough time to set up the
cafasho steamer. Only two minutes remained before the first attacks of
the battle were scheduled to begin, and that meant they had drifted
completely into the sphere of combat improvisation. That was just fine
with Vestara. She had been trained to be unpredictable when she
fought, and sometimes the only way to do that was to toss the plan
aside.

Vestara was surprised to see the Senator's private office furnished
sparely but elegantly in blatant Keshiri style, with sculptures of ropy

glass resting on display tables throughout the room. The pieces were done in a new style known as flying storm back on Kesh, and they usually depicted a hurricane or cyclone rolling over an alien landscape.

To the initiated, at least, the conquest symbology was clear, and Vestara found herself shaking her head at its open display. It was the kind of arrogance that would be the Sith's greatest vulnerability in the coming war. Her people simply did not understand how dangerous the Jedi truly were—or how determined the Masters were to destroy the Lost Tribe of the Sith.

Workan's redheaded assistant motioned Vestara and Ben toward a clear spot in the center of the room, then followed close behind as Ben pushed the float pallet forward. When two more red-caped guards stepped out of a corner and fell in behind them, Vestara knew it had been her ploy—the silent *I'm Vestara Khai* she had secretly mouthed to the guard in the pages' closet—that had finally won them admittance. She was taking a terrible risk exposing her identity like that, but she wanted to be sure that Luke Skywalker killed Workan, and that meant getting herself and Ben into the High Lord's office.

Ben stopped the float pallet at the indicated location, then drew his shoulders square and stood at attention. Workan studied the pallet from behind a large glass desk at the far end of the room. He was a distinguished-looking man with dark hair and darker eyes. Though Vestara had not revealed this to the Jedi's mission planners, she had met the High Lord once before, back on Kesh when she had been summoned to become Lady Rhea's apprentice. He had struck her as a cunning and observant man, and the venom in his gaze suggested that he had seen through her disguise and confirmed her identity for himself.

Finally, Workan gestured toward the tray in Vestara's hands, using the Force to summon the small envelope she was carrying. Ben let out a gasp of surprise that managed to sound spontaneous enough to be credible. Had Workan and his fellow impostors not already known that they were looking at a pair of spies, the act might have fooled them. As it was, two of the High Lord's bodyguards were on Ben before his mouth closed, one holding the heavy, curved blade of a glass parang to his throat while the other pressed the emitter nozzle of an unlit lightsaber to his back.

In the same instant, Vestara felt the sharp tip of a shikkar pricking the flesh over her left kidney. "Not a word, traitor," the redhead warned. "Don't even flinch."

Vestara obeyed, watching in silence as Workan inspected the envelope for signs of poison. By now, Luke Skywalker would be starting across the visitors' parlor with the other two members of the assault team. It would take them less than a minute to overpower the sentries in the outer office and reach the security door. Yet even thirty seconds was a long time for Vestara and Ben to survive as unarmed captives, and the safe thing would have been to abort the operation back in the pages' closet, when it grew apparent they weren't going to be admitted before the Jedi surprise attack began.

But aborting the operation would have meant allowing Workan to live, and allowing Workan to live was not an option. Vestara had realized back on the Sith world of Upekzar, when she had sacrificed Jedi Knight Natua Wan to the ancient Dream Singer in order to save Ben, that she would not be able to hide among the Jedi forever. And as a High Lord, Workan was bound by Sith custom to hunt down and slay Vestara for daring to kill High Lord Sarasu Taalon on Pydyr. Therefore, Workan—like all of his fellow High Lords—had to die before Vestara could safely leave the protection of the Jedi Order.

Finally satisfied that the envelope was not a death trap, Workan read the exterior salutation aloud. " 'My dear friend Kameron.' "

At this point, less than a minute remained before the first Jedi assaults began and Workan started to feel Sith dying across all of Coruscant. Vestara and Ben were supposed to be serving cafasho, doing whatever it took to hold the High Lord's attention while Luke and the rest of the team stormed the outer offices. Well, they might not be serving cafasho now, but Vestara was pretty sure that they had captured Workan's *complete* attention.

Workan removed a folded flimsiplast from inside the envelope and read that aloud, too: " 'Did you truly think I wouldn't know who you are?' "

A ripple of alarm rolled through the Force as Workan's subordinates grasped the significance of Wuul's message. The High Lord himself looked almost as though he had been expecting such a note, merely cocking a thin black brow and looking at Ben.

"Is this some sort of joke?"

"Not at all."

As Ben spoke, muffled voices began to sound in the outer office. Knowing the next few moments would determine whether Ben lived or died, Vestara started to address Workan in an attempt to distract him . . . and felt a tiny stab of pain as the shikkar broke the surface of her skin.

If Ben noticed, he showed no sign. "Turn the note over," he said. "I think that will explain things."

Workan did as Ben instructed, then read, " 'Surrender or die.' " His face grew crimson, and he read the second part. " 'Decide *now.*' "

The High Lord lifted his eyes to glare at Ben, but before he could speak, the muffled voices beyond the security door gave way to cries of alarm. The sizzle of clashing lightsabers began to sound outside the door.

"If you're going to surrender, I'd recommend doing it soon," Ben said, clearly trying to hold Workan's attention inside the room. "You don't have much time."

Workan's eyes narrowed. "*I* am not the one with a parang to his throat."

A hint of cockiness came into Ben's voice. "No, but you *are* the one who drank two cups of cafasho in Senator Wuul's office yesterday morning," he said. "You're already dead, High Lord Workan."

The lie came so smoothly that even Vestara did not sense it in Ben's Force aura, and she *knew* it was a fabrication. The cafasho steamer had only been a ruse to get Ben and Vestara inside Workan's office, but the High Lord wouldn't realize that—not if he was relying on the Force to tell whether Ben was lying. He glanced again at Wuul's note, and fear began to blossom across his face.

The sound of the fighting beyond the door began to subside even sooner than Vestara had expected, but Workan's attention remained fixed on Ben.

"I see." The High Lord rose from behind his desk. "If Wuul has already poisoned me, why go to so much trouble to tell me? Gloating is hardly the Jedi's style."

"Neither is killing in cold blood," Ben said. "As the note says, you *do* have the option of surrender. There's an antidote."

Workan glanced back toward the flimsiplast, and—not for the first time—Vestara found herself in awe of Ben's quick thinking. He was using the High Lord's abilities against him, making Workan question his own common sense by hiding an obvious lie in the Force. The trick wouldn't work for long . . . but it wouldn't need to.

A loud thud sounded from the security door, and a guard said, "Milord, perhaps we should kill the prisoners and—"

"That door is hatch-steel," Workan said, waving the man silent. He started around his desk. "This antidote—is it in the cafasho steamer?"

"Shall I take that as a surrender?" Ben sounded far too cocky for his circumstances—and Vestara had to admit she kind of liked it. "Your people will need to lay down their—"

"Enough." Workan pulled a lightsaber from beneath his robes. "We are done playing games, Jedi."

And that was when a compression wave blew across the room.

Vestara did not wonder what had happened or wait to hear the blast. She simply spun away from the shikkar, using one hand to trap the redhead's wrist and the other to slam a palm-heel into the base of the woman's jaw. She glimpsed an orange flash and heard the sharp clap of a detonite explosion, then brought her knee up beneath her foe's arm—and saw the glass dagger float free.

She continued her attack anyway, snapping the elbow across her thigh. The woman cried out and used the Force to send the dagger flying toward Vestara's throat.

Why did Sith *always* overreach? Vestara pivoted aside, easily dodging an attack she could never have avoided if the woman had settled for a leg attack, then grabbed the redhead by the chin and killed her with a Force punch to the throat.

"Down *now*!"

Recognizing Ben's voice, Vestara dropped. A crimson blade flashed past a meter overhead. Her gaze followed the blade to the lightsaber, the lightsaber to the arm, and at the other end she found the guard from the pages' closet. She glanced at the float-pallet hovering behind him and reached for the cafasho machine in the Force.

The guard pivoted away—straight into Ben, who shoved the shikkar that had almost killed Vestara into the man's neck.

The guard collapsed, and Vestara saw a second gold-armored figure stepping toward Ben. She sent the cafasho machine flying in that guard's direction. He activated a crimson lightsaber and cleaved it apart before it hit him.

By then she was snatching the lightsaber from beneath the dead redhead's robes, and Ben was taking another from the impostor he had just killed. Vestara sprang to her feet, then stepped away from Ben so they could flank their new opponent.

She glanced toward the door and found it standing next to a smoking hole that had once been a wall. Seha and Doran were just rushing through the breach, angling toward the last guard, while Luke and Workan had already joined battle in a whirling tempest of color and smashed office furnishings. With only three Sith left, there was no question of the final outcome—even a High Lord could not overcome those odds, not when Luke and Ben Skywalker were on the other side.

Vestara sprang to the attack, swinging high to prevent the guard from leaping into a Force tumble. He blocked and spun, bringing his blade around in time to deflect a leg slash from Ben, then glanced toward a display table near the wall. Guessing that a glass sculpture would already be flying toward her head, Vestara dived into a forward roll, then locked her lightsaber into the ON position and tossed it at her attacker's legs.

The guard dropped his own blade to deflect the one flying toward his thighs—then simply divided along the spine as Ben's lightsaber cleaved him from collar to belt. The body did not fall so much as peel apart, and the sculpture crashed to the floor three meters away.

Vestara called her own weapon back into her hand and then looked up to find Ben stepping across the body toward her.

"So," she said, glancing down at the dead Sith. "I guess you *do* care."

"Of course I care." Ben smiled and reached down to take her hand. "Good teammates are hard to find."

"And you two certainly make a good team," Doran Tainer said, joining them. He studied the three Sith they had killed. "Did you even *have* weapons when this thing started?"

"A Jedi is always armed," Vestara said, quoting a maxim that was a favorite of the Sith as well as the Jedi.

She held Ben's hand for a moment, enjoying its strength and

warmth—and knowing that one day soon, she would have to turn her back on his touch. Finally, she allowed him to help her to her feet, then turned toward the battle between Luke and Workan. A swath of shattered glass and smoking furniture marked the path their fight had taken to the rear part of the room. It seemed clear from the crooked route that the fight had been both desperate and well matched, but now Workan was finally being forced to retreat past his desk. With Seha Dorvald rushing to join the fight, he would eventually be pushed into a corner and perhaps even taken for interrogation.

And *that*, Vestara could not allow—not after the trick she had used to get them into the office in the first place. She thought for a moment, then pulled a blaster pistol from the holster of a dead guard.

"Something's wrong!" She started toward the back of the room. "We've got to stop him."

A large hand caught her by the shoulder. "Stop him from what?" Doran demanded. "Luke wants to take Workan—"

Vestara shook free. "Look at where he is—he's trying to get to his desk." She raised the blaster pistol and began to fire into the combat, not so much trying to kill Workan herself as to force him away from the desk—and onto Luke's blade. "He must have a detonator switch back there!"

Doran released her shoulder, and a moment later two more streams of blasterfire joined Vestara's.

"Dad, trap!" Ben yelled. "Back off!"

"Seha—you, too!" Doran added.

Both Jedi dived away at once, leaving a badly confused Workan struggling to bat aside the storm of blasterfire coming his way. Already exhausted and wounded, with one arm hanging limp and a smoking slash across his chest, he was no match for three attackers trained to coordinate their fire to overwhelm his defenses. It took only six shots for Ben to burn a hole through his head.

"Quick thinking, Ves." Ben squeezed her arm, then added, "And thanks. You just might have saved us again."

Chapter Four

THE PLANET OSSUS HUNG LIMNED IN FIRE, A GIANT GRAY PEARL FLOAT-
ing between the orange globes of two suns. It was gray because the entire world was covered in clouds. It was covered in clouds because,
twice each year, Ossus passed directly between its two stars. Blasted by
radiant energy from opposite sides, it went several weeks without
night. Planetary temperatures skyrocketed, changing most of the surface water into atmospheric vapor.

Allana Solo knew all that because she had read it in the Intelligence
Ministry briefing file, along with a warning that conditions were so
steamy during this period that pilots departing the surface would be
flying blind until they reached space. But to nine-year-old Allana, staring out at the world from the Royal Stateroom aboard the *Dragon
Queen II*, it seemed like Ossus was trying to keep the Jedi young ones
home, to prevent the Jedi academy from being evacuated even if it
meant the death of every last student.

"There's no need to worry." Allana's mother came to stand in the observation bubble next to her. "Your grandparents have been doing this sort of thing since before *I* was born."

Allana nodded and glanced at her mother's reflection in the transparisteel. Wearing a gray flight suit with a rancor-tooth lightsaber hanging from a belt across her hips, she looked more like a Jedi Knight than the Queen Mother of the Hapes Consortium. It was a style of attire that Tenel Ka wore only in private—and a rare glimpse, Allana knew, into the life that one of the most powerful women in the galaxy *wished* she could live.

When Allana did not reply, her mother took her hand. "They're going to be fine. If anyone can do this, it's Han and Leia Solo."

"I don't think you can promise that," Allana said, continuing to study the cloud-veiled planet in front of them. "Even Grandpa and Grandma don't usually fly *into* the middle of a Sith ambush—at least not on purpose."

"No, not usually," her mother allowed. "But . . . that's why we're here. With a Hapan battle flotilla waiting to pounce, the Sith might decide not to attack at all."

Allana rolled her eyes. "Even I understand the Sith better than that, and I'm only nine."

Her mother chuckled. "Well, perhaps it was more of a hope than a belief," she allowed. "But we both know what a mistake it is to underestimate your grandparents."

Allana started to agree, but stopped when her pet nexu, Anji, growled a warning. Allana glanced toward the interior of the stateroom and saw her mother's cousin and confidante, Trista Zel, approaching. Knowing that Trista would not be interrupting unless it was important, Allana silenced Anji with a hand signal, then stepped aside to make room in the little observation bubble.

Trista flashed an apologetic smile. "Sorry to interrupt, cousin," she said. Had anyone else addressed the Queen Mother so casually, they would have been banished to the Transitory Mists. "But you wanted to be informed when the Sith make their move."

Tenel Ka raised her brow. "Already?"

Trista nodded. "The scouts have spotted a wing of Skipray twelve-jays entering the atmosphere on the far side of the planet."

"*Twelve*-jays?" Tenel Ka echoed. "Where'd they come up with something that old?"

Trista shrugged. "We're still working on that, Majesty," she said. "What's important is that TacCon thinks they'll use the cloud cover to hit the convoy as it leaves the academy. Commander Skela recommends launching two wings of Miy'tils to support Vhork Squadron and protect the convoy."

Tenel Ka thought for a moment, then nodded. "Inform the Solos—but send four wings instead."

Trista's eyes widened. "*Four* wings?"

None of the Queen Mother's other advisers would have dared to question her judgment, but Trista and Taryn Zel—and Jedi Knight Zekk, too, now that he and Taryn were a couple—were members of something called the Lorellian Court. Allana suspected that the Lorellian Court was an ultra-secret unit of Hapan Security. But she knew only three things about the organization for sure: First, she was forbidden to mention its existence, even to her grandparents. Second, she could trust anyone who flashed the secret face-code. And third, she would be introduced to that court on her eighteenth birthday.

When the Queen Mother did not immediately reply, Trista said, "Majesty, four wings is half the task force's fighter complement—and those twelve-jays are older than we are."

"Those twelve-jays are being flown by Sith pilots," Tenel Ka said. "Until we understand their capabilities, I want to err on the side of caution."

The tone of command in the Queen Mother's voice was unmistakable.

"Four wings it is." Trista inclined her head, but made no move to leave. "I also have a message from Lady Maluri."

Tenel Ka gave a weary sigh. "Must I?"

"I'm afraid so," Trista said. "She asked me to relay her concern that risking Hapan lives to protect Jedi younglings is a flagrant misuse of royal authority."

Tenel Ka rolled her eyes. "Please remind Lady Maluri that the Sith attempted to assassinate her queen," she said. "Inform her that if *she* is not willing to punish such an affront to Hapan sovereignty, then I will replace her with someone who is."

"With pleasure, cousin."

Trista bowed and started to withdraw, but Tenel Ka raised a finger to stop her.

"And see that this is the *last* time Lady Maluri needs to be warned about the astonishing lack of affection she displays for her queen," Tenel Ka added. "Tell her I threw something."

Trista smiled. "I'll make the situation clear, Majesty."

Tenel Ka nodded, and Trista departed.

After she was out of earshot, Allana caught her mother's eye. "You're risking a lot to help Grandma and Grandpa evacuate the Jedi academy," she said. "Lady Maluri can't be the only noble who doesn't like helping the Jedi."

Her mother thought for a moment, then nodded. "Yes, that's correct. I *am* risking a lot—my life, and probably even yours." She looked out the observation bubble again. "And what reason would I have for taking a risk like that? What is the *only* reason I would risk your life?"

Allana did not need to ponder the answer—it had been drilled into her since she was old enough to remember the phrase. "To protect the realm."

"That's right," her mother said. "Had the Sith succeeded in their assassination attempt on me, there would have been a war of succession—a war that you're not ready to fight."

"I know," Allana said. Sometimes it seemed like her life was just one long lesson. But she always did her best to pay attention, because she knew that someday trillions of lives would depend on her decisions. "And while our people were fighting one another, the realm would have been an easy target for outsiders."

"For the *Sith*," her mother corrected. "Whether Lady Maluri and her friends care to admit it or not, the Lost Tribe is *already* making war on us. All I'm doing now is lining up allies."

"And *nobody* is a better ally than the Jedi," Allana agreed. She turned back toward the cloud-swaddled planet hanging beyond the transparisteel. "Which is really good, because the Jedi are our friends.

And Grandpa always says that you have to stick by your friends—no matter what."

"Your grandfather is very wise," her mother agreed. "And he's right. Even if the Sith *hadn't* attacked me, we would have found . . .'"

But Allana was no longer listening, for a small hole had just opened in the Ossan clouds. It started to expand rapidly, growing from the size of her fist to larger than Anji's head in the space of two breaths, and suddenly Allana felt her stomach rising. The hole swelled to an enormous black pit, and she realized she was falling, plummeting into a darkness deeper than space. A damp, fetid smell filled her nostrils, and the rush of passing air whispered in her ears.

Except it wasn't a whisper. It was more of a hiss, like the sound of an angry Barabel, and Allana realized she wasn't falling at all. But she wasn't standing on the *Dragon Queen II,* either. She was in a dark corridor beneath the Jedi Temple, peeking through an open hatchway into a murky room filled with a huge nest of rodent bones.

Peering out among the bones were dozens of tiny heads. They had stubby snouts and long, flickering tongues, and their slit-pupiled eyes were shining with fear and anger. They began to pour from the nest, leaping and screeching and clawing. Allana backed away—and found herself trapped against a wall.

The young reptiles never reached her. A storm of blaster bolts erupted behind her, pouring through a durasteel wall to send the little creatures flying back into their nest, charred and smoking and dead.

Allana screamed, calling for Tesar and Wilyem to return to their hatchlings. But the Barabels never came. The nest vanished in the murk, and Allana realized she was back aboard the *Dragon Queen II,* locked tight in her mother's arms. Pressed flat to the observation bubble was Anji, growling and clawing at the transparisteel.

"Allana?" her mother gasped. "What is it? What's wrong?"

Allana glanced around, her confusion only growing as she recognized the familiar opulence of the Royal Stateroom. "Mom, I have to talk to Master Sebatyne—now!"

Her mother cocked a brow. "Master Sebatyne?" she asked. "But she's on Coruscant—in the middle of a battle, most likely."

"That doesn't matter. They're killing the—" Allana stopped herself, realizing she couldn't say more without breaking the promise she had made to Tesar Sebatyne, that she would never, *ever* reveal the existence of the Barabel nest beneath the Jedi Temple. "Someone is blasting my friends' young ones!"

"What friends?"

"My friends on Coruscant," Allana said. "They need our help!"

"And we'll get it to them," her mother assured her. "But we can't help anyone until you calm down. Now, start from the beginning and tell me everything."

Allana took a deep breath and held it briefly, using a Jedi relaxation technique to clear her mind and drive away the panic. Because panic was the enemy—her aunt Jaina was always telling her that. Panic had killed more people than all the blasters in the galaxy, and it would go on killing, even after there were no more wars.

After a couple of breaths, Allana felt calm enough to explain what she had seen—how she had been looking out at Ossus when a hole opened in the clouds, and how she'd fallen into it and found herself standing in a darkened corridor deep in the basement of the Jedi Temple.

"But that's all I can tell you," Allana said. "I promised to keep the rest secret."

"Promised whom?"

Allana scowled. "Mom! We don't have time for the Grees Gambit," she said. "Hatchlings are being killed."

Her mother's expression grew more patient than concerned. "Allana, you know you weren't actually in that corridor, don't you?"

"I . . . I know," Allana said. "It was another Force vision, like the one I had on Klatooine."

Tenel Ka considered this, then said, "You're clearly very strong in the Force. That's two visions in less than six months."

Allana didn't know whether to be overjoyed—or scared to death. Her father was Jacen Solo. She had not known him well, but she had read enough about his life to know that Force visions had led to his downfall, and she certainly didn't want to follow him to the dark side. But she also knew that Grand Master Skywalker had Force visions, too, and that he seemed to accept them as guidance from the Force.

Neither of which told Allana what she should do. "If it's a Force vision, then I'm supposed to make sure it doesn't happen, right?" she asked. "Like I did when I saw the burning man with you?"

Her mother's eyes flashed in alarm, but she didn't tell Allana she was wrong. Instead, she merely turned her palms up in a gesture of helplessness.

"I wish I knew," she said. "Every vision means something different. All I can say for certain is that this one means you're strong in the Force."

Allana considered this, recalling something she had overheard Luke Skywalker tell her grandmother, that Jacen had turned to the dark side because he thought it was his destiny to change what he saw. The last thing she wanted to do was make the same mistake—but she couldn't ignore what she had seen happening to the hatchlings, either. Letting them die seemed even worse than trying to change the future.

After a moment, Allana frowned up at her mother. "Mother, that's not much help," she said. "How am I supposed to know what the Force is telling me to do?"

"Maybe it wasn't telling you to *do* anything," her mother said. "Force visions aren't commands, Allana. They're just glimpses of a future that's always in motion. The most important thing about them is what you do after you've had one. That's what determines who you're going to become inside—and who you become is far more important to the future than any one choice you'll ever make."

"Grandpa calls that Lando's Dodge," Allana said, none too happy with her mother's advice. "He says people use it when they don't know what to tell you."

Her mother smiled. "Well, the truth is that I *don't* know what to tell you. You have to decide for yourself. That's the way the Force works."

"But what if I choose wrong?"

"Listen to your heart, and you won't," her mother promised. "No one can see the future, Allana—not even Grand Master Skywalker. But we shape it every day with the choices we make. All you need to do is listen to your heart. Your heart tells you what is right and just. If you do that, the future will take care of itself."

Allana did not need to listen long. "That's pretty easy," she said. "I can't turn my back on my friends. I've got to warn them about the danger to their young ones."

"Then that's what we'll do," her mother said. "Do you think you can warn Master Sebatyne through the Force?"

Allana thought for a moment. She could usually find her mother in the Force, even across all of the light-years that separated Coruscant and the Consortium. And sometimes she could find her grandmother. But she had never been able to locate Barv, or even Jaina, and she knew them a lot better than she did Master Sebatyne.

Finally, she shook her head. "I don't think I can."

"In that case, we would have to use the HoloNet," her mother said. "And if we do that, the Sith might intercept the message. Would that matter?"

"That would be very bad," Allana said instantly. So far, she had heard nothing to indicate that the Barabel nest had been discovered. But if the Sith intercepted a message warning Master Sebatyne of the danger to the hatchlings, they would be certain to mount a thorough search. "It would ruin everything."

"Then maybe we should wait until after the evacuation is finished," her mother said. "As soon as your grandparents return, we'll ask Princess Leia to warn Master Sebatyne through the Force. Will that be okay?"

Allana thought for a moment, then nodded. "I think it has to be."

Chapter Five

THE GRAY MIASMA THAT FILLED ACADEMY SQUARE WAS MORE STEAM than fog. It condensed on the climate-controlled coolness of the *Falcon*'s flight deck canopy and ran down the transparisteel in long shimmering runnels, and it was impossible to see anything outside clearly. Woodoo Hall, just twenty meters away, was a crooked gray box, and the long line of beings emerging from it were shapeless swirls in the fog. The rest of the convoy—eleven Olanjii *Sharmok*-class troop transports arrayed at various points around the parade ground—were not visible at all.

It was going to be a tough run—maybe the toughest run Han Solo had ever made. The Sith were going to send the best pilots they had, and in the dense fog their Force abilities would more than neutralize the Hapan advantage in equipment and training. The sooner the convoy ran for the safety of the Battle Dragons' turbolaser umbrella, the better its chances of survival would be.

Han activated the intercom and opened a channel to the *Falcon*'s rear freight ramp. "Are we loaded yet?"

The din of a hold being loaded quickly came over the cockpit speaker, then Leia said, "Almost, Han."

"That's what you said ten minutes ago."

"Ten minutes *is* almost," Leia said. "We're working as fast as we can back here."

"Well, work faster," Han said. "I don't like this fog. Things can hide in it."

"Things like *us,* Captain Solo," a silky Hapan voice said. "Will you stop worrying? You're beginning to show your age."

"Sweetheart, you're confusing age and experience again," Han replied, deliberately using a term that would rile a proud Hapan woman like Taryn Zel. "And my experience tells me that if you don't get moving back there, we won't *have* a chance to hide. We've been on the ground thirty minutes already."

Leia's voice came over the speaker, sharp as a vibroknife. "Han, how many students are we collecting?"

"Three hundred and twenty-two," Han replied. He had been over the logistics of the operation a hundred times, trying to convince himself they could get it done before the Sith arrived from their not-so-secret staging base in the Colsassan moons. "But that's only twenty-six point eight students *per transport.* It shouldn't take—"

"And how many family members do they have?" Leia interrupted.

"Nine hundred and twenty-three," Han said. "It still shouldn't take—"

"And support staff?"

"Twelve hundred, give or take," Han said. "But they were supposed to be—"

"And how many thousands of tons of matériel are we loading?"

"Don't talk to me about the matériel," Han said. "I wanted to vape that stuff."

"And replace it with *what?*" Leia demanded. "The academy is moving—perhaps permanently. People are going to need a place to sleep. The students are going to need training equipment. The technicians are going to need tools and parts, and we don't have the resources—"

"All right, all right," Han interrupted. He knew Leia's side of the argument as well as his own. With the GA government in the hands of the Sith, the days of unlimited funding were gone. The Jedi Order was going to need everything it could carry off of Ossus. "I just wish we didn't have to take *everything*."

"It wouldn't be a problem if you hadn't insisted on waiting until the last minute," Taryn pointed out. "Commander Luvalle wanted to start this operation four hours ago."

"What she *wanted* to do was spoil Luke's play on Coruscant," Han retorted. During the planning session, he and Luvalle had butted heads repeatedly, with the commander arguing that thirty minutes on the ground wasn't enough time, while Han insisted they couldn't begin the evacuation until *after* the Jedi had launched the attack on Coruscant. "How sure are you *she* isn't Sith?"

"Quite sure, Captain Solo." There was a coolness in Taryn's voice that suggested she had better things to do than defend the commander's reputation. "If you don't mind, we're busy back here. Princess Leia will inform you when the cargo is stowed."

A sharp *pop* sounded from the speaker, and then the intercom fell silent. Han's jaw dropped, and he spun around in the pilot's chair, looking toward the back of the flight deck where R2-D2 was monitoring the comm station.

"Did you hear that?" he demanded. "She deactivated me!"

R2-D2 spun his dome toward the front of the flight deck, then emitted a long series of urgent whistles.

"What's wrong?" Han demanded. C-3PO was out on loan, helping Raynar Thul figure out exactly what Abeloth was—and, with any luck, where she had disappeared to—so Han didn't have anyone to translate the little droid's beeps and whistles. "If she used a blaster on that intercom station, she's riding out of here in a strut well!"

An alert chime sounded from the main display, and Han turned around to find a message from R2-D2 scrolling across the screen. THE NEWS IS WORSE THAN THAT. VHORK LEADER REPORTS THAT A WING OF SKIPRAY BLASTBOATS HAS RECENTLY EMERGED FROM HYPERSPACE.

Han's heart began to pound ferociously, but he forced himself to remain calm. Vhork Squadron—named for a giant Daruvvian hawk that took a dim view of airspeeders encroaching on its territory—was the best starfighter squadron in the Hapan Royal Navy, and that was why they were flying top cover for the mission.

"Okay," Han said cautiously. "So Vhork Squadron is moving to engage, right?"

R2 gave a negative chirp, then followed it with an explanatory note: INTERCEPTION FAILED. THE ENEMY ACTIVATED A JAMMING DEVICE AND DROPPED INTO THE ATMOSPHERE. VHORK LEADER REPORTS THREE TARGETS ELIMINATED, BUT THE OTHER BLASTBOATS ESCAPED, FORTY-SEVEN SECONDS AGO.

"And they're just telling us now?"

VHORK SQUADRON IS ATTEMPTING TO REACQUIRE THE ENEMY, AND HER MAJESTY HAS DISPATCHED FOUR MIY'TIL WINGS TO SUPPORT THE EFFORT.

"Okay, plot a launch vector and have the starfighter wings assemble at the other end. We'll bring the Sith to *them*."

R2-D2 gave a confirming tweedle, then Han slapped the activation switch on the *Falcon*'s comm unit and opened a channel to the rest of the convoy.

"Listen up . . ." He relayed the details of the report he had just received. "My guess is we've got about five minutes before those blastboats pop out of the rift valley and start vaping anything with an ion drive. So get your cargo stowed, your hatches secured, and launch . . ."

Han checked his primary display for the vector.

". . . local north at a seventy-degree climb. *Don't* stray out of that ascension corridor, or you'll be entering the free-fire zone."

"What free-fire zone?" a Hapan pilot asked. "No one mentioned any free-fire zones in the briefing."

"Plan B," Han said. "Our fighter cover is going to zone defense."

"Plan B called for us to drop into the rift valley and wait for an escort," a second pilot reminded him.

"This is the *new* Plan B," Han replied. "Trust me, the last thing you want is to be down in that valley with a bunch of Sith hunting you in the fog."

Han tried to raise Leia again on the cargo hold intercom, but all he got was dead air. "Blast!" He turned to R2-D2. "Take a holo."

The droid spun his dome around until the cam lens was pointed in Han's direction. When the red RECORD light activated, Han began to speak.

"Leia, we've got a bunch of blastboats on their way. We need to be locked down and launched in five minutes. And while you're at it, re-activate the intercom back there!" He paused until the RECORD light darkened, then addressed R2-D2 himself. "Show that to Leia—and *don't* let her ignore you. Get in her way if you have to."

Another alert chime sounded from the main display, and Han turned to find another message from R2-D2.

FIVE MINUTES CUTS THE ESCAPE SAFETY MARGIN TO ZERO.

"I hate to break this to you, Artoo," Han said, "but we never *had* a safety margin."

UNDERSTOOD. EVACUATION PROCEEDING AS PLANNED.

The droid retracted his interface arm and started down the access corridor toward the main cabin. Han began to prep the *Falcon* for a hot launch. The fusion core was already on standby, so he slowly began to feed it more fuel, trying to preheat the inner housing to minimize temperature stress when the big laser cannons began to suck power. At the same time, he brought the targeting computers online and engaged his active sensors. The Sith would be using the Force to find their targets anyway, so he had nothing to lose by pinging electromagnetic signals off their hulls. Finally, he activated the ion drive and brought the throttles up until the *Falcon* dropped her nose and began to rock and shudder on her struts.

Beyond the viewport, the blocky gray shape of a departing transport began to move through the fog on the invisible cushion of its repulsor drives. A few hundred meters ahead, a trio of blue circles flared to life and began to glow more brightly as a second vessel activated its ion engines, preparing, like Han, for an emergency launch that would turn a wide swath of Jedi academy grounds into a kilometer-long furrow of charred dirt. Given the tons of Jedi equipment that the convoy would be leaving behind on the parade ground to be captured, Han wished he'd thought to instruct all of the transports to make emergency launches—but it was already too late. The gray rectangles of two more transports began to rise through the fog, and another set of ion engines flared to life off to port.

An alert buzzer chimed from the *Falcon*'s control panel, and Han glanced over at the tactical display to see a line of jamming static rolling out of the nearby rift valley. He hit the general-quarters alarm—and that was when he saw Taryn Zel's reflection in the viewport.

"Captain Solo." She bustled onto the flight deck, with R2-D2 close behind. "We're doing the best we can back there. If you think you can—"

She was interrupted by the distant thunder of accelerating ion engines. Han activated both sets of upper shields—forward and aft—and was still pushing the control glides to FULL when the fog grew crimson with shrieking cannon bolts. The *Falcon* reverberated with the crackle of shields taking hits, and the lights dimmed as power was diverted to the shield generators.

"Stang!" Taryn gasped. She spun and started back down the access corridor, already yelling back toward the main cabin. "Zekk, get those ramps up and take the belly turret. I'll take top."

"No, stay here and take the copilot's chair." Han had to yell loudly to make himself heard above the battle noise. "Have Leia take top turret. Artoo, hook yourself into the tactical net."

Taryn paused two steps down the corridor and turned to meet his gaze in the viewport reflection. "But the Princess is—"

"A Jedi. And the Force is going to work a lot better than a targeting computer when our sensors are being jammed." Han pointed at the copilot's seat. "So sit."

Taryn's reply was lost to the deafening crackle of half a dozen simultaneous hits, and the entire flight deck strobed gold and white with dissipation static.

Taryn merely nodded and yelled something into the main cabin that Han could not hear, then hurried into the copilot's seat and strapped in. Han checked the tactical display and found that the wall of jamming static had advanced to the edge of the academy grounds.

"Do we have everyone aboard?" he asked, still yelling to make himself heard.

Taryn shot him a tense look. "I hope so." She fixed her attention on the ramp indicator lights, then finally nodded. "We must. The ramps are up, and I can't imagine Zekk or Princess Leia leaving any Woodoos behind."

Han activated the intercom again and was relieved to hear the voice of a young Jedi issuing orders in the cargo hold. There was still too much noise to make out exactly what he was saying, but he seemed to be giving orders rather than shouting in alarm, and that was good enough for Han.

He opened the shipwide channel and said, "Grab something and hold on back there. This is gonna be a *very* rough ride."

As he spoke, two columns of boiling blue ions appeared in the fog and shot skyward. A heartbeat later a dozen Sith-piloted blastboats opened fire on the fleeing transports, their efflux tails curving sharply as they turned to pursue. Han checked his tactical display and saw only one Sharmok left on the ground. It launched before his eyes, vanishing from the screen, then streaked past so low overhead that it left the *Falcon* rocking in thrust-wash.

Han pulled the yoke back and slammed the throttles forward. The *Falcon* leapt after the departing convoy, though not quickly enough to prevent a dozen blastboats from slipping into line between them and the last Sharmok.

"Taryn, retract the struts and bring up the belly shields," Han ordered. "Leia, you and Zekk clear those Skiprays off that—"

A cacophony of lock alarms screeched to life, and a series of sharp thuds reverberated through the hull as cannon bolts stitched a line of hits across the *Falcon*'s belly armor. Taryn hissed something angrily in Hapan, then the cabin lights flickered as the lower shields finally began to absorb damage.

Han resisted the urge to blame Taryn for being too slow and settled for a muttered curse instead.

"Not my fault, Solo," she said anyway. "You're the one who said retract the struts first."

"You hear me complaining?"

"As a matter of fact, yes," Taryn said. "What *is* a three-fingered shenbit wrangler, anyway?"

"Seven fingers too slow," Han replied. "Shift seventy percent of power to our rear shields, then arm the concussion missiles. See if you can get a heat-lock on one of those blastboats."

As he spoke, all eight of the *Falcon*'s big laser cannons began to chug, and the blastboats ahead started to blossom into fireballs. At the same time, the crackle of stressed shield generators began to reverberate through the ship. Han held a steady course, giving Zekk and Leia a stable firing platform that allowed them to destroy eight blastboats in as many breaths.

Finally, the load meters on both rear shields shot into the danger range, and Han knew they had run out of time. He rolled into an evasive helix, then activated the aft landing cams. He was not at all surprised to find a swarm of blue rings—blastboats silhouetted by their own exhaust plumes—glowing in the fog behind the *Falcon*. The gunners were obviously using the Force to aid their targeting, as his corkscrewing climb was doing nothing to diminish their accuracy.

"Can we *take* this kind of damage?" Taryn asked, clearly looking at the same thing Han was.

"Sure, no problem," Han assured her. "As long as the shields hold—"

Both rear shield-overload alarms began to buzz.

Han started to pull the throttles back in an effort to trick his pursuers into overflying them—then recalled that the blastboats were being piloted by *Sith*, and they would see through that maneuver just as easily as their gunners were anticipating his evasive rolls.

"Okay," Taryn said. "So what happens if the shields don't hold?"

"Did you get that heat-lock yet?"

"Don't get testy, old man." Taryn said. "I'm working on it."

"Well, stop," Han said. "Set a pair of fuses for half a second and dump two missiles without—"

"Igniting their propulsion units," Taryn finished. Her voice assumed a note of admiration. "You *were* a pretty good smuggler once, weren't you?"

Before Han could answer—or add *on my mark*—he felt the drag of the Ossan atmosphere rushing into the open missile tubes. He shoved the throttles past the overload stops, then heard the muffled *bang . . . bang* of the launching charges expelling two missiles from the weapons bay.

Han did not even hear the detonation. The steering yoke simply pushed itself back into his lap, and the *Falcon* went into a slewing, almost-vertical climb as the vector plates were lifted by the shock wave. Damage alarms began to ring in all corners of the control panel, and Leia's voice came over the intercom.

"Han? How bad is—"

"We're fine." Han began to slap the damage alarms silent, looking at each indicator just long enough to be sure that the *Falcon* hadn't taken any catastrophic damage. "I think."

"Captain Solo had me dump a pair of concussion missiles on our pursuers," Taryn said, smiling across the flight deck at him. "You did well when you chose him, Jedi Solo. He's quite an asset in a bad situation."

"He does have his moments," Leia agreed.

A deactivated damage alarm began to chime again, and Han saw that they were losing pressure in the number two sleeping cabin.

"All right, enough with the flattery." He eased the yoke forward again—and was alarmed to feel more resistance than he should have. "We didn't come through that exactly untouched, so keep those blastboats off our tail."

"What blastboats?" Zekk asked. "I don't see any down here."

"And there aren't any above us," Leia added. "I think you must have gotten—"

The viewport went crimson as a pair of cannon bolts blossomed against the underpowered forward shields, and then the golden light of dissipation static began to strobe through the entire flight deck.

"They're up here!" Han yelled, trying to figure out how the blastboats had managed to get ahead of him so quickly. He shoved the sluggish yoke forward, forcing the *Falcon* into an unstable dive, then glanced over and saw that Taryn was not nearly as good at reading his mind as Leia was. "What are you waiting for? Shift power to the forward shields. Launch some concussion missiles!"

A negative tweedle sounded from the comm station behind him, then a message from R2-D2 scrolled across Han's display. HOLD YOUR FIRE. THE ATTACK IS A MISTAKE.

"A mistake?" he echoed. "Who makes a mistake like *that*?"

A flurry of blaster bolts flashed through the fog, missing the *Falcon* by more than a dozen meters, and Han realized that whoever was shooting at them didn't have the Force—and if they didn't have the Force, they couldn't be Sith. He opened a hailing channel.

"Miy'til squadron, hold your fire!" he said. The blue dots of a dozen starfighter engines appeared in the fog ahead, growing larger and brighter as they approached. "We're the good guys!"

There was a short silence, during which time the blue dots resolved themselves into blue rings, then the icy voice of a Hapan officer replied, "How do we know that?"

Taryn activated her mike and said something in ancient Lorellian.

Another pause followed, and then the woman responded in a chastened tone. "We apologize for the misunderstanding, *Millennium Falcon*, but you *did* stray into the free-fire zone." The squadron veered away. "Continue climbing on your former vector. You'll be clear of the sensor jamming in a minute, and then you can catch the rest of the convoy."

"So they made it?" Leia asked. "All of them?"

"You're number ten," the officer replied. "So far."

Han's heart sank. "We were the last to launch," he said. "If you haven't seen the other two, that means they're in trouble."

The officer fell silent for a moment, then said, "We outnumber the enemy four to one, and we're flying the latest Miy'tils. If anyone is still down there, we'll find them."

It was Taryn who asked the obvious question. "What if you find them too late?"

"Then the Sith *will* pay," the woman said. "That I promise."

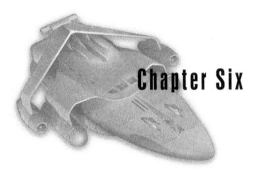

Chapter Six

STARING OUT ACROSS FELLOWSHIP PLAZA, WYNN DORVAN SAW LITTLE evidence that war had come to Coruscant. Pedestrians still wandered through the Walking Garden, inhaling the sweet scent of lycandis and blartree blossoms. Tourists still lingered at their tables in Wenbas Court, enjoying a leisurely lunch in the shadow of the Jedi Temple. Children continued to float in the air above Mungo Park, laughing and squealing as they turned somersaults above the giant negrav trampoline. Everywhere he looked, beings were out enjoying themselves, blissfully ignorant of the hundreds of little battles secretly raging in every corner of the planet.

And Wynn intended to keep it that way—provided, of course, he could convince his Beloved Queen of the Stars that letting her capital world slip into open warfare would not win the hearts of her subjects.

Without looking from the window, the Beloved Queen said, "I do not like all these Jedi on my planet."

To everyone else, she appeared to be Roki Kem, an elegant Jessar female dressed in a formal white gown. But Wynn saw her in her true form. To him, she was Abeloth, a tentacle-armed monster with eyes as tiny as stars and a mouth so broad it could swallow a human head.

The Beloved Queen turned away from the window, facing a tall Keshiri woman with dark lilac skin almost as blue as Roki Kem's. "How many of the creatures have infested us, Lady Korelei?"

A glimmer of fear showed in Korelei's long oval eyes. "That is difficult to say, Beloved Queen," she said. "The Jedi attack us everywhere, and yet we have not been able to find *them* anywhere."

"Because you are on *their* world, Lady Korelei." Wynn forced himself to meet his torturer's gaze as he spoke, then could not quite suppress a shudder as he turned to address the Beloved Queen herself. "There can be a few hundred warriors at most. The whole Jedi Order numbers barely more than a thousand, and that includes the students they removed from beneath the Lost Tribe's guard at Ossus."

The Beloved Queen's tentacle-arms rippled with her displeasure. "And yet they have slain how many Sith, Lady Korelei?"

"Less than a thousand, Beloved Queen." As Korelei spoke, her gaze remained fixed on Wynn. "The number remains uncertain."

"But near enough to call it a thousand?" the Beloved Queen clarified. When Korelei nodded, she continued, "Still, that leaves you five thousand Sith. I would think that would be enough to clear the problem by dawn tomorrow."

The Beloved Queen's words were, of course, less a question than an order. But that did not stop Korelei from dropping her chin in shame. "That I cannot do, Beloved Queen."

"You cannot?" Her voice turned as sharp as a Sith shikkar. "I fail to see the problem."

"The Jedi have intelligence on us." Korelei raised her chin again. "They know our secret identities, and we know nothing of them. It gives them a permanent advantage of surprise."

"And you have done nothing to nullify that advantage?" the Beloved Queen asked. "Surely, you have captured *one*?"

Unable to force herself to answer, Korelei merely looked away.

"I see." The Beloved Queen stared at the Sith just long enough to make the woman grow pale, then asked, "What are you going to do about that?"

Korelei fixed her gaze on Wynn. "There is much that your adviser has not told us."

"How can that be? You had more than a month with him." The Beloved Queen turned on Wynn and studied him for many moments, until he could see nothing but the silver pinpoints of her gaze. Cold tentacles of fear began to snake down inside him, and still she did not look away. Finally she said, "Yes, there is much he has hidden from you. But if you could not get it from him in a month, you will not get it from him tonight—and by tomorrow it will be too late."

Korelei's slender face went gaunt with fear. "Then we have only one option, Beloved Queen," she said. "We must reveal ourselves to the people of Coruscant. We must tell them that they are now ruled by Sith."

Wynn's chest tightened. "Why would you do that?" he asked. "So the entire population of Coruscant will rise against you?"

"The people of Coruscant will rise against nothing," Korelei retorted. "They will suffer and obey—and we will know the Jedi by those who fail to tremble beneath our lash."

Wynn's pulse began to pound so hard it felt like his temples might burst. There was a cruel simplicity to the Sith's plan—and one that just might succeed. If the invaders began to behave brutally enough, the Jedi would be forced to reveal themselves—to step onto the field and fight in the open, no matter how bad the odds.

The Beloved Queen smiled, her gruesome mouth stretching wide. "It will not work quickly," she said. "But it *will* work."

Wynn could tell by the excitement in her voice that it was more than Korelei's plan his Beloved Queen liked. He had accompanied her into the undercity several times in the past day alone, and he did not need to be a Jedi to recognize how she fed on the fear and the suffering down there. It literally seemed to flow into her, making her stronger and healthier—and the more she drank in, the more she seemed to want. Korelei's plan would give her an endless supply of fear and pain, and the entire planet would become her feeding grounds.

And that, Wynn Dorvan could not allow.

Taking a deep breath, he asked, "Beloved Queen, is this what you really want? To win the battle . . . and lose the war?"

The Beloved Queen's eyes blazed white. "Lose *how*? The people will obey the Sith." She turned to Korelei. "Is that not so?"

Korelei dipped her chin. "We will make it so."

Wynn shook his head. "The people will fight," he said. "And they won't stop until they're dead."

"Then we will oblige them," Korelei said. "They will stop fighting when we have killed enough of them."

Wynn was not surprised to see the Beloved Queen scowl in disapproval. She was a being who fed on fear and anguish, not on death, and anything that reduced the population of Coruscant also reduced *her*. He stepped to the viewport and peered out across the crowded plaza, trying to think of a way to use her dark hunger to prevent all those innocent beings from being drawn into the secret war between the Jedi and the Sith—or at least to keep them ignorant of it for a while longer.

"Those beings are *Coruscanti*," Wynn said, touching a finger to the transparisteel. "They're accustomed to being the masters of the galaxy, not its slaves—and if Korelei does not understand that about your subjects, she understands nothing."

Korelei's expression did not darken, nor did she hiss a curse or telegraph her attack by stepping toward Wynn. Her shikkar simply slipped from its sheath and sailed toward his belly in a glassy gleam so fast he barely had time to go cold inside.

But one of the Beloved Queen's tentacles was already curling through the air in front of him, and in the next instant Wynn was not crying out in anguish, or gasping for breath—he was, in fact, still standing on his own two feet, not even bleeding and hardly even shaking.

He forced himself to meet Korelei's hate-filled eyes. "You need to add some new problem-solving strategies to your repertoire, Lady Korelei," he said. "Silencing the opposition is not always the best solution."

Korelei's face grew stormy, and she started to raise a hand to hit Wynn with some sort of Force blast.

"Not yet," the Beloved Queen said, stopping Korelei's attack with a glance. "If Chief Dorvan has a better idea, I wish to hear it."

"I do," Wynn said, forcing himself to breathe again. He and the

Bwua'tus had discussed many times how to save Coruscant from the Sith without destroying it, and it had always come down to keeping the battle confined, to setting the fight someplace from which there could be no withdrawal . . . for either side. "If you want the people to remain docile, Beloved Queen, you must defeat the Jedi quietly. The people must never know what you have done."

"That's impossible," Korelei protested. "The only way to kill the Jedi is to find them, and the only way to find them is to flush them into the open."

"Forgive me, but you're wrong." Wynn glanced down at the shikkar still hanging in the tentacle in front of him, then turned to the Beloved Queen and said, "There is only one way to find the Jedi, and that is to bring them to *us*."

"To us?" the Beloved Queen echoed. "Inside my Temple?"

"Exactly," Wynn said. He waited for a dozen heartbeats as the shikkar continued to hang in front of him—then finally sighed in relief as the tentacle withdrew and returned the weapon to Korelei. "The Sith must withdraw into the Temple—and force the Jedi to come inside after them."

Chapter Seven

THE *MILLENNIUM FALCON* SAT SHUDDERING IN THE HANGAR, A MILKY drop of durasteel resting on a deck so dark and expansive it looked like a drift of open space. The vessel's rear corner sagged over a collapsed strut, her white hull armor was pocked from cannon strikes, and the ion drives were jetting hot coolant. Yellow smoke kept billowing from the exhaust vents, and every few seconds the upper turret would shake as though the power core were about to blow. And still, the battered transport was the most beautiful thing Queen Mother Tenel Ka had seen in a long time. It was hissing, pinging, carbon-scorched proof that Han and Leia Solo had survived another close call, that they had cheated death yet again and escaped an ambush that should have left their atoms flying in the Ossan winds.

Emergency sleds and fire carts started to float out of the hangar's dark corners, and passengers began to stream down the ramp beneath the *Falcon*'s hull. Several were limping or holding their arms, but no one seemed seriously injured or in a hurry. Finally, the Solos themselves emerged from the ship, Han turning to speak to the service crew and Leia bending down to say a few words to the Jedi younglings, and Tenel Ka finally began to breathe again.

"I don't see why you were so afraid," Allana said. She had not left Tenel Ka's side since Aegel Squadron had reported damage to the *Falcon*. "You *said* it would be a mistake to underestimate Han and Leia Solo."

"As it would." Tenel Ka flashed her daughter a reassuring smile. "But of course I'm still concerned. You know how fond I am of the Solos."

Before answering, Allana glanced across the salon toward the command center, where Trista Zel was helping Kam and Tionne Solusar assemble a report on the evacuation's outcome. Tenel Ka was fairly certain that both Masters had deduced her daughter's true identity long ago, but no one had said as much to Allana herself, and so Allana continued to play the Solos' adopted daughter even in their presence.

Seeing that both Masters were busy taking reports over their headsets, she took Tenel Ka's hand. "Grandma and Grandpa worry about *you*, too," she whispered. "And so do I."

A pang of loneliness shot through Tenel Ka's heart, and she found herself wishing she had not been born the daughter of a Hapan prince, that she were free to raise her own daughter in her own modest apartment. But any attempt to abdicate her responsibility would only get them both killed. Anyone taking Tenel Ka's place would not feel secure on the throne until her agents had eliminated every possible rival—especially the child of a former Queen Mother. So there was nothing to be done except what Tenel Ka *was* doing, and that meant continuing to pretend that her daughter was someone else's child until Allana grew old enough to defend herself from the daggers—political and actual—that were so much a part of life in the Hapan court.

Tenel Ka squeezed her daughter's hand. "Thank you," she whispered. "But you don't have to worry about me. I have a whole army of secret friends keeping watch over me."

Allana cocked an eyebrow. "Like Trista and Taryn?"

Tenel Ka nodded. "That's right."

A soft *swoosh* sounded from the back of the salon, and Tenel Ka turned to see Han Solo stepping out of the lift tube. He paused just

long enough to scan the room and locate Allana, then spread his arms
and started across the salon.

"See?" There was a forced cheerfulness to Han's voice that betrayed the concern Tenel Ka sensed in his presence. "I told you we'd
be fine!"

Allana stepped into Han's hug and squeezed him hard. "I knew *you*
would. I was just afraid that without me to keep watch on things, the
Falcon would get all banged up." She released him, then put her hands
on her hips and turned toward the viewport. "And it looks like I was
right!"

"You certainly were," Leia said, joining them. She leaned down and
kissed Allana's cheek. "The way Han wobbled in, we're lucky we only
broke one strut."

Han flashed a scowl, but it was more of a forced grin than a true
frown. "Hey, after you let all those blastboats potshot us, I was doing
good just to land right-side up." He turned back to Allana. "Isn't that
right?"

"Sure," Allana said, smiling. "If you call bouncing across the
hangar deck a *landing*."

Han dropped his jaw in feigned dejection, then returned her smile.
"You got me there, kid. We did come in a little rough." He ruffled her
hair, then turned to Tenel Ka and allowed his expression to show the
concern she had already sensed. "So, how bad is it?"

"The Masters Solusar only arrived a few minutes ago, and they are
still assembling reports," Tenel Ka said, pointing toward the command
center. "I'm sure they would be happy to give you a preview."

Han nodded and started across the salon, but Allana caught Leia by
a handful of robe and held her back. "Can you find Master Sebatyne in
the Force?"

Leia stopped and said, "I can certainly try. But you know she's
probably very busy right now."

"This is important," Allana said. "You need to warn her about
something."

"Then of course I'll do my best," Leia said. "What am I warning
her about?"

"The *Sith*. They're going to find Tesar and the others."

Leia's expression grew confused. "What makes you think that?"

"Because I saw it happen," Allana said. "In a viewport."

Leia glanced at Tenel Ka, clearly looking for a hint.

"Another Force vision," Tenel Ka explained. "Apparently, she saw Tesar and the other Barabels being discovered inside the Temple."

A flicker of understanding came to Leia's eyes. "I see." When she turned back to Allana, there was a calm acceptance in her expression that suggested some stray bit of information had just fallen into place for her. "But you know I can't actually talk to Master Sebatyne through the Force, right?"

Allana nodded. "That's okay, as long as you make sure she understands."

"I'll do my best," Leia said. "But we'd have to use the HoloNet to be sure."

"No, we can't do that," Allana said, shaking her head. "The Sith might intercept the message, and that would only make what I saw happen sooner. It would be like I *made* it happen."

"Well then . . ." Leia glanced toward a pair of luxurious nerf-hide chairs flanking a low beverage table in the salon's near corner. "I'd better see what I can do."

"We'll give you some quiet," Tenel Ka said. Sensing a burst of joyful surprise in the Solusars' Force aura, she took her daughter's hand and started toward the command center. "Perhaps you and I should check the evacuation after-reports while Princess Leia reaches out to Master Sebatyne."

"Okay," Allana said, allowing herself to be drawn along. "But I already know the after-reports are good."

"Because you felt it in the Force?" Tenel Ka asked.

"That," Allana said, "and I haven't heard any Corellian curse words."

And good news it was. As they approached, Kam Solusar looked up from his station and touched a button on his headset. His face was as chiseled and ruggedly handsome as ever, but the wounds he had suffered defending the Jedi academy during the Second Civil War had left him a little thinner than before.

"We're doing well," Kam said, smiling. "We haven't lost anyone so far."

The news was even better than Tenel Ka had hoped—especially

considering the difficult circumstances of the mission, and the enemy's cleverness in attacking under cover of the Ossan fog.

"When you say anyone," she asked, "do you mean transports or people?"

"Both," Tionne clarified. With her silver hair and white eyes, she remained a woman of ethereal beauty—despite the subtle imperfections of the prosthetic arm and leg she wore in place of the limbs she had lost during the same incident that had wounded her husband. "Sharmok seven-eighteen took some heavy damage and has lost communications. But Volgh Squadron is escorting her in, and the leader is relaying visual now. It looks like seven-eighteen will make it, too."

Tenel Ka smiled. "That is very good news."

"It is." Tionne's face grew more somber. "Though I'm afraid your Miy'til pilots have taken some casualties, and two squadrons remain engaged."

Tenel Ka felt her stomach knot, but nodded. "We expected that," she said. "But this is more than a rescue mission, Master Solusar. It's a chance for the Hapan Royal Navy to assess the enemy's capabilities."

"I'll bet that wasn't an easy sell with Lady Maluri and Ducha Luvalle in the room," Han commented. "So thanks—and I mean for everything."

"The Consortium appreciates your gratitude, Captain Solo," Trista Zel said, looking up from her data display. "But I assure you, the Queen Mother has no need to *sell* anything."

Han raised his hands as though to apologize, then scowled and suddenly turned back to Tionne. "Did you say seven-eighteen?"

She nodded. "That's correct."

"And we didn't lose any other transports?" he asked. "You're sure?"

"We're sure, Han," Kam said. "We're Jedi Masters. We *can* count to twelve."

"Yeah—but it shouldn't have been this easy." Han circled around to the back of the crescent-shaped console, then leaned over Trista's shoulder to study the data display. "It was a mess down there, and seven-eighteen got jumped in front of us. She got jumped *hard*."

Trista craned her neck to look up at him. "Captain Solo, are you suggesting—"

"I'm not suggesting anything. Seven-eighteen launched ahead of the *Falcon*. Now she's the straggler." Han stabbed a finger at the display. "And it looks like she's making for the flagship. You figure it out."

Trista spoke into her throat-mike, then her face paled as she listened to the reply. A second later she began to snap orders.

"Have Volgh Leader signal seven-eighteen to veer off *now*," she said. "And no excuses. Warn the pilot that if she's still on this vector in sixty seconds, she *will* be vaped."

"Vaped?" Allana looked up at Tenel Ka. "But she's carrying academy students!"

"She's *supposed* to be." Tenel Ka extended her Force awareness in the transport's direction, but there were fifteen Battle Dragons and close to a dozen clusters of Jedi students in the area, and it was impossible to tell whether the presences she sensed were aboard Sharmok 718. "But her behavior is suspicious. Something is very wrong."

Tenel Ka stepped around behind the console, and her heart fell when she saw the display. One of the screens showed a close-up image of a Sharmok transport gliding through a starry drift of space. With a line of scorch holes angling up her stern quarter, a pair of jagged rings where the cannon turrets used to be, and a hull crumple behind her main hatch, the vessel had clearly seen some savage close-quarters combat.

A dot of white light appeared against the flight deck viewport and began to blink on and off in the staccato rhythm of the Hapan military's flash code.

"Any sign they were boarded?" Tenel Ka asked.

"None reported," Trista replied.

"There wouldn't be," Han said. "Sharmok air locks use a standard two-stage touch pad, right?"

Tenel Ka considered the hull-crumple behind the hatch and, realizing that it looked more like collision damage than a missile strike, saw what Han was saying.

"You're suggesting the Sith used the Force to open the air lock?" She glanced at the identification strip at the bottom of the display and saw that the image was coming to them from the battle cam of Volgh Leader. "I must agree. Trista, instruct Volgh Leader to open fire on Sharmok seven-eighteen's ion drives immediately."

Tenel Ka felt the Force shudder with the shock of her companions, but the precision of the command left no opportunity to question its wisdom. Han gave her a quick, tight-lipped nod, and Trista spoke into her throat-mike, relaying the order. The Solusars merely exchanged a wide-eyed glance—no doubt checking with each other to see if either thought Tenel might be overreacting.

"But what if there are still academy students aboard?" Allana objected. "They could be killed!"

"That's why Volgh Leader is targeting the ion drives." Han took Allana by the shoulders and pulled her close. "If that Sharmok is being flown by Sith, no way can we let her get near the flagship. So we're going to disable her and send a boarding party to take control." He looked back to Tenel Ka. "Right, Your Majesty?"

"Correct." Tenel Ka smiled a silent thanks to Han, then checked the tactical display to find the Battle Dragon closest to the transport. "Trista, have the *Daphoros* execute a tractor beam capture of Sharmok seven-eighteen as soon as the engines have been disabled, then send a boarding company to retake—"

"If I may, Your Majesty," Kam said, interrupting as politely as possible. "Given the Sith involvement, it might be wise for me to take some Jedi along."

"Excellent point, Master Solusar," Tenel Ka said, feeling a pang of regret that she could not join the Jedi Knights going to fight the Sith. "Trista, inform the *Daphoros* that Master Solusar will be joining the boarding company as its commander. And suggest to the Lady Commander that she send her best assault team on this mission."

As Tenel Ka spoke, she kept one eye on the tactical display, watching as Volgh Leader and her wingmate came in for their attack run. Rather than dropping back behind the target and risking an engine detonation by firing directly up the thrust nozzles, the Miy'tils were swinging in from the flank. For a moment, as the Sharmok continued toward the *Dragon Queen II* without altering her vector, Tenel Ka began to think Han might be wrong, that perhaps 718 had merely lost her Hapan crew and was now being piloted by some terrified Jedi apprentice.

But half a second before the Miy'tils opened fire, the transport's designator symbol jerked left as the pilot took evasive action. The first

Miy'til symbol flashed white as the starfighter opened fire, then shot past without a hit. The wingmate opened fire in the next heartbeat, and the Sharmok's color changed to yellow, for "damaged." Sighing in relief, Tenel Ka switched her attention to the visual display and saw only whirling stars as Volgh Leader wheeled back around toward the target.

"Report," Tenel Ka ordered. "Did they disable the engines?"

"Patience, Majesty," Trista said. "They need time to evaluate."

Taking her cousin's gentle chide in stride—*someone* had to keep her humble, after all—Tenel Ka fixed her gaze on the visual display, hardly daring to breathe as stars whirled past. Finally, the Sharmok's ion tail drifted into view, flickering and flashing as her sublight drives flamed out. By the time the entire stern appeared, the last engine had stopped, and the image showed only a trio of red-hot exhaust nozzles.

Tenel Ka let her breath out—and the screen went white with a detonation flash. She felt a terrible ripping in the Force and heard her Jedi companions gasping in shock—then she heard a small, frightened cry and knew her daughter had felt it, too, the searing pain of three hundred lives coming to a single end.

Tenel Ka pivoted around and knelt before Allana, folding her into her embrace. "Come here."

Allana remained limp in her arms. "I felt them end," she said. "I felt them—"

"I know, sweetheart." Tenel Ka resisted the temptation to tell her daughter not to think about it, because she knew that was impossible. No one could feel the deaths of several hundred people and simply forget about it—especially not a nine-year-old girl. "The Sharmok's ion drives must have taken a critical—"

"No way," Han said from behind Tenel Ka. "That was no engine blast. Engine blasts don't take out whole starfighter squadrons."

"What?" Tenel Ka craned her neck, but did not rise to look. Allana needed to be held right now. "We lost Volgh Squadron? How much of it?"

"All of it," Han reported. "The blast radius was three kilometers. They don't make ion drives big enough to cause that kind of blast. Had to be baradium—a *lot* of it. That ship was rigged."

Allana looked over Tenel Ka's shoulder. "You mean the Sith did it?"

she asked. "They blew everyone up because we wouldn't let them aboard?"

Han's face grew sad. "Yeah, sweetheart, that's what I mean." His gaze shifted from Allana to Tenel Ka. "That bomb was meant for the Queen Mother."

Allana's posture grew rigid. "They were trying to trick us?" She slipped free of Tenel Ka's embrace and looked her in the eye. "Again?"

Tenel Ka nodded. "That's what Sith do," she said. "That's why we need to be so careful around them."

As Tenel Ka spoke, Leia approached from the corner of the salon. Her expression was calm, but the concern in her Force aura suggested that she had felt the deaths as clearly as the others. She took one look at the somber faces gathered around the console and dropped her gaze in sorrow.

"How bad is it?" she asked.

"They captured Sharmok seven-eighteen." Tionne's voice was filled with grief. "It appears they were trying to use it to sneak a baradium device aboard the flagship . . . to eliminate Queen Mother Tenel Ka."

Leia's eyes flashed, and she could not help glancing in Allana's direction. Like Tenel Ka, the Solos had been warned by the Skywalkers about what had happened at the Pool of Knowledge, when a Sith High Lord had seen an image of a Jedi queen sitting on the Throne of Balance. Obsessed with preventing the vision, the Sith believed Tenel Ka to be that queen, and their mistake had resulted in a series of misguided assassination attempts. It was a burden she gladly carried in order to protect her daughter.

After a moment, Leia said, "We should certainly count ourselves fortunate they didn't succeed." She stepped around the console and began to study the tactical display. "But I can't help thinking of the passengers—of all those students and their families. Do we know for sure they were aboard?"

"Yeah, we do," Han said. "Seven-eighteen was just ahead of us when we launched, and it wasn't far behind when we landed. The Sith didn't have time to off-load three hundred prisoners—even if they had wanted to."

Kam nodded. "My guess is the whole blastboat attack was designed to cut a transport out of the convoy and conceal a bomb on it," he said. "Still, there were over two dozen students aboard who were old enough to put up a fight. The Sith would have needed a sizable force to capture their target so quickly, and we don't actually know who died on that Sharmok."

"Right. The bomb might have been Plan B." Han paused and glanced in Allana's direction, then apparently decided there was no need to spell out the possible alternative—that the Sith's Plan A had been to land an elite boarding company and capture the *Dragon Queen II* for their navy. He turned to Tenel Ka and said, "It wouldn't hurt to have someone check along seven-eighteen's trajectory to see what they find."

"Are you trying to be clever again?" Allana asked, looking at Han. "Because I know what you're saying—that they might have dumped the passengers out an air lock."

"It's certainly worth checking," Tenel Ka said. She nodded to her cousin. "Trista will see to it."

Trista acknowledged the order with a quick nod and began to speak into her throat-mike. When Tenel Ka turned back to her daughter, she found Allana looking more worried than ever.

"There's nothing to fear," Tenel Ka said. "That Sharmok was never going to come aboard. That's why we have Royal Protocol."

"I'm not worrying about *us*," Allana said. "It's the Barabels. The Sith just killed almost thirty Jedi and their families, and pretty soon they're going to kill Tesar and his—"

Her eyes went wide, and she ended the sentence without finishing the thought. Instead, she turned toward Leia. "Does Master Sebatyne understand about my vision?"

Leia's expression grew apologetic, and she shook her head. "I don't think so. She seemed to be, well, *hunting,* and when I tried to make her think of Tesar, she just withdrew. I was trying to reach her again when . . ." She finished with a glance toward the console, then added, "I don't think it's going to work."

"It doesn't sound like it," Allana agreed. Her face grew serious, then she said, "I guess I have to do this myself."

Leia's brow rose. "Do *what* yourself?"

"Go to Coruscant," Allana said simply. She turned to Han. "How soon can you have the *Falcon* repaired?"

Han scowled. "Never, if you're expecting to fly to Coruscant in it," he said. "Haven't you heard? The place is crawling with Sith."

"We won't be there long," Allana said. "All I need to do is find Barv. *He* can warn Tesar."

Han looked relieved. "Why didn't you say so? *I* can find Barv. What's the message?"

"That I need to speak to him," Allana said. "Aboard the *Falcon*."

Han shook his head. "No way," he said. "You're wasting your breath, kid. The message or nothing."

Allana scowled at Han for a moment, then exhaled sharply and turned to Leia. "He doesn't understand," she said. "This is about the Force. I have to warn Tesar myself."

"Isn't Tesar hiding inside the Temple?" Leia asked.

Allana looked more worried than ever. "I didn't say that."

"You didn't have to," Leia said. "It's rather obvious, now that I've had a chance to put everything together."

Allana looked crestfallen. "You mean I let their secret out?"

"Not at all," Tionne said. Her voice was warm and comforting, and Tenel Ka could tell she was using the Force to help calm Allana. "The Masters have suspected there's a nest for quite some time."

"And that has *nothing* to do with you," Kam assured her. "Tesar and the other young Barabels disappeared months ago, and Master Sebatyne has been *very* touchy about the subject. We'd have to be fools not to figure it out."

"But only you and Barv know where to find the nest, right?" Tenel Ka asked. "So you haven't betrayed the Barabels' trust at all."

"She's right, Allana," Leia said. "And we'll make sure Barv explains that when we sneak him into the Temple to warn the Barabels. No one will be angry with you, I promise."

Allana frowned. "What if you can't find Barv?"

"We'll find him," Han said. "We're good at that sort of thing, in case you hadn't noticed."

"What if Barv is dead?" Allana countered. "The place is crawling with Sith, and he's fighting them—probably a lot of them, as big as he is."

Han's face went blank, and Leia looked at him with a she's-got-you-there expression.

"You see?" Allana insisted. "Bringing me is the only way to be sure."

Han's expression only hardened. "Then we're just gonna have to gamble," he said. "Because you're not coming. That's final."

Allana rolled her eyes, then turned to Tenel Ka. "Tell him," she said. "It's my Force vision, and that means *I* have to decide what to do about it."

"Perhaps, but it's Captain Solo's ship, and that means only he decides who flies on it," Tenel Ka said. "Why don't we give your guardians a chance to handle this? I really do think it's for the best."

Allana gave Tenel Ka such a look of betrayal that it made her heart ache, and then the little girl turned to Leia with beseeching eyes.

Leia merely shrugged. "Han said final. You know what that means."

"Yes, I do." Allana fixed an exasperated glare on Han, then said, "It means he's being a ronto-head."

"Fine," Han retorted. "I'm a ronto-head. And you're still not coming."

"Fine." She spun away from him and started for the chairs in the corner. "But don't blame me if Tesar bites your arm off. He doesn't like ronto-heads, either."

Chapter Eight

LUKE STOOD WATCHING THE OLD BOTHAN LIMP BACK AND FORTH across the grimy floor of the undercity industrial hangar. The Bothan was addressing three brigades of elite space marines, explaining why he had asked them to volunteer for a mission to overthrow the Galactic Alliance's current Chief of State, Roki Kem. Whether human, Bothan, or another species, all of the soldiers had the steady gaze of veterans who had seen too much to doubt their commander's incredible story of infiltration and deception. Their shoulder patches represented units from a hundred different vessels stationed near Coruscant, and their average age skewed ten standard years older than that of a typical combat unit. And they all had at least two things in common: they had all served aboard a ship personally commanded by Admiral Nek Bwua'tu, and when he had commed to ask them to help him save the Galactic Alliance, they had all answered with an unwavering yes.

"... the enemy has retreated into the Jedi Temple with seventy-five percent of its forces." The admiral's words seemed to reverberate from every corner of the hangar as a small mike in his tunic collar relayed his voice to a network of speakers spaced throughout the formation. "This withdrawal is certainly a trap, designed to lure our Jedi friends into an ambush against a superior Sith force . . ."

Luke turned to another Bothan standing at his side, Admiral Bwua'tu's dapper uncle, Eramuth. "To tell the truth, Counselor, I'm not sure why you waited for the Jedi to return," he said quietly. "Club Bwua'tu seems to have the war well in hand without us."

"I'm surprised you haven't figured that out by now, Master Sky-walker," Eramuth replied, maintaining a straight face. "We needed the cannon fodder."

"Cannon fodder?" Luke echoed, almost taking the old Bothan seriously. "You couldn't have hired Mandalorians?"

The Bothan shook his gray-furred head. "Of course," he said. "But they didn't manage very well the last time they tried to storm the Temple."

"I see," Luke said. "It's nice to know you have more faith in the Jedi Order."

"There's that." A crooked smile snaked along Eramuth's muzzle, then he added, "And you *do* work for free."

Luke cocked a brow, then chuckled and turned back toward the marine brigades. He knew as well as Eramuth did that the vast majority of today's casualties would be space marines—and that the admiral had made the danger clear before asking anyone to volunteer. That so many had accepted his call to overthrow the Galactic Alliance Chief of State—a mission that was, at first glance, an act of treason—was a testament to the soldiers' faith in the honor and ability of their beloved admiral.

". . . are going to turn Roki Kem's trap against her," Bwua'tu was explaining. He stopped pacing and turned to face his space marines, and the corners of his long mouth rose into a cunning grin. "We're going to launch simultaneous assaults against the Temple at thirty different points, with the objective of forcing Kem to redeploy the bulk of her forces to the Temple perimeter."

Bwua'tu stopped and extended his new prosthetic arm toward Luke. "Grand Master Skywalker will brief you on the rest of the mission."

Luke activated the mike on his own collar and stepped to the admiral's side. "First, I want to thank you all for volunteering for this mission. As Admiral Bwua'tu has explained, it's not just the Jedi Temple we are liberating. The Lost Tribe of the Sith has infiltrated every level of the Galactic Alliance government, and our victory today will prevent them from achieving their goal of dominion over the entire galaxy."

A barely audible rustle rippled through the brigade as the space marines shifted their weight from one foot to another, and Luke realized these soldiers were no strangers to assignments in which the fate of the galaxy hung in the balance. He took a deep breath, and then continued.

"Your objective is to draw the Sith forces to the Temple's outer shell. Once you have succeeded, I will be able to deactivate the Temple shields and open the blast doors from a central location. When that occurs, Admiral Bwua'tu expects the Sith to stand their ground and continue fighting. Assuming he's correct, the Jedi will launch a series of attacks from the Temple interior, driving the enemy out onto the Temple exterior, where they will be exposed to fire from your assault carriers' heavy weapons."

Sensing a tide of uncertainty rising inside the minds of the veteran soldiers, Luke opened his palm and motioned for patience, acknowledging their questions before the first one could be asked.

"If they don't do as the admiral anticipates—"

"They will," Bwua'tu interrupted, drawing a chorus of good-natured chuckles. "Of that, you may be certain."

Luke smiled, then shrugged. "Of course the admiral is right," he said. "But if the Sith *do* fall back, make sure that your Jedi liaison makes contact with a Master before dismounting to press the attack. Whether we push the Sith out of the Temple or into it, our goal is to trap them between the fist and the wall."

Luke illustrated the remark by bringing his fist down into his open palm. He sensed another question rising in a marine standing near him, a Duros female in the third rank. Before she could request permission to speak, he pointed to her.

"Yes, Sergeant?"

The Duros' eyes widened slightly, then she smiled and asked,

"How certain are you that you'll be able to bring the shields down and open those blast doors?"

"Not as certain as I'd like to be," Luke admitted. "But if the first attempt fails, we'll keep trying."

"Until?"

Luke grew somber. "Until we can't anymore," he said. "And if that happens, there'll be a baradium strike."

"*After* I call off the Temple assault, of course," Bwua'tu clarified. "If I order a withdrawal, waste no time before obeying. We won't be giving the enemy time to escape, so the missiles will be on the way as I speak."

The hangar reverberated with the *crump* of thousands of boot heels cracking together, and Bwua'tu nodded in satisfaction.

"Good." The admiral turned to Luke, then said, "I think we're ready to assign the liaisons."

Luke nodded and turned toward the hangar wall, where a line of fifteen Jedi stood at attention. He motioned to the first Jedi Knight in line, Admiral Bwua'tu's young nephew Yantahar, then turned back to the space marines.

"Your commanders have already been briefed on this, but you should all know that a Jedi Knight will accompany each battalion into battle," Luke said. "Their role is strictly advisory, but I urge you to pay attention to their advice. You'll be fighting in a Force-heavy environ-ment, and they will be able to sense many things you cannot—including the location of the Jedi Order's own assault teams."

Yantahar presented himself at Luke's side, standing tall and straight in a Jedi robe over light battle armor, then executed a formal bow to the marines.

"Yantahar Bwua'tu," Yantahar said, using the Force to project his voice across the hangar. "At your service."

The admiral beamed at him for a moment, then called, "Brigade one, Battalion One!"

"Here, sir!" answered a dark-skinned human female in a colonel's uniform.

Yantahar went to stand next to the woman. Luke called out the next Jedi Knight in line, another Bothan named Yaqeel Saav'etu, who presented herself in the same manner and was assigned to the next brigade. But when the time came to call out the third Jedi Knight in line, Bazel Warv, Luke skipped ahead to the next Jedi.

Immediately a wave of confusion and concern rippled through the Force, and Luke regretted that there had been no opportunity to speak with the big Ramoan before the briefing began. He caught Bazel's eye and raised a finger, signaling him to remain patient, then introduced the rest of the Jedi liaisons.

When there was only one Jedi left, Luke turned to Admiral Bwua'tu. "I'm afraid your liaison hasn't arrived yet."

Bwua'tu frowned and glanced over at Bazel, who was watching the exchange with the lips of his huge muzzle curled into an expression that seemed caught halfway between eagerness and puzzlement.

"Is there some reason that Jedi Warv is unavailable?" Bwua'tu asked. "My nephew says that Jedi Saav'etu holds him in high regard. Apparently, he's quite resourceful."

"That he is," Luke agreed. "But I'm afraid something has come up that will prevent him from taking part in the battle."

Luke had barely uttered the words before a wave of disappointment rolled through the Force, and he knew without doubt that Bazel had been eavesdropping on the exchange—despite the fact that his big ears had been turned toward the sides of his enormous head.

"That's too bad," Bwua'tu said, offering his hand to Luke. "Perhaps I should allow you to go explain the situation. He seems quite disappointed, and we both have a lot to do."

"Very true, Admiral." Luke shook Bwua'tu's hand. "I'll send Jedi Dorvald to replace Jedi Warv soon. May the Force be with you until we meet again."

"You're the one who's going to need it, my friend," Bwua'tu replied. "All I have to do is sit in the command post and watch."

"All the same," Luke said. "You know how to contact Master Sebatyne, if the need arises?"

"Certainly," Bwua'tu said. "Just watch for Sith falling out of the sky."

Luke smiled, fully aware that the admiral was only half joking. Saba was keeping the pressure on the Sith who had not retreated into the

Temple, leading Izal Waz and a small team of younger Jedi Knights on what she called "the never-ending hunt."

"A comlink will work, too," Luke said. He started toward the grimy durasteel wall where Bazel Warv stood, at the same time drawing his comlink and opening a channel to Ben. "Is Jedi Dorvald still with you?"

"Affirmative," Ben replied. "We just got the speeder locked down. But this is a rough neighborhood, so Doran is staying behind."

"Good," Luke said. "Bring Seha with you when you join me."

"Affirmative," Ben said. "See you soon."

As Ben signed off, Luke reached the wall where Bazel stood waiting. The big Ramoan was standing next to a doorway, which opened into a dark corridor that led out to the docking balcony. He looked dejected, his huge green shoulders sagging so far that his knuckles hung next to his knees.

"Did I do something wrong, Master Skywalker?" he asked in his gravelly voice. "I just want to—"

"You did nothing wrong." Luke reached up and placed a hand on one of Bazel's huge biceps. "But I've received a message from the Solos. They're on their way here to see you."

"Me?"

Luke nodded. "Yes. They need you to do something for Amelia."

Bazel's long ears went out sideways from his head. "For Amelia?" he asked. "What?"

"I was hoping you could tell *me*," Luke replied. "They said they couldn't explain it over the HoloNet, but that you were the only one who could do it."

Bazel's ears swung back flat against his head, and his big bulbous eyes shifted away from Luke.

"Bazel," Luke asked, putting some durasteel in his voice, "what do they want?"

The Ramoan spread his huge hands. "I don't know," he said. "How could I? They're not even here yet."

"You have an idea," Luke pressed. "What is it?"

Bazel let out a sigh that felt like a hot breeze against Luke's face. "It must have something to do with the secret."

Luke's heart rose into his throat. "*Amelia*'s secret?" he asked. "How did you find—"

"The *other* secret, Master Skywalker!" Bazel interrupted, shaking his big head from side to side. "Not her secret name!"

"You know her real name?" Luke asked, stunned. *"How?"*

Bazel's voice grew soft. "Master Skywalker, I can't tell you that right now."

Realizing that Bazel was no longer looking at him, but *over* him toward the doorway, Luke scowled. He, too, could sense a trio of presences coming through the doorway behind him—and if Bazel knew enough about Allana's secret to be *that* careful with it, he probably knew who Allana really was. Fighting to keeping his alarm from bleeding into the Force, Luke pivoted around to see his son stepping into the hangar.

"Sorry to interrupt," Ben said, stepping aside to allow Seha Dorvald's lithe form through the door. "But I *said* we'd see you soon."

"No problem, son." Luke nodded to Seha, but continued to watch the door. "Is Vestara—"

"Right here, Master Skywalker," Vestara said. She entered the room, being careful to avoid looking in Bazel's direction. "I hope we didn't miss anything important."

Chapter Nine

THE ASSAULT WOULD SUCCEED, VESTARA KNEW, FOR ONE SIMPLE REASON: the Jedi knew their ancient Temple better than its Sith occupiers ever could. Within the hour, the Jedi would penetrate the immense structure in force, and the Circle of Lords would come to understand how badly they had underestimated Luke Skywalker. By the time Skywalker was finished, there wouldn't be a High Lord left alive on Coruscant, and any survivors back on Kesh would be too busy worrying about him to even *think* about hunting her down.

At least that was Vestara's hope. If the Jedi attack proved successful enough, she might even consider sending a message to the surviving High Lords, promising to reveal Kesh's location if she so much as *smelled* a Sith looking for her. Such a threat would work only if the High Lords were truly frightened of Luke and his Jedi—and after today, they would be.

A dull clang echoed through the crowded pumping station, and the large bypass pipe in front of Vestara trembled with an internal pressure change. The upper half rotated away, exposing the damp interior of a water main roughly one and a half meters in diameter. Ben and his cousin Jaina hoisted a maintenance capsule into the main, then opened the hatch. Inside the capsule was a cramped passenger cabin, complete with dual couches and a pilot's yoke. Ben activated the control panel and waited while it ran a two-second systems check, then put a foot on the access step and turned to Vestara.

"Ready?"

"As ready as I'll ever be." Vestara touched the empty lightsaber hook on her hip. "I just wish I had a weapon—even a blaster."

Ben's face fell, but before he could speak, Jaina stepped forward.

"Sorry, Vestara. That's the way it has to be." Her voice was firm without being combative. "If being without a weapon worries you, you can always stay behind."

"Not really," Vestara said, putting a hint of understanding in her voice. "I need to prove my loyalty."

Ben shook his head. "Ves, you shouldn't take—"

"Please don't, Ben," she said. "I understand why the Masters find it hard to trust me. Truly, I do."

"This isn't just about the Masters," Jaina said, taking another step closer. Vestara began to have the unpleasant feeling that Jaina understood her game better than she did herself. "Not everyone in the Jedi Order has spent time with you. For a lot of us, it's hard to trust a Sith."

"A *former* Sith," Ben corrected. "Come on, Jaina. Her own father tried to kill her."

"Okay, a former Sith," Jaina said, barely glancing at him. "I'm serious, Vestara. If going into battle unarmed bothers you, then stay here."

"And how will the Jedi know who the High Lords are?" Vestara asked. "How will they know when they have found the Grand Lord?"

"We'll get by," Jaina replied.

"Or blame *me* when something goes wrong." Vestara climbed the step and placed a hand on Ben's hip. "You're not going anywhere without me. I need to be there to watch your back—even if I don't have a weapon to defend it."

An impatient tweedle sounded from the pumping station's interface panel, and the R9 unit plugged into the dataport began to flash its projection lamp at them.

"I guess we'd better get in," Ben said. "We're holding things up."

Vestara climbed into the capsule and stretched out on the passenger's couch, then waited in the antiseptic-tinged air as Ben slipped in beside her and pulled the pilot's yoke up between his knees. The hatch sealed automatically, and a soft green light filled the interior. As soon as Vestara had strapped in and brought the navigation display online, Ben activated the control thrusters.

A muffled *thump* sounded behind them as the droid opened the pipe again, then a loud gurgling echoed through the capsule, and Vestara felt her stomach rise as they slowly accelerated. Ben's gaze went straight to the navigation display. It showed nothing ahead but a long stretch of uninterrupted pipe.

Vestara allowed an uncomfortable silence to hang between them for the first hundred meters of travel, then asked, "So, where are we going? Besides the Jedi Temple, I mean."

Ben didn't reply for a moment, keeping his eyes on the display and obviously struggling over how much to tell her.

"Oh, right. I'll find out when we get there." Vestara turned her gaze back to the padded hatch cover hanging just a dozen centimeters above her face. "And I'll be sure to tell Jaina how careful you were to keep me in the dark."

Ben sighed. "It's not that, Ves," he said. "I'm just not sure how to explain it to you."

"It's okay, Ben." She pulled her arm away from her side, so that it was no longer touching him, and folded it across her stomach. "I understand."

"Look, all I know is that it's Level One-seventy-five, Sector Twelve, Twenty-two North Eighteen," Ben said. "Does that mean anything to you? Because it sure doesn't to me."

"Level One-seventy-five?" Vestara asked. "That's pretty high up, isn't it?"

"Sure—if you're a granite slug," Ben scoffed. "But it's still farther down than I usually go. It's one of the mechanical cores, I think."

"Core?" Vestara echoed. "As in, *central core?*"

"Yeah, Ves," Ben replied. "That's where the 'core' usually is. In the center."

"I suppose so," Vestara said, allowing some of her growing—and very real—fear to seep into her voice. "Maybe I should have listened to Jaina."

Ben glanced over at her, his brow arched. "What makes you say that?"

"I don't think the Masters have thought this through," she said. "Ben, I come from a planet with *tens of thousands* of Sith. And half of them are probably right here on this planet, hiding inside the Jedi Temple."

Ben dipped his chin, trying to conceal a smile. "That's kind of what we're counting on, Vestara."

Vestara's stomach went hollow. She had expected their team's objective to be the capture of a cargo dock, so the Jedi would have a bridgehead from which to invade the rest of the Temple. But this sounded like they planned to emerge well inside the Sith perimeter and attack outward—and if that was their intention, it could only mean that the Jedi knew a way to disable the shields and open the Temple remotely.

"The Jedi have a secret override, don't they?" she asked. "You're just going to open the doors and let all those space marines come in shooting?"

"Something like that." Ben looked over at her, his eyes soft with concern. "Does that bother you?"

Vestara hesitated for a moment, then nodded. "Yes, I guess it does." It would have been useless to say anything else; Ben would have sensed the lie in two heartbeats. "There's not one Saber in there who wouldn't ignite a lightsaber through the back of my head, so I know it shouldn't. But . . ."

"But they're your own people." Ben nodded. "You wouldn't be human if seeing them killed didn't bother you."

"Thanks, Ben. I'm glad you understand."

"No problem," he replied. "I know it's not easy."

An alert ping sounded from the navigation unit, and a Y-intersection appeared on the screen ahead. Ben's knuckles paled as his grasp tightened on the steering yoke, and Vestara saw him begin a silent count as he prepared to make the turn into the Temple. She found herself trying to imagine a life with him that didn't involve being a Jedi *or* Sith, just two regular people trying to make their way in the galaxy. Of course, they would never be *too* regular. But she could see them being happy as professional gamblers, or even a husband-and-wife bounty hunter team—providing, of course, that she could persuade Ben to use the Force for something other than saving the galaxy.

Ben's gaze locked on the navigation screen, and he eased them through the turn, bouncing off the pipe wall just once before he brought the capsule back under control. Almost instantly another intersection appeared at the bottom of the display, along with a small inset schematic showing a tangled network of navigable conduits.

"It won't be long now, I guess," Vestara said.

"Only a couple of minutes," Ben answered. "We just crossed into the Temple."

"Ben?" Vestara asked. Her dream of making a life together outside the Jedi Order was as much a fantasy as had been those letters she had written to an imaginary loving father, but she had to know—to be *certain*—before the battle began. Ben deserved that much. "Have you ever thought about not being a Jedi?"

"Sure," Ben said, surprising her. "But not since I was a kid."

"You didn't want to be a Jedi when you were young?"

Ben shook his head. "Not at all." He rolled the capsule up on its side, preparing to enter a riser pipe they were approaching. "I was in Shelter when Abeloth contacted the younglings."

"And you weren't affected?"

"Only because I withdrew from the Force." Ben's gaze remained fixed on the display, and he seemed to be only half listening. "I don't remember a lot about it."

"What about now?" Vestara asked. "Can you see yourself doing something else?"

Ben tipped the steering yoke away, his brow furrowing in concentration as he swung them into the riser.

"Why *would* I?" A knell rang through the capsule as it slammed into the pipe, then it hit the other side, and Ben cursed under his breath. "I need to concentrate on piloting this thing. Can we talk about this later?"

"No need," Vestara said. "It was a silly question anyway."

She had her answer—and it made her feel like a black hole inside.

Vestara could never be a Jedi, not in any true sense of the word. Ben could be nothing else. Their love had been doomed from the start—from five thousand years before they were born—and now all that remained was for her to accept reality and find a way to survive without the Jedi to protect her from the Lost Tribe's vengeance.

Fortunately, if it came to it, Vestara would have something to trade. At first, she had not understood the significance of the conversation between Master Skywalker and Bazel Warv. Most young girls had secrets, so it had taken her a moment to grasp the significance of Amelia Solo's "secret name." But Master Skywalker's reaction—and how quickly he had ended the conversation when he realized they were not alone—had certainly suggested to Vestara that Amelia's secret was one the Jedi themselves took *very* seriously. The final confirmation had been the wave of alarm she had felt when she rounded the corner and stepped through the door with Ben, when Master Skywalker—and even Ben, to a certain extent—had realized what she had just overheard.

After that, it had been a simple matter for Vestara to complete the puzzle. At the Pool of Knowledge, she had glimpsed enough of the face that High Lord Taalon had seen on the Throne of Balance, and that glimpse had been enough to know the Jedi Queen was a redhead who bore a striking resemblance to the Hapan Queen Mother, Tenel Ka. It was well known that Tenel Ka and Jacen Solo had been classmates at the Jedi academy on Yavin 4, and the gossip media suggested they had remained "friends" until Jacen set fire to Kashyyyk.

It was a fact that Tenel Ka had given birth to a baby girl name Allana, whose father she refused to identify. Allana had reportedly been killed during the Second Civil War, when Moffs attempted to assassinate Tenel Ka's entire family with one of their nanoviruses. At about the same time, the Solos had adopted a Force-sensitive war orphan of the same age.

But most telling, now that Vestara thought back, was the day she had seen Han and Amelia together in a hologram. She had been aboard the *Jade Shadow* when Han Solo commed to report that Leia had been arrested, and Amelia had been in the holo with him. Vestara had suggested that Han take the child along when he went to seek his wife's release from Chiefs of State Padnel Ovin and Wynn Dorvan. At the time, she had thought she was merely reacting to how cute Amelia was. But now she realized it was more than that—she had been reacting to a family resemblance.

Amelia Solo had Han Solo's eyes and mouth. Even more telling, there was a hint of a crooked grin in Amelia's smile. Vestara closed her eyes and looked back in her memory, using meditation and the Force to sharpen her recall, to bring every detail of the little girl's head into clearer focus—and she saw the last bit of proof.

Amelia's hair was not naturally black. It had red roots—golden-red, as a matter of fact. And golden-red was the color of the Hapan Queen Mother's famous tresses.

So Amelia Solo was destined to become the queen whom Lord Taalon had seen in the Pool of Knowledge. The Skywalkers knew it. Bazel Warv knew it. And now Vestara Khai knew it, too.

For the time being, she would keep the knowledge to herself. Until she knew the circumstances of her new life, there was nothing to be gained by revealing it to anyone, and she owed it to Ben to hold the secret—at least until she could trade it for something very important.

Like saving her own skin.

They banged through a dozen more intersections, then the entire display flashed yellow and Ben eased back on the throttle. He slipped the capsule into a bypass line and came to a dead stop. A liquid squeal reverberated through the hull as the control valves were adjusted, and the water began to gurgle away.

Ben unbuckled his restraint harness and glanced over at Vestara. "Ready?"

Vestara nodded. "You have no idea *how* ready," she said, unbuckling her own harness. "After today, no Jedi will have any doubts about me. I promise you that."

A look of concern came to Ben's face. "Don't do anything reckless, Ves," he said. "Just point out the High Mugwumps. You don't have anything to prove."

Vestara forced a smile. "Not to you, maybe."

The muffled clang of a shifting access panel sounded from above, then the capsule's hatch broke its seal and hissed open. Ben let his gaze linger on Vestara and whispered, "I mean it—be careful," then climbed out.

Vestara followed a moment later and found herself standing on the bypass platform next to Ben and the Horn siblings, Valin and Jysella. Valin extended a hand to Ben.

"Welcome home."

"Thanks," Ben said. "It's good to be back."

Jysella eyed Vestara as though considering whether to offer a similar greeting, then simply gestured toward the inspection capsule.

"Come on," she said. "Help me pull this out of the way."

"Of course."

Vestara extended a hand toward the crane hook affixed to the rear end of the capsule and used the Force to lift it out of the bypass pipe. Jysella did the same with the front, and together they stowed it atop a growing stack of capsules piled at the far end of the platform.

"Thanks." Jysella turned to Ben and pointed toward the front of the murk-filled chamber. It was packed with filtering units, pump motors, and purification tanks. "Your father's somewhere in front. He said to see him for assignments as soon as you arrived."

Ben acknowledged the message with a quick nod and motioned for Vestara to lead the way. Instead she remained where she was, slowly expanding her Force awareness out into the gloom. Something felt wrong, but she could not quite decide what it was.

The room was the size of a starfighter hangar, but so packed with equipment, cabinetry, and spare parts that it felt more like an underground labyrinth than the huge chamber it was. Everywhere she looked, dripping pipes ran from one processing unit to another, then climbed into the overhead darkness in bundles as big around as tree trunks. Some pieces of equipment were the size of cargo sleds, and the noise level was loud enough to make her wish she had a pair of sonic dampeners handy. The conditions were ideal for hiding a sentry or a spy. Considering the importance of the room—and the direct access to it from outside the Temple—Vestara could not believe the Sith would have failed to take such a basic precaution.

When she did not sense any dark presences lurking in the area, she asked, "How many guards did the first Jedi Knights kill in here?"

"None," Jysella replied. "The place was empty."

Vestara turned to look at her. "And that doesn't strike you as strange?"

"Master Skywalker did have a team search the entire room, just in case," Valin said. "But right now, there are Jedi-led companies of space marines outside the Temple, assaulting thirty different entrances. Master Skywalker thinks the Sith have moved all their sentries to the exterior doors and down into the underlevels."

"That *was* the plan," Jysella added, flashing a half smile. "And sometimes, plans actually work."

The joke did little to lift Vestara's heart. If Master Skywalker's assault team met a disastrous end here, her life expectancy would drop by a factor of ten—and she had learned enough about the Temple defenses to realize that a determined host of Sith would be able to hold off the space marine assault indefinitely. And even if they could not, the High Lords would have plenty of time to escape alive. Vestara needed Skywalker and his team to succeed and succeed quickly, so they could disrupt the Circle of Lords and make possible a life for her other than pretending to be a Jedi hopeful.

She took Ben's arm and started toward the far end of the platform. "We need to have a look around," she said. "The Sith understand diversions as well as the Jedi, and they wouldn't make the mistake of leaving this room unguarded."

"Master Skywalker's orders were clear," Jysella called after them. "You're to report at once."

"Thank you, Jedi Horn," Vestara said, speaking over her shoulder. "We understand."

She led the way down a short metal staircase to a durasteel deck grating suspended about a meter above the true floor, which was covered in some sort of dark membrane. Vestara was confused about its purpose, until she noticed that the entire floor sloped toward a depression in the center of the room. Apparently, leaks and flooding were enough of a concern that a central drain had been installed.

Ben stepped off the staircase and stopped at Vestara's side. "Ves, we need to follow orders. I'm sure they checked the place over."

"I'm sure they tried," Vestara said, starting toward a speeder-sized pump motor. "But something is definitely wrong here. Don't you feel it?"

Ben fell quiet and began to look around, no doubt expanding his own Force awareness into the dark recesses of the room. Finally, he shook his head.

"No, I don't feel anything," he said. "But that doesn't mean much one way or another. I'm sure most Sith know how to hide their Force presences as well as we do."

"That's not what I'm saying. It's just too calm . . ." Vestara let her sentence trail off as she finally realized what was missing. "Where are the droids?"

Ben frowned. "Droids?"

"You can't walk a hundred steps on Coruscant without running into a droid," she said. "And you're telling me the Jedi didn't use any to run this place?"

Ben's brow rose. "I see your point." He glanced around again. The room was too packed with equipment to see all the way to the front, but that was where Jysella had told them his father was waiting. "Let's check with Dad anyway. Maybe there's something he forgot to tell us at the briefing."

"You go ahead," Vestara said. "I'm going to have a look around."

Ben caught her arm and started her toward the front of the room. "Ves, come on."

Catching the note of warning in his voice, Vestara allowed him to pull her along. "Why, Ben?" As she walked, she continued to reach out in the Force, searching for any hint of the sentry that had to be somewhere in the darkness spying on them. "So the rest of the team won't grow suspicious of me showing some initiative?"

"Because Jedi obey orders, too," Ben said, picking up the pace. "Especially in battle situations."

Vestara started to remind Ben that he had once urged her to think for herself—then felt the deck grating wobble beneath her foot. Normally, she would not have given the sensation a second thought. But her Master, Lady Rhea, had taught her to pay attention to *everything* going into a fight, to remember that even the smallest detail could save her life, so Vestara dropped her gaze.

She saw the weapons first, a pair of blasters and a trio of lightsabers, all partially hidden in the fold of a black robe or the crook of a dark elbow. The people holding the weapons were on their backs, resting two abreast with their faces wrapped in dark scarves. Their eyes were squeezed to mere slits to prevent the whites from showing, and they were remaining absolutely still to avoid attracting attention.

Vestara glanced away, trying to act as though she hadn't seen the figures beneath the grating. But she had noted at least half a dozen in a mere glance, and there was no reason to believe that was the entire force. The Jedi were walking into an ambush—and that could only mean the Sith had known they were coming.

Vestara had no idea how her people had learned of the Jedi assault plan, but she *did* know who would be blamed for it—provided she was lucky enough to live that long. Sith were nothing if not first-rate assassins, and this ambush appeared to be a variation on the Quiet Return. When they expected the target to be alert and wary upon entering the killing zone, Sith assassins preferred to remain somewhere else until the victim relaxed, then return via a secret entrance to launch the attack. She was guessing that this group had come from the chamber below, through a hole cut a few hours earlier, and hidden beneath the drainage membrane.

Vestara continued to walk at Ben's side, trying to figure out how the ambush affected her. The Sith would be watching her more closely than any of the Jedi except Grand Master Skywalker, so it would be impossible to disappear before the attack began. Besides, she needed the Jedi assault force intact to make her own plan work.

"Ves?" Ben asked. "Wake up, will you? We're about to go into battle."

"Oh yes, the battle," she said. Now that she knew where the ambush was coming from, she just wanted to reach the control panel as quickly as possible. "You're right, of course."

"I am?" Ben asked, turning his head to look over at her. "What happened to change . . ."

His sentence faded into an unexpected silence—as did the sound of their footfalls, and the swishing of Vestara's robe. But when she glanced over at Ben, she saw that his mouth was continuing to move as though he were still hearing his words inside his own head. Someone was using the Force to quiet the air and prevent it from carrying sound waves—and that could mean only one thing.

Vestara reached out to Master Skywalker in the Force, flooding her presence with alarm, then grabbed Ben by the arm and spun around to find a ten-meter section of deck grating flying toward them. A blast wave of shock and confusion raced through the Force as Ben struggled to comprehend what he was seeing, and Vestara knew he would never react in time. She slammed her forearm across his chest and kicked his heels out from beneath him, then flung her own legs out in front of her.

They landed side by side on their backs an instant before the grating slashed past, passing a handbreadth from their faces. Ben's eyes bulged wide and his mouth opened in a soundless cry of surprise— then Vestara began to slide across the grating back toward their attackers. She raised her head and saw a wall of dark-cloaked ambushers leaping from their hiding places, blasters flashing and lightsabers ignited.

Suddenly Vestara stopped sliding. She glanced back and saw Ben's hand extended toward her, holding her in the Force, trying to drag her back.

A ferocious ache began to throb through her hips and shoulders, and Vestara felt as though she was coming apart. Then she realized she probably was. She screamed in pain and shook her head, yelling at Ben to let her go.

Whether Ben actually heard her above the battle din—the screaming of blaster bolts and the growling of lightsabers—Vestara could not tell. She simply started to slide faster than before.

Behind her, Ben snapped his lightsaber off its belt hook and sprang to his feet, then quickly dived into a somersault as a flurry of blaster bolts burned into the grating around him. For an instant, Vestara thought he would ignite the blade and get them both killed by attempting to fight his way toward her.

She should have known better than to underestimate Ben Skywalker. He simply continued to somersault, using the Force to trace a zigzag course across the deck. When he came up, his weapon hand snapped in her direction, flinging his lightsaber toward her. Vestara reached for it in the Force, at the same time looking back toward the ambushers.

The first Sith were already charging past, using their crimson lightsabers to bat aside the torrent of bolts coming from a group of

Jedi charging back from the front of the room. Ben's lightsaber landed in her hand. She thumbed the activation switch, then rolled to her belly and swung the sizzling blade through two sets of running legs. When a cold shiver raced down her spine, she continued the roll and brought the weapon up to block.

A shower of sparks erupted as Vestara's blade clashed with another, and she glimpsed a lavender Keshiri face snarling down from the other side of the blazing cross above her. The two blades locked, and Vestara lay beneath her attacker, struggling to keep the woman's lightsaber away. The *crump-crump* of detonating grenades began to sound somewhere near the front of the room, and in the back of her mind she realized the Jedi were being attacked from two sides.

Vestara relaxed her arms a little, and the Keshiri woman's lightsaber began to descend toward her face.

"First, I take your beauty," the woman said. "Then I—"

Vestara hit her with a Force blast and sent her flying back into a rank of Sith climbing up through the missing section of grating. The Keshiri's blade, still ignited, sliced one warrior in half, and her body knocked two more off their feet.

Beyond the tangle of limbs and blades, Vestara glimpsed Valin and Jysella Horn still up on the bypass platform, Valin using his lightsaber to defend Jysella from Sith blaster bolts while she leaned through an open access panel. Vestara traced back the stream of bolts until she spotted a Sith warrior firing from between a pair of pump housings. She sent him tumbling with a Force shove.

That was all the respite Valin Horn needed. He leapt off the bypass platform in a flying cartwheel. Beginning to think she and the Jedi just might survive this ambush after all, Vestara sprang to her own feet—and heard a deep voice behind her.

"Enough."

The base of her skull exploded into dull throbbing pain as something hard and heavy—the hilt of a lightsaber, no doubt—struck. She spun and caught only a glimpse of black cloth as her attacker moved behind her.

The hilt descended again.

Her knees buckled, spinning her around, away from her unseen attacker. Her vision began to narrow, but fifteen meters away up on the water main bypass platform, she saw a small female Jedi climbing out of an open access panel. The woman ignited her lightsaber, then came leaping over the platform's safety rail, brown hair flying and violet blade whirling, and Vestara knew the battle was on.

Jaina Solo, Sword of the Jedi, had just arrived.

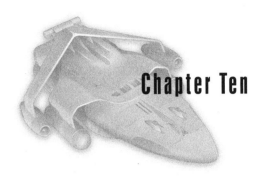

Chapter Ten

A FORK OF FORCE LIGHTNING FLASHED PAST BELOW JAINA'S CORKSCREW-ing body, so close that the sting of its heat penetrated the thin molytex armor beneath her robes. She twisted into another whorl, her wrists turning almost of their own accord as she swung her lightsaber around to catch the next bolt, and then she sensed the floor rising up beneath her. She brought her feet around and landed hard, the durasteel deck grating shuddering beneath her boots as a dozen dark-robed figures spun to face her, their wide eyes betraying the confusion and alarm they felt at seeing a Jedi Knight deliberately jump into the heart of a Sith mob.

How a mission could go sour so fast, Jaina had no idea. The Sith were everywhere, crawling beneath the deck grating, dropping down from the pipes, darting out from between the filter cabinets and pump housings. Clearly, the Jedi had walked into an ambush, and their battle plan had fallen into chaos.

No problem. In a situation like this, Jaina thrived on chaos. She *became* chaos.

Jaina leapt over an incoming leg slash, then dropped her attacker with a quick snap-kick to the temple. She blocked a strike at her neck and, still in the air, turned her jump into a cartwheel. She shifted to a one-handed grip and swung her free arm in an arc, using the Force to sweep two more Sith off their feet. Landing in their midst, she stomped on the throat of the first and jammed her lightsaber through the chest of the other, then pulled a concussion grenade off her combat harness and thumbed it active.

She dropped it at her feet and began to count. *One.*

The melee went still. All eyes dropped to the grenade, noted the absence of a safety pin, the arming light blinking red. The Sith looked at her with wide eyes, then spun away and tried to hurl themselves beyond the blast radius.

Jaina's count reached *Two.* She caught the grenade on the toe of her boot and kicked it toward a missing section of deck grating, where a fresh stream of Sith warriors were climbing into view.

Her count reached *Three,* and Jaina dropped.

The detonation hit her like a hoverbus, rolling her across the deck, flinging flesh and durasteel through the air above her. Why the Sith had sprung their trap so early, Jaina could not imagine. The largest part of the Jedi assault force had not even reached the killing zone, and while dozens of Sith were already in the room, they seemed almost as confused and poorly positioned as their targets. Maybe Luke had sensed the danger and forced the issue—or maybe he had been their true target all along. Perhaps they feared Luke Skywalker just that much.

And that was a mistake.

Luke Skywalker was not the Sword of the Jedi. *Jaina* was, and now the Sith had trapped themselves inside a locked Temple with her.

Jaina stopped rolling and raised her head, trying to decide who to take on next. Strewn with overturned equipment and severed pipes, the chamber was too tangled with streaking bolts and sweeping arcs of color for her to see anything clearly. The floor was littered with bodies, some motionless, more writhing, too many with faces she recognized as fellow Jedi. Her droid, Rowdy, had managed to extract himself from the inspection capsule and descend the stairs from the bypass platform. Now he was working his way toward the computer interface at the front of the chamber, where the original plan had called for him to contact the Temple's central computer, ordering it to lower the shields and open the blast doors.

Off to one side of the battle, Vestara lay unconscious between a flocculation mixer and the adjacent sedimentation basin. Standing over her was a tall, slender Sith Lord wearing a black cape atop black blast armor. His thin lips were sneering as he spoke into a throat-mike. Luke and Master Horn were nowhere to be seen, but Valin and Jysella Horn were atop a narrow pipe, fighting back-to-back while standing three meters above the floor.

And Ben . . . Ben seemed to think he was invincible, Force-tumbling through the air toward Vestara, dodging blaster bolts and Force lightning with no lightsaber to protect him. He extended an arm, hooking his elbow around a small transfer pipe that crossed the room about two meters above the deck, and allowed his momentum to swing him downward just in time to avoid a fork of blue Force lightning. He came arcing back up, one hand sending a Force blast back toward the woman who had attacked him. She went flying into the gloom, and Ben released his arm and went arcing away, corkscrewing and somersaulting until he dropped out of sight behind a settling tank.

Three Sith were already leaping up onto the transfer pipe to take the woman's place, and Jaina had her next set of victims. She used the Force to launch herself off the deck grating . . . and was still in the air when her targets sensed their danger. The leader jumped off the pipe—another woman, her long red hair trailing behind her as she raced to intercept Ben. The two men, one with a dark beard and one clean-shaven, spun to defend themselves.

Jaina's lightsaber was already coming down, severing Dark Beard's sword arm at the elbow. She used the Force to send the limb and lightsaber flying in Ben's direction, then glimpsed the crimson arc of Square Chin's blade curving toward her lead leg. She flipped her own weapon down to block the attack . . . but, before she could Force-stick her boot in place, she felt her foot sliding across the transfer pipe. In the next instant Jaina was plummeting toward the deck, with one Sith screaming in pain below her and the other jumping down from above.

Chaos.

Jaina shoved off in the Force, sending Square Chin floating back toward the transfer pipe—and pushing herself in the opposite direction. She slammed down atop Dark Beard, driving her elbow into his ribs and snapping her head back into his face. She felt his nose shatter, then rolled to her side.

Square Chin was dropping toward her again, his eyes narrowing as she extended her sword arm, pushing the tip as high into the air as she could. He brought his own weapon around to block, and Jaina used the Force to spin him backward, making his parry impossible.

The tip of her lightsaber caught the Sith just below the shoulder blade, then he was sliding down the blade to land atop her, as heavy and limp as a sack of gravel. Jaina's breath left her in a pained gasp, and her chest felt like a rancor had stomped it. But she had no time to wonder about broken ribs. She deactivated her lightsaber and, using the Force to boost her strength, flung the body off.

The silver arc of a glass parang was already slicing toward her from the direction of Dark Beard's belt, held in the invisible grasp of the Force. Jaina reactivated her lightsaber, intercepting the weapon—and barely altering its trajectory as her blade melted through it. The two halves flashed past her face, so close they stung her jaw before they shattered against the deck grating.

Jaina brought her lightsaber down across the Sith's torso. The stench of charred flesh grew overwhelming, and only adrenaline kept her from gagging. She jumped to her feet and raced after the red-haired Sith who had gone to attack Ben.

She needn't have worried. Ben had collected the lightsaber that Jaina had sent flying his way, and now he was using it to press his attack, combining strength and speed to push Red Hair back. Jaina extended a hand, hitting the Sith with a Force shove that sent her stumbling into Ben's lightsaber.

Ben staggered, then quickly finished the woman by flicking his weapon up through her torso. She seemed to peel away from the blade, dropping to her knees and collapsing backward onto the grating. He kicked her weapon aside, then gave a quick salute with the crimson lightsaber in his hand.

"Thanks," he said.

"Glad to help," Jaina said. She pointed down a narrow aisle between two nearby settling basins. "Let's go."

Ben turned in the opposite direction. "They have Vestara."

He started to add something else, but Jaina stopped listening when a tall figure in a dark robe dropped onto an evaporation cabinet behind him. By the time the Sith raised a hand to launch a Force attack, Jaina was leaping to her cousin's defense.

Ben must have sensed his danger, too, because he was already moving. They bumped shoulders as he pivoted around, then a deafening crackle split the air and Jaina found herself flying backward on a bolt of Force lightning. She slammed into the wall of a settling tank and remained pinned there, teeth grinding, nerves burning, limbs paralyzed—until Ben shoved his crimson lightsaber into the dancing fork of energy.

Jaina collapsed to her knees, muscles throbbing and quivering and generally useless. Her attacker let his lightning sizzle out and reached for his lightsaber, but she was already grabbing him in the Force. She jerked him off the cabinet and down into the aisle. The Sith was still crying out in shock when her cousin finished him off.

Ben took a heartbeat to check for other attackers, but the battle had progressed from the initial "confusion-and-carnage" phase to the "hidden-death" stage, and there were no longer any Sith out in the open. Even the din of the battle had dwindled to sporadic outbreaks of thunder, shriek, and sizzle.

Ben stepped to Jaina's side. "You okay?"

"Why wouldn't I be?"

Jaina tried to stand, but her still-quivering legs wouldn't obey. She extended her hand for help—and felt her entire shoulder erupt in a fiery ache unlike anything she had ever felt before.

"Just a little shaky," she added. "Get me up."

Ben pulled her to her feet, then cast a furtive glance back toward the basin where they had last seen Vestara. Her captor had retreated deeper behind cover, but one of Vestara's feet could still be seen lying against the wall of the mixing station.

"Hold on, Ben." Jaina slipped an arm around Ben's waist, then grabbed a handful of robe and put more weight on him than was really necessary. "You're not going to help her by getting yourself killed."

"Who's going to get himself killed?"

"Who do you *think*?" Jaina demanded. "We're outnumbered ten to one here, and that guy with Vestara looks like he's in charge."

"So?"

"*So* that makes him at least a Lord, and probably a High Lord," Jaina said, realizing her objective had changed from killing the enemy to keeping Ben from being killed by the enemy. Battles were unpredictable like that. "Are you really ready to go after a Sith High Lord? Because I'm not—not when he has all the advantages."

Ben sighed, but continued to look toward the basin. "What if it was Jag?" he asked. "Would you leave him behind?"

He was right, of course. If it had been Jagged Fel back there, Jaina wouldn't be wasting time talking about it. She would be working her way toward the mixing station to rescue him—or to die trying.

But it wasn't Jag. It was a Sith girl who had betrayed Ben half a dozen times already, who had been working her way into the Skywalkers' confidence for months—and who might actually be waiting for a chance like this one to deal a body blow to the entire Jedi Order. Unfortunately, Jaina couldn't say as much to Ben. He was a teenager in love, and teenagers in love did not like to hear that their sweethearts might be lying, cheating assassins.

Chaos.

"You have a point," Jaina said, pretending to consider his argument. "But if that were Jag, he would want me to do the smart thing and not get myself killed while attempting an impossible rescue."

She turned away, trying to get Ben started in the opposite direction.

Ben stayed where he was. "I didn't ask what *Jag* would do. I asked what *you* would do." He tried to free himself from Jaina's grasp, but she clamped down hard and pulled him back. He scowled and said, "I thought you were shaky."

"I'm getting better," Jaina said, grabbing a handful of molytex armor through his robe. "And whatever I might do, it would be smart. So I wouldn't charge in without a plan, and I wouldn't get someone *else* killed with me."

Ben frowned. "I'm not asking you to come."

"Right," Jaina replied. "And you expect that to square me with your father? That you didn't *invite* me to walk into an obvious trap right along with you?"

Ben stopped pulling, and Jaina knew she had him. He might be willing to throw away his own life on a lost cause, but he wouldn't take her with him.

"Trap?" Ben asked.

"*Think,* Ben. The Sith commander alone, Vestara lying unconscious at his feet? It's too much temptation. He wants you to go after her." Jaina tugged him toward the circular wall of a sludge tank. "Come on. We need to find the others and regroup. Then we'll figure out how to save Vestara."

Ben reluctantly allowed her to pull him along. "You'd better mean that, Jaina. I'm not going to abandon her."

"Ben, I can't promise we'll save her," Jaina said. "You know better. But we'll do what we can, okay? We just need to be smart about it."

Taking care to keep their heads beneath the top edge of the tank, they crept around to the other side—and found themselves facing a metal ladder affixed to a large feeder pipe rising into the darkness above. A narrow catwalk ran between the ladder and the chamber's forward wall, about eight meters above their heads. Kneeling at the near end were two black-robed figures, one holding a long-muzzled version of a Verpine shatter gun, the other wearing a pair of night-vision goggles. The sludge tank had prevented them from seeing the area Jaina and Ben had just departed, but both Sith were scanning the killing zone in front of Vestara's still-motionless feet.

Jaina glanced over and saw that Ben's face had gone pale. He clearly understood what he was seeing—a sniper nest waiting to attack anyone who tried to reach Vestara. Jaina started to pull a frag grenade off her combat harness, but Ben touched her forearm and shook his head, signaling her to move on. He knew as well as she did that taking out a single sniper nest was unlikely to defang the Sith trap. And even if it did, as soon as Vestara's captor realized what had happened, Vestara would change from bait to liability, and her likelihood of being killed would rise tenfold. If they wanted to rescue Vestara alive, they needed a plan—and now Ben knew it, too.

Jaina motioned her cousin to follow, then slipped away from the settling basin and began to work her way toward the front of the chamber. Their best hope of saving themselves—and Vestara—lay in giving the Sith something else to worry about. The best move was to complete their mission and get the Temple's blast doors open. To do that, they would have to find her droid, Rowdy, and get him plugged into the computer interface panel—then keep him in one piece long enough to convince the Temple computer to override the lockdown command.

The interface station came into view. A meter-wide panel with a display screen and a keyboard located above a row of droid-accessible dataports, it had two rows of status lights running down one side. Most of the lights were blinking or glowing in colors ranging from red to amber, but there was nothing on the display screen to suggest that Rowdy had already contacted the Temple computer.

"At least it's been activated already," Ben observed. "Now all we have to—"

The sentence came to an abrupt end when a brilliant flash lit the chamber. The deafening crackle of a thermal detonator filled the air, and the chamber grew instantly damp and cold. Then the deck grating started to vibrate beneath their feet, and the muffled roar of a waterfall began to rise from the direction of the bypass platform. They ducked behind a pump motor, then carefully raised their heads high enough to peer back over the top.

Shooting into a hole where the platform used to be was a column of water two meters thick.

Chaos.

"No more reinforcements," Ben observed. "A break like that's going to trigger gate shutdowns all the way back to the main."

Jaina nodded. "It's just as well," she said. "We can't bring in enough Jedi to outnumber them, so a large force only makes us easier to locate."

As she spoke, a shiver of danger sense chilled her spine. She reached for Ben's collar and ducked back down—only to hear his lightsaber already sizzling to life. She activated her own weapon, barely bringing it around in time to catch the fork of Force lightning that came dancing her way. At the other end stood a lavender-skinned Keshiri female, flanked by a cadre of human Sith, six on each side. Their crimson blades snapped to life as one, and they began to fan out, cutting off all hope of slipping past.

"Go your way, Ben," Jaina ordered, still fighting to hold the Force lightning back. "Now!"

"Can't!" Ben said. "We've got a dozen Sith here."

He put his back against Jaina's, but making a stand was the last thing she wanted to do. She glanced over at the pump and, seeing that it was still running, came up with a different idea.

"Ben, follow me!"

By the time Jaina said this, a trio of glass parangs were flying in her direction. She reached out to Ben, making sure he sensed where she was going, then dived toward a twenty-centimeter outflow pipe that exited on her side of the pump.

As soon as her blade tipped down, the Force lightning blasted her in the leg and sent her spinning. Concentrating on keeping her fists clenched around the hilt of her weapon, she allowed the lightsaber to slice through the outflow pipe where it turned to pass down through the deck grating.

Water sprayed in all directions, and the Force lightning died away. Ben brushed past behind her, amid the tingling of shattering parangs. Jaina rolled onto her back, bringing her blade around until it was above her head. She slashed through the outflow pipe again, this time closer to where it left the pump housing. A meter-long section of pipe exploded outward, riding a jet of water as big around as Jaina's leg, and went spinning toward the Keshiri woman.

The ear-piercing cracks of two grenade detonations sounded from the far side of the pump, announcing that Ben had been busy himself. Then Jaina's entire body began to prickle with danger sense. Shouting for him to come along, she sprang to her feet and executed a series of Force flips more or less following the column of water toward her first attacker.

Having just redirected the flying pipe, but still struggling to keep her balance in the water jet, the Keshiri was in no position to defend herself. Jaina beheaded the woman on the way past, then felt the invisible punch of a concussion wave as a Sith grenade exploded back at the pump.

Jaina tumbled through the air, completely out of control, ears aching and head spinning, then crashed down on a hip. Her entire leg exploded in pain, and she continued to roll, sometimes sideways and sometimes over her shoulders, until she finally slammed into the curved wall of some sort of settling basin.

She was still trying to orient herself—and find Ben—when she felt something ping off the basin wall next to her head. She spun away and came around in a crouch, searching for the source of her attacker. A spark flashed off the deck where she had been sitting, and a dent appeared in the grating.

The shatter gun.

Jaina rolled again, and this time, she came up looking back toward the sniper nest. The shatter gun barrel was swinging in her direction.

Where was Ben?

Jaina backflipped away, keeping her hand extended, and felt the air whisper as the pellet passed beneath her.

The sniper was good.

Then Jaina came around again and saw the barrel trying to follow her, and this time it was the Sith who was slow. Jaina grabbed the shatter gun in the Force and jerked, hard. The sniper pitched forward out of his firing crouch, following his weapon toward the sludge tank below. They hit the edge and broke together.

Jaina had no time to look for her cousin. A wall of Sith was charging in her direction, their crimson lightsabers dancing in their hands as they ran. Hoping to find some hint of what had become of Ben, she reached for him in the Force, then crouched down below the edge of the settling basin—and felt Luke reaching out to her, urging her to leave the cover of the basin and turn toward the interface panel.

But there remained no sign of Ben.

Jaina paused just long enough to take one last look back toward the pump motor. Half a dozen glass blades came flying in her direction. She swept them aside with a Force blast, then turned and sprinted for the interface panel, dodging and somersaulting as Force lightning and blaster bolts streaked into the gloom ahead.

Then she was only a step away from the interface panel, with only two places to go—right toward the main door, or left down a small service aisle flanked by two banks of equipment cabinets. She felt Luke pull her to the left, and so she charged down a passage so narrow she would have almost no hope of dodging anything after she entered.

Jaina managed three steps before her spine grew icy with danger sense and fear. She dropped to her belly and felt the heat as a flurry of blaster bolts shrieked past overhead. Then she rolled to her back—and saw Ben somersaulting down the aisle toward her, just three steps ahead of the Sith who had opened fire.

Jaina sprang up, using the Force to launch herself high enough for Ben to tumble past beneath her, then ignited her lightsaber—and barely managed to catch a fork of Force lightning on the blade. She yelled for Ben to keep going and started to advance on her attacker.

She felt Luke touch her in the Force again, gently tugging her down the aisle. She retreated as quickly as she could, running backward and pivoting from side to side, pressing her back and shoulders flat against the equipment cabinets whenever blaster bolts and Force-hurled parangs went sailing past.

The aisle opened up into a comparatively small storage room cluttered with stacks of enormous spare valves and pipe fittings—most over a meter in diameter. Luke continued to draw Jaina onward, so she kept dodging and retreating, and an instant later she was one step from the back wall, standing at Ben's side. They were trapped, with nowhere to go.

Then Luke and Corran Horn emerged from behind a stack of giant valves, igniting their lightsabers and stepping forward to ricochet bolts toward her attackers. Instead of charging directly to the attack, the Sith began to spread out again, hoping to outflank the Jedi and attack from all sides at once.

Jaina glanced over at the two Jedi Masters. Both were watching the Sith with smug expressions on their faces.

"Thanks for coming," Luke said, speaking in a Force-enhanced voice. "I'm Luke Skywalker, Grand Master of the Jedi Order. And I'm only going to say this once: drop your weapons."

Most of the Sith looked confused or worried, but their apparent leader—a stocky blond man with a dagger-shaped beard—glared in open hatred.

"I don't care who you are." He raised his hand, preparing to wave the others forward. "You can't be *that* good."

"I thought you'd say that," Luke replied.

He glanced into the darkness above the enemy's head—and drew a scornful snort from the Sith.

"Come now, Master Skywalker," he said, raising his hand to wave his warriors forward. "If that is the best—"

His retort was cut short when a pair of figures in dark molytex armor dropped out of the gloom above the narrow aisle. The *snap-hiss* of igniting lightsabers sounded behind the band of Sith, and startled voices began to cry out in pain.

Jaina did not wait for Luke to order the attack. She simply leapt forward, Force-hurling the closest Sith into the one behind him, bringing her blade down in a vicious overhand slash that he managed to block despite the confusion. He spat at her eyes in a desperate attempt to blind her and then, as she leaned away, drove a knee into her ribs so hard it rocked her up on one foot.

Jaina swept her other foot across in front of her, hooking his ankle just as he shifted his weight back to catch his balance. His foot flew out and he went down on his side, trying to twist around so he could bring his lightsaber back up to block.

Jaina planted her boot on his hip, driving him into the deck face-first. At the same time, she whipped her lightsaber up to block a strike from a dark-haired woman stepping forward to take the spitter's place. Still standing on his back, Jaina pivoted around and snapped her foot up sideways, catching the woman at the base of the chin. She felt the sharp crackle of shattering jawbones, and the Sith flew backward off her feet.

Not even taking the time to lower her foot, Jaina flipped her lightsaber down and drove it into the man upon whom she was standing. She whipped the tip around inside—just to make sure the Sith was done fighting for good—then brought her leg down and turned back to the dark-haired woman.

A blue lightsaber was already protruding from the Sith woman's sternum, slicing down toward her hip. The anguish in her eyes faded to emptiness, then she collapsed and landed in a heap on the deck. Behind the corpse, standing shoulder-to-shoulder with Valin Horn and staring at the dead body with an expression halfway between horror and relief, was Jysella.

Jaina dipped her head in acknowledgment, then spun to meet her next attacker—and found Luke picking his way toward her. His lightsaber was already deactivated, and his expression was serene, as though fighting Sith at three-to-one odds was only meditation for him. Following a step behind him was Ben. The young man looked a bit awestruck, but he was spattered with enough blood to suggest he had not been idle.

In the opposite direction, Jaina found Corran coming to join them. His nose was wrinkled at the stench of so much death, but he seemed no more troubled by the fight than did Luke. Jaina deactivated her own lightsaber and turned back to Valin and Jysella, who must have cut their way through at least four Sith before reaching Jaina's side.

"Nice work, guys," she said. "Even I didn't feel you hiding up there."

Jysella smiled. "It's easy to be stealthy when the enemy is focused on you and Dad and Master Skywalker."

"Not that easy," Luke said. "You did well. Both of you."

Valin beamed, but distant boots could already be heard running in their direction. More Sith.

"We'd better get going," Luke said. "The way Rowdy has been acting, he's going to leave without us."

Jaina's brow shot up. "You've seen Rowdy?"

Luke nodded, then waved them toward the back of the storage area. "We managed to hold the computer interface long enough for him to learn that it's been disabled."

"Disabled?" It was Ben who asked this. "But it looked active when we saw it."

"It certainly did," Corran replied. "And I think we know what that means."

"They had time to plan this ambush," Jaina said, not quite able to keep from glancing in Ben's direction. "A *lot* of time."

Ben scowled. "I know what you're thinking," he said. "But it couldn't have been Vestara. She didn't even know where we were going."

"And you know that *how*?" Corran asked.

"Because she asked me about it while we were in the capsule," Ben replied. "About two minutes before the ambush."

"Questions are not always what they seem," Corran said. "You're a good enough investigator to understand that."

"And I'm good enough to know that assumptions aren't facts," Ben replied. He turned to his father. "Vestara is *not* the one who betrayed us. You know that."

Luke remained silent for an instant, then shrugged. "All I know is we're going after a Sith Grand Lord. Whatever we think we know, we're probably fooling ourselves." As he spoke, muffled Sith voices began to sound from the far end of the aisle. "We'll sort that out later. For now, we just need to keep moving."

He motioned to Corran and Valin, and the two Horns quickly moved a two-meter stack of valves and pipe elbows away from the wall. Behind it, at the end of a short aisle, a freestanding lift tube emerged from the floor and vanished into the gloom above. A crude portal about one and a half meters high had been cut into the wall of the tube, revealing a sporadic flow of canisters, crates, and soft-sided bags rising inside it. Next to the opening stood Rowdy, rocking back and forth and trilling impatiently.

"A *cargo* tube?" Jaina asked.

"Rowdy seems to think it will take us to another interface station," Corran said, glancing back to Jaina. "At least, I assume that's why he had us cut a big hole into it."

Rowdy gave an affirmative tweedle, and the voices grew louder and more urgent as Sith began to come down the aisle toward them. A heartbeat later the first blaster bolts started to ping around the storage area, ricocheting off pipe fittings and equipment cabinets.

"It's got to be better than staying here," Jaina said. Worried that Ben would do something foolish, she turned to find him staring back down the aisle. "Ben—"

"I know," he said. Ben's Force aura began to sizzle with frustration and anger, then he waved a hand and sent a control valve tumbling down the aisle toward the Sith. "We have to go."

Chapter Eleven

HOW THE SCOUTSHIP HAD MANAGED TO SLIP INSIDE THE BLOCKADE, Head of State Jagged Fel could not imagine. He had a thousand Sienar Sentinel picket boats watching all approaches to the planet Exodo II. He had six Star Destroyer task forces crowded into an area of space barely a thousand kilometers in diameter. He had a hundred turbolaser crews pouring fire into the cluster of sunlit megaliths that had once been Exodo II's moon Boreleo, and he had three sensor crews monitoring every cubic meter between the target zone and the cordon perimeter. And yet there it was on the bridge display: the golden sliver of a KDY Star Ranger, slipping into a dark chasm between a trio of kilometer-long moon fragments.

The most likely explanation for the infiltration was also the most alarming: that someone had deliberately allowed the craft through. His siege of ex–Galactic Alliance Chief of State and would-be Imperial Head of State Natasi Daala was about to enter its second month, and Jag was acutely aware that his power was hanging by a thread. Every Moff in the Empire was mobilizing his private fleet, and there had already been several border clashes as old enemies took advantage of Jag's distraction to make star grabs. His spies reported that the Moffs who were not attacking one another were as likely to join the fight against him as to support him against Daala. The Imperial Navy itself could not be trusted, either. In fact, Jag had been forced to dispatch entire fleets to the most remote corners of the Empire, for fear that their officers would side with Lecersen or Vansyn rather than Jag, the legitimate Head of State.

And now someone in the Home Fleet was letting blockade-runners slip through the cordon. He had no doubt that they were messengers, carrying offers of support that Daala and Lecersen would eagerly accept, no matter what they had to promise in return. If Jag did not end this insurrection soon, he was going to have a civil war on his hands. Perhaps he would have something even worse, with the Empire collapsing into anarchy and the Moffs turning on one another.

As Jag pondered the difficulties of keeping the Empire together, a dozen turbolaser beams flashed across the bridge display, targeting the Star Ranger as it entered Boreleo's debris field. Stone sprayed everywhere, then the screen went white with luminous overload, and the image of the Star Ranger vanished before it grew obvious whether the little scoutship had been destroyed.

Jag waited, staring at the screen. When it did not clear after a couple of seconds, he turned to the task force commander, Admiral Vitor Reige, and cocked an expectant brow.

"I'll have a report for you as soon as possible, Head of State."

Reige, a tall, hook-nosed man with dark hair and piercing blue eyes, shot a glance toward his aide, who started across the bridge to relay the inquiry to the *Bloodfin*'s captain. It was a frustratingly slow way to get a simple answer, but in the military, chain of command was all.

"Thank you, Admiral Reige." Jag was fairly certain that the admiral remained loyal to the Empire's legitimate Head of State. But Reige's mentor had been Gilad Pellaeon himself, and it was impossible not to wonder what kind of effect the friendship between Pellaeon and Daala was having on the admiral's judgment. "And you might ask for a tracking report. Whatever the Star Ranger's fate, I'd be very interested to know how it slipped through our blockade."

"As would I, Head of State," Reige said. "At the moment, all I can think of is that the craft has been outfitted with stealth technology."

"Sorry, Admiral—I only wish that was it," said Tahiri Veila.

Standing at Jag's shoulder on the side opposite Reige, she was un-armed and wearing bright red confinement bracelets around both wrists. Though Jag had every confidence that Tahiri intended to honor her promise to stand trial for murder, the brig gear was an overt state-ment of her status as an Imperial prisoner—and her idea. It had been aboard this very ship that she had killed Gilad Pellaeon. So Tahiri had offered to wear the restraints as a concession to the feelings of Vitor Reige and the many others who had loved Pellaeon as a father. Thus far, the strategy seemed to be working. There were plenty of sour looks and muttered insults, but the crew seemed to accept that she was merely on parole until a proper trial could be organized.

After a tense silence, Reige grudgingly acknowledged the comment by turning his head in her direction. "I take it you have another expla-nation, Prisoner Veila?"

"The Force," Tahiri replied. "A powerful presence has entered the debris field—one I haven't felt here before."

"A *powerful presence?*" Reige scoffed. "And that would mean what, precisely?"

"Sith," Jag said, trying to ignore the cold knot that had begun to form in his stomach. He turned to Tahiri. "Is that what you're sug-gesting?"

Tahiri hesitated, her eyes fixed on the bridge display as the image returned to normal. Two of the kilometer-long massifs had been re-duced to a collection of red-glowing boulders, and there was nothing of the Star Ranger to be seen.

Finally she said, "I certainly feel a darkness, but whether it's Sith . . ." Her gaze shifted toward the forward viewport, beyond which the shat-tered moon appeared to be little more than a tiny ball of flame at the convergence point of a steady stream of turbolaser strikes. "All I can say is that whoever's out there, they are strong in the Force. Very strong."

"And still alive." The remark came from directly behind Tahiri, where Jag's Chiss aide and bodyguard, Ashik, was standing. "You feel that, as well?"

Tahiri nodded. "I do."

"Most impressive, prisoner Veila," Reige said drily. "With you aboard, one wonders why we need sensor crews at all."

"I was wondering that *before* the prisoner spoke, Admiral," Jag said, putting a little durasteel in his voice. He could understand Reige's indignation at having Tahiri walking free aboard the *Bloodfin,* but her Jedi abilities were too useful at the moment to leave her locked in the brig—and it was time for Reige to recognize that. "Had *she* been sitting at a sensor station, perhaps she would have spotted the infiltrator before it was silhouetted against the debris field."

As Jag spoke, Reige's aide returned and whispered something into the admiral's ear. The look of puzzlement that came to Reige's face quickly changed to one of vindication, and he turned back to Jag with a look approaching defiance.

"I doubt it would have made any difference *who* was at the sensor stations, Head of State." Reige pointed to a holopad in the fleet admiral's salon at the back of the bridge, then said, "The Star Ranger seems to be using a new form of jamming technology. If you would care to join me, I'll explain."

By the time Jag and the others had retreated into the salon, the tactical hologram of the Exodo II planetary system was already on display. The image portrayed an outer shell of designator symbols beginning with the letters *ISS*—for "Imperial Sienar Sentinel"—surrounding a mottled green-and-black sphere. Save for the lack of clouds, the planet looked identical to the world Jag saw every night outside his stateroom window. The task force, hanging in orbit where the moon Boreleo used to be, was a knot of designator symbols too tangled to read.

Reige nodded, and his aide pointed a remote control at the holopad. A moment later a circle of perhaps thirty ISS symbols dissolved into static.

"The time scale has been compressed a thousandfold," Reige explained. "Every second on the holo represents a little over a quarter hour in real time."

The static circle continued to expand for a couple of moments, then quickly began to shrink and elongate in the direction opposite Exodo II's spin. Within three seconds—about three-quarters of a standard real-time hour—the circle had narrowed into a short, slender band that was traveling around the planet toward the task force.

"The static resulted from an energy flash that traveled along this route, temporarily blinding sensors," Reige's aide explained. "At the time, the reconnaissance officers attributed it to a solar flare and didn't worry about it."

"Which is a very bad mistake, and one they had better not make again," Jag said. He turned to Tahiri. "Would you care to explain what we're seeing?"

"Of course, Head of State." Tahiri's gaze remained fixed on the holo. "It's a Force flash."

"A *Force flash,* prisoner Veila?" Reige said. "I'm afraid you'll need to define the term for those of us who aren't on intimate terms with members of the Jedi Order."

"It's a countersurveillance technique," Jag said, doing the explaining himself. "The Jedi use it to temporarily blind security cams and intrusion alarms. On the vids, it looks like a minor glitch."

Tahiri nodded. "Exactly. But this one . . ." She fell silent as the hologram changed scales to depict the inner cordon of the blockade, and then she turned to face Jag. "This one is very powerful. Even Grand Master Skywalker isn't strong enough to blind a picket boat's sensors at those kinds of ranges."

"If you're trying to tell us it was no Jedi piloting that Star Ranger, there's no need," Jag said. "I have it on good authority that the Jedi like Daala even less than I do at the moment."

This drew a polite laugh—no more—from the staff officers.

But Tahiri's expression remained serious. "Actually, Head of State Fel, what I'm trying to suggest is that the pilot can't be Sith, either."

She pointed at the hologram, which now showed the designator symbols of six destroyers and thirty escort vessels arrayed around the shattered remnants of the moon Boreleo. Fully half of the vessels were engulfed in static.

"Not with enough strength to blind that many starships."

Jag saw the fear come into her eyes and knew what she was thinking. "Go ahead and say it, Tahiri," he said. "Admiral Reige will need to know."

"Very well." Tahiri swallowed, then said, "I think we've found Abeloth."

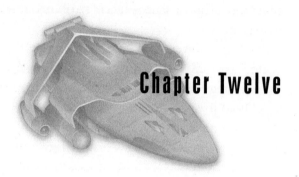

Chapter Twelve

OUTSIDE THE *CHIMAERA* RAGED A SILENT STORM OF TUMBLING MEGA-liths and flashing turbolaser strikes, a hell of Daala's own making erupting inside the shattered pieces of the moon Boreleo. Vansyn's flagship, the *Wyvard,* hung only a few kilometers away, blocking the mouth of a semi-permanent passage and venting black smoke from the cavity that had once been her bridge. Long streams of bodies and flot-sam were jetting from the melt holes in her forward hull, and hundred-meter tongues of flame were shooting through the splits in her sagging midsection. And still Fel's Chiss allies continued to pour maserfire into the flagship's lifeless hulk, trying in vain to blast her out of the way so they could at last enter the heart of the debris field and attack the *Chimaera.*

But at the moment, Daala's attention was not on the battle. Instead she was sitting in her command salon, where an Imperial News Net-work report was playing on a pop-up display at the end of the confer-ence table. The report was a day old, but with Fel's fleet jamming all transmissions into or out of Exodo II's vicinity, it was the first newscast she had seen in a nearly a month—and the closest thing to an intelligence briefing she had received since taking refuge inside Boreleo's remnants.

". . . the Moffs are seizing this opportunity to settle old scores," reported an intelligent-looking woman with an oversized nose.

Her image was replaced by the flashing web of a turbolaser battle in deep space.

"When Moff Garreter mobilized his fleet to assist Head of State Fel, Moff Woolbam attempted to annex Rimcee Station. Garreter was forced to divert to protect the integrity of his holdings. The situation is the same across the entire Empire, with Moffs skirmishing over border systems that have been contested since before Palpatine was Emperor."

The newscaster's image reappeared, this time with a chart of the modern Empire hanging above her right shoulder. Red starbursts began to dot the map as she continued.

"Battles and invasions have been reported in more than a dozen systems. Imperial fleets are being forced to intervene in the Vexta Belt, Entralla, Dactruria, and Tovarskl. At Muunilinst, a three-way fleet battle rages among forces loyal to Head of State Fel and Moffs Woolbam and Callron the Younger."

The newscaster's face expanded to fill the entire display.

"The instability has caused turmoil in financial markets in every sector as investors brace for a descent into chaos. Unconfirmed reports suggest that two fleets of the Imperial Navy have been approached by powerful Moffs attempting to buy the loyalty of their commanders."

"Pause report," Daala said, bringing the newscast to a temporary halt.

She shook her head in dismay, unable to believe how badly her plan to liberate the Empire was floundering. Had she foreseen the stalemate between herself and Jagged Fel, she would never have attempted to unseat him. As bad as it was to leave the Empire in the hands of a Jedi puppet, even that would have been better than allowing it to disintegrate into anarchy. And truth be told, Daala was not merely *allowing* it to happen—she had *caused* it when she had failed to remove Fel.

To be fair, though, she was guilty only of bad timing. Fel simply wasn't up to the job of ruling a dynamic civilization like the Empire.

Sooner or later, the Moffs would have sensed his weakness and rebelled anyway. Daala took a calming breath, then faced the young Star Ranger pilot who had risked her life to deliver the report.

"This is madness," Daala said. "The Empire is sinking into barbarism."

"Exactly." The young woman had narrow blue eyes and a wide mouth that seemed just a little too large for her face. "That's why I felt I had to come to you, Admiral. Head of State Fel is not up to the job of holding the Empire together."

"That shouldn't surprise anyone," Lecersen observed. Seated in the chair next to Daala, he looked on the verge of cracking himself, with purple circles beneath his eyes and skin as gray as a fleet officer's uniform. "And that's all the more reason we need to find a way to slip out of here—*now*."

Daala answered without taking her eyes from the young lieutenant. "Escaping is easier said than done, Drikl."

"If Lieutenant Pagorski can sneak *into* this rubble pile, I dare say we can find a way to sneak *out*." Lecersen stood. "And the sooner, the better. We need to get back out there and take charge."

"Take charge of what, exactly?" As Daala spoke, she continued to study Pagorski, trying to figure out why a young woman who had only recently been released from a Galactic Alliance prison would risk her life to join the remains of a cornered, badly battered fleet. "The Final Fall of the Empire?"

"Not at all," Lecersen insisted. "I have friends—a great many friends. And as soon as they learn of my escape, they'll rally to our cause."

"Assuming we *do* escape." Daala locked gazes with Pagorski. "Assuming that Lieutenant Pagorski's miraculous infiltration of a very tight blockade isn't just a ruse to avoid a bloody assault by luring *us* into a foolish attempt."

The look of puzzlement that shot through Pagorski's eyes lasted just long enough to appear sincere, then the corners of her wide mouth lifted into an approving smile.

"I knew I was right to come to you, Admiral Daala," she said. "No one understands how the Imperial mind works better than you."

"Your flattery is duly noted, Lieutenant," Daala replied. "It won't, however, lull me into a foolish decision. If Head of State Fel didn't *allow* you to slip through the blockade—one that even the Rebel Alliance could have kept sealed tight—how did you manage?"

"Isn't that obvious, Admiral?" Pagorski answered immediately. "Jagged Fel didn't let me through. Someone else did."

Daala cocked her brow, impressed—but not certain yet whether it was with Pagorski's coolness under fire, or her resourcefulness in accomplishing a goal.

"And does this someone have a name?"

"Not one that I'm going to share with the next Supreme Commander of the Imperial Navy," Pagorski said. "You're a woman who values duty as much as she does loyalty, and I wouldn't want a black mark placed in his file for doing me a favor."

"Of course not," Daala said. The lieutenant was smarter than she looked, for that was exactly how Daala would have reacted to someone betraying his commander and his ship. "But if you're not here trying to lure us into a trap, why *did* you come?"

"To deliver a situation report," Pagorski replied simply. "Which I've done. The rest is up to you. You're the admiral."

"Be that as it may, you still made it alive," Lecersen said. "I assume you have a plan for leaving in the same condition?"

"I'm afraid that would be a poor assumption." Pagorski's gaze shifted toward the main viewport, where the *Wyvard*'s lifeless hulk could be seen drifting backward under the steady maser barrage. "As I'm sure Admiral Daala has surmised by now, my arrival did not go entirely unnoticed. In fact, it appears I may have caused them to come after you. My apologies."

"Don't flatter yourself, Lieutenant," Lecersen said. "You're the last reason Fel is coming after us now."

A twinkle of wry amusement came to Pagorski's eyes. "Is that so?"

"Absolutely," Lecersen said. "It's the chaos in the Empire forcing his hand. Fel is desperate to turn his full attention to the Moffs."

"Who are probably carving off pieces of your sector as we speak," Daala pointed out. "And no doubt making a crippled mess of the rest of the Empire, too."

"All the more reason to be certain that *one* of us escapes to take charge," Lecersen said, turning toward the exit. "I'll be returning to the *Empire Maker* to make my attempt now, Admiral Daala."

Daala shook her head. "Not yet." Even were one of them to survive the escape attempt and convince a few of the other Moffs to rally around them, it would only turn the current crisis into a full-out civil war—and one far more likely to result in the Empire's final disintegration than her own victory. "It's too early for that."

"I'm afraid my mind is made up, Admiral," Lecersen said. "I wish you the best of luck in your own attempt."

"I said *not yet,* Drikl." She shot a commanding glance toward Pagorski, and the lieutenant had a hold-out blaster in her grasp so fast that her hand did not even seem to move. Daala caught herself staring and turned back to Lecersen. "Perhaps you could give me another half an hour?"

Lecersen eyed the blaster for a moment, then said, "I don't see how I can refuse."

Daala smiled, quietly relieved that Lecersen had not forced her to have him killed. She was beginning to see an opportunity in the Empire's current situation, and if her idea developed into a full-blown solution, she was going to need Lecersen to serve as her puppet.

"Thank you, Moff Lecersen."

Before she could motion him back to his seat, the voice of the *Chimaera*'s captain came over the intercom.

"Admiral Daala, it's time. The masers are beginning to push the *Wyvard* back."

Daala activated the TRANSMIT switch. "Very well, Captain. We'll be right there." She rose and motioned for Lecersen and Pagorski to follow her. "You'll want to see this."

She stepped out of the command salon onto a bridge acrid with the smell of fear and exhaustion, then led the way to her command post. The *Chimaera*'s captain stood at the combat information console, three days of gray stubble on his face, his bloodshot eyes bulging with caf overdose as he looked out over the frenzied discipline of a ship's bridge in full battle.

"Captain Remal, how do our chances look?" Daala asked.

"We'll know in a minute, Admiral."

Remal pointed at a tactical display that showed a ten-kilometer pocket of empty space surrounded by tumbling boulders. The remnants of Daala's battered fleet were scattered around the makeshift redoubt. At the center of the formation was the cruiser *Kagcatcher,* her projection crews keeping the pocket more or less stable by carefully modulating the ship's four gravity-well generators. Lecersen's flagship, the *Empire Maker,* was positioned along the back wall, ready to attempt a desperate escape through a hundred-kilometer maze of shifting megaliths. The derelict *Wyvard* was still blocking the entrance tunnel, slowly drifting backward under the maserfire pouring into the molten mess of its bow.

Not shown on the display were two dozen smaller vessels out in the labyrinth maze, operating independently and doing whatever they could to harass the attacking forces. Daala doubted the ambushes would actually repel Fel's assault, but they would at least extract a heavy price in ships and lives.

Finally, the *Wyvard* was pushed completely out of the passage. Twenty starfighter squadrons appeared on the display, their designator symbols going active as they broke away from their mother ships and swarmed to defend the redoubt. They had barely arrived before Imperial squadrons began to pour out of the tunnel, and the mouth vanished into a swirling cloud of designator symbols.

"Admiral Daala," Lecersen said. "I really must insist that you release me at once. The time has come to take our chances and hope one of us survives this mess."

"And that will serve the Empire *how,* Moff Lecersen?" Daala asked.

"By providing a figure for the Moffs to rally around," Lecersen said. "So we can organize and counterattack."

"And turn chaos into cataclysm." Daala shook her head. "An Empire at war with itself is as weak as an Empire in anarchy, and I have no interest in ruling an empty shell."

"Ruling an empty shell is better than dying here," Lecersen retorted.

"For you, perhaps," Daala replied. "But I'm beginning to see another way to defeat Head of State Fel—a way that won't destroy the very thing I'm trying to save."

As Daala spoke, the maserfire resumed, pushing the *Wyvard* farther back. She shifted her gaze from the display to the viewport. She could no longer even see the wrecked Star Destroyer, only a long pillar of flame shooting ever deeper into the redoubt.

"So what do you propose?" Lecersen demanded, paying no attention to the battle outside. "At this point, the only way to prevent a civil war is to surrender so Fel can turn his full attention to the Moffs—and surrender has never been my style."

"Nor mine," Daala said, almost absently. She turned to Remal. "I believe the time has come, wouldn't you agree?"

The captain nodded. "I would," he said. "It's a pity we don't have sensor data in there, but they've got at least one of the Chiss Star Destroyers coming through. That should be enough to make them think twice."

"Very well, Captain," Daala said. "You may commence Operation Crate Crusher."

"Commencing Crate Crusher now," Remal acknowledged.

As the captain opened a channel to the *Kagcatcher*, Daala turned to Lecersen and continued her conversation. "You're wrong about surrender being the only way to prevent a civil war," she said. "Very wrong."

Lecersen frowned, his gaze drifting toward the viewport. "You're saying you have another way?"

"There is *always* another way, Drikl," Daala said. "I learned that from the Jedi."

As Daala spoke, an excited murmur began to build on the bridge. She glanced back toward the viewport and saw the entrance tunnel to their redoubt collapsing. Two of the huge megaliths were swinging together as the *Kagcatcher* used its gravity-well projectors to pull the third out of alignment. As the gap closed, the maserfire grew more intense—then finally ceased in a single blue-white flash as the two pieces of moon came together.

A rousing cheer shook the bridge, and Daala gave an approving nod to Remal. "Well, done, Captain. How many squadrons of enemy starfighters do we have trapped inside?"

"Close to twenty," Remal replied.

"Excellent," Daala said. "Any pilot willing to surrender his craft to us will be offered a comfortable cell or an officer's commission in my fleet, his choice."

"Very good, Admiral," Remal said. "And for those who prefer to fight on or destroy their craft?"

"They will be left to die in their vac suits," Daala replied. "Make that *very* clear when you hail them."

A hard smile came to Remal's mouth. "As you command."

Daala turned back to Lecersen. "Now, where were we?" she asked, motioning him to follow her back to the salon. "As I recall, discussing how *neither* of us intends to surrender."

"Destroying one of the Empire of the Hand's big toys is hardly going to turn the battle in our favor, Admiral," Lecersen said. "And if you're thinking it might buy us a truce—that *is* surrender. Fel will only use the time to consolidate his power."

"Not a truce, Drikl." Daala stepped into the command salon ahead of him. "I was actually thinking of an election."

"An *election*?" Lecersen stopped at the threshold behind her. "Why in the blazes would Fel agree to that?"

"For the same reason I would," Daala said. "Because he doesn't want the Empire to dismantle itself—and because he believes he will win it."

"And he *will*," Lecersen said, finally following her into the salon. "He has more resources than you do—and he *is* the current Head of State."

"A Head of State appointed by a *Jedi*," Daala reminded him. "Nothing is more unpredictable than an election, Drikl—not even a battle."

"In this case, I must disagree," Lecersen said. "You seem to be forgetting the low esteem in which the Moffs hold women—myself excluded, of course."

"What makes you think I'm forgetting anything?" Daala asked. "With you standing at my side, the Moffs will be persuaded to overcome their prejudice. Between your planetary resources and my military assets, we'll clearly be a strong candidate."

"But strong enough?" Lecersen asked. "Moff votes are bought, not earned—and Fel can deliver now. We'll have only promises."

"Which is why you should suggest a *general* election, Admiral Daala," Pagorski said, stepping forward. "Then you wouldn't have to settle for sharing the throne, since most Imperial commoners think more highly of women than they do Moffs. Moreover, a general election would appeal to Fel's democratic inclinations. He might even prefer it over a military victory, because it's the kind of reform he would like to bring to the Empire anyway."

"A *general* election?" Lecersen scoffed. "The Moff Council will never approve that."

"The Moffs are too busy clawing at one another's throats to stop us," Daala said, growing even more enthusiastic. She nodded to Pagorski. "Well done, Lieutenant. I like it."

"*You?* Beat Jagged Fel in a popularity contest?" Lecersen shook his head in disbelief. "That will never happen."

"But it *will*," Pagorski said. "I can guarantee it."

Lecersen shot her a withering glare. "I suggest you remain silent, Lieutenant. Your delusions are becoming an embarrassment."

Pagorski's eyes flashed white. "They're not delusions, Moff." Without looking away, she asked, "Admiral, would you permit me to prove it?"

"By all means," Daala said. "I'd welcome it."

"Thank you." Pagorski's smile grew wide, and then her hand slithered up to rest on Lecersen's shoulder. "Moff Lecersen, you may prostrate yourself before your new Head of State."

"Prostrate myself?" Lecersen demanded. "On *your* command?"

"It's more of a suggestion." Pagorski squeezed his shoulder, her fingers digging in so hard they seemed to actually sink into his flesh. "For your own good."

As she spoke, Lecersen's eyes widened and his face paled. A cold sweat began to pour down his brow. After a few breaths, he finally collapsed to his knees and placed his palms at Daala's feet.

"That's better." Pagorski smiled, then shifted her gaze back to Daala. "We can win this, Admiral—I promise you."

Chapter Thirteen

DOWN ON LEVEL 351 OF THE JEDI TEMPLE, WYNN DORVAN STOOD pressing himself into the corner of the computer core decontamination chamber. This was not because he objected to being misted with a dust fixative, but because he was trying to keep his Sith escorts from noticing his excitement. Directly ahead, the grip of a hold-out blaster was hanging out of the sleeve of a Sith Saber, as though the weapon were ready to fall from its secret holster.

The accessibility of the hold-out blaster was almost certainly a trap, of course, designed to test Wynn's loyalties. But there was a slim chance that the weapon had simply been jarred loose, and that its owner did not realize it had become visible.

And Wynn was ready to take that chance. When he had suggested that Lydea Pagorski be released to build goodwill with the Empire, the Beloved Queen of the Stars had destroyed the poor woman and taken over her body. When he had tried to trick her into playing into Admiral Bwua'tu's hands by suggesting that the Sith withdraw into the Temple, she had used her strange Force powers to anticipate the Jedi battle plan and arrange a devastating ambush. Abeloth was something beyond Wynn's understanding, a monster of unimaginable power and capable of unthinkable evil, and he had been a fool to think he could play her.

There had never been any hope of stopping her, Wynn could see that now. And there was no realistic hope of escaping her and the Sith alive, either. The best Wynn could hope for was to avoid the same fate Pagorski had suffered—to end his unwitting collaboration, one way or another, before the Beloved Queen of the Stars decided to push her tentacles into his head, too.

All he had to do was get his hands on that hold-out blaster.

The inner door slid aside, and the Beloved Queen of the Stars stepped out of the crowded decontamination chamber into some much cooler space Wynn could not see. He started to ease forward, angling toward the hold-out blaster—then had to draw up short when the entire group stopped just one step later.

"Chief Dorvan and I will be fine here alone," the Beloved Queen said, speaking in the voice of her Roki Kem manifestation. "The rest of you may return with Lady Korelei to prepare the ambush."

The Sith in front of Wynn—the one with the loose blaster—said, "Beloved Queen, allow me to stay, I beg you." He turned to glance back at Wynn, his eyes smoldering with contempt. "There is something amiss with your adviser today. I can feel a lie in his aura."

Wynn steeled himself to make a lunge for the hold-out blaster, but the Beloved Queen's voice stopped him.

"That is of no concern, Master Tsiat," she said. "I have no need to fear Chief Dorvan."

Wynn felt the cold pressure on his face, and though he could not see past the shoulders of the Sith in front of him, he knew the Beloved Queen was looking in his direction.

"Do I?" asked the Beloved Queen.

"Not from me," Wynn said. Even as he spoke, he felt sure that she knew he was lying—that she could hear it in his voice and sense it in his aura. "I'm simply not capable."

"Everyone is capable, Chief Dorvan." It was not the Beloved Queen who said this, but Lady Korelei, the Keshiri High Lord who had been Wynn's torturer. "All one needs is courage."

"I fear that's one quality I lack," Wynn said. His heart had climbed into his throat, but he was enough of a sabacc player to know the time had come to gamble everything. "I'm an administrator, not a warrior."

"Then our Beloved Queen will be safe with you, I am sure." A faint smile came to Lady Korelei's lavender lips, and she motioned to the Sith standing between Wynn and the exit. "Let him pass."

Wynn was more certain than ever that his captors were trying to test him, but he was determined to take his chances. Even dying would be preferable to what awaited him as Abeloth's servant. He nodded to Korelei.

"Thank you."

Wynn stepped forward, deliberately tripping over a nearby heel. He cried out and went sprawling, grabbing the first sleeve within reach to prevent himself from falling. Of course, that sleeve belonged to the Sith with the hold-out blaster, Master Tsiat.

Tsiat roared in rage and used the Force to fling Dorvan back into the corner. "Clumsy ugwum!"

Dorvan wailed and cowered, curling into a ball—to hide the little weapon he had just stolen. "It was an accident!" He slipped the blaster into the sleeve of his tunic. "I apologize!"

He heard a boot step toward him, and then Tsiat's foot slammed into his ribs. "Apology accepted."

The foot drew back as though to kick again, but Lady Korelei's voice split the rising din. "You've made your point, Master Tsiat. I'm sure Chief Dorvan will be more careful in the future."

Wynn felt himself rising off the floor, and he continued to rise until he was above the heads of the Sith. When he glanced back, he found Korelei's oval eyes watching him with the same cold emptiness he had often seen in those of the Beloved Queen. His stomach began to churn with a queasy terror as a pair of silver flickers appeared in the depths of her gaze. Her smile grew as wide as her face. All her teeth suddenly seemed to be fangs, and a relentless tide of despair welled up inside Wynn. He knew what he was seeing.

The Beloved Queen of the Stars had taken a *third* body.

Now Abeloth had *three* manifestations—Roki Kem, Lydea Pagorski, and Lady Korelei. Wynn grew so cold that he started to shake, and he did not recognize the sensation as despair until he found himself praying that he was hallucinating, that he had finally lost his mind under Korelei's torture and escaped into the oblivion of insanity.

Because even madness would be better than three Abeloths.

Wynn stopped descending, and he found himself hovering in the air before the Roki Kem manifestation, fighting hard not to burst out wailing, too frightened to meet her gaze and see, written in the cruel truth of her face, the pitiful futility of his resistance.

"Chief Dorvan, will you please put your feet down?" the Roki Kem manifestation asked. "Or do you expect Lady Korelei to continue holding you there for the rest of the day?"

Wynn put his feet down and was a little surprised to feel a solid floor beneath his shoes. His fear had grown so strong that he was starting to doubt his own perceptions, and it occurred to him that perhaps this was how Abeloth invaded minds, by terrifying and confusing people so badly they finally went insane.

"Thank you," said the Roki Kem manifestation. Waving a dismissive hand toward the others, she used the Force to pull Wynn a few steps forward. "Chief Dorvan and I will continue alone."

Wynn heard the decontamination chamber hiss close behind him, and then he found himself standing in the Jedi Temple's computer core, staring at Roki Kem's back . . . at *Abeloth's* back . . . with a holdout blaster up his sleeve.

Wynn experienced no sudden wave of relief. The situation had the stink of a trap to it, like having a sabacc hand that was *nearly* the best possible and an opponent happy to call any bet. It felt too good to be true, and it probably was. The blaster might well have a depleted energy cell or a disabled XCiter chamber, but he was determined to play the hand he had—and that meant staying patient until he knew which card he was holding up his sleeve: the Legate or the Idiot.

So Wynn followed the Kem manifestation forward into the computer core. It seemed to be a vast, spherical cavity filled with drifting clouds of radiance and flashing streaks of light. He and the Beloved Queen were on a transparisteel service balcony that protruded about a dozen meters into the chamber. At the forward end of the balcony sat several banks of display screens and interface consoles. There was no sign anywhere of the systems administrators who had once used the equipment to communicate with the Temple's computer core.

The Kem manifestation went to the primary equipment bank and took a seat in a swiveling chair, the middle of a trio.

"Don't lag, Chief Dorvan," she said. "You have no reason to be frightened. You're still much too valuable for me to kill."

"I'm not frightened, just confused," Wynn lied. He continued forward until he was standing at the arm of the chair adjacent to the one the Beloved Queen now occupied. "Might I ask what am I doing here?"

"Remaining available," she said. "I will need your advice again soon."

"About what?"

"You will know when I am ready for you to know."

"My apologies," Wynn said. Either the Beloved Queen was lying about needing his advice, or she did not yet know what kind of advice she would be seeking. "I didn't realize you were unaware yourself."

A pair of silver points began to burn deep in the Queen's eyes, and for a moment her arms seem to writhe like tentacles. "I said you were too valuable to *kill*," she warned. "Now be silent."

Wynn remained standing, confident that the blaster was no test. The Beloved Queen had a habit of covering her weakness with a threat whenever she felt vulnerable. And the only time she ever seemed vulnerable was when she entered one of her revelatory trances. He had no idea where her mind went during such episodes, whether she was flow-walking like Jacen Solo had done or simply spying on her enemies through the Force—but he did know that while she was away, she was oblivious to her surroundings.

Wynn waited as the Beloved Queen's breathing turned shallow and her eyes grew distant and glassy. And then he continued to wait, counting to a hundred and watching for any movement that would suggest she was not deep in her trance.

When he saw none, he asked, "Beloved Queen?" He waited another twenty heartbeats, then spoke louder. "Beloved Queen!"

She remained motionless, her blue Jessar skin as smooth as stone and her gaze fixed somewhere beyond the chamber. Wynn stepped behind the chairs, then pulled the hold-out blaster from his sleeve and checked the energy cell.

Charged.

He checked the gas canister. Full.

He glanced over his shoulder at the decontamination chamber door. Closed. Wynn pointed the blaster at the chair, and the Beloved Queen did not stir. Was it really going to be this easy?

Wynn pulled the trigger, and an energy bolt screamed into the seat back. He pulled the trigger again. This time, the bolt shot completely through the chair and through her body, then vanished into the darkness above the equipment bank.

He smelled scorched flesh and began to hope that it really *was* that easy. He circled to the front of the chairs and saw the Beloved Queen slumped in her seat, her hands hanging over the armrests, her chin on her chest, and a smoking hole through the center of her torso. Clearly dead.

Still, better to be sure.

Wynn stepped closer and pointed the blaster at her head.

A low animal groan rumbled up from her chest, and then blood splashed his face and tunic. He heard someone screaming and realized it was him, and he pulled the blaster trigger again. A screaming bolt burned through her forehead just above the eyes. Her head rocked back, fell forward again, and then rolled to the side.

Wynn pulled the trigger one more time and sent another bolt burning into her head, this time through the temple. Her head did not move, and he stumbled back, away from the smoke and the smell and the oozing gore.

For a moment, he stood there. Waiting.

Nothing happened.

The Beloved Queen was dead, and Wynn had survived. He couldn't really believe it.

He felt the equipment bank against his back and realized he was still backing away. He stopped and shifted his gaze toward the decontamination chamber, remembering the dozens of Sith who were setting up their ambush out in the corridor. He had no idea what to do about them. He hadn't expected to survive the assassination attempt, so he hadn't thought that far ahead.

A voice behind him, cold and familiar, said, "You will never slip past them, Chief. There is no escape."

Wynn sprang away from the equipment bank, moving faster and

leaping farther than he would have believed possible, and landed beyond the chairs. He spun around, already knowing what he would
see . . . and he saw it: a face of pure radiance, the size of a bantha and
as wispy as a cloud, floating out in the darkness of the computer core.
She appeared vaguely human, with a long cascade of coarse yellow hair
and tiny, deep-sunken eyes that shone from their sockets like stars at
the bottom of a well. She had a nose so small it was almost absent, and
a large, full-lipped mouth so broad that it reached from ear to ear.

Abeloth.

"Yes," she assured him. "Your Beloved Queen of the Stars."

Wynn shook his head. "You're no queen of mine." He raised the
blaster pistol and pressed the emitter nozzle to the side of his head.
"And you're wrong. There *is* an escape."

He pulled the trigger in the same instant he felt his hand jerk. A
blaster bolt screamed past above his temple. He felt searing heat across
the top of his skull and smelled his own singed hair, and Wynn knew
he had failed. He had survived.

"I am never wrong," Abeloth said.

The blaster twisted free of Wynn's hand and went flying. Then a
blast of Force energy hit him in the chest, and he went flying, too.

"There is no escape . . . for any of you."

Chapter Fourteen

CARGO DID NOT NEED LIGHT OR FRESH AIR. IT DID NOT GRAY OUT DURing high-g accelerations, nor did it suffer ringing ears every time it shot through a grav-control halo. Cargo did not feel its gorge rise when the transfer tunnels took an unseen turn, and it did not grow dizzy with dehydration as it sailed through the stifling heat of a repulsor-driven freight-handling system.

But Ben did.

And that made the journey from the water-intake plant a real test of endurance and courage. For what seemed an hour, Ben sailed through the sweltering cargo tube, lurching and turning through the darkness, consumed by his growing fear for Vestara. He could only imagine the agony she would suffer at the hands of her Sith captors, the punishments she would endure for killing so many of her own kind—especially High Lord Taalon and her father. But it was more than just fear eating at him. It was anger, too. Everyone had been so fast to blame Vestara for the ambush . . . and no one faster than Corran Horn. Considering how his own children had betrayed the Jedi while under Abeloth's control back on Nam Chorios, Master Horn ought to have known better than to pass judgment based on nothing but a guess. Vestara deserved better than that.

A spine-jamming deceleration jerked Ben's thoughts back to his own situation, and he felt the air stir ahead as a freight canister sped through an unseen intersection just centimeters from his head. He hung there motionless for a few moments, listening to surprised groans and involuntary grunts echoing through the passage as his five companions endured their own sudden stops and unexpected accelerations. Then he felt his face beginning to stretch as he shot forward again, and once more he was flying helplessly through the darkness.

The worst part was the control rings. Every hundred meters, Ben would pass through one of the repulsorlift control rings that lined the shaft. If he was lucky, the ring would be on standby, and he would suffer only a moment of unpleasant queasiness as he passed through a wafer-thin antigravity field. But as he approached an active ring, a crashing roar would fill the tunnel. There would be a moment of silence as he passed through, then an excruciating *pop* deep inside his ears, followed by a maddening ringing that made his whole head ache.

So far, Ben had passed through fifteen active rings and endured more twists and turns than he could track. His stomach felt like he had been practicing wingovers with a deactivated inertial compensator, and he was so thirsty that he was almost ready to start sucking the sweat out of his own robes. And he had no idea how much longer the journey would last—or what they would find when they finally reached the computer interface located at the other end.

Ben felt his stomach flutter as he passed through an inactive control ring; then the muffled thump of a shifting guidance door sounded in the darkness ahead. A moment later his spine bent backward as he was drawn upward into a vertical shaft. A cloud of blue light appeared above his head and rapidly brightened into a reflection on the interior wall of another bend in the tube—this one back to the horizontal. Ben barely managed to spin around before passing through a final pair of control rings. He decelerated so hard his kidneys ached, and then he was spat out of the freight tunnel and dropped onto the padded bed of a receiving bench.

A bar of brilliant white light appeared a few centimeters ahead and started to glide along the pad toward Ben. He rolled away, only to find himself trapped on his side, his back pressed against the guide-rail on the far side of the bench. The beam swept across his face, bright and blinding as it shone into his eyes, then continued toward his feet. As his vision began to clear, Ben saw that the light was being projected from a saucer-shaped silhouette sitting atop the squat, blocky torso of an STK-CLR stock-keeping droid.

The subtle whine of a pneumatic motor sounded from the droid's shoulder and waist areas, and four telescoping arms extended toward the guide-rail. Ben rolled beneath them, then swung his legs around and dropped off the bench to stand next to the droid.

It spun around its head-disk so that the projection slot was facing Ben. "Your universal stocking code is not evident," it said, speaking in a deep, clattering voice. "Please display it for proper shelf assignment."

Ben shook his head. "I'm not a stock item."

"Of course you are," STK-CLR responded. Another whine sounded, and before Ben could react a set of servogrips closed around his wrists and ankles. "You came through the freight system."

"Not everything that comes through the freight system is a stock item." When Ben tried to pull free, the droid's arms suddenly extended farther, and he found himself hanging spread-eagled in the gloom. "Put me down! And that's an override command."

"Stock items are not authorized to issue override commands," STK-CLR countered. A small panel opened in the droid's chest, and a slender hose ending in a tiny nozzle shot out and sprayed a bar code down the front of Ben's robe. "You have been marked DEFECTIVE UNIT. Present yourself to the routing station on the far side of the delivery portal for return to your supplier."

Rather than continue the argument, Ben simply hung his head. "Sure, whatever you want."

"Good." The droid lowered Ben to the floor. "And relay my displeasure to your manufacturer. This is the Jedi Temple. We have acceptance specifications."

As soon as his boots hit the floor, Ben pivoted around and tripped the primary circuit breaker in the back of the droid's neck. A surprised squawk sounded from the STK-CLR's vocabulator; its arms retracted into their sockets, and its frame hissed down to settle over its legs. Ben pushed the droid away from the receiving pad, then snapped his lightsaber off its belt hook and turned to see if he could figure out where the freight-handling system had deposited him.

He was not surprised to find himself in a dimly lit warehouse filled with row after row of high, gloom-swaddled shelves. The Jedi Temple had at least a hundred such rooms, devoted to storage for laboratories, armories, fabrication shops, communications centers, even routine maintenance functions necessary to keep any building of its size in good repair. But this room smelled faintly of Tibanna gas and hyperdrive coolant, and it was reverberating to the muffled thunder of artillery strikes crashing against the shields outside a nearby chamber.

All of that told Ben that he was in the parts locker of a spacecraft repair bay. Judging by the size of the locker, and by the steady battle rumble he was hearing, it was a repair bay that served an extremely large and busy hangar.

The muffled growl of activating control rings sounded deep within the freight-handling system and grew instantly louder, and Ben looked back in time to see the meter-long silhouette of an astromech droid shooting out of the delivery portal. It decelerated almost instantly, then settled gently onto the receiving pad.

Ben used the Force to lift the little astromech onto the floor next to him. "Rowdy?"

The droid responded with an indignant tweedle.

"Sorry," Ben said. "Not much light in here."

A ceiling lamp activated, illuminating the vicinity in a cone of brightness—and leaving no doubt about the identity of the battered little unit in front of Ben.

"Turn that off!" Ben ordered. "We're trying to stay hidden here."

The lamp remained on, and Rowdy whistled a question.

"From the Sith, of course," Ben hissed. "I can't believe you brought us to the Main Operations Hangar! There are probably a couple hundred Sith manning the cannon batteries—right out there!"

Rowdy tweedled in agreement. Then, without deactivating the lamp, he dropped his third tread and began to roll along behind the shelving units. Ben followed along until they reached the eighth row, at the far end of which he saw another cone of light shining down on his father and Corran. The two Jedi Masters were twenty meters away, standing next to a computer interface panel, but staring over the parts counter out into a massive repair bay as brightly lit as it was empty. Given their lack of caution, it seemed apparent that Ben's fear of discovery was unwarranted. The Sith were simply too busy defending the exterior of the Temple to worry about what was in the parts locker behind them.

"Okay, Rowdy. Sorry." Ben pointed toward the interface panel. "You obviously know what to do. I'll go back and let the others know the situation."

Rowdy replied with a good-natured trill, and Ben returned to the receiving area, where Jysella Horn stood peering into the delivery portal with her lightsaber in hand. Her jaw was set, her feet were braced, and her Force aura was humming with anticipation.

"There was a lot of blasterfire behind me," Jysella said as Ben approached. "I think Jaina and Valin have been trading bolts with the enemy the whole way."

"Blasted Sith." Ben vaulted over the receiving bench, then turned to face the delivery portal. "Don't they recognize a desperate escape when they see it?"

Jysella shrugged. "Maybe they're just as desperate to catch us."

The sound of activating control rings began to growl up from the depths of the freight-handling system, and an instant later Jysella's brother, Valin, came shooting out of the delivery portal. His attention was fixed behind him, and he was holding a blaster pistol with a pinging depletion alarm.

Ben began to have a very bad feeling. "Valin, is Jaina—"

"Jaina's in trouble," Valin interrupted. He rolled off the bench toward Jysella, then ejected the blaster's energy cell, popped in a new one, and holstered the weapon. "She kept calling for cover, but it's hard to fire past someone's head when you keep taking g-loads. I might have hit her a couple of times."

"If she was still firing herself, you did great," Ben assured him. " 'In trouble' is better than 'dead' any day."

"I'll feel better when she tells me that herself," Valin said. He snapped his lightsaber off its hook and took a position at Jysella's side. "But this is going to get even messier. It sounded like there were dozens of Sith in the tube behind her."

"It doesn't matter how many there are," Jysella said. She stepped over to the control panel on the side of the delivery portal. "Not if they never get here."

Ben smiled. "I like your thinking." He looked toward Valin. "But we have another problem. There must be a couple hundred Sith out in the Main Operations Hangar, and this storage locker is a dead end. We need an escape route."

Valin nodded and started for the back corner of the warehouse. "I'll cut a bolt-hole."

Ben activated his comlink and opened a channel to his father. "We've got Sith following us through the freight system," he said. "We're trying to strand them, but no promises. How are you and Rowdy coming with the interface?"

"If stranding them doesn't work, try to buy some time," Luke replied. "Rowdy is plugged into the droid socket, but he can't find the computer core."

An angry whistle sounded over the channel as Rowdy objected to the characterization of the problem, but the groan of control rings was already building down in the cargo tubes, and Ben began to hear the muffled squeal of blasterfire.

"Okay," he said. "We're about to make a lot of noise back here, so be ready to turn back reinforcements. Let us know as soon as you get those blast doors open."

By the time he finished speaking, the blasterfire had grown louder and more distinct. Ben activated his lightsaber, then positioned himself within easy reach of the delivery portal and drew in a deep breath, trying to clear his mind before the combat began. He still felt angry and frightened for Vestara—and he had to put that aside. Fear led to mistakes, and anger led to . . . well, someplace he did not want to go.

Ben was still trying to center himself when Jaina shot out of the delivery portal. She stank of singed molytex and charred flesh, and she was firing back into the delivery portal even as the freight system dropped her onto the receiving bench. Ben gathered himself to leap up beside her, but her eyes snapped in his direction, and she shook her head.

"Stay clear!" Jaina rolled off the other side of the bench, yelling, "Grenade!"

Ben reacted instantly, his hand rising as he reached out in the Force. He caught something heavy and fist-sized as it shot from the delivery portal, then swept his hand toward the far wall and felt the tiny orb go sailing.

In the next instant a yellow blast seared the side of his face, and he felt himself slam into the nearby shelves even before he realized he had been sent flying. His ears were ringing and his ribs ached, but he could still feel all of his limbs—and one of them was holding a lightsaber. He extracted himself from the toppled shelving, then turned back to find a Sith warrior already jumping off the bench toward Jaina. Two more—one with a pointed dark beard and the other with an old scar across his nose—were turning to face Ben. Their eyes shone with the anticipation of an easy kill.

Ben didn't care for their attitude.

He Force-blasted Scarnose back across the receiving bench, then leapt at Pointed-Beard. The bearded Sith pivoted forward, whipping his lightsaber around, and their weapons met in a spray of sparks.

Guessing what would come next, Ben launched himself into a cart-wheel over their locked blades and watched Pointed-Beard's Force-hurled glass parang spin harmlessly past. He came down behind his foe and pivoted hard, dragging his lightsaber through the Sith's shoulder and torso.

The man collapsed, screaming and stinking of charred flesh, and Ben found himself looking down on Jaina from his perch on the bench. She was standing over the corpses of Scarnose and the third Sith, her shoulders heaving as she struggled to catch her breath. For a moment, Ben thought she was just tired from killing two Sith in the three seconds it had taken him to kill one.

Then he noticed the large circle of blood-soaked cloth on the side of her robe. At the center was a deep, thumb-sized burn hole.

"Jaina, are you okay?"

Ben's ears were still ringing from the grenade blast, and he could barely hear his own words—much less Jaina's reply. But the alarm in her eyes was plain to see, and when her gaze slid toward the delivery portal, he realized what *she* must be hearing: the growl of activating control rings.

Ben glanced toward the control panel and found Jysella holding her lightsaber with both hands, dragging it back and forth as fast as she could. He pulled a thermal detonator off his combat harness.

"Jysella!" Ben could barely hear his own voice, but it was loud enough to make Jysella look in his direction. He tossed the thermal detonator to her. "Blow it!"

Jaina suddenly leapt onto the bench, her lightsaber igniting barely in time to intercept a fork of Force lightning that came crackling out of the delivery portal. Ben spun to the other side, activating his own blade and moving in for the kill as their Sith attacker shot out into the open.

Ben did not strike.

The Sith was too familiar, a tall slender Lord with thin sneering lips, wearing a black cape over blast armor. His hands were extended in front of him, continuing to pour Force lightning into Jaina's flagging guard even after the freight-handling system dropped him facedown on the receiving bench. Ben waved his blade past the Sith's eyes to catch his attention, then lowered the tip to within a few centimeters of the man's temple.

"Surrender or die," Ben ordered. "Decide now."

Jaina's outrage hit like a Force blast, but Ben did not care. This was the Lord who had taken Vestara prisoner—who had been trying to use her to lure Ben into an ambush. If Ben had any chance at all of rescuing her, it lay with this Sith. So even when the man was slow to stop attacking Jaina, Ben did not kill him. Instead he placed a boot in the center of the Sith's back and repeated his order.

"Surrender or die."

The Lord let his chin drop, and the Force lightning fizzled out. He turned to look up at Ben.

"What is it you want, Jedi?" The words would have been soft under the best of circumstances. But with the ringing in Ben's ears, he had to stoop down to hear them clearly. "A trade?"

Ben nodded. "The thought had crossed my mind." It appeared it might be easier to strike a deal than he expected. "Your life for—"

"Ben!"

Ben had no time to wonder who had called out, or even to wonder why. He simply sensed a blast of alarm, then felt Jaina grab him in the Force and Jysella reaching for his attention. In the same breath, his leg exploded in pain, and Ben looked down to see a finger-length shikkar lodged in his thigh.

The Sith used the Force to snap off the hilt, then took advantage of his victim's shock to roll away from the lightsaber hovering at his temple. Ben lunged after him, but stopped when Jysella clutched at him through the Force.

"No, Ben!" This time, it was clearly her voice. "Detonator!"

Ben glanced over to see her backing away from the smoking control panel, one hand held above her head with two fingers raised. She lowered one finger, then flung herself away from the delivery portal. By the time he turned to do likewise, Jaina had already grabbed him in the Force and hurled them both away from the freight system.

They hit together, crashing into a shelf full of heavy boxes just before a blinding white flash filled the room. There was a thunderous crackle that seemed to last forever, and the heat grew so intense that Ben feared they had been caught inside the blast radius.

That particular fear vanished an instant later, when he dropped to the floor and drove the shikkar against his femur. His entire leg erupted into the kind of anguish that made weak men wish they were dead, and he felt his mouth open to scream.

Jaina landed at his side, her hand already clamping his mouth. "Quiet!"

She used the Force to pin him down, then raised herself up just enough to look back toward the detonation site. Shooting from the flaming delivery portal was a fountain of blood and bone—all that remained of their Sith pursuers after they passed through the wrecked deceleration rings.

"We don't know if that mugwump cleared the blast," Jaina said. "He might still be alive."

Ben nodded and swallowed his unvoiced scream, then reached up and gently pulled her hand away from his mouth. "I wasn't actually going to scream."

Jaina eyed him doubtfully. "If you say so."

She grabbed his leg above and below the wound, then used the

Force to start extracting the glass blade. The pain grew even more unbearable as the jagged top began to tear through muscle and sinew. Ben clamped his jaw shut, drawing on the Force for strength.

Jaina's expression was devoid of sympathy. "You deserved that, you know." She kept her voice low, but her tone was harsh. "What were you thinking, trying to capture a Sith Lord? In the middle of hand-to-hand combat?"

Ben couldn't answer without risking a scream, but he had been thinking about Vestara, of course. The Lord had been using her as bait, so he probably knew what had become of her. Ben only hoped the Sith had other uses for her, too, or she would soon be dead.

Jaina continued to draw the blade out slowly, deliberately prolonging Ben's anguish—or so it seemed to him.

"You're lucky," she said. "A little to the left, and you'd be dead."

The blade slipped free with a final *pop* of tendon. The pain faded from the unendurable to the merely excruciating, and blood started to flow out of the wound, fast and dark. But Jaina was right. Had the shikkar penetrated a few centimeters to the left, it would have severed his femoral artery. Frankly, Ben could not understand how that had failed to happen. The Sith Lord had struck from an ideal angle, he had been using the Force to guide his shikkar, and he'd taken Ben completely by surprise. By all rights, Ben should have been watching the last of his life's blood spurt out in a long, bright jet. The fact that he *wasn't* could only mean one thing: the Sith had not wanted to kill Ben, either.

"He didn't miss, Jaina," Ben said. "He didn't *want* to finish me."

Jaina shook her head. "Don't kid yourself, Ben. Sith don't play nice. You shouldn't, either." She pulled a clean bacta patch from a belt pouch and pressed it over his wound, then took his hand and placed it on top. "Pressure."

Ben did as she instructed. "He wasn't being nice," he said. "I think he wanted to take me prisoner. That's why he went for my thigh, instead of my heart or my abdomen."

Jaina remained silent as she secured the patch with a self-snugging bandage, then finally nodded. "Okay, you've got a point," she said. "You're Luke Skywalker's son. You'd make a pretty good hostage."

She slipped an arm under his shoulder and helped him to his feet. They were still looking back toward the gaping hole where the delivery portal had been, and as they watched, the familiar growling of activating control rings sounded down in the freight-handling system. A muffled scream came next, followed by a fountain of pinkish ooze that had once been a living being.

"You guys took out the deceleration series," Jaina said. "Nice thinking."

"Jysella's idea," Ben admitted. "I'm not sure she thought about goo geysers, though."

Jaina shrugged. "It buys us enough time to join your dad and the others," she said. "That's what counts."

But instead of starting forward again, Jaina paused at the edge of the aisle, no doubt looking for any sign of Ben's attacker. Ben extended his own Force awareness into the surrounding area, searching for any hint of danger that would suggest the Sith was lying in wait for them. It certainly seemed possible that Jaina had guessed correctly about wanting to take Ben hostage, but something did not feel quite right about that. The Sith had hurt his own odds of surviving by failing to eliminate an enemy when he had the chance. And back in the waterworks, he had also taken a big risk by dangling Vestara as bait. Together the two ploys seemed like a deliberate plan, and Ben was starting to feel hunted.

Ben and Jaina were still searching for any sign of the missing Sith Lord when Jysella poked her head out of an aisle on the other side of the crater. "You'd better hurry," she called. "They've got problems at the interface station."

In the distance, an exchange of blasterfire could be heard. Evidently, the Sith out in the hangar had finally realized they had trouble in the parts locker and launched an attack.

"Be right there," Jaina called. She slowly withdrew her support from under Ben's arm. "Can you move on your own?"

Ben took his own weight, calling on the Force to fortify his injured leg—and using a Jedi meditation technique to handle the pain. When his knee did not buckle, he removed his arm from her shoulders.

"I'm good." He gestured at the blaster burn in her side. "How about you?"

Jaina glanced down at the hole. "A little trouble breathing," she said. "But not much blood loss. I'll be fine."

"Are you sure?" Ben asked. "Because if you're having trouble breathing—"

"I'm fine," Jaina insisted. She gave him a look that suggested she might be talking to a five-year-old. "I've been doing this a long time."

With that she nudged him forward, and together they limped cautiously around the crater. When no Sith Lords emerged from hiding to attack them, they fell in behind Jysella and went forward to the interface station. Luke and Master Horn were crouched behind the service counter, ducking Force lightning and trading blasterfire with a rapidly growing contingent of Sith warriors out in the repair bay. Rowdy was still plugged into the data socket, tweeting and chirping and rocking back and forth on his treads in what looked suspiciously close to frustration.

As they drew near, Ben and his two companions began to add their own fire to the storm of flying bolts, and Ben went to crouch next to his father. He fired blindly over the counter three times, then dropped out of sight as a flurry of bolts came streaking back over his head.

"Problems?" he asked.

"You could say that," Luke replied, almost yelling to make himself heard over the screeching torrent. "Rowdy seems to think that *all* of the interface panels have been disabled."

"So?" Ben popped his head up and saw a white orb sailing toward the parts locker. Trusting his aim to the Force, he opened fire and was rewarded with an orange fireball as the grenade detonated twenty meters from the counter. "It's not like we can get out there to use another one anyway."

"No," Corran said, dropping back behind the counter with a pinging depletion alarm and ejecting his useless power cell. "You're not understanding. It's not just the hangar stations that are disabled. It's all of them—in the entire Jedi Temple."

Ben's heart sank, but it was Jysella who asked, "Then how are we going to lower the shields? And get the blast doors open?"

No one spoke for a moment, then Ben said, "There's only one way, at least if we want to open them all at once." He turned toward the corner of the parts locker, where Valin Horn was still dragging his lightsaber blade through the durasteel wall, just putting the final touches on the bolt-hole. "Rowdy needs to talk directly to the Temple computer."

His father nodded. "We need to enter the computer core itself." Luke signaled Ben and Jaina to lead the way toward Valin's bolt-hole. "And you can bet the Sith will be expecting us."

Chapter Fifteen

THE PILLARS STOOD SCATTERED ACROSS THE FACE OF THE DISTANT mountain, their pale shafts cropping out of the blue-gray slopes like cliffs. Their columns looked a hundred stories tall, but the mysterious edifice they had been erected to support remained buried beneath a kilometer-high mound of silt. No road crossed the endless sweep of scrub-dotted plain that surrounded the dust-mountain, and no craft could be seen streaking across the orange sky above it. And yet the pillars were the sole hint of civilization in the Reo system—in the whole Maraqoo sector—so this had to be the place.

Raynar Thul eased the landspeeder forward. Though he had played an important part in several recent Jedi missions, he did not feel ready for this one. Master Skywalker had asked him to return to the Killik Colony he had once led as the Joiner UnuThul. But Raynar had literally not been himself back then. He had been a wounded combat survivor who had allowed himself to become lost in the shared mind of a Killik hive—to become a Joiner. It was an experience that had totally destroyed his sense of identity and left his mind a shattered wreck, and Raynar continued to feel tenuous and incomplete in his recovery.

But now the Jedi were facing an enemy as enigmatic as she was powerful, and their only hope of survival was to coax some answers from the jumbled hive-minds of the Killiks. *Someone* had to convince them to reveal everything they knew about the mysterious Celestials they had once served, and Raynar was the only Jedi who could do it. So he had accepted the assignment and promised to succeed . . . even if it meant losing the mind he had spent eight long years trying to reassemble.

As the landspeeder drew closer to the mountain of dust, Raynar saw that the giant pillars were decorated with reliefs of winged beasts and horned fiends. Twined around the feet of these figures were ropy shapes that might have been serpents or vines.

Lowbacca, two and a quarter meters of Wookiee, hunched in the front passenger seat with his knees in his chest, growled the opinion that the vines were a good sign.

"I quite disagree, Master Lowbacca," C-3PO said, speaking from directly behind the Wookiee. "In this context, the tendrils are symbols of inevitable destruction. If the ruins weren't so obviously deserted, I would suggest that we turn around immediately and erase them from our memory chips."

"I think Lowie means that we're in the right place," Tekli said. Sitting in the passenger seat behind Raynar, the furry little Chadra-Fan was probably the only one in the crowded landspeeder who was even remotely comfortable. "The vines suggest that we've finally found a hive with a direct association to Abeloth. But the winged figures are something new. Is there a record of ophidian grotesques appearing with other symbols?"

"Not in my data banks," C-3PO assured her. "And I have cached every available reference to the subject. In fact, I have available two point three million articles and seven point one million images—"

Lowbacca interrupted with an impatient rumble.

"No, I would not prefer to ride on the stowage cover," C-3PO replied. "Do you have any idea what all that dust would do to my servomotors?"

Lowbacca rumbled again.

"I am not experiencing a problem with my vocabulator, Jedi Lowbacca," C-3PO answered. "And even if I were, I assure you that more dust would only make it worse."

Raynar chuckled, glad to have his friends along to keep his mind off his fears. Officially, Master Skywalker had assigned Tekli and Lowbacca to the mission as its medic and technical officer. But Raynar was pretty sure their most important duty was to keep him sane—at least, he *hoped* it was. C-3PO was on loan to serve as a translator, so it wouldn't be necessary for Raynar to risk becoming a Joiner again just to communicate with the Killiks. Whether it was part of Master Skywalker's plan or not, the droid had also acted as a constant annoyance—and a diversion. The three Jedi had been living in close quarters for over a month now, and C-3PO had given them a handy place to redirect any irritation they felt with one another. It was a job at which the droid had never failed to excel.

The landspeeder was still a kilometer away from the mountain when dark specks began to appear in the spaces between exposed pillars. At first, the flecks seemed to be some sort of decoration, but as the companions drew closer the shapes grew more squarish, then swelled into distant window openings. A path appeared in the dust at the base of the mountain, running through a narrow channel toward a tall black arch that looked a lot like an open gateway.

Deciding the black arch *was* a gateway, Raynar turned toward it . . . and felt a cold prickle of danger sense race up his neck. He expanded his Force awareness and sensed something much nearer, a huge hungry presence moving toward the landspeeder almost as fast as the landspeeder was moving toward the mountain.

The sensation made no sense. There was a steady breeze blowing across the plain, raising a thin veil of smoke-blue dust that hung about a meter above the ground, but visibility was still close to three hundred meters, and the presence was a lot nearer than that. Raynar brought the landspeeder to a halt.

"I feel it, too," Tekli said. "Something is eager to get at us before we reach the mountain."

Lowbacca groaned a question.

"Well, I can't see anything except the back of your enormous and furry head," C-3PO answered. "Perhaps I would be of more use if you didn't insist on making the droid ride in back."

"I don't think it's an illusion," Tekli said, ignoring C-3PO and replying to Lowbacca. "It can be sensed only through the Force. And any illusion that can be sensed only through the Force won't turn away many threats."

Lowbacca moaned his agreement, and the hungry presence continued to draw nearer. Raynar popped the canopy latch on his side of the landspeeder—then saw the soil settling and understood. He put the landspeeder in reverse and pushed the throttles to maximum.

Too late.

Twenty meters ahead, a giant pair of serrated pincers burst from the ground and spread apart, revealing a slimy red maw about twice as wide as the speeder. The maw led into a long sinuous throat lined by concentric rings of spines. Out of the depths of this cavern shot a spray of gray, ropy tongues that slapped down on the front end of the vehicle. The pincers snapped shut, burying their tips deep in the side panels.

The landspeeder started to slide forward. Raynar pushed the throttles past maximum to overload, clear to the end of the lever guides. The vehicle continued to slide toward the fang-filled maw.

"Out!" Raynar yelled.

Lowbacca popped the latch on his side. He exploded from his seat so swiftly that he caught the canopy bubble on his neck and shoulders, snapping it off at the hinges. Tekli yelled that she was also free. By then, Raynar was already pushing off the steering wheel, using the Force to send himself tumbling out of the landspeeder.

When he looked back, the maw had engulfed the landspeeder almost to the passenger compartment and was dragging it down into the dusty pit from which it had emerged. Still in the back, C-3PO was leaning away from the ropy tongues, waving both arms at Raynar.

"Jedi Thul, why are you just standing there? Please *do* something quickly!"

The landspeeder passed over the edge of the pit and tipped forward.

C-3PO pointed down into the pit. "I suggest that you kill it *immediately!*"

Killing the creature was out of the question—and not only because of its size. Instead, Raynar extended a hand and used the Force to lift the droid out of the landspeeder—then found himself struggling against Lowbacca, who'd had the same idea.

Raynar released his Force grasp. C-3PO went sailing, then hit Lowbacca in the chest, bounced off, and landed in the dust at the Wookiee's feet.

Lowbacca dropped his chin and studied the droid for a moment, then moaned a question.

"I could not possibly know that yet," C-3PO replied. "I'm still running my diagnostics!"

Lowbacca shrugged and set the droid on his feet, then growled and rubbed his chest.

"It's not *my* fault my elbow gave you a bruise," C-3PO said. "I was merely trying to minimize my own damage."

The shriek of folding metal sounded from the pit. Raynar stepped to the edge and, through a veil of blowing blue dust, saw a huge heart-shaped head poking out of the bottom. It was rolling the crumpled landspeeder around in its mandibles, using its mouth to tear off pieces and crush them into meter-wide spheres—which it quickly found unpalatable and spat out.

A small hand grasped Raynar's arm and tried to pull him away from the pit. He pulled back just hard enough to stay where he was, and Tekli stepped to his side.

"Raynar?" Tekli whispered. "Is it really wise to stand where that thing can see you?"

Raynar shrugged. He wasn't sure what that thing was—but there was a reasonable chance it was a Killik. He took a deep breath, both calming himself and filling his lungs, then raised both forearms in greeting.

"Thuruht?" he called.

The insect stopped chewing and pushed its head another meter out of the pit, revealing a huge bulb that was probably a vestigial eye. The ground trembled beneath Raynar's feet, and he felt a faint rumbling deep in his stomach.

"Oh, my!" C-3PO said, speaking from three meters away. "She would like to know who is asking—and why you are disturbing her work."

Raynar smiled as much as the flesh of his burn-scarred face allowed. "Tell her I'm an old friend," he said. "UnuThul needs help."

"Jedi Thul, I'm not sure that's wise," C-3PO said. "Killiks rarely cooperate with liars, and you haven't been UnuThul for quite—"

Lowbacca growled, warning C-3PO to be careful about what he said.

Raynar glanced over at the droid. "Tell her, Threepio."

Before C-3PO had a chance to obey, the ground trembled again.

The droid cocked his head, then said, "As it happens, that won't be necessary. Thuruht comprehends Basic quite well. She has invited us to the Celestial Palace."

Raynar looked into the pit and dipped his head. "We're grateful."

As the ground trembled in reply, Raynar led the way around the pit and started toward the palace. The air was arid and choking hot, and with a haze of blue dust obscuring everything below their waists, it was difficult to find the best path across the plain. Twice, Raynar sank to his thigh when he inadvertently stepped into another pit.

Several times, he glimpsed a ridge rising in the dust ahead as one of Thuruht's giant guardians burrowed across the plain to greet him and his companions. Usually, the greeting consisted of little more than coming alongside them and emitting a subterranean rumble so deep they felt it in their stomachs. But about three hundred meters from the palace, a huge head burst from the ground, blocking their way and clacking its mandibles.

It had been a long time since Raynar had been part of a Killik hivemind, but he didn't think the creature was trying to threaten them. He motioned his companions to lower their weapons and stepped forward. Keeping his prosthetic arm at his side, he raised his flesh-and-blood hand in greeting. The insect responded by dipping its head and rubbing its worm-like antennae across his forearm. Then it emitted a soft, muffled *boom* and withdrew.

As soon as the creature vanished into the ground again, Tekli stepped to Raynar's side. "You'll be coated in pheromones now," she observed. "You still have your nasal filters in place, yes?"

Raynar sniffed hard. Finding it difficult to draw air, he nodded. "No worries," he said, starting toward the palace again. "No one who's been a Joiner wants to become a Joiner again—including me."

Lowbacca observed that no one ever wanted to become a Joiner in the first place. The pheromones just made it happen.

"We'll be okay," Tekli assured the Wookiee. "Even if the filters overload, the counteragents will give us enough protection to get through a week of exposure."

Lowbacca turned to Raynar and growled a question.

"Hard to say," Raynar answered. "But a week is probably long enough."

"And if it isn't, I have more counteragents aboard the *Long Trek*," Tekli said. "We can always return and take another injection."

Lowbacca glanced over his shoulder, looking back toward the distant ridge where they had landed the scoutship, then grumbled unhappily.

"I quite agree," C-3PO replied. "That's a very long walk, indeed. My actuators simply won't tolerate it."

"*You* won't need to," Raynar said. "Pheromones don't affect droids. You can just wait with Thuruht."

"Alone?" C-3PO objected. "I'm quite sure that's not what Princess Leia had in mind when she offered to send me along."

"Probably not," Raynar agreed.

As they entered the channel at the base of the dust-mountain, Raynar realized the scale of the place was even larger than it had appeared from the landspeeder. The channel stretched two hundred meters to the gate, and its walls were easily seventy meters high. The archway at the far end was large enough to accommodate a Lancer frigate, and the enormous support columns flanking the entrance rose a hundred meters before vanishing into an overhang of wind-packed dust.

The figures on the pillars were largely hidden by the dust. On the left-hand column, all that could be seen were two sharp-taloned feet dangling beneath the overhang, tangled in the coils of what was either a serpent or a tentacle. On the right-hand column, even less was visible—only a single wing dipping out of the dust, wrapped in what was a length of either vine or rope.

The air grew dank and humid as they drew within a couple dozen steps of the archway. Raynar sensed the fused Force presence of a group of Killiks loitering in the passages near the entrance, and his pulse started to pound in his ears.

"Don't worry," Tekli said, stepping to his side. "We're here with you."

Lowbacca added his owned reassurances, promising to drag Raynar out by his feet at the first hint that he was becoming a Joiner again. The words were offered in kindness, but Raynar found them to be of little comfort. There *was* something to fear. If becoming a Joiner again was the only way to learn what Thuruht knew of Abeloth and the Celestials, then become a Joiner he would. And he knew the same was true of Lowbacca and Tekli. The Order needed the intelligence they had been sent to gather far more than it needed them.

The trick, of course, would be making sure that at least one of them stayed sane enough to report back to the Jedi Council.

Together they stepped through the archway into the cool darkness of the ruins. Raynar heard the clatter of approaching insects, and a moment later he began to feel their antennae brushing over him, paying particular attention to his real forearm. They were careful to avoid the prosthetic, however. Killiks did not like artificial body parts. The devices blurred the line between living being and droid, and Killiks did not understand droids. Droids were alien and never to be welcomed, because droids never became Joiners.

As his eyes adjusted to the darkness, Raynar found himself facing a trio of Killiks with mottled-blue exoskeletons and four delicate arms. They had the same heart-shaped heads as their giant hive mates outside, but they were only about a meter and a half tall and lacked the huge mandibles of the guardians. When they saw Raynar studying them, all three folded their arms against their thoraxes and dipped their heads.

"*Ruur ubb unuwul burur,*" said one. "*Uru rur rruru bub.*"

"Thuruht welcomes the wise UnuThul and his followers to the Celestial Palace," C-3PO translated. "The hive is honored that he has chosen to rejoin the Kind through them."

Lowbacca let out a quick growl, informing Thuruht that they weren't there to join anything.

"Are you certain you wish me to translate that, Jedi Lowbacca?" C-3PO asked. "You're actually being rather—"

Thuruht interrupted with a short thrum, and the droid turned to face the insect. After a moment, he looked back to Lowbacca.

"Thuruht says it doesn't matter why you came, the hive will be honored to have you." He shifted his attention to Raynar. "We are asked to attend the queen in her chamber."

Had his burn scars permitted it, Raynar would have raised his brow. Modern Killik hives were no longer organized around a queen, but he supposed it only made sense that Thuruht's social structure would reflect its great age. He inclined his head to the blue insects.

"If you'll show us the way."

All three turned and led the Jedi and C-3PO up a stale-smelling passage that ascended along the outer walls of the palace. The climb was steep and lonely, rising in a rough spiral that felt five kilometers long.

They frequently passed through musty-smelling areas where a side tunnel led into the depths of the palace. The few insects they encountered seemed to be wandering about aimlessly rather than executing the business of the hive. Most of the time, the balls of luminescent wax hanging along the walls were too dim to see much more than the silhouettes of the three guides ahead. Every so often, however, they would pass one of the huge windows they had seen from outside, and the light would spill in to reveal archways decorated with bas-relief carvings of plants and animals from a thousand different worlds.

But it was the panels between the arches that put a flutter in Raynar's stomach. The images depicted the grandeur of deep space, always with some peculiar twist that seemed unlikely to occur in nature. There was a supernova exploding in only one direction, a ring of nine planets circling their sun along a single orbital path, a nebula hanging like a curtain between two star systems. Finally came a scene that looked all too familiar—a system with five planets orbiting the same star in very similar orbits, with the third and fourth locked in a tight twin-planet formation.

Raynar stopped. "What's that picture?"

The insects answered without stopping or looking back. *"Urrub."*

"Our work," C-3PO translated. The droid paused, waiting in vain for a more thorough explanation, then said, "I'm sorry, Jedi Thul, but Thuruht doesn't seem to be in a very informative mood right now. Perhaps they've been offended by Lowbacca's rudeness."

Lowbacca moaned a halfhearted apology.

Thuruht continued to ascend the corridor. Raynar remained where he was and called, "Is this one the Corellian system?"

The insects stopped five meters up the passage, then reluctantly turned around. *"Buurub uu ruub ur ru ub."*

"Thuruht wouldn't know what it is called by lesser beings," C-3PO translated. "But to Thuruht, it is known as Five Rocks."

Tekli stood on her toes, reaching up to wipe the dust away from the third and fourth planets—the twins—then asked, "Does Thuruht know why the system was constructed?"

"Ub."

The insects turned and walked on.

"Thuruht said 'yes,'" C-3PO translated. "May I suggest we follow? They seem to be growing impatient with us."

Lowbacca shrugged and started up the passage. Raynar and Tekli fell in behind the Wookiee. A few minutes later they turned toward the center of the palace, traveling down a long hall even larger and more ornate than the one they had just ascended. The air grew warmer and more humid, and the glow-balls started to shine more brightly. Dozens of workers began to appear, scurrying in and out of side passages, carrying tools and bales of a stringy yellow fungus, or waxy orbs of golden membrosia, one of the Killiks' favorite nourishments. Raynar started to feel thirsty, and he noticed Lowbacca eyeing a membrosia bearer as she crossed the corridor ahead.

"*That* I miss about being Taat," Tekli said. Taat was the hive she and Lowbacca had inadvertently joined years before, after Raynar had summoned them to help the Killiks fight the Chiss. "It will almost be worth the trip to have some again."

"They sell it in Restaurant Galatina on Coruscant, you know," C-3PO offered helpfully. "I understand the Horoh is especially fine this year."

"And a thousand credits a liter," Tekli said. "I'm a Jedi Knight, not an investment banker."

They reached the end of the hall, where two huge guards stood to either side of the corridor, their long mandibles locked across an entrance ten meters wide. They looked much the same as the one that had eaten the landspeeder, except there was nothing vestigial about their eyes. The pair glared at the procession as it approached, and Raynar began to fear that he and his companions would not be permitted to enter the queen's chamber.

Then a deep drumming sounded from the interior. The guardians lifted their mandibles, and the guides led the way into a vast chamber containing hundreds of empty floor pits. In a healthy hive, the pits would have been filled with incubation cells. But the deep drifts of dust in the bottom of these cells suggested they had not been used in centuries. Unlike the rest of the palace, the room was well lit, with the sun's orange light spilling in through a transparent membrane stretched across the vaulted ceiling.

The guides stopped a few steps inside, leaving Raynar and his companions to continue down a large center aisle toward the queen. Almost as large as the entrance sentries, she lay stretched across a massive dais, with six sturdy legs curled against a bantha-sized abdomen and a mouth flanked by a pair of multijointed mandibles. Standing on the floor in front of her were four guardians identical to those outside the entrance.

Closer to the dais were a pair of floor pits filled with the familiar comb of incubation cells. Raynar saw no more than thirty compartments, and only three nursery Killiks to attend them. The hive wasn't quite dead, but it wasn't thriving, either.

As Raynar and his companions passed the last nursery pit, the guardians shuffled away from the center of the dais, revealing a wide set of stairs. The queen's abdomen rippled, filling the chamber with a long, low rumble barely audible to human hearing.

"I must say, this is quite unexpected," C-3PO said. "The queen is inviting Lowbacca and Tekli to groom her."

Lowbacca emitted an uncertain groan.

"It means you remove her external parasites," Raynar explained. Lowbacca and Tekli's old hive, Taat, had been much more egalitarian in social structure, so they had probably never participated in the ritual. "It's an honor. Yoggoy used to groom me—"

Lowbacca huffed in disgust.

"Just think of it as a medical procedure," Tekli whispered. "And remember why we're here."

The Wookiee sighed and dropped his head, and the group ascended the stairs. An attendant emerged from behind the queen, appearing atop her giant abdomen with a bucket in one hand and a cloth and a bottle of antiseptic spray in two of her others, then motioned for the groomers to join her. As former Joiners themselves, Lowbacca and Tekli had enough experience to realize Killiks weren't shy about crawling over one another, so they scrambled up to join the attendant.

Raynar watched them ascend, then stepped over to present himself to the queen. Her head was small compared with the rest of her body, but it was still half the size of Raynar himself, with eyes as big as shock-balls and slender mandibles the length of a Wookiee's arm. Raynar raised his flesh-and-blood hand in greeting. In return, the queen dipped her head, then rubbed a feathery antenna along his wrist.

"Wuur uu rur uu," she thrummed. *"Ubub ruub uru."*

"Thuruht welcomes you back to the Kind," C-3PO translated. "The hive will be honored to have you."

Raynar felt a nervous flutter in his stomach. Lowbacca had clearly stated they had not come to join the hive, yet Thuruht was speaking as if it were already fact. All Killiks had a tendency to confuse belief with reality, so the queen might simply be saying she believed the three Jedi would eventually become Joiners again. But her tone was insistent, and it struck Raynar as an assertion of will—a warning that Thuruht would not be defied.

Raynar continued to hold his arm aloft until the queen withdrew her antenna. Then he said, "You know we are not here to join the hive."

The queen lifted her head above his, clapped her mandibles together, and let out a short rumble.

" 'Yes, but it *will* happen,' " C-3PO translated. "She seems quite sure of it."

Raynar let out his breath, taking a moment to calm himself, then looked into the queen's nearest eye. "That can't happen," he said. "You remember last time, when I became UnuThul."

The queen dipped her head a little and let out a series of soft booms.

" 'You won't make the same mistake again,' " C-3PO translated. " 'You have grown in years and in wisdom.' "

"It doesn't matter," Raynar said. "The Chiss wouldn't like it. They would go to war."

The queen's reply grew a little softer.

" 'What the Chiss don't know will never hurt us,' " C-3PO said. "They already know."

A low rumble sounded from the insect's thorax, and C-3PO translated, " 'You told them?' "

Raynar shook his head. "No, but they have spies everywhere." As he spoke, he was trying to figure out why Thuruht seemed so determined to have him as a Joiner. Visitors became Joiners after they had been exposed to Killik pheromones for enough time. But hives rarely engaged in deliberate recruitment—not unless they were in need of something a new Joiner could provide. "If I don't return to the Galactic Alliance soon, the Chiss will mobilize for war—and they *will* attack the Kind."

The queen studied him for a time, then tipped her head and rumbled a question.

"Thuruht asks why you came, if your presence is such a danger?"

"Because a greater danger threatens the Galactic Alliance, and we need Thuruht's help to defeat it," Raynar explained. "We need to know everything Thuruht can tell us about the Celestials—and a being who calls herself—"

The queen's entire body shuddered. *"Ruur ub?"*

"It seems we're in luck, Jedi Thul," C-3PO said. "She asks if the name is Abeloth?"

Raynar nodded. "Then you know who Abeloth is?"

The queen gave several short, nervous booms.

"Indeed she does," C-3PO responded. "Thuruht is the one who imprisoned her."

Raynar's heart began to pound. "Good. The Jedi need to know everything Thuruht can tell us about her."

"Ub?"

Raynar needed no translation. "Because Abeloth has escaped," he said. "And we don't know where she went."

The queen raised her head and let out a rumble so thunderous that Raynar's own torso began to reverberate. Workers started to pour into the chamber from all sides, some bearing orbs of membrosia and others rushing to clean the dust from the cell pits in the floor. The nursery attendants dropped into the nearest clean pit and began to exude wax, creating a comb of fresh incubation cells.

Raynar turned to C-3PO, who was watching the sudden flurry of activity with an attentiveness that suggested a major portion of his processing power was engaged to make sense of it.

"Threepio," Raynar shouted, trying to make himself heard above the rumbling queen. "What's all the booming about?"

"I'm afraid it makes no sense, Jedi Thul," the droid replied. "I must be misunderstanding."

"Tell me anyway," Raynar ordered.

"Very well," C-3PO said. "Thuruht keeps saying that the hive must prepare."

"Prepare?" Raynar asked. "For what?"

"That's the part I must be misunderstanding," C-3PO answered. "Thuruht seems convinced that the galaxy is about to perish. She keeps saying that the end of time has come."

Chapter Sixteen

OUTSIDE THE AIRTIGHT DOOR OF THE COMPUTER CORE STOOD TWO Sith sentries, both holding their lightsabers in hand. Wearing black robes over black torso armor, they were scanning the long access corridor and speaking frequently into their headset comlinks. Clearly, they would not be easy to surprise.

Jysella watched the two guards on her screen for a moment longer, then thumbed the control-ball at the base of the remote display unit. The two Sith seemed to shrink and pull away as the tiny spy droid widened its angle of vision. Around the perimeter of the screen, a bright green border continued to flash, indicating that the unit's molecular sampler was still finding traces of detonite—a prime ingredient in most antipersonnel mines.

She smiled. The mines weren't going to be a problem.

Jysella studied the screen a moment longer. There wasn't much else to see in the wide-angle view, only the white corridor that led to the decontamination chamber outside their objective—the Jedi Temple's computer core. Once her team breached the core, the battle was—for all practical purposes—won. Their droid, Rowdy, would plug into a data socket and convince the central computer to lower the shields and open the blast doors. Three brigades of Jedi-led space marines would storm the Temple. The battle would be bloody and costly, but the Sith had no place to run. They would be found and eliminated.

Simple.

Jysella switched to thermal imaging. The two guards smudged into bright yellow man-blobs. The corridor itself turned medium blue, with the orange stripes of electrical conduits running through the walls. Behind the stripes, she could make out the red ghost-shapes of another twenty Sith warriors, hiding in the cramped cavities behind the wall panels.

Sith were patient, she had to give them that. It had been thirty-six hours since her father and Master Skywalker had decided to break into the computer core, and the ambushers had probably been hiding behind the walls for most of that time. With any luck, they would be groggy and slow from the ordeal, and it would be easy to trick them— at least, as easy as it *ever* was to trick Sith.

Jysella opened a comlink channel to Master Skywalker. "No change."

She wasn't concerned about being overheard. She and Ben and Valin were hiding inside a closed room, more than a hundred meters from the nearest Sith. Jysella wasn't sure where her father and Luke and Jaina were hiding, but she knew it would be where they, too, could not be overheard.

The comm channel itself was even more secure, encrypted using the Jedi's own unbreakable logarithms. The strike team had been using their comlinks to coordinate with Admiral Bwua'tu and his staff. Once, during a rest break, Jysella and her brother had used the channel to let their mother, Mirax, know they had survived the disastrous ambush in the water treatment plant. Jaina Solo had even managed to link to the HoloNet so she could talk to Jagged Fel—*in the Imperial Remnant.*

Alone in here, they were not.

After a few seconds, Master Skywalker acknowledged, "Copy, no change. All clear?"

"You're good to move," Jysella confirmed. "May the Force be with you."

"And with you, too," Luke answered. "If something doesn't feel right—"

"Don't worry, Dad," Ben said. He was standing next to Valin behind Jysella, watching the remote display over her shoulder. "No heroes here."

The voice in Jysella's earbud changed to that of her own father. "You three are already heroes, just *trying* this," he said. "What we don't need are dead heroes. Understood?"

"That goes double for you guys," Jysella said. "Now can we *please* get this done? It's been ages since I had a decent sanisteam."

An awkward silence fell over the channel—mostly because no one really wanted to sign off. After nearly two days of nerve-racking evasion, heavy fighting, and rushed healing trances, the entire team was feeling a little punchy.

The silence continued until Jysella finally sighed. "*Joke,* okay?" She shook her head, then added, "See you in a few."

"Yes," Jaina replied from the other end. "See you in a few."

The channel went silent again. Jysella slid a control glide down, and the blobby images of the Sith ambushers began to diminish as the spy droid retreated. The droid was barely the size of a flitnat, but she was careful to keep its speed down to avoid drawing attention to it. This was their last chance to make the Temple assault work, and if it failed, the best they could hope for would be to die fighting rather than have the Sith take them alive.

Still, Jysella would not have wanted to be anywhere else. When she and Valin had volunteered to enter the Temple with the first wave of Jedi, Master Skywalker himself had said that he would be proud to have the Horn siblings guarding his back—despite the Abeloth-induced psychosis that had caused them to betray him and Ben on Nam Chorios. And if Luke Skywalker could show that kind of loyalty to *them,* then Jysella could sure as the Void do the same for him.

After a few seconds, a trio of yellow ghost-shapes entered the thermal image and began to advance up the corridor. The two sentry-blobs guarding the computer core stepped to the front of the decontamination chamber, then vanished behind the white-hot brightness of ignited lightsabers.

Jysella reactivated her throat-mike. "Seven meters," she said, estimating the distance to the antipersonnel mines the spy droid had detected. "Stop there."

All three figures—one small and female, the other two large and male—stopped. The taller male extended a hand, and Jysella barely managed to switch back to conventional imaging before a Force-generated pressure wave triggered the first mine. A cone of orange fire shot up to mushroom against the ceiling, then a second one erupted, and a third, and a fourth. The image on the display deteriorated into a wild blur as the shock waves sent the spy droid tumbling.

"Trap defanged," Jysella commented. She glanced back at Ben. "Good plan. Let's hope the rest works this well."

"It wasn't mine alone," Ben said.

Ben's original suggestion had called for him and Jysella to draw the ambushers off, but their fathers had believed the Sith would be more likely to fall for the ploy if they knew where both Masters and Jaina were.

"But it will work," Ben said. "You can count on it."

No sooner had he spoken than the muffled crack of Force lightning sounded from the computer core. Jysella used the thumb-ball to resume control of the spy droid, then reoriented it until they could see the Sith ambushers. All twenty appeared to be racing down the corridor behind a rolling storm of blasterfire and Force lightning. There was no sign of either Ben's father or her own, but Jaina's small form could be glimpsed up near the ceiling, Force-tumbling through the air as she batted colored bolts back into the pursuing mob.

Jysella rotated the spy droid back toward the computer core. On her display screen appeared a smoky, blast-pocked corridor showing stretches of exposed conduit and ductwork. Six bodies—all Sith—lay scattered along the passage. The heavy door that guarded the decontamination chamber stood sealed but unguarded, the control panel keypad casting a faint green glow into the battle haze.

"Too easy," Jysella said. "Even your plans aren't *that* good, Jedi Skywalker."

"Another trap," Ben agreed. "No sentries, and that's a lot of bodies for three people to leave behind while running in the other direction."

"That wasn't just *anyone* running in the other direction," Valin reminded him. "It was the Sword of the Jedi and two Council Masters."

"All the same." Ben reached over Jysella's shoulder to tap the screen. "Run the droid past and see which ones are faking."

Jysella elevated the droid's auditory sensors to maximum and did as Ben suggested. They heard a lot of crackling and hissing from broken conduits and breached ductwork, but nothing that sounded remotely like a heartbeat—not even a weak one. She stopped the droid a few meters from the computer core.

"We're just going to have to accept it," Valin said. "Our dads are awesome in a fight."

"Jaina, too," Jysella added. "But let's play it safe—I'll scout ahead."

Before Ben or her brother could object, Jysella hit the door control and stepped out into the corridor. Twenty seconds later, she entered the smoke-filled passage that led to the computer core. She paused at the intersection, then slowly extended her Force awareness toward the door and sensed nothing—not even a tenuous sign of life.

And that was when she heard the soft whir of droid wheels approaching behind her. Jysella glanced back and found Rowdy following a few meters behind. Whether the little droid had misinterpreted an instruction or slipped away from Ben and Valin on its own was impossible to say, but there was no question of sending him back. They didn't have time, and even issuing the instruction would draw more attention to them than she cared for.

Motioning Rowdy to wait behind her, Jysella pulled her blaster pistol and advanced up the corridor to the first body. A Sith male with a blaster hole still smoking in his forehead, he was obviously no threat. She put two more bolts into the corpse, hoping to encourage anyone playing dead to reveal themselves *now.*

When no one moved, Jysella continued to the next corpse and found that this one, too, had a blaster hole in the center of his forehead. So did the next one, and the one after that, and the last of the six. She tried to tell herself it was only natural, that with the Sith wearing armor beneath their robes, the only place to hit them *was* the head. But no matter how she looked at it, that was amazing marksmanship for someone on the run.

Jysella was just a few steps from the computer core when a soft whir sounded behind her again. She spun, igniting her lightsaber and bringing it around less than a centimeter above Rowdy's dome. The little droid gave an alarmed screech and rocked back on his treads—then suddenly extended his welding arm and started to roll forward again, shooting sparks in Jysella's direction.

"Stop that!" Jysella pointed her lightsaber down the corridor toward the intersection. "Didn't I order you to wait back there?"

Rowdy ignored her and rolled under the sizzling blade toward the computer core. He exchanged his welding arm for an interface arm and went to work slicing the lock.

Jysella took the chance to comm Ben. "Are you missing something?"

"Rowdy." Ben sounded exasperated. "He went out the door about ten seconds after you did, then started to make too much noise when I tried to haul him back. In the end, Valin and I decided it was safer just to let him follow."

"I guess it worked out," Jysella said. "There was nothing in the corridor, and I would have needed him to slice the decontamination chamber lock anyway. I'll let you know how it feels once I'm in the core."

"Okay," Ben replied. "We're moving up for support now."

Jysella closed the channel, and five seconds later she and Rowdy were standing inside a small chamber being air-blasted and coated with a dust fixative. Once the decontamination ended, the inner door opened, and Jysella found herself looking out into a huge, spherical chamber lined by flickers of blue current.

A semicircular service balcony extended about fifteen meters into the chamber, supporting several display banks and interface stations. Just beyond the balcony rail, constellations of holographic status indicators hung twinkling in red and green and yellow; in the distance, the soft blue glow of memory clouds floated between the crackling orbs of processing clusters.

Jysella's heart began to hammer as she realized how close they were to achieving the mission. All they had to do was cross a dozen meters and plug Rowdy into a computer interface console. The droid clearly realized the same thing, for he emitted an excited chirp and rolled out onto the balcony floor.

"Not so fast, Shortstuff." Jysella used the Force to draw him back into the decontamination chamber. "This feels too easy."

The droid whistled in protest, but Jysella ignored him and began to expand her Force awareness into the room. There was a weak, anguished presence floating somewhere above her, near the entrance. But there was also a dark presence in the chamber, diffuse and powerful and everywhere, as though the computer core itself had become Sith.

Unable to use her comlink inside the mag-shielded confines of the computer core, Jysella reached out in the Force and found Ben and Valin close by, coming up the corridor toward the decontamination chamber. She filled her presence first with a sense of accomplishment—to let them know she had entered—then with uneasiness. She felt her brother's presence respond almost at once, cautious and worried. Ben added patience, and she knew they wanted her to wait.

"No arguments there," Jysella said aloud.

Still not leaving the chamber, she reached over Rowdy toward the control panel. He emitted a disappointed chirp and sank onto his treads. Then, as Jysella pressed the button to close the airtight door, the little droid emitted a taunting buzz and shot out onto the balcony.

"Rowdy!"

Jysella barely had time to dive through the opening before the door *snick*ed shut behind her. She landed just outside the decontamination chamber and rolled to her feet in a fighting crouch, alert for the faintest prickle of danger sense. She felt only the anguished presence above and behind her, weak and barely alert, and beyond the balcony railing, the same miasma of dark energy she had detected before.

Rowdy continued forward. His goal seemed to be a trio of swiveling chairs that sat facing the primary interface console. On the back of the middle chair was a star-shaped scorch, surrounding a dark hole about where the heart of a seated human would be. Jysella pressed her back against the door of the decontamination chamber and again expanded her Force awareness. She still felt no hint of an impending attack.

When Rowdy reached the primary administration console and plugged into the droid socket with no hint of trouble, Jysella decided she could risk looking away from him for a moment. She stepped away from the door and turned back toward the decontamination chamber.

A familiar figure was hanging a few meters away, suspended upside down and watching her from a pair of eyes that had been blackened by a severe beating. His face was bruised and swollen almost beyond recognition, and one of his shoulders was jutting out from the socket at an impossible angle. But there was no mistaking the conservative cut of his short brown hair or the reserved style of his gray business tabard.

"Chief Dorvan?" Jysella gasped. She resisted the urge to rush to his aid, preferring instead to remain where she was until she had some idea of what had happened. "What happened?"

"She . . . she underestimated me," Dorvan answered. A crease that might have been a smile crept across his swollen face. "Everyone does."

"Who?" Jysella asked.

Dorvan's gaze shifted toward the primary interface console, where Rowdy was still at work—and where the chair with the scorch hole was located.

"She did."

"Who?" Jysella asked.

"Her." Dorvan looked as though he wanted to point, but it was impossible in his position. "Look."

Jysella spent a moment debating the possibility of a trap, then finally decided that whatever had happened there was already over. Being careful to stay alert to Dorvan's presence, she advanced until she came to the primary interface console, where Rowdy was blinking and beeping with the computer core.

She turned to inspect the administrators' chairs. Two of the seats were empty, but the one in the center was occupied by a blue-skinned Jessar female. There was a blackened scorch hole in the center of her chest, another between her eyes, and yet a third in the side of her head.

Roki Kem.

"Be . . . careful." From this far away, Dorvan's voice was so weak and filled with pain that it was barely audible. "She's not dead."

Jysella turned back to the man, whom she was beginning to think had lost his mind to Sith torture. "Did *you* kill Roki Kem?"

"I told you!" Dorvan snapped. "She's not dead! And that's *not* Chief Kem."

Before Jysella could reply, Rowdy interrupted with an urgent whistle. She raised a hand for Dorvan to wait and turned back to Rowdy.

"What's wrong?"

The droid emitted an impatient tweedle, then a display screen above the interface station suddenly *snick*ed to life. The image was dark and fuzzy, but it looked to Jysella as if the droid was showing her a corridor. Judging by the dim lighting and the curtains of corrosion and moss clinging to the durasteel walls, it was probably deep in the depths of the Jedi Temple—or possibly even in some other building.

"Don't be fooled," Dorvan called from the back of the balcony. "That *isn't* . . . Roki Kem!"

"Okay, if you say so." Jysella did not look up as she replied, for she already knew what Dorvan probably wanted to tell her—that Roki Kem was a powerful Sith impostor. Still looking at the display screen, she asked Rowdy, "What am I supposed to be looking at here? Does it have something to do with the shields or the blast doors?"

A message began to scroll down one side of the screen, next to the image of the corridor. I FOUND VESTARA KHAI. As the words appeared, so did a small female figure dressed in a Jedi robe, running along the passage from the screen bottom toward the top. SHE IS FLEEING INTO THE TEMPLE SUBSTRUCTURE, CURRENTLY ON LEVEL 30 CORRIDOR N300X.

"The substructure?" Jysella echoed. "What the blazes is she doing down there?"

Even before she had finished asking the question, a dozen Sith warriors appeared on the display, racing up the corridor in pursuit of Vestara.

RUNNING FOR HER LIFE, Rowdy replied.

"So I see," Jysella said. "Okay, keep an eye on her if you can—Ben's going to want to know what happens to her. But our priorities are the shields and the blast doors."

She felt Valin reach for her in the Force, puzzled and concerned. Clearly, he and Ben had entered the decontamination chamber and were alarmed not to find her there. She replied with a short burst of frustration—*Rowdy*—followed by a feeling of calm.

The exchange came to an abrupt end when a pained screech erupted from the wall where Dorvan was suspended. Expecting to see something more horribly wrong than what was already hanging there, Jysella looked—and was surprised to see that it was merely the tormented bureaucrat, trying to get her attention.

"You're playing into her hands!" Dorvan cried.

"Whose hands?" Jysella motioned at Kem's corpse. "Hers?"

"Yes!" Dorvan replied. "Don't you see? She's manipulating you!"

Jysella looked at the body. Finding it still dead, she decided that Dorvan's mind had clearly snapped.

"Chief Dorvan," Jysella asked in a deliberately calm voice, "I already know who Chief Kem really is."

Dorvan's eyes widened in fear. "You do?"

Jysella nodded. "Yes. She's a High Lord of the Sith." As she spoke, Rowdy tweedled for attention. She motioned the droid to wait a moment, then added, "She might even be Heir Grand Lord on Coruscant."

The fear in Dorvan's face changed to terror. "No." His complexion went gray, and it looked like he might be going into shock. "You *don't* understand!"

Rowdy asked for attention again, this time with an urgent screech. Deciding to focus on her mission rather than a prisoner's shattered mind, Jysella reached out to Dorvan in the Force.

"I *do* understand, Chief Dorvan," she said, bathing him in a heavy flow of the same soothing Force energies that she used to make any kind of Force suggestion. "Everything will be fine."

Dorvan's voice trailed off into incoherence—which was close enough to calm for Jysella's purposes. She turned back to the display above Rowdy's interface socket. Almost immediately, words began to scroll across the screen.

THE COMPUTER CORE IS MALFUNCTIONING. SHE INSISTS THAT SHE IS THE MASTER OF THE JEDI TEMPLE. SHE INSISTS THAT SHE IS THE BELOVED QUEEN OF THE STARS, AND SHE INSISTS THAT SHE HAS LOCKED ALL SHIELDS AND DISABLED EVERY BLAST DOOR IN THE JEDI TEMPLE.

Jysella began to have a sick, hollow feeling inside. "The Beloved Queen of the Stars?" Her voice was a mere gasp, so low that even *she* barely heard it. "Ask the computer for her name."

A gout of flame shot from the interface socket, and Rowdy shot across the balcony trailing sparks, smoke, and the acrid stench of melting circuit boards. He continued until he slammed into the balcony safety rail, then toppled over and began to ooze molten metal and extinguishing foam from every seam in his casing.

An attention chime sounded from the display, and an answer to Jysella's question scrolled across the screen.

YOU KNOW WHO I AM.

And Jysella *did* know.

The Jedi had come for the Sith—and found Abeloth.

Jysella's entire body went cold. Her thoughts grew sluggish and her emotions became muddled, and she began to tremble. Abeloth had taken her mind once already. She could not let that happen again— *would* not. She snapped a thermal detonator off her combat harness and disengaged the safety, then began to back toward the air lock . . .

. . . and remembered her brother and Ben.

They should have been standing at her side by now, lending her strength and courage and helping her decide what to do. But she had heard nothing yet—not even a distress cry in the Force.

Jysella spun around and saw that the light above the air lock remained yellow. The exchange pumps were still engaged, filtering air— or simply removing it.

She reached for them in the Force—and found only a single presence, too weak and near death to tell whether it was Ben or her brother.

Jysella set the thermal detonator's fuse to one second, then turned back toward the computer core . . . toward *Abeloth.*

"Open the air lock . . . *now.*"

To Jysella's surprise, the door slid aside at once, emitting a loud, hissing pop that suggested the air lock had already been depressurized. Ben was nowhere to be seen, but her brother's body lay motionless on the floor. She reached out to him in the Force and, finding that he was still alive, started to shake him.

"Valin! Wake up!" Still holding the detonator in her hand, she stepped into the air lock and knelt at his side. "Where's Ben?"

A loud keen sounded from over the air lock door, and Wynn Dorvan's voice rang down from above.

"Didn't I warn you?" he cried. "She *sees* the future!"

Chapter Seventeen

THE PEARLY IRIDESCENCE OF HYPERSPACE COALESCED INTO STREAKS OF blue light, then the lines became stars, and the *Millennium Falcon* was in realspace again. Coruscant went from a distant fleck to a beldon-sized disk in less than a minute. By the time Leia brought up the sensors, the planet filled the entire viewport—a vast ball sparkling so bright it flooded the flight deck with its golden glow.

She activated the tactical display and was astonished to see a schematic that she could actually understand at a glance. That just wasn't normal. Usually, the Coruscant approach was so choked with traffic that only an astromech droid could work through the swirling layers of designator symbols and find a safe trajectory.

But today Leia could have chosen a route just by looking. There were the usual bands of satellite designators, which marked orbital facilities such as manufacturing plants, battle platforms, and solar mirrors. Most of the other symbols represented military task forces, usually a single Star Destroyer surrounded by its escorts.

The military vessels were arrayed across the planet in no deployment pattern that Leia could recognize. In places, three or four task forces seemed to be circling one another, as though a battle might erupt at any moment. In other areas, there were huge unprotected voids where the sparse civilian traffic was making mad dashes both to and from the surface.

Han barely seemed to notice the unusual pattern. He simply swung the *Falcon* toward one of the unguarded areas, then tipped his head back toward the navigator's station.

"Go ahead and send that message now, Jayk," he said. Jayk was one of thirty brand-new Jedi Knights aboard the *Falcon*. The Masters Solusar had sent them along to reinforce the Jedi on Coruscant. "Amelia's got to be worried sick about her furry buddy."

"Very well, Captain," Jayk said. A slender Ryn female, she had red hair and a nose so small that it barely resembled a beak at all. Like most of the young Jedi aboard, she had been promoted from apprentice to full Jedi Knighthood just before the hastily repaired *Falcon* parted ways with the *Dragon Queen II* at Taanab. "I've already prepared a burst transmission with a vid of Anji playing with Jedi Rivai. I hope that will reassure her."

The pet nexu had shown up in Allana's empty bunk just before the last hyperspace jump. Unfortunately, the *Falcon* had been under strict comm silence until now, so this was their first chance to send word to Allana, aboard the *Dragon Queen II,* that they had Anji.

"Let me know if they acknowledge," Han said. He hit the deceleration thrusters so hard that Leia was thrown against her crash webbing. "I'm expecting a message."

"Hey, flyboy, take it easy," Leia said. "Slamming the passengers around isn't going to make Amelia apologize to you."

"Who's asking for an apology?" Han replied. "I just wish she had shown up to say good-bye."

"She was angry with us," Leia said. "And maybe she had reason to be. We did end the discussion pretty quickly."

Han glanced over. "What's to discuss? Coruscant is a war zone. We *weren't* going to take a nine-year-old into a war zone—and certainly not *her.*"

"Of course not," Leia agreed. "But there's more than one way to say no."

"I think my way worked pretty well." Han glanced around the cabin. "You don't see her here, do you?"

"That's not the point," Leia said. "I didn't get a chance to say good-bye before we left the *Dragon Queen*. How do you think she'll feel if we don't come back from this?"

Han rolled his eyes at her. "Like *that's* going to happen."

They hit Coruscant's atmosphere much too fast, and the *Falcon* decelerated again, harder than before. Friction flames began to shoot past the viewport, then the ship began to buck and grow warm inside. Because of the Sith occupation, they were literally coming in as hot and bright as a meteor, trying to take advantage of the enemy's disorganization so they could disappear into the city before anyone jumped them.

Leia returned her gaze to the tactical display. The nearest task force was a light cruiser escorted by three frigates. They were wheeling around and spraying a squadron of XJ5 ChaseX starfighters in the *Falcon*'s direction. Leia plotted an estimated interception point and was relieved to find that the *Falcon* would already be down in Coruscant's skylanes.

"How are we doing?" Han asked.

"We'll make it," Leia said. "But don't slow down."

"What if our hull starts to melt?"

"Find rain." Leia studied the designator symbols on the display, trying to figure out whether the task force's commanding officer was allied with the Jedi or the Sith. "Any idea who commands the *Regalle*?"

Han shook his head. "Artoo, see if you can access the Fifth Fleet database and—"

A message chime sounded from the navigator's station, and Jayk said, "Hold on. We're being hailed."

"By the *Regalle*?" Leia asked.

"By the *Lady Worbi*," Jayk replied. "She's a Charubah *Stella*-class frigate from the—"

"I know who flies Stellas, Jayk," Leia interrupted mildly. "What I *don't* know is why the Hapan Royal Navy is here."

"Shall I ask them?" Jayk inquired.

"Just open the channel," Han said, clearly impatient with the young Jedi Knight's inability to read his mind. "It's not like we're trying to dodge *them*."

"Very well, Captain."

A soft *pop* sounded as Jayk opened the channel, then Taryn Zel's familiar Hapan voice came over the cockpit speaker. "I hope you'll forgive the interruption," she said. "But we seem to have misplaced one of our female passengers. And our, uh, commander dispatched the *Lady Worbi* to inquire if she might have sneaked aboard your vessel while no one was looking."

Leia could not help smiling at the careful choice of the word *commander*. Almost certainly, Taryn was referring to Allana, who had no doubt been raising quite a fuss on the *Dragon Queen II* over her lost nexu. She activated her mike.

"As a matter of fact, we *did* find an unauthorized passenger," Leia said. "She was curled up in her customary spot. Tell your commander that her furry friend is just fine."

"Her *furry* friend?" This from Zekk. "When you say unauthorized passenger, how many legs did she have?"

Leia had a sinking feeling. "Four," she answered. "How many legs does—"

"Two," Taryn answered. "We noticed a certain young lady's absence after we departed Taanab."

"Young lady?" Han stormed. He pulled back on the pilot's yoke, bringing the *Falcon* out of its meteoric plunge. "Are you telling me Amelia stowed away? On *this* trip?"

On the tactical display, the ChaseX squadron's interception point drifted upward, into the highest levels of the city.

"Han—don't slow down!" Leia said. They had passed the point of no return, for they did not dare allow the *Regalle* and its task force within firing range—not with Allana on board. "Keep diving!"

Han glanced at his own display and scowled. "What do you suppose the odds are that those guys are on *our* side?"

"Fifty–fifty," Leia replied. "And that's not good enough."

"I guess not." Han shoved the yoke forward again, then opened a shipwide intercom channel. "Amelia Solo to the flight deck—now!"

"We're checking on the stowaway," Leia informed the *Lady Worbi*. "If her pet nexu is here, she's probably here, too."

"That's also our feeling," Taryn replied. "Can you return for a rendezvous?"

Leia checked the tactical display and saw that the ChaseX squadron was continuing to accelerate after the *Falcon,* while the *Regalle* and its escorts were fanning out to spread their turbolaser fire.

"I think that's negative," Leia replied. "We don't know who that is behind us, but so far they don't look very friendly."

"Very well," Taryn said. "We'll cover your descent and assess our options later. Keep us informed."

"Affirmative," Leia said. She hadn't felt her granddaughter's presence aboard the *Falcon,* but that wasn't surprising. After the close call on Klatooine, she had been working with Allana on concealment techniques—and that included hiding her presence in the Force. "We'll let you know as soon as we find her."

The *Falcon* started to shudder and slew in the thickening atmosphere, and then a warning buzzer announced that the hull temperature had climbed into the failure zone. Tongues of white flame appeared in the orange glow outside, flakes of corroded metal starting to disintegrate in the heat. Han had no choice but to swing away from the ChaseX squadron and decrease their dive angle. He pulled the throttles back, using the repulsorlift drives to slow their descent.

R2-D2 tweedled an alert, and lock alarms began to screech almost instantly.

"See if you can get a friend-or-foe ID on those ChaseXs, Artoo," Leia ordered. She activated the intercom. "Brace for battle back there. Ramud and Huli, go weapons-live, but don't initiate. Amelia, if you're not on the flight deck in—"

"I'm *coming!*" a small voice shouted from the back of the access tunnel. "Be patient! Dad just called a minute ago."

"That's because we didn't know you were aboard." Leia turned to find her granddaughter scurrying down the corridor with Anji padding along beside her. Dressed in an insulated jumpsuit, Allana was coated from head to foot in various colors of grease. Leia pointed at the empty seat across from Jayk. "You have a lot of explaining to do, young lady."

"I already explained," Allana said. She climbed into the seat and began to buckle herself in. "You just didn't listen back on the *Dragon Queen.*"

"Because we're your parents," Han said. "We don't need to listen."

"That's a bunch of poodoo," Allana shot back. "You're the one who's always saying you can't let other people tell you what to do."

"We're not other people," Han replied. "We're *supposed* to tell you what to do. That's our job."

Allana rolled her eyes, then looked to Leia. "I had a *vision*," she said. "Just like on . . ."

She glanced over at Jayk, clearly uncertain of how much to let slip in front of a Jedi she didn't know very well.

"We'll finish this discussion later," Leia said, turning forward again. "Right now, we need to figure out whether those starfighters on our tail are friends or—"

R2-D2 interrupted with a sharp whistle, and a single word scrolled across the copilot's display: FOE.

"*Bloah*," Leia said. "You're sure?"

THE PROBABILITY IS 93.4 PERCENT, R2-D2 reported. THE TASK FORCE IS COMMANDED BY ADMIRAL POLOW, A GRADUATE OF THE GALACTIC ALLIANCE SPACE ACADEMY.

"The *Galactic Alliance* Space Academy?" Leia repeated. "Not the New Republic?"

R2-D2 emitted an affirming whistle.

"Thank you, Artoo," Leia said, seeing the problem. The Galactic Alliance Space Academy was only three years old. That meant an officer who had graduated from it would be no higher than a lieutenant commander. She opened a channel to the *Lady Worbi*. "*Lady Worbi*, the good news is that we found that stowaway. She's sitting right behind me, in fine condition."

"That *is* good news," Taryn replied. "What's the bad news?"

"Do you see that task force pursuing us?"

"Of course." Taryn sounded almost insulted. "Are they a problem?"

"They still haven't hailed us," Leia said. "And we're pretty sure their commander isn't one of ours."

"I see." Taryn went silent for a moment, then said, "We can't do much about the ChaseX squadron, but we'll give the cruiser and her escorts something to worry about."

"Thank you," Leia said. "That would be a great deal of help."

She closed the channel and saw that the *Falcon* was only seconds from starting to scrape her belly on tower pinnacles. Soon they would begin setting fire to the buildings they passed, and even Han was not skilled enough to fly a YT-1300 transport through Coruscant's crowded skylanes at this kind of speed. But the tactical display showed an estimated attack point hovering in the upper margin of the city, with the ChaseX squadron already matching the *Falcon*'s speed and continuing to accelerate. Fortunately, Taryn had launched all three of the *Worbi*'s Miy'til squadrons and was circling behind the task force, giving the *Regalle* and her escorts plenty to think about.

The *Falcon* tipped up on her side as Han swerved to avoid a residence tower, then he said, "Sweetheart, you *do* know I'm gonna have to slow down eventually, right?"

"The thought had crossed my mind," Leia admitted, keeping her eyes on the tactical display. "Just be ready to evade. Those ChaseXs are closing fast."

"How long before they open fire?"

"Whenever they want," Leia replied. "That last swerve brought them into range."

"And they're not opening fire?" Han pulled the throttles back, and the orange glow beyond the viewport quickly vanished as the flames died away. "No problem, then."

"Han!" Leia watched the tactical display in horror as the ChaseX squadron closed to medium range. "Have you lost your mind?"

"Relax," he said. "Not everybody in the Alliance Navy is Sith. If those guys aren't opening fire yet—"

"It's because they want to avoid collateral damage," Leia finished, nodding. She opened a hailing channel. "ChaseX leader, please state the reason for your pursuit and be advised that we are Coruscant natives."

"We know who you are," replied a clipped voice. "And that's why we're pursuing. You Jedi spicerunners aren't welcome here on Coruscant anymore. You can surrender now, or we open fire."

Han scowled at the cockpit speaker. "Thanks for the warning."

He pushed the yoke forward, dropping the *Falcon* between two skytowers, then rolled into a half-deserted skylane and dived through three levels of hover vehicles. Almost immediately a new voice came over the traffic channel. It was a female controller.

"*Longshot,* what do you think you're doing?" she demanded, using the false transponder code under which the *Falcon* was traveling. "You are not cleared to fly that thing in general traffic!"

"Sorry about that," Leia replied, continuing to watch the tactical display. Rather than start a cannon battle in the narrow confines between Coruscant's looming towers, most of the ChaseX squadron had pulled up and spread out to fly top cover. But three starfighters had followed the *Falcon* down into the skylane. Now they were flying between traffic levels, ducking under pedbridges and swinging from one wall to another in an effort to get a shot. "But I think you'd better clear the lane for us. This is beginning to look dangerous."

"And whose fault is that?" the controller demanded. "You're going to lose entry rights over this. I hope you know that!"

"Hey, get those guys off my tail and we're outta here," Han replied. He began to juke and jink, trying to make the *Falcon* a difficult target. "All I'm trying to do is land this crate."

A loud *thwung* rang through the *Falcon* as a cannon bolt burned into the hull. Then the entire ship shuddered as the big quad cannons returned fire.

"Is that cannon fire?" the controller asked. "Please tell me you haven't started a dogfight in the middle of Seventh Lane Seventeen Fifty."

"Okay, I won't," Han said.

"*We're* not the ones who started it," Leia added. She closed the channel and called up a skylane schematic for her main display, then asked Han, "Shields?"

Han shook his head. "Things are tight enough in here without bouncing off every pedbridge and hoversled we pass."

A trio of cannon bolts flashed past Leia's side of the flight deck and vanished down the skylane, sending airspeeders diving for the undercity or whipping around corners. The *Falcon*'s cannons fired again, and Ramud's deep Duros voice came over the cabin speaker.

"Vape one ChaseX." He sounded more relieved than excited. "I saw the canopy blow and an ejection plume, so maybe the pilot will survive."

Leia was glad to hear the concern in the young Jedi's voice. Luke had taken pains to emphasize that the Jedi were at war with no one but the Sith. She found it heartening to see that the message had been received.

Another *thwung* sounded from the stern. Leia felt the *Falcon* slew as Han struggled to stay in control. She kept her eyes on the skylane schematic, searching for a way to disappear into the labyrinth of dark lanes that ran beneath Fellowship Plaza.

"How are those repairs holding up?" she asked.

"Not well enough to keep taking cannon bolts," Han said. "Will you guys in the turrets stop playing nice and get those ChaseXs off our tails? It's them or us, fellas!"

Han tipped the *Falcon* up on its side and sliced down through a dozen levels of traffic, giving both gunners clear shots at their pursuers. The quad cannons began to chuff steadily while a torrent of color flashed past as the ChaseXs returned fire. A loud ping echoed through the ship when a bolt glanced off the upper hull, then an Arcona hiss came over the intercom.

"Vape ChaseX two!" Huli's voice grew rueful. "The pilot didn't make it."

Incredibly, the third pilot stayed on their tail. Another hit tolled up from the stern, and Han's hands began to shudder as the *Falcon* went into a spin that Leia doubted was intentional.

Finally, Leia found what she was looking for. "Han, there's a barge tunnel three hundred meters ahead to starboard."

"Are you c-c-crazy?" Han demanded, stuttering because the yoke was vibrating so badly. "We can't m-m-make that turn at this—"

"Then slow down!" Leia said. "It's that turn or a dash across Blemmer Circle."

By the time she finished the sentence, she was pressing into her crash harness as the *Falcon* slowed to make the turn. The belly gunner lost sight of the target, and the chuffing of the lower quad cannons quieted. The dark oval of the tunnel entrance appeared on the right, then began to broaden into a circle as Han tried to make the turn. A collision alarm broke into a screech.

"Blast!" Han cursed. "We're not going to make—"

And then they were in the darkness, a deafening shriek filling their ears as the hull scraped along the tunnel wall. A tremendous roar sounded behind them, then the upper quad cannons went quiet, too. Ramud did not bother to report the crash that had destroyed the last ChaseX.

Han looked over at Leia, his face pale. "What next?"

"Don't hit anything," Leia said. "Those barges are robotic. They don't use running lights, and our sensors are worthless down here."

Han's eyes widened. He hit a switch on the instrument console, and a trio of floodlight beams stabbed through the darkness ahead.

"And don't slow down," Leia added, still studying the schematic. "If any of those other ChaseXs come after us, we've got ten kilometers before we have a chance to lose them."

Han squeezed the yoke so hard his knuckles grew white. "I don't know why I let you navigate," he said. "Don't you have any *good* news?"

"Sure," Leia said. "Once we make it through the tunnel, we'll be a hundred kilometers from the hangar."

"And *that's* the good news?" Han asked. "Really?"

It was Allana who replied. "Don't be scared, Dad. We can do it."

Han glanced at her reflection in the viewport. "Who's scared?"

"You are," Allana said. "You're sweating . . . and I can feel it in the Force."

Han sighed. "Okay, so I'm a little bit scared."

"I don't know why," Allana said. "The Queen Mother told me you guys do this stuff all the time."

"We do," Han said, continuing to look at her reflection. "But not with *you* aboard. The next time I tell you to stay—"

"Why don't we talk about that later?" Leia interrupted. "After we've all had a chance to calm down?"

"I'm not *going* to calm down," Han said, still looking at Allana. "You're in big trouble, young lady."

"I know," Allana said, her tone as confident as it was subdued. "But at least I'm here."

The *Falcon* continued through the barge tunnel. It wasn't long before they began to encounter boxy barge-silhouettes moving in both directions. Undulating through the darkness, they ducked beneath all oncoming traffic and flew up and over the ones they were overtaking.

Leia kept expecting the barge traffic to come to a standstill as the control center initiated a safety shutdown—but the operators were either panicking or not paying attention. A few tense minutes later, the

Falcon finally shot out of the tunnel and entered the cluttered darkness beneath Fellowship Plaza, and Leia breathed a sigh of relief.

After a series of evasive maneuvers designed to detect anyone trying to follow them, Leia ran a thorough signal analysis to make sure the ChaseXs had not tagged the *Falcon* with a tracking device. After that, she ran a powerful degaussing current through the outer hull—just to be certain she hadn't missed anything. Then she checked again for unauthorized transmissions, and finally she decided that the *Falcon* was, indeed, clean.

"Artoo, bounce a burst message to Jedi Command," Leia ordered. "Tell him we're en route, and we need safe-approach charts."

R2-D2 tweedled a response, and Han began to thread his way into the lowest levels of the undercity. Just half a kilometer down, the structures were so crusted in yorik coral that it was impossible to see the buildings themselves. Curtains of moss dangled hundreds of meters from pedbridges, and ten-meter stalks of fungi grew on balconies. Strange four-winged reptiles soared through the darkness, their claws clutching still-struggling rodents—or limbs torn from decaying corpses. In many ways, it looked as though the Yuuzhan Vong had never left this part of the planet—and in some ways, that was true. With its attention focused on rebuilding the rest of the galaxy—and just keeping order—for most of the last two decades, the Galactic Alliance had never had the political will to repair what the extragalactic invaders had done to Coruscant's hidden slums.

R2-D2 chirped an alert, and then a map of the undercity appeared on the copilot's display. They were closer to the rendezvous point than Leia had imagined, and it took only a few minutes to slip through the tangled labyrinth to a dark hollow in the yorik coral. At first, she mistook the cavity for a cavern entrance, but when the *Falcon*'s floodlights illuminated it, she saw that it was actually a hangar door painted matte black.

Leia felt a welcoming brush in the Force, and she knew they were being watched by a group of Jedi sentries. She replied by reaching out in the Force herself, allowing them to sense her relief at having arrived. The door retracted into the wall. On the other side was a loading bay. It looked deserted, but Leia could sense several Jedi presences lurking in hiding places.

"I don't know about this," Han said, holding the *Falcon* outside the entrance. "Are you sure it's the right place?"

"Yes." Leia and Jayk both responded at the same time.

"Dad," Allana added. "The Jedi are at war. You don't expect them to post a *sign*, do you?"

"Don't be silly." Han eased the *Falcon* across the threshold, raising a thick cloud of dust as they moved toward the berthing circles. "I'm just saying . . . would it've killed them to do some cleaning?"

He shut down the cooling fans, then lowered the struts and quickly set the *Falcon* down near the back of the small chamber. Behind them, the doors closed with a muffled clang. By the time Leia and the others had unbuckled and traveled down the access corridor to the main cabin, their Jedi passengers had lowered the boarding ramp. They had arrayed themselves in a neat line and were awaiting the captain's permission to debark. Han rolled his eyes at their formality, then motioned for them to fall in behind him and led the way down the ramp.

As soon as the Solos stepped foot on the floor of the loading bay, the entire rear wall began to rise. Beyond lay a much larger, brightly lit hangar that was bustling with combat-support activity. Maintenance crews were reloading dozens of assault cars with ammunition and fuel, while repair droids swarmed the exteriors applying hasty battlefield patches. There were even medical droids on the floor, evaluating injuries and dressing minor wounds.

In one corner, Admiral Nek Bwua'tu was interrogating a platoon of soot-stained space marines, no doubt trying to put together an accurate picture of combat conditions. Scattered around the chamber were half a dozen Jedi Masters, each speaking quietly with a small band of Jedi Knights in color-shifting robes.

Leia was starting to wonder why there were so many Jedi in the hangar, instead of out fighting, when she sensed her former Master approaching. She turned to find Saba Sebatyne emerging from a doorway on the near side of the room, her scaly face showing none of the surprise that Leia could feel in the Barabel's Force aura.

Accompanying Saba were Bazel Warv and Mirax Horn. Bazel wore a combat harness loaded with a couple of casefuls of grenades. Mirax wore space marine battle fatigues, with a general's insignia attached to the collar. The rank, Leia assumed, was provisional—no doubt bestowed by Nek Bwua'tu so Mirax would have the proper authority to oversee the search for Sith sleeper agents.

When Saba had approached to within a couple of paces, she stopped and peered over Leia's head toward Jayk, Ramud, and all the other new Jedi Knights.

"This one thought apprentices were to go to Shedu Maad," she said.

"That was the plan," Leia admitted. "But these apprentices have been promoted. They're Jedi Knights now."

"The Masters Solusar say they're ready," Han added. "And since we had to drop by anyway, we thought we'd bring you some reinforcements."

Saba shifted her gaze to Han, her forked tongue flicking out between her lips. "Yes, reinforcementz are good." She looked back to the Jedi Knights, giving them a slit-eyed Barabel appraisal. Finally, she nodded and pointed across the hangar to where a towering wall of Yuzzem fur stood dressed in a Jedi robe. "Master Barratk'l is charged with lair security. Present yourselves to her."

The young Jedi Knights bowed as one. "Yes, Master."

Saba waited until they were gone, then pointed a talon in Allana's direction. "This one is surprised to see your foundling with you. She is small for a fight, is she not?"

Han nodded. "Yeah, but she's stubborn enough to be a teenage Wookiee."

Allana smiled, clearly recognizing a compliment when she heard one. She stepped closer to Saba and said, "I need to talk to you about something."

Saba studied the girl with a huge eye. "Yes?"

Allana didn't flinch. "I can't tell you here." She glanced past Saba toward Bazel's mountainous green bulk, then spoke more quietly. "That would be breaking a promise."

"What promise?" Saba asked, following Allana's gaze toward Bazel. "Does it concern Jedi Warv?"

"It's the reason we came to see him," Allana answered. "Grand Master Skywalker was *supposed* to tell him to meet us."

Saba turned her head and studied Allana out of one eye, a gesture of Barabel suspicion. "To meet *you*?" she asked. "Really?"

Allana let her chin drop, clearly realizing she had been caught in an exaggeration. "Well, to meet my parents," she corrected. "Master Skywalker wasn't expecting me to be here, but I *had* to come. I'm the one who had the vision."

"And Jedi Warv was in your vision?" Saba asked, going from suspicious to confused. "A vision about breaking a promise?"

"Actually, Amelia's vision concerned a Barabel nest," Leia said. The time had come to cut to the chase. "The Sith were attacking it."

Saba's scales bristled, and she glared down at Allana with bared fangs. "*What* nest?"

Allana surprised Leia by ignoring the menace in Saba's voice. Instead she stepped forward until she was nose-to-abdomen with the Barabel, then said, "I think you *know* what nest. Do I need to say names?"

"Tesar?" Saba gasped. "Dordi?"

Allana nodded. "And Wilyem and Zal. *Now* can we talk?"

Saba stumbled back a step, clearly astonished. "You know?"

"Master Sebatyne," Leia said, "we *all* know."

Most Jedi understood why the younger Barabels had disappeared, and Leia had assumed that Saba realized that. But it was growing apparent that the Master had been fooling herself about how well the secret of the nest was being kept.

"It's really not that difficult to figure out," she added.

"Yeah, give us some credit," Han added. "Your son disappears with a bunch of other Barabels for a few months. You get all grouchy and nervous. What else could it be? They're making a nest."

Saba let her shoulders slump. "This one hoped that you would believe they were on a secret mission."

"I'm afraid we know you too well for that, Master Sebatyne," Leia said. "You'd never go around the chain of command and launch a secret mission."

Saba eyed Leia as though she were a shenbit, then finally asked, "*Everyone* knowz?"

Leia nodded. "All of the Masters," she confirmed. "And a fair number of Jedi Knights."

"So it's no use trying to silence everyone who knows," Han replied. "You can't kill *all* of us."

Saba glared at Han as though contemplating the truth of his assertion, then finally nodded and turned back to Allana. "And you came
here to warn Tesar and his nestmates of your vision?"

Allana nodded. "I can't just let it happen," she said. "Tesar is my
friend."

Saba let her head drop. "And Tesar is this one's son," she said. "But
she is sorry—this one does not know where to find the nest."

Allana frowned. "Really?" she asked. "You don't where it is?"

Saba shook her head. "Barabelz do not tell nest locationz to anyone," she said. "Especially motherz."

Allana exchanged glances with Bazel. They both fell silent, and
then Allana glanced away, looking guilty.

Saba's head bobbed forward. "*You* know?"

Allana reluctantly said, "I don't think I can tell you that without
breaking my promise."

The Barabel folded her scaly brow and looked from Allana to Bazel,
her head cocking ever farther sideways as she tried to make sense of
what she was hearing.

Finally, she drew back. "This one does not understand. You are a
strange pair to make a life-promise." She looked to Bazel, then
dropped her snout and bared her fangs, presenting the huge Ramoan
with the nearest thing to a sympathetic gesture that Barabels had.
"This one does not think it will work."

"We're *not* a promise pair!" Allana exclaimed. "We didn't *mean* to
find the nest. It was just a big accident!"

"But I can find it again," Bazel rumbled, "if you think I should?"

"Yes, it must be you," Saba said, not even hesitating. She looked
back to Allana, turning her head to study her out of one eye again,
then returned her gaze to Bazel. "*This* one has not been accepted into
the nest."

The note of admiration in Saba's voice was hard to miss, and Leia
was suddenly hit by the magnitude of what her granddaughter had
achieved. Barabels were by nature a fierce and cautious species. Yet Allana had coaxed four of them into trusting her *and* Bazel—and with a
secret they would not share with their own mothers. If Allana could
achieve that at nine, perhaps there was hope for a peaceful galaxy, after
all. Perhaps *Allana* was that hope.

After a moment, Bazel nodded. "Good. Then I volunteer." He paused a moment, then glanced over at Leia. "But how am I going to get into the Temple?"

Han smiled and reached up to slap him on the shoulder. "Don't worry about that, big fella," he said. "After all the trouble we had smuggling supplies in during the Mando siege, Luke had me set up a secret entrance. We can drop you at the other end of the evacuation route. It won't be fast going in, but it will get you into the lower levels with no problem."

"Speaking of problems," Leia said, eager to change the subject before Allana decided she had to go with Bazel, "I see a lot of Jedi here still being briefed. I thought they would all be inside the Temple fighting by now."

Saba nodded. "This one, too. The shieldz are not yet down. The blast doorz are still closed."

"Our first wave of attackers ran into a Sith ambush," Mirax explained. "We haven't been able to insert the rest of the company."

Leia's stomach went hollow. "How bad was the ambush?"

"Bad," Saba replied. "We lost ten Knightz . . . so far."

"But Luke and Jaina escaped the initial attack," Mirax added. "We're *sure* of that. Ben, too."

Leia did not sense any grief in Mirax's voice, so she felt comfortable asking, "Corran and your children, too?"

Mirax nodded. "They're okay, the last time they checked in."

"But no one else remainz," Saba added. "Master Skywalker and his team are alone."

"You're telling me there are six Jedi in there on their own?" Han demanded. "Against four thousand Sith?"

Leia could feel how frightened Han was growing, and she understood why. Jaina was their last surviving child, and the thought of losing her—and Luke, too—was almost more than she could bear.

"And you aren't doing anything about it?" Han continued.

"This one *is* doing something, Captain Solo," Saba said. "She is obeying orderz. Master Skywalker has told her he needz more time to open the blast doorz."

"And if that doesn't happen?" Han demanded. "You could be waiting for—"

"Then they go in the hard way," Mirax said, putting a little dura-steel in her voice. "But you know as well as I do, that has to be a last resort. If we start lobbing baradium bombs into the Jedi Temple, no one has control over who gets killed."

Mirax's stern tone and good sense seemed to bring Han back to his senses. He fell silent for a moment, then spoke in a calmer tone. "Okay. You gotta wait for Luke—when it comes to long shots, nobody is better than him. But six against four thousand is pretty bad. Why don't we use the evacuation tunnel and send in a little help?"

"The entrances are in the undercity, yes?" Saba asked. "That is fine for the lower levelz, but it would take dayz to fight up into the main part of the Temple. We would lose too many Jedi Knightz."

"And we don't have days," Mirax said. "Admiral Bwua'tu's troops don't have the fuel or ammunition to continue their assault that long."

"Nor is that the only problem," Leia said, recalling the admiral in command of the *Regalle* task force. "Nek Bwua'tu can't keep the rest of the military sidelined forever. Sooner or later, the Sith impostors in the officer corps will start convincing their subordinates to ignore the admiral's order. Then they'll start bringing *their* assets into action around the Temple."

Leia saw Han's hand close in a fist and knew she was getting through to him. When he felt helpless, he started to look for soft walls to punch. Unfortunately, he wasn't going to find any in an undercity industrial hangar. She took his arm.

"Han, I just don't think there's any way we *can* help them," she said. "If Luke and the others can't get those blast doors open, their only chance will be to escape before the baradium drops."

Han tensed as though he had found his wall, then glanced at Allana and merely lowered his chin. "Yeah, I know." There was more resignation than resentment in his voice—but the resentment *was* there. "They're Jedi. They're on their own."

Han had barely finished speaking before Allana stepped to his side. "They're not just any Jedi, Dad. They're two of the best Masters ever—and they've got four *really* good Jedi to back them up. And that means they're going to be okay." She took his big hand in hers, then added, "Trust me."

Chapter Eighteen

DOWN THIS DEEP IN ITS SUBLEVELS, THE JEDI TEMPLE SEEMED MORE cave than building. The corridors were so crusted in yorik coral that Vestara sometimes had to turn sideways to squeeze through narrow sections. Fungi grew everywhere, clinging to the walls and ceilings in long shelves and stringy curtains. The air reeked of mildew and vermin. The glow panels still activated on approach, but the light they cast had to pass through several centimeters of grime, resulting in a gloomy pall that usually seemed more shadow than illumination.

Even so, Vestara wasn't lost. The guidance beacons were chirping steadily in the earbud of her salvaged comlink, so this *had* to be the evacuation route. According to the mission briefing, the route led to a secret access tunnel that Han Solo had developed after the Mandalorian siege. Everyone in the assault company had been shown how to use his or her comlink to access a special chirp-code that could be used to find the tunnel entrance.

Of course, Vestara's original comlink had been confiscated after she'd been taken prisoner. But it had been easy enough to Force-summon a new comlink from a dead Jedi Knight while her captors were busy in the water treatment plant, trying to lure Ben into their trap. It had been even easier to slip away during the confusion following the Jedi survivors' daring escape into the freight-handling system.

What had not been easy, however, was staying ahead of her own pursuers. She had expected the Sith to fixate on the Skywalkers. So she had fled in the opposite direction, with the intention of rejoining them later—if it served her. Vestara had barely finished cutting her way through the floor before some Sabers started to give chase, and she had been running ever since.

They seemed to anticipate her every move. They fired at her from intersecting corridors. They sprang out of hidden alcoves. They dropped out of the ceiling or appeared mysteriously ahead. There had to be a dozen of them by now.

And why? It just didn't make sense. An entire division of space marines was pounding the Temple exterior, and Luke Skywalker himself was loose in the interior. Surely the Circle of Lords had more important things to worry about. Vestara was one little Sith girl, fleeing for her life. Not much of a threat. So either the Grand Lord believed punishing her to be more important than defending the Sith foothold on Coruscant—or they believed recapturing her to be worth the drain on their defenses.

But again, *why?* She was just one girl.

A cloaked silhouette appeared ahead, stepping out from the shadows along the wall. He was tall and broad-shouldered, and Vestara feared for a moment that he had gotten ahead of her and been lying in wait. But the man turned in the opposite direction and started down the corridor away from her, and the shadow from which he had come broadened into an intersecting passage.

Vestara did not even break stride. She just raised her hand and unleashed a blast of Force energy. The man's spine arced backward, and he flew down the passage with limbs flung wide. By then, she was five steps from the intersection and wishing she had a grenade—because her pursuers never came alone, and they were seldom fools or cowards.

When no one else emerged from the intersection, Vestara slipped close to the same wall and launched herself into a high, arcing dive over its entrance. She landed hard in a forward roll that was more of a forward *slam* and still managed to come back onto her feet. She extended one leg and pirouetted on the other, coming around just as an emerald-eyed woman stepped from the intersection. Vestara hit Emerald-Eyes with a Force shove and sent her stumbling into the wall.

Then a lightsaber snapped to life behind Vestara. She finished her pirouette and found the Force-blasted man rushing back, his crimson blade already sweeping down at her knee.

Vestara sprang into a one-handed cartwheel, landing a vicious roundhouse kick on the way past his head, then ignited her own blade and brought it sweeping up to finish the fight.

Her moves would have been perfect—except her attacker wasn't there.

He was standing just beyond her reach, shaking his head clear and holding his lightsaber in a low guard that seemed a little too careless. Vestara should have killed him anyway, but that would have taken time—and time she did not have. Back at the intersection, his companion was leaping to her feet, and the sound of running boots was beginning to build in the corridor beyond the intersection. Vestara flashed the man a wry smile and shook her head.

"Sorry." She was winded, so winded she could barely gasp the words. "Not that . . . dumb."

She gave him a Force shove that failed to rock him on his heels, then turned and sprang away. He was after her in a heartbeat, trailing a few steps behind, so close she could hear the weapon sheaths rasping against his trouser legs.

"This is foolish." He was not out of breath at all. "Surrender now, and you won't suffer."

Vestara did not waste her breath on a reply. She had been running and fighting for hours. The only thing keeping her on her feet was the Force itself, and even the Force would fail her soon. Her legs burned and her lungs ached. She had coughed so much phlegm her chest felt like a volcanic eruption. Her vision narrowed at bad moments, and her hearing faded even at good moments, until all that remained was the steady chirping of the guidance beacons.

"There's no escape," her pursuer called, only two paces behind. "Not for you."

Vestara lengthened her stride and pumped her arms harder.

Her pursuer laughed. "You are doing our work for us, little girl," he called. "How long before even the Force betrays you?"

The next time Vestara's right arm came forward, she turned her shoulder to hide her hand from view. She flipped her lightsaber around, pointing its emitter nozzle to the rear. When her hand swung back, she grabbed him in the Force and pulled hard.

She activated her blade.

Her pursuer screamed. Vestara flicked her wrist, dragging the blade through his body. She did not break stride.

Three steps later, she dared to glance back. Emerald-Eyes was a dozen paces behind, pushing hard but not overtaking, running Vestara down.

Twenty meters beyond followed a whole column of dark-cloaked Sith. They were running two abreast, jostling and twisting in the narrow confines, a stream of angry eyes, all fixed on Vestara. There had to be twenty of them now, with a Keshiri woman in the second row whom Vestara recognized as Lady Sashal.

Twenty warriors and a High Lord, all to chase down a single girl. Had the Circle gone mad?

Emerald-Eyes put on a burst of speed, and Vestara felt the hand of the Force close around her. Knowing she needed to break free while she still could, she stopped, changed directions, and launched herself down the corridor behind a Force-enhanced side kick.

A kick that *should* have caught the woman square in the chest.

But the kick missed—and left Vestara standing on one leg, with Emerald-Eyes behind her.

An arm snaked around Vestara's waist, and the cold circle of a lightsaber emitter nozzle touched the side of her neck.

"Drop your lightsaber," the woman ordered. "Move, and you die!"

Vestara dropped her lightsaber and stood very still on one leg. Then she began to think. Sith were not the kind to show mercy, not after a long and grueling chase, not when they had lost several companions to their quarry.

Maybe her pursuers wanted her alive. That would explain all the talking, and the lack of blaster bolts and Force lightning.

"Move and . . . die?" Vestara gasped, still breathing hard. "Really?"

"Try me."

"Sure."

Vestara let her leg collapse, and her weight fell on the arm around her waist. Taken by surprise, Emerald-Eyes failed to catch her, and Vestara dropped like a bag of rocks. When the lightsaber pressed to her throat did not ignite, Vestara knew she was right about the huge effort to capture her. The Sith wanted her—but they wanted her alive.

By the time she hit the floor, Vestara was rolling back toward her captor. She drove an elbow into Emerald-Eyes's knee and heard a *pop*. A nice loud *pop*. The woman screamed, and the crack-siss of an igniting lightsaber sounded above Vestara's head.

Too late.

Vestara was already grabbing for the wrist. She snapped it at the joint, forcing the blade away as Emerald-Eyes collapsed. Vestara accelerated into her roll, driving her foe down hard, and the hollow crack of skull hitting yorik coral echoed off the walls. Yorik coral was harder. Emerald-Eyes went into seizure, body shaking and mouth foaming.

Blaster bolts and Force lightning began to flash up the corridor, some hitting a meter short, most screaming well overhead—suppression fire, meant to keep Vestara pinned until they could recapture her. She pulled Emerald-Eyes's blaster and began to spray bolts back down the corridor . . . *not* suppression fire.

The first shot took out the man in front of Sashal. The second would have taken the High Lord herself had the Saber next to her not used his own arm to deflect the bolt.

The close call was enough to make Sashal and her followers hesitate—only for a second, but that was all the time Vestara needed. Still firing, she grabbed Emerald-Eyes's lightsaber and raced down the corridor.

At least, *racing* was her intent. Instead Vestara's exhausted body began to stumble and stagger. She drew on the Force even more heavily. Every part of her burned. Every part ached. The Force was feeding on *her* now, bursting cell after cell, and it would not be much longer before it devoured her completely.

Better that than be taken alive. Whatever the Circle of Lords wanted with her, she had no illusions about how they would extract it. Her torture would be a violation of body and spirit that would leave her a broken, empty vessel unable to recall her own name.

Blasterfire began to screech past her knees. Sashal was trying to cripple her. Vestara hurled herself into a Force tumble, making it impossible to fire at her legs without risking a head hit. The blasterfire stopped at once, but Vestara could not keep tumbling as fast as her pursuers could run.

She came up on her feet and began to pour blaster bolts into the ceiling ahead, aiming for the glow panels. Her pursuers fired on her legs again. The fiery sizzle of a graze burned her thigh, and then she was running in a pool of darkness. Behind her, the blasterfire ceased.

Vestara ran another ten meters before the sensors activated the next glow panel. Her pursuers managed to snap off a couple of shots before she plunged them back into darkness. Sooner or later, a shot would bring her down—and even if it didn't, the Sith were gaining.

Vestara tipped the blaster pistol over her shoulder and squeezed the trigger, firing blindly. Two shots later, she heard a scream and a thud. She stepped to the other side of the corridor and fired again, and another scream sounded over the steady chirping in her earbud.

Another glow panel activated ahead. Before she could darken it, a blaster screamed behind her. A fiery stabbing took her below the knee. Her leg buckled, and Vestara launched herself into a forward roll and came up firing. The glow panel finally went dark.

Then the guidance chirping began to slow.

Vestara kept rolling, and the chirping in her earbud became even slower. There was a turn coming. She rolled again, then fired back down the corridor. Someone close screamed.

Vestara sprang up on her good leg and limped two steps, then the chirping grew steady. She turned left . . . and felt the floor disappear.

Forcing herself not to cry out, she tucked herself into a ball and bounced down a steep, rugged ramp. It had probably once been a stairwell, but it lay crusted beneath so much dirt and yorik coral it felt more like a hillside. The fall seemed to last forever, and she did what she could to protect herself, using the Force to slow herself and cushion the blow. Still, every time her wounded leg came down, the impact sent a pang of anguish through her entire body.

Finally, Vestara reached a level surface and stopped. She was lying on her back in the darkness. Her head was spinning and her body felt like one big bruise. She had lumps rising on her forearms and on the shin of her uninjured leg, and the wounded leg felt like the bone was on fire. But at least she was alone, and the only sound in her ears was the chirping of the guidance beacons, now rapid and insistent, telling her to turn right.

Vestara rolled to her stomach and looked back up the stairs—or tried to. The automatic illumination was not working in this part of the Temple, and all she could see was darkness. She removed one chirping earbud and listened to the patter of running boots, somewhere above.

They had missed the stairwell—for now. They would discover their mistake as soon as they activated the next set of glow panels. She returned the earbud to its place and followed the chirp signals into the darkness. The space felt large and open, with warm swirling air and faint plopping sounds that seemed to come from every direction.

A dozen painful steps later, the warm air began to puff directly into her face. The plopping sounds grew more infrequent and more likely to come from behind her. She seemed to be entering some sort of broad passage. She thought about using the lightsaber for illumination, but in that echoing labyrinth the distinctive sizzle would be heard hundreds of meters distant. So she continued to limp into the darkness.

And then she heard it: the soft *buphoot* of a puff-fungus expelling its spores.

Vespara clamped her mouth shut and exhaled through her nose, then Force-sprang three paces backward.

She ignited her lightsaber. As she had expected, before her was a slender, knee-high mushroom with a web of sticky feeder-threads draping out of a freshly burst cap, still engulfed in its yellow cloud of paralyzing spores. Just beyond was the mouth of a tunnel about three meters high. The passage had probably been completely round before the yorik coral had taken hold, but now it was more of a lopsided oval. Two more of the deadly fungi stood just inside the tunnel mouth, their caps not yet swollen enough to explode.

Vestara spun in a slow circle, using her lightsaber to illuminate the surrounding area. She was standing on a large platform that ended at the mouth of the tunnel. In the small area that she could see, there were at least six more fungi, along with several large patches of gray

moss. The mosses were probably acid mats, which enwrapped anything that stepped on them.

Lying just at the edge of the light, she saw a large gray cocoon. The
half-meter-long tail of a giant slashrat trailed out of the end, and where
it entered the cocoon, the flesh had been eaten to the bone. Vestara's
heart sank. She had seen such things before, and she knew exactly what
they meant.

Abeloth had come to Coruscant.

From the darkness back near the coral-encrusted staircase came a
distant Keshiri voice, lyrical but angry. "Back here, you fools! I see a
light."

Vestara did not hesitate. She circled past the puff-fungus—she and
Ahri Raas had called them deathstalks on the jungle world—and began
to limp down the ancient tunnel. As far as she could tell, the passage
had been part of some ancient transportation system. It ran straight
and true for over fifty meters, then made a gradual bend to the left and
ran straight for another fifty before starting to descend at a gentle
angle. By then, she could hear the voices of her pursuers crying out in
pain and astonishment as they fell victim to the death fungi. Meanwhile, the guidance chirping was growing stronger. She dared to hope
she was at last nearing the end of the evacuation route.

Then the concussion wave hit.

At first, Vestara didn't understand what had happened. She simply
found herself lying on the tunnel floor with ringing ears and a queasy
stomach. The air felt inexplicably warm and dry, and she could see a
rapidly fading orange glow around the bend behind her.

Grenades.

Vestara hadn't counted on that. She scrambled to her feet and began
to call on the Force again, drawing it into her in a hot torrent of invig-
orating energy. The time had come to escape or die—and it no longer
mattered which, as long as she did not let Sashal take her alive. Using the
Force to leap the acid mats and her blaster to clear the deathstalks and
smotherveils from her path, she broke into an awkward sprint that was
as much hopping and skipping as it was running. Another concussion
wave hit even harder than the last, but this time Vestara was ready. She
simply threw herself into the air and let the wave carry her an extra couple of meters before she landed on her one good leg . . . on a level floor.

Three meters ahead stood an iris hatch. It was too covered in mold and mildew to be called shiny, but it was completely free of yorik coral and equipped with a glowing control panel.

The guidance chirping ceased, and a faintly female computerized voice sounded in Vestara's earbud. "Passcode, please."

"Ees set nesh oh nee wees," Vestara barked. She had a memory for numbers, and she had taken care to rehearse the passcode until she could rattle it off in her sleep. *"Wees nee oh ees set nesh."*

"I am sorry," the voice replied. "That is not the passcode. Would you care to try again?"

"Ese!"

"I am sorry," the voice said again. "The language—"

"Yes!" Vestara interrupted, realizing her mistake. Sashal and her company had been speaking Keshiri, and Vestara had slipped into thinking in her native language without even realizing it. "I would like to try again. Now!"

"Very well," the voice replied. "But this is your last attempt. Your voice pattern has been recorded and—"

The rest of the warning vanished into static as her pursuers set off another grenade. Vestara used the Force to brace herself against the concussion wave, but they were so close now that the durasteel flashed orange with reflected flame, and she was knocked into the hatch anyway.

"Three seven four zero nine two!" Vestara yelled into her throat-mike. "Two nine zero three seven four."

"Passcode accepted."

Vestara stepped away from the hatch, ready to leap through and order it shut behind her.

The hatch remained closed.

A cold prickle raced down Vestara's spine, and she glanced back up the tunnel to see a trio of Sith Sabers racing into view. The one in the middle was holding a live grenade, while the two flanking him were armed to defend him, one with a blaster pistol and the other an activated lightsaber.

Vestara fired three bolts at the Sith in the center, but his companion with the lightsaber simply stepped forward and deflected the attacks into the walls. She was not surprised when the three men stayed long enough to evaluate her situation, then disappeared back up the tunnel just beyond her view.

"Computer?" Vestara whispered into her throat-mike. "What's wrong? The code was correct! I know it was!"

"Affirmative," the voice replied. "The passcode was correct."

"Then open the *sharstung* hatch!" Vestara ordered. "This is an emergency!"

"Emergency acknowledged," the voice replied. "The hatch will open as soon as the outer doors are secure."

"Override!" Vestara ordered. "Open now!"

"Override authorization code, please."

"Three seven four . . ." Vestara stopped herself, realizing that any attempt to bluff her way through an override code was bound to backfire. "Cancel. Just open the hatch at the earliest opportunity."

"Of course," the voice replied. "That *is* the nature of an emergency declaration."

Vestara put her back against the hatch, then sat on her heels and aimed her blaster pistol up the tunnel. Her situation wasn't all *that* bad. All she had to do was hold off the Sabers until the computer sealed the hangar's outer doors. How long could that take? Five seconds? Thirty, at most?

That might have been a problem, had her pursuers been trying to kill her. But they wanted her alive, and they thought they had her trapped. With that kind of advantage, she could hold them off five *minutes,* easy.

A woman's boots came into view, standing on the tunnel floor high enough up the slope that they were all that was visible. Vestara took aim and fired. The tip of a crimson lightsaber swung into view and batted the bolts back toward the hatch. They landed well above her head—but close enough to the control box that she did not want to risk it again.

The boots continued forward another few steps, until Vestara could see the thighs above them. Lady Sashal's voice rang down the passage.

"We can play this game until you deplete your blaster's power cell." The Keshiri dropped to her haunches and met Vestara's gaze. "The only thing you will accomplish is to make me angry. Surrender now, and you will not suffer while you are in my custody."

"What about *after*?" Vestara scoffed, realizing there was more than one way to stall. "Can you guarantee my safety until I speak to Grand Lord Vol?"

A chorus of laughter sounded behind Sashal, and she shook her head. "No one can do that," she said. "Grand Lord Vol has been replaced."

"Replaced?" Though Vestara felt not even the slightest inclination to mourn Vol's passing, her surprise was genuine. "Who could do *that*?"

"Come and see," Sashal replied. "The new Grand Lord is most eager to grant you an audience."

"I'd like to." Vestara glanced up at the control box, wondering how long it would be before the red status light on its face turned green. "But I'm afraid that would interfere with my mission."

"Which mission is that?" Sashal scoffed. "The one to reveal all our secrets to the Jedi? Or the one to kill another High Lord?"

"The one to kill the Jedi queen," Vestara answered. It *had* been her original assignment, and the claim was just audacious enough to sound plausible. "It was assigned to me by High Lord Taalon."

This drew a snort of laughter even from Sashal. "When? Just before you ran a lightsaber through his back?"

"In the Maw," Vestara said. "Shortly before I persuaded the Skywalkers to protect me from him and my father."

A muffled *thunk* sounded on the other side of the hatch, loud enough that Sashal's eyes flicked away from Vestara's face toward the durasteel she was leaning against.

"Lord Taalon died because Abeloth had taken him," Vestara said, trying to hold Sashal's attention for just a few seconds longer. Surely, the hatch would be open by then. "As did my father. I had no other choice."

"There is always a choice, *Jedi* Khai."

Sashal stood, and more boots appeared next to hers. Vestara holstered her blaster pistol and also rose, her lightsaber gripped tight in both hands.

"My mission is the key to the Sith conquest!" she yelled. She felt a slight vibration, as though something heavy had just settled onto the floor on the other side of the hatch. "Let me prove it!"

Sashal stepped into view, surrounded by her Sith. Some were armed with lightsabers and some with blasters, and a couple were still holding grenades—a sure sign, Vestara knew, that they, too, had sensed the activity on the other side of the hatch.

But the High Lord did not order a charge. She simply locked gazes with Vestara and said, "Very well. Prove it to me."

Vestara couldn't believe it. Was her stalling tactic actually going to save her?

"And if I do?" she asked. "You'll let me go so I can complete my mission?"

A mocking sneer came to Sashal's face. "Of course," she said. "If you prove to me that this mission is real, how could I refuse you?"

"You couldn't," Vestara agreed. She was beginning to think that her position just might be better than she had dared to hope—that it might even be possible for her to return to the Lost Tribe as a hero and a Lord herself. "I can tell you the identity of the Jedi queen. Would that be proof enough of my mission?"

An astonished silence fell over the entire Sith company, and Sashal's eyes went wide. The Keshiri studied Vestara for several moments, probing with the Force to see whether she was being truthful. And Vestara let her, because she *was* telling the truth. She knew the identity of the Jedi queen. And if revealing that secret was the only way to survive and go free, then reveal it she would.

A loud *thunk* reverberated through the hatch, and Vestara knew she was out of time. "When that hatch opens, it will be too late," she said. "After I'm seen with you, I'll never be able to get close to the Jedi queen again."

Finally, Sashal nodded. "*If* I believe what you tell me," she said. "But there can be no doubts. I must believe you."

"You will." Vestara deactivated her lightsaber. Hoping to appear more confident than she was, she hung it from her belt. "The Jedi queen's name is Allana Solo."

Sashal frowned, obviously sensing the truth of what Vestara claimed but still struggling to put all the pieces together. "*Amelia* Solo?" she asked. "The adopted daughter of Han and Leia Solo?"

Vestara shook her head. "Her real name isn't Amelia." She was starting to feel hollow and sick inside, for she was well aware of how terribly she had just betrayed Ben—but better to betray him than to die at the hands of a Force torturer herself. "It's *Allana* Solo, and she's not the Solos' adopted anything. She's actually the daughter of Queen Mother Tenel Ka."

Sashal's eyes shone in sudden comprehension, and she deactivated her own lightsaber. "The heir to the Hapan throne lives?" she asked. "And the Solos are raising her?"

"That is what I am saying," Vestara confirmed. "And more. It's common knowledge among the Jedi that Queen Mother Tenel Ka and Jacen Solo were close when they were young. There are those who believe they stayed close even after she assumed the Hapan throne."

"Then Allana is the daughter of the Hapan queen and Jacen Solo?" Sashal started down the tunnel toward the hatch, her company following close behind. "You are certain?"

"What I am *certain* of is that the girl living with the Solos is the Jedi queen," Vestara said. She was more than a little alarmed to see Sashal coming down the tunnel, but she was gambling for everything now— for her life and more, for complete redemption in the eyes of the Lost Tribe and a return to her people as a hero. "And the Jedi are determined to keep her identity secret. It explains everything that happened on Klatooine."

"It's plausible," Sasha agreed, still thinking. "It would explain why your father failed when he tried to kill the Queen Mother. And it makes sense for the Jedi queen to be the child of a Queen Mother and a powerful Jedi Knight."

"A powerful Jedi Knight who became the Sith Lord Caedus," Vestara reminded Sashal. "If the Force has not been at work in this, then I have no idea what the Force is."

"Indeed." As Sashal spoke, the metallic hiss of a retracting iris hatch sounded behind Vestara. The High Lord stopped five paces away—far enough from her to defend or attack. Then she looked through the open hatch into whatever lay beyond . . . and flashed a spiteful grin. "You have done well, Saber Khai. *Very* well."

Sashal extended her arm. Fearing the worst, Vestara snapped the lightsaber off her belt hook. But the High Lord barely seemed to notice. She was still staring over Vestara's shoulder, sneering in open delight.

"Detonator, *now!*" Sashal commanded. She extended an arm behind her. "Five-second fuse!"

The Sith behind Sashal immediatly pressed an armed detonator into her hand—making certain to place the safety pin beneath the High Lord's thumb.

Sashal's gaze shifted to Vestara. She used the Force to turn Vestara's hand palm-upward, then slapped the detonator into her grasp—without the safety pin secured.

"It's your mission, Saber Khai," the High Lord said. "You finish it."

"Of course," Vestara said.

She tried to secure the safety pin again—and failed. Spinning around to locate her target, she found herself looking through the open hatchway into a cramped loading bay. Nearly filling the tiny space was the distinctive teardrop hull of a famous YT-1300 light transport, the *Millennium Falcon,* with the giant green bulk of the Ramoan Jedi, Bazel Warv, just stepping off the boarding ramp onto the loading bay floor. And running down the ramp behind him was a little gray-eyed girl followed by a pet nexu.

"Lady Sashal, you are too generous," Vestara said. Trying to conceal her astonishment, she drew her arm back to throw. "It will be a great honor to be the one who kills the Jedi queen."

Chapter Nineteen

THE VOICE COMING OVER THE FLIGHT DECK SPEAKER WAS CLIPPED AND condescending, with a crisp Hapan accent that made Han's scalp crawl.

". . . is no place for the Chume'da right now," the voice was saying. "She should be on her way home."

"Coruscant *is* her home, in case you've forgotten," Han retorted. Of course, he knew that Taryn Zel would never forget anything about Allana. But when she fired up *the voice* and started in with the Hapan-aristocrat act, he got stubborn. He just couldn't help himself—probably because he had a secret fear that Allana might act the same way someday, after she grew up and returned to live on Hapes. "She's been living here for the last seven years—with *us*."

"I know where she *has* been living, Captain Solo," Taryn said. "That doesn't mean it's safe for her to be with you on Coruscant *now*."

As Taryn spoke, Han was looking through the corner of the view-port, watching the loading bay's coral-encrusted door slowly crawl closed. He thought it had probably been a mistake not to install a faster door when he built the Jedi Temple's secret access tunnel.

He *knew* it had been a mistake not to expand the entire bay. At the time, he had thought that a lot of visible construction would draw too much attention from the denizens of the undercity. But it had been a real trick to squeeze the *Falcon* into such a cramped space. With only four meters of clearance, he had been forced to ease the stern in backward, then spin the nose around and slip in sideways—a complicated maneuver that had drawn attention of its own. Once the Jedi got their Temple back, they were going to need a new secret tunnel—*if* they got their Temple back.

"*Captain Solo?*" Taryn's voice was full of annoyance. "I'm waiting. Are you going to explain yourself?"

"I never explain myself," Han said. "It's a bad habit."

Han heard someone with a deep voice chuckling in the background—probably Zekk, who seemed to take dealing with the arrogance of Hapan women as some kind of sport.

Taryn was silent for a moment, then said, "Then would you please be kind enough to inform me what you're doing down there?"

"I already explained all that," Han said. "Bwua'tu was fresh out of assault cars big enough to carry Jedi Warv. We were the only ones who could deliver him to the tunnel entrance."

"Yes, I understand that part," Taryn said. "What I don't understand is why you had to bring the Chume'da *with* you. Couldn't you have left her at the Jedi headquarters?"

"Not really. But stop worrying. This place is a lot more secure than HQ. There's way less traffic down here, and only a few dozen Jedi even *know* about it."

"How very reassuring," Taryn said, not sounding reassured at all. "Now please stop dodging the question. Why couldn't you leave her with Master Sebatyne back at headquarters?"

Han paused to consider his words. It wasn't going to be easy to convince the woman in charge of the Chume'da's secret bodyguards that Allana was safe—not when he wasn't absolutely sure of that himself.

Finally, he said, "Well, think about it. Leaving her behind didn't exactly work out last time."

Taryn's voice grew incredulous. "You're saying she sneaked aboard the *Falcon* . . . again?"

"It was more like *stomping* aboard than sneaking," Han said. "She wouldn't take no for an answer." .

"And you let her get away with that?" Taryn demanded. "You and Princess Leia are the adults, Captain Solo. At least, you're supposed to be."

"And *she*'s the Chume'da," Han retorted. To tell the truth, he was actually kind of proud of Allana's stubbornness. It showed character. "Besides, after a while Leia said we had to go with it. Some sort of Force thing."

Taryn's voice grew cold. "*Some sort of Force thing* is no reason to risk the Chume'da's life."

"Actually, it is." It was Zekk's deep voice that interrupted, coming over the same channel as Taryn's. "Whether we like it or not, the Chume'da has a destiny tied to the Force. When the Force sends her a vision, it's not our place to question how she responds to it. All *we* can do is be on hand to protect her."

Taryn fell silent, and Han could almost see her biting her lip as she allowed herself to see the wisdom in Zekk's words. Like Han, Taryn was a normal person in love with a Jedi, and like Han, that meant accepting that certain things just had to be taken on faith.

After a moment, a heavy female sigh sounded over the speaker. "Very well, Captain Solo. But you *are* protecting her, are you not?"

"Of course. Stop worrying. Just stay up there and fly top cover for us." Han activated the exterior cam to check on Allana. She was standing just outside the ship, on the boarding ramp with Bazel. Her brow was furrowed and her neck craned as she looked up at her huge friend. She was issuing instructions and tapping her index finger into the Ramoan's giant green thigh. "She's just giving Bazel some last-minute orders before he heads off to warn the Barabels. We'll be on our way in no time."

As he spoke, the loading bay's slow-moving door *finally* crawled its way closed, then settled into its seat with a loud boom. Han glanced over his shoulder to where R2-D2 stood at the droid station.

"Okay, Artoo, tell security to open that door again *now*," Han said. After the *Falcon* had entered the loading bay, the facility's stubborn security computer had insisted on closing the door—even refusing an override command to leave it open. "We'll be ready to leave before it clears."

R2-D2 tweeted an acknowledgment. A second later he added a notification tweedle. Han turned forward again and saw a message scrolling across his primary display.

SECURITY IS UNABLE TO COMPLY IMMEDIATELY. THERE IS AN EMERGENCY ACCESS REQUEST AT THE TUNNEL HATCH.

"An emergency request?" Han turned toward the back of the loading bay, where the access tunnel began its run into the Jedi Temple. The iris hatch was already half dilated, revealing the torso of a young woman in light molytex armor. She seemed to be turned half away, as though looking at something behind her. "What the blazes?"

"Captain Solo?" Taryn's voice was filled with alarm. "What's wrong?"

"Stand by," Han said, still watching as the hatch completed its dilation. "We've got company."

"What kind of company?"

"Jedi, I think. Maybe an emergency evacuation."

As Han spoke, the figure turned. She was an attractive female of about sixteen, with brown eyes much darker than her hair. She had a small scar at the corner of her mouth that suggested a cruel smile, and in her hand, she held a small silver orb that looked all too familiar.

"Vestara Khai?" Han gasped.

His gaze went back to the silver orb, and his confusion vanished in a flash of understanding and rage. He activated the external speakers.

"Detonator!" he yelled. "Everyone, get back in here—"

Before Han could add the word *now,* Vestara stepped through the open hatch. For a moment, Han thought she wasn't going to attack after all, that he was misinterpreting what he was seeing and this was just some strange sequence of events that did not yet make sense.

Then Vestara moved aside, revealing a long line of dark-robed warriors behind her. Han activated the ship's automatic blaster cannon and designated the hatch as the target area. Vestara used a gentle underhand pitch to toss the detonator toward the *Falcon,* then continued to hold her hand up, using the Force to guide the silver orb toward the boarding ramp. Han glanced back at his cam display, hoping to see Leia and Bazel leaping to safety with Allana in tow.

Instead he saw Anji, springing toward the tunnel mouth, and Bazel, extending a big green arm in the detonator's direction. The Ramoan waved his hand toward the loading bay wall, and the silver orb veered . . . straight toward the *Falcon*'s flight deck. Han didn't need an astromech droid to tell him its new trajectory would carry it within a few meters of the pilot's seat.

"*Fierfek!*" Han leapt up and sprang toward the access corridor at the rear of the flight deck. "Go, Artoo! Go-go-g—"

A deafening crackle—

—erupted at the far end of the *Falcon*'s flight deck outrigger. Leia jerked her head around and saw the blinding white flash of a thermal detonator explosion. She raised a hand, half shielding her eyes, then stood staring in shock, heart breaking as the ball contracted on itself and vanished, leaving only the truncated end of an access corridor to mark the last place she had seen Han—on the flight deck of his *Millenium Falcon*.

"Grandpa?" Allana's voice grew shrill. "*Grandpa!*"

Allana turned to rush up the boarding ramp, jolting Leia out of her own shock—reminding her that even if the worst *had* happened, Allana still needed her. Leia whirled and lunged, catching the girl by a shoulder.

"Stop! Think!" Leia had to squeeze hard to keep Allana from breaking free. "We're fighting for our lives here. What would your grandfather tell you to do?"

Allana stopped struggling, and her eyes grew strong. "Figure the game."

"That's right." Leia glanced toward the back of the loading bay, where two dark-cloaked Sith were stepping through the open hatch. "Assess, *then* act. And retreating into a disabled vessel—"

"Is dumb," Allana finished. She spun around and started back down the boarding ramp. "Barv! We're in big—"

"*Trouble,*" Bazel finished. His lightsaber was already crackling to life. "I know."

The first blasterfire erupted from the tunnel mouth, and Bazel started to bat energy bolts back toward the Sith. Leia hesitated a heart-beat, torn between protecting Allana and retreating to check on Han. Then she ignited her own blade and raced to defend her granddaughter.

Allana was already darting into position behind Bazel, using his pivoting bulk as a shield while she reached for the huge blaster pistol strapped to his thigh. Before Leia could yell at her to stop, the Ramoan froze, and Allana pulled the weapon from its holster.

"Got it?" Bazel asked.

"Got it."

Allana dropped to a knee behind Bazel's huge leg and shouldered the weapon. She opened fire, loosing bolts so rapidly they seemed to flow out in a steady stream. The closest Sith swung his lightsaber low to defend his ankle, brought it high to protect his head, then pivoted away and swept it low again to deflect a knee shot. The fourth bolt caught him in the ear, and Leia felt the Force shudder with the shock and confusion of a little girl who had just killed a man.

Leia took a position to Allana's left and started to send energy bolts flying back toward the Sith. She was not surprised that Allana and Bazel had rehearsed a few maneuvers, or even that someone—no doubt Taryn Zel—had taught her granddaughter to shoot so well. But that didn't mean Allana was prepared for the guilt and fear and relief that came of killing a person at close range.

Allana didn't freeze. She just switched to the next Sith and put him down as quickly as the first. Leia felt a pang of sorrow in the Force— but also determination, and even a little anger. Allana understood their situation. She knew what to do.

Leia just wished *she* knew what to do. The Sith were slipping from the tunnel in two-person teams and working their way along the walls, trying to flank the little girl and her protectors before attacking. Running for cover would only trigger a charge, and trying to hole up aboard the *Falcon* would be suicide.

An imperious Keshiri female emerged from the tunnel alone. Allana opened fire on her, but the lavender-skinned woman sent the bolts streaking back so accurately that Leia had to step in to help defend her granddaughter from her own fire. Even then, two bolts slipped past in two seconds, and Allana wisely stopped firing and rolled behind Bazel's massive leg.

Already well trained, she snatched a fresh power cell from the storage pouch on the Ramoan's thigh holster. She ejected the old power cell, slipped the fresh one into place, then called, "What now, Grandma?"

"We hold on until Taryn and Zekk get here," Leia said, though she had no idea how they would manage *that*. A dozen Sith were firing on them already, and more came out of the tunnel every second. "Hit your panic alarm."

"Grandma!" Allana's voice was indignant. "I did *that* a long time ago."

"Okay, well . . ." A bolt screamed past, so close that Leia smelled her own scorched hair. "We need cover."

"Good idea," Allana agreed. "Where?"

"You pick," Leia replied. A flurry of bolts erupted from Leia's left, and she barely pivoted around in time to deflect them into the *Falcon*'s belly. "Can't stop to look."

"Plan C," Bazel rumbled.

"Yeah," Allana said. She popped up behind Bazel, then cradled the huge blaster pistol in her elbow and extended one hand above her head. "It's what Grandpa would do."

"Plan C?" Leia asked, not sure she really wanted to know. "What's Plan—"

"The last thing they'll ever expect," Allana explained. As she spoke, Bazel dropped to a knee in front of her. She grabbed a handful of collar and dug her feet into his waist belt, then pulled herself up and rested the barrel of the huge blaster pistol across his shoulder. "We charge!"

Bazel stood and thundered toward the tunnel, his jade bulk twisting and turning behind the whirling brilliance of his lightsaber. Allana poured blaster bolts over his shoulder. Sith danced and dived out of their path, some with fresh holes smoking in their throats or knees. Realizing that her granddaughter was right—that charging was *exactly* what Han Solo would do—Leia cast a last glance up the boarding ramp, silently willing Han to appear—to come racing down to join the charge.

But Han was nowhere to be seen.

Now that she had half a second, when not busy batting blaster bolts

away from Allana, Leia reached for Han in the Force . . . and felt him
alive, inside his beloved ship. He wasn't in pain, but he wasn't moving.
He was angry and determined and almost smug.

As usual, Han Solo had something up his sleeve.

Leia filled her presence with a love she knew he wouldn't feel, then
sprang after her granddaughter, confident that she was doing exactly
what he would have told her to do, had he been able.

But that didn't make leaving any easier.

A smoking hole erupted in Bazel's enormous shoulder. He whirled
so fast Allana would have been thrown free had she not been using the
Force to keep herself stuck to her huge green friend. Another bolt took
him in the chest, and Leia realized the Ramoan was spinning to shield
Allana. She reached his side and began to bat bolts back toward the Sith.

"Go!" she ordered. "I've got your back!"

Bazel pivoted toward the tunnel entrance, now only a few steps
away, and thundered forward. Leia spun into position behind him,
running backward, her lightsaber painting loops of color above her
head as she defended Allana.

By now the Sith had them outflanked. Leia heard the *thud-sizzle* of
a dozen bolts burning into Ramoan flesh. Her own leg swung back of
its own accord, and she nearly fell, catching her balance on a wounded
leg that felt like boiling oil. Allana's blasterfire became a constant
shriek, and the growl of clashing lightsabers sounded on the other side
of Bazel's dancing bulk.

Then the Force lightning came.

Leia caught the first fork on her own lightsaber. Less than ten paces
away, a second Sith stopped and raised her hands, her fingertips curling toward Allana.

Leia grabbed for her granddaughter in the Force. "Off!" she commanded, trying to pull Allana from Bazel's shoulders. *"Now!"*

Allana came sliding down, and the lightning crackled past only centimeters above Leia's head. Bazel's voice boomed in surprise and anguish.

Allana knelt next to Leia. She opened fire, and three shots later the
woman who had just tried to kill her was down. So was the man who
had wounded Leia.

The floor shuddered, and even before Leia heard the *snip-sizzle* of a hot blade popping through flesh, she knew Bazel was down. Taking her granddaughter by the arm, Leia spun around his kneeling bulk and emerged on the other side—and found herself facing half a dozen crimson blades. Allana's blaster pistol shrieked twice, and a tall Sith dropped sideways, releasing a lightsaber that had been buried in Bazel's chest.

Amazingly, the Ramoan wasn't finished. His green blade swept across in front of him, smashing through the guard of two Sith—slicing them apart at the shoulders—before a powerful dark-bearded man finally blocked the attack.

Bazel's free arm shot out, collapsing the man's chest around a massive fist.

"Behind me," Bazel ordered. He began to rise. "We stop for—"

A thunderous chuffing erupted behind them. The entire ceiling of the loading bay flashed blue, and four geysers of molten durasteel erupted near the ceiling on the wall ahead. Leia turned. She saw R2-D2 coming down the boarding ramp toward them—and a familiar face winking at her through the *Falcon*'s belly turret.

"*Han!*"

The weapon barrels began to depress, and Leia saw what he intended. She spun back around to find Bazel on his feet again. He was sweeping his long lightsaber back and forth like a scythe—not actually *killing* any Sith, but knocking them off-balance and sending them flying out of his path. Allana was a pace behind him, facing the *Falcon* and staring at the belly turret with a gaping mouth.

"*Wait!*" Allana gasped. "Grandpa's *alive?*"

"Of course, dear." Leia threw herself over Allana, at the same time hitting Bazel with the most powerful Force shove she could manage. "Now get down so Grandpa can shoot!"

They were still falling when the chuffing started again. She extended her arms to keep from flattening Allana, but even so she heard a loud gasp as they hit the floor together.

"Are you hurt?"

"No . . . way!" Allana's voice was barely audible over the roaring and crashing of the laser cannons. She began to squirm beneath Leia, no doubt trying to see what was happening around them. "But I'm worried about Barv."

"Me, too."

Leia put a hand on Allana's back to keep her from lifting her head too high, then looked forward and—beneath the fiery sheet of crashing cannon fire—saw that the big Ramoan was *still* battling Sith. He had at least three trapped beneath his huge green body, which was jerking and twitching as they hacked at his belly and chest with their parangs and whatever else they could bring to bear. But the Ramoan was giving better than he took. He had one man's throat squeezed shut, another one's skull locked in his crushing grasp, and a third pinned beneath his slashing tusks.

Between the Ramoan and the tunnel lay a smoking tangle of body parts that had once been Sith warriors. Some of the pieces were still moving, and a couple were even clutching lightsabers in their twitching hands. But none was in any condition to be a threat to Allana—or to anyone else.

Leia could tell by the molten metal and jagged holes around the tunnel mouth that Han had poured a lot of fire down it, but that didn't mean there were no survivors lurking inside. On the other hand, there were probably a lot of nooks and crannies in the loading bay itself where their Sith enemies could have taken cover—and it wouldn't be long before they recovered from the initial shock of the cannon attack.

She glanced back toward the *Falcon*. The laser cannons were still sweeping toward the right side of the loading bay, firing on full automatic and cutting down anything that moved—and most of what didn't. R2-D2 was already within a couple of meters of her, coming out of the smoke with his grasping arm extended and a grenade in the pincer claw.

Leia tried to catch sight of her husband inside the belly turret, but the smoke was too thick and the flashing of the cannons too bright. She shook her head. *He really* does *think of everything!*

She extended her hand and used the Force to gently tug at the grenade. To her relief, R2-D2 seemed to understand and opened his claw. The grenade was a Merr-Sonn C-20 concussion model, perfect for clearing the tunnel without rendering it impassable. Leia set the fuse for two seconds and removed the safety pin, then finally took her weight off Allana.

"When I run—"

"I follow," Allana yelled back. "I *have* had evasion training, you know!"

Leia *did* know, and it broke her heart to realize just how essential that training had been. Her nine-year-old granddaughter was already a veteran of several assassination attempts and practically an old hand at close-quarters combat.

R2-D2 rolled past, making straight for the tunnel. Leia released the firing handle and tossed the grenade ahead of the droid, then used the Force to float it into the mouth of the passage—where it stopped dead as someone inside caught it in the Force. Leia pushed harder and felt the Sith pushing back. Then a white flash filled the tunnel, and Leia felt nothing inside the passage at all.

Pulling Allana up beside her, Leia jumped to her feet—and felt a cold ripple race up her spine. She shoved Allana forward.

"Go!" she yelled. "And blast anything that moves in there!"

As Leia spun around, Sith heads started to pop into view, peering over smoking bodies and from behind the *Falcon*'s struts. Bolts of energy began to streak toward her from half a dozen directions. She deflected the first three, then launched herself into a backward Force flip—and nearly collapsed when she came down hard on her injured leg.

Bazel was two meters away from Leia, trailing long loops of intestine as he crawled toward her—and the tunnel—on hands and knees. She switched to a one-handed grip and extended her free hand toward the Ramoan, trying to use the Force to help him to his feet.

A fork of Force lightning crackled past a fist's width above his back, and Leia barely managed to catch it with her one-handed lightsaber grip. Bazel looked up and shook his head.

"No." A pained smile creased his wide mouth, and one of his tiny eyes squeezed shut in a weary wink. "It's an . . . act."

Leia felt her grasp slipping and had to grab her lightsaber with both hands. Bazel slumped, but instead of dropping back to his belly, he lifted himself higher, into the path of the Force lightning.

"Go!" he boomed. "Allana needs . . ."

Allowing the sentence to trail off, he simply pointed at the tunnel. Then, incredibly, he rose to his feet again and turned, bringing his lightsaber up to catch the Force lightning. Somehow, over the roar of the *Falcon*'s cannon turrets and the screaming blasters and the hissing lightsabers, Leia heard Allana crying out for her friend, begging him to come back.

Bazel was right. Allana needed her.

Leia turned and raced into the tunnel mouth. There she found Allana kneeling among the corpses, Bazel's huge blaster pistol braced atop R2-D2's grimy dome and tears streaking down her face. She was continuing to pour fire out into the loading bay, trying to help her big green friend. Judging by the blaster wounds in some of the bodies strewn around Allana, Leia could tell that at least a few of those Sith had still been alive when Allana entered the passage.

"I *told* them to surrender," Allana said, almost shouting to make herself heard over her screaming blaster pistol. "But they just kept reaching for their weapons."

"Then you had no choice," Leia said. She glanced up the tunnel. "Did any—"

"No," Allana yelled, shaking her head. "No one escaped. I killed them. All of them."

"It's okay, Allana." In truth, Leia didn't know if it would ever be okay. The despair and cold detachment in her granddaughter's voice tore at her inside—perhaps because it reminded Leia of what Allana's father had become—but she could offer no comfort or wisdom until they were safe. "You did the right thing."

Leia turned back toward the loading bay and was astonished to see Bazel still on his feet, spinning through a storm of blasterfire. His robe had been reduced to smoking tatters, and his green hide was pocked by so many burn holes that he appeared to be spotted. Meanwhile a steady stream of cannon bolts continued to pour from the *Falcon*'s belly turret, melting a long furrow into the loading bay's durasteel wall.

Bazel seemed to be following the cannon barrage as it continued to sweep away from the tunnel mouth. Leia thought he was simply trying to draw the enemy away from her and Allana—until four more Sith emerged from the smoke. They were angling toward the place where the *Falcon*'s flight deck used to be, no doubt preparing to board through the now-open access corridor and end the fire from the belly turret.

Leia deactivated her lightsaber and reached for Bazel's oversized blaster. Allana shook her head.

"No." She continued to fire, slipping a stream of bolts past Bazel's flank and forcing the four Sith to slow their advance. "I'm a *really* good shot, Grandma."

"Yes, you are," Leia agreed. "But you're only nine, and—"

"You're just afraid I'll see Grandpa and Bazel die," Allana finished. "And I'm afraid I *won't.*"

"Allana." Leia continued to hold out her hand, her heart breaking at the thought of losing Han—and having her granddaughter see it. "Please."

"They're doing this for me," Allana said. She managed to put a bolt through the leader's knee, and a tall blond woman stepped forward to take the man's place. "And I want to remember it. I *need* to remember it."

The blond woman began to bat Allana's fire back toward the tunnel, and there was no debating the issue. Leia activated her own lightsaber just in time to deflect the bolts, and then Bazel closed with the remaining Sith and vanished into a tangle of swirling color.

The chugging cannons continued their deadly sweep, taking out a forward landing strut as they raked the area beneath the cargo mandibles. The *Falcon*'s nose dipped toward the missing strut.

Then a trio of blue flashes appeared from the *Falcon*'s stern, taking the blond in the flank and driving her into Bazel's flashing blade. Leia glanced over to see the aft cargo lift dropping out of the *Falcon*'s belly. Naturally, her husband was kneeling behind a corner post, pouring fire into the swarm attacking Bazel. The *Falcon*'s big quad cannons, obviously locked on automatic mode, continued to burn furrows into the loading bay walls.

A Sith quickly stepped away from the fight with Bazel and began to bat Han's blasterfire back toward him. He dived off the lift into a forward roll and came up on one knee, less than five paces from the tunnel mouth.

Then Han stopped firing and spun back around, facing the *Falcon*'s belly turret. He began to fumble for something inside his vest pocket.

"What the . . ." Leia gasped. Thinking he must be disoriented or wounded, she put the Force behind her voice and added, *"Han! Get over here!"*

When he merely continued to fumble in his pocket, she reached for him in the Force and started to drag him toward the tunnel mouth—until Han withdrew his hand holding a silver rectangle that Leia recognized as an electronic droid caller.

Han pointed the caller toward the *Falcon*'s sensor dish. The belly turret suddenly reversed direction, and cannon fire began to sweep back toward Bazel and his attackers. Most of the Sith simply broke off and dashed for cover, but the one who had turned to defend the group against Han's blasterfire rushed to intercept him.

Bazel roared in fury and charged after him. With one arm gone and his flesh burned and bleeding, the big Ramoan should have been dead by now. Leia had no doubt that he already *was,* by some medical definitions of the word. But Bazel was still drawing on the Force, calling on its power—and no doubt his devotion to Allana—to keep fighting. He caught up in a step and a half, bringing his lightsaber in for a low leg-slash that the Sith barely managed to spin around and block.

Too exhausted to launch another attack, Bazel fell to his knees, roaring in rage and pain as the *Falcon*'s laser cannons continued to sweep toward him. Seeing what was about to happen, the Sith turned to flee. Bazel dropped his lightsaber and extended his hand, using the Force to summon his last enemy back into his grasp.

The Sith counterattacked wildly, using a powerful two-handed lightsaber strike to hack at Bazel's arm and shoulder. The Ramoan ignored him and merely looked toward the tunnel mouth, his small sad eyes dropping to where Allana was kneeling at Leia's side. He flicked his chin toward her, motioning her to go.

Han stumbled into the safety of the tunnel mouth, out of breath and huffing. Leia caught him by the arm and held him up, and then they both turned and saw that the laser cannons would soon cut through Bazel and his attacker. Han quickly raised his hand, pointing the droid caller toward the *Falcon*'s sensor dish, but Allana grabbed his arm.

"No, Grandpa!" she shouted. Her voice was barely audible over the roaring of the cannons. "That's how he wants to go."

Han's gaze shifted back toward the Ramoan, who had just lost his second arm and part of his skull to his foe's lightsaber, then nodded and lowered his hand.

Allana pushed in tight between Leia and Han, then raised three fingers to her lips and held them there until the cannon fire reached Bazel Warv, her best friend ever.

Chapter Twenty

IT WAS A RELIC OF THE OLD IMPERIAL ARROGANCE, TAHIRI THOUGHT, that Vitor Reige would allow the *Bloodfin*'s communications officer to waste so much bandwidth on an Imperial News Network report that obviously held no interest for his commander in chief. Seated at the head of the conference table in the admiral's salon, Jagged Fel was paying more attention to the personal datapad on his lap than to the holographic riot raging above the transceiver pad, and if he was listening to the droning voice of the political operations instructor he had drafted from the Imperial military academy, there was no indication of it in his distracted manner.

"... can see, the unrest continues to spread," said the instructor, a gray-haired commodore named Selma Djor.

As she spoke, Djor used a laser pointer to draw attention to the mob of thugs above the holopad. The image showed them charging into a line of political supporters, most of whom were carrying signs with Jag's name above a slogan too small to be legible in the image.

"To tell the truth," Djor continued, "I'm beginning to believe a general election isn't appropriate for Imperial citizens. Most of our subjects simply aren't capable of participating in the democratic process."

As Djor spoke, Tahiri expanded her Force awareness toward Jagged. Finding his presence filled with loneliness and fear, she understood the reason for his preoccupation. The assault on the Jedi Temple was well under way, and it was not going well. It only made sense that he would be checking for an update from Jaina. That was probably why he had scheduled Djor's briefing for this time slot—because he had known he would be distracted by his concern and did not want to have to concentrate on anything important. It was so *Jag* to plan ahead like that, and Tahiri couldn't help feeling a bit envious of Jaina. Not that she wanted Jagged for herself—she just wanted to feel that kind of love again, to know there was someone out there who cared for her so much he actually planned time to worry about her.

Djor abruptly fell silent and frowned at Jagged. She looked like a headmistress who had caught one of her charges watching the latest episode of *Flame Flicker* on his datapad.

"Please continue, Commodore," Jagged said, not bothering to look up. "I *am* listening."

"You may be listening, Head of State Fel," Djor replied. "But without actually seeing these images, I doubt you can comprehend the situation fully."

Jagged's Force aura blazed with a sudden anger, and he looked up to meet Djor's gaze.

"Commodore Djor," Jagged began, "your orders were to remain on Bastion to oversee the development of a *proper* electoral apparatus. Yet you have come all the way to Exodo Two to do . . . what, exactly? To persuade me that the Imperial populace is too ignorant to participate in a general election? That the Empire does such a poor job of educating its citizens that they are simply too *ignorant* to vote for their own leader?"

Djor drew herself to attention. "Not at all, Head of State Fel," she said. "But the evidence suggests that the citizenry isn't prepared to act responsibly at this time. There's a good possibility that . . . well, that they might not make a wise decision."

"And by 'not make a wise decision,' you mean the citizens might choose Daala?" asked Ashik. Jagged's chief aide and head bodyguard, the blue-skinned Chiss was standing at his superior's shoulder, directly opposite Tahiri. "Is that correct?"

Djor glanced at Ashik, then returned her gaze to Jagged. "I'm afraid that Lieutenant Pagorski's efforts are turning public opinion against you, Head of State," she said. No sooner had an election been announced than Lydea Pagorski—the same security officer who had given false testimony at Tahiri's murder trial on Coruscant—had turned up as Daala's primary campaign coordinator. "Your insistence on keeping Daala and her allies inside the blockade is being perceived as weakness. Most people assume you're simply afraid of her fleet strength."

"Or that she's the better tactician?" Jagged asked.

Djor dipped her head in acknowledgment. "That, too, Head of State," she said. "It simply makes you look . . . *frightened*."

"Yet you believe the citizenry isn't ready for an election," Jagged said, looking surprisingly satisfied. He glanced over at Ashik. "It certainly *sounds* as though they're paying attention."

Ashik nodded. "Indeed it does, Head of State."

Djor glanced in confusion from Jagged to the Chiss, then said, "Forgive me if I'm wrong, but I *do* assume that we all agree Head of State Fel is the superior choice. Otherwise, what's the point of opposing Daala at all?"

"Exactly, Commodore," Jagged said. "What *would* the point be?"

Tahiri could see by the gleam in Jagged's eye that there was more to his plan than he had shared—even with her. Not only had he anticipated the doubts Djor had mentioned, he was *counting* on them.

When Jagged did not elaborate, Admiral Reige said, "I'm afraid I agree with Commodore Djor." Seated on Jagged's right-hand side, he was the only other person in the cabin who was not standing. "I fail to see how this kind of mob violence benefits you—or the Empire."

Jagged gave him a confident smile. "Only because you've never lived in a democracy, Admiral." He took his datapad out of his lap and placed it on the table, then finally glanced at the holographic riot. "In a real democracy, it's not the result that is important. It's the process."

Reige's eyes betrayed his doubt, and he and Djor exchanged worried glances.

Jag smiled patiently. "People will only truly follow a leader if they choose that leader themselves."

Djor rolled her eyes, and Reige looked even more worried.

"If I may," Tahiri said, addressing Jagged, "perhaps I should explain the *real* reason you agreed to this election."

Jag's smile changed to a smirk, and he actually looked impressed. "Be my guest." He glanced at a pair of puzzled-looking Imperials, then said, "I'm looking forward to hearing this as much as you are."

Tahiri started to feel less confident of her conclusion, but said, "Clearly, you're laying a trap."

"And?" Jag steepled his fingers and looked at her expectantly. "I hope you can do better than that, Tahiri. I'd hate to think Jaina's confidence in you is misplaced."

Tahiri frowned. "*Jaina*'s confidence?" She glanced down at the datapad. "I thought she was still inside the Jedi Temple."

"She is," Jagged said. "And no, I haven't heard if the shields are down yet. This is something she suggested after their last attempt failed."

"You commed to ask her for *advice*?" Tahiri asked. "In the middle of a battle?"

"Not quite," Jagged said. "She commed *me*. They were trying to regroup, and she had a few minutes. So she asked HQ to set her up with an S-thread feed."

There was a hint of sorrow in his eyes, and Tahiri knew there had been more to the conversation than Jag would share in front of his subordinates. Probably, Jaina had asked to speak with him because she feared it might be her last chance to say good-bye. Tahiri held Jag's gaze a bit longer than was needed, letting him know she understood how difficult it must be for him to be *here*—instead of helping Jaina on Coruscant—then flashed him a supportive smile.

"And when you and Jaina ran out of other things to talk about, the conversation naturally turned to Daala," Tahiri said. "Jaina suggested a way to deal with her."

"Something like that," Jagged said. He turned to Reige and Djor. "Jedi Solo has a wonderfully devious mind, when the occasion demands."

"Behind every great leader stands a great adviser," Djor said tightly.

"However, you might want to keep her role confidential until *after* she becomes an Imperial citizen, don't you think?"

"*Jaina?*" Tahiri gasped, unable to contain her shock at the idea. "An Imperial citizen?"

"Of course," Reige said, scowling at her. "If she's going to marry the Head of State, she'll become a citizen of the Empire."

Trying not to laugh, Tahiri looked to Jagged. "I'll bet *that* conversation went well," she said. "I'd give anything to see Han's face when someone tells him that his only daughter will have to join the Empire to marry you."

"We haven't actually discussed that yet." Jagged paled at the thought, then gathered himself with a shudder. "And stop trying to change the subject. Do you know what I need you to do, or don't you?"

Tahiri thought for a moment, trying to imagine how Jaina would handle a problem such as Daala. "She arranged for the Jedi to loan you a StealthX, didn't she?"

Jagged nodded. "She did."

"And shadow bombs?" Tahiri asked.

"An entire rack," Ashik replied.

"I see," Tahiri said. She took a deep breath, trying to decide how she felt about what Jagged was asking her to do, then finally shook her head. "I'm sorry, Head of State Fel. Attacking the *Chimaera* during the battle would have been one thing. But now that you and Daala have agreed to a truce, I'd be committing the same crime I'm accused of in Admiral—"

"It's not Daala," Jagged interrupted. "It's nothing that easy."

Tahiri frowned. "Then I don't understand," she said. "If you're not sending me after Daala, then who *are* you trying to trap?"

Jagged pointed to the holographic riot still raging above the transceiver pad. "The one who's behind *that*," he said. "I'm sending you after Abeloth."

"*Abeloth?*" Reige gasped. He leaned closer to the holo, as though he actually expected to see her in the riot, then finally nodded. "Of course. She is on Daala's side."

"I wouldn't assume *that*," Jagged said. "But she's certainly not on ours."

"That does seem doubtful, from what you have told me of her." Reige turned to Tahiri. "And you can find this Abeloth?"

Tahiri remained quiet, mentally sorting through all the Imperial Intelligence reports she had been reading lately, then realized she had a decent idea of where to start looking.

"Didn't I see something about a certain Mandalorian who was seen on Hagamoor Three?" she asked.

Reige frowned at Jagged. "That communiqué was Utmost Secret," he said. "Am I to assume that you are now in the habit of granting unvetted security clearances to prisoners?"

Jagged shrugged. "Tahiri *was* a Jedi, Admiral. Who's to say how she knows what she knows?"

Reige's eyes smoldered, and he turned back to Tahiri. "I don't suppose *you'd* care to enlighten us?"

"The thing is, Boba Fett is the one who broke Daala out of the Galactic Alliance's detention center," Tahiri said, dodging Reige's question. "So if *Abeloth* is working with Daala . . ."

Irritated though he was, Reige was quick to see the connection. "Then Abeloth might be on Hagamoor Three with Fett," he said. "Though I *should* mention that the Mandalorian's identity wasn't established. We don't know for certain that it was Fett."

"But Hagamoor Three is part of the Getelles holdings, correct?" Jagged asked. "It's a moon orbiting Antemeridias?"

Reige nodded. "It is."

"And that would be the same moon where the nanovirus scientists have gone into hiding?" Jagged asked. "The ones who developed the strain that targeted the Hapan Chume'da?"

Tahiri had not seen *that* detail in the reports.

"That's what Eye-eye reports," Reige said, using the common acronym for Imperial Intelligence. "And everything certainly points in that direction. But the reports haven't been confirmed."

"Of course not," Jagged said. "Otherwise, those scientists would all be under arrest." He turned to Tahiri. "These would be the same scientists who developed the nanovirus strain that Admiral Atoko released into Mandalore's atmosphere."

"Then I think we know the identity of the Mandalorian on Hagamoor Three," Tahiri said. "And if that's where Boba Fett is, it's as good a place as any to start looking. If I can pick up his trail, maybe I'll be able to trace it—or *him*—back to Abeloth's hiding place."

"Then you'll be going to Hagamoor Three?" Reige asked. "To find Boba Fett—so you can use *him* to find Abeloth?"

His expression was equal parts disbelief and respect.

Tahiri nodded. "So it seems," she said. "If you'll return my lightsaber."

"Of course, Prisoner Veila," Reige said. For the first time since Tahiri had met him, he gave her a broad smile. "Quite honestly, I can say that returning your lightsaber will be my great pleasure."

"Uh, thanks . . . I think," Tahiri said. She turned to Jagged. "And assuming I find her?"

"I don't care about Fett one way or another, but do whatever it takes to stop Abeloth," Jagged said. "I'll assign you a frigate—with my full authorization to use it however you must."

Tahiri cocked her brow. "As in *vape* her?"

"Back to her atoms," Jag said. "All I ask is that you do what you can to limit collateral loss of life."

"Of course," Tahiri replied. "And thank you for trusting me with something like that."

"We *all* want Abeloth destroyed, prisoner Veila. And if you succeed, you'll have a pardon for any and all crimes against the Empire." Jagged turned to look at Reige. "Is that acceptable, Admiral Reige?"

Reige's brow rose in surprise. "I'm grateful that you would ask, Head of State." He fell silent and regarded Tahiri for a moment, then finally said, "Fett *and* Abeloth? If she survives *that*, I'd sign the pardon myself."

Jagged smiled. "Thank you, Admiral," he said. "And if you *should* happen to become the next Head of State, I'll expect you to honor your word."

Reige's smirk turned worried. "Sir?"

"My trap," Jagged said. "Prisoner Veila hasn't explained *your* part in it yet."

Reige looked back to Tahiri, who quickly looked back to Jagged.

"You want *me* to explain this?" she asked. "You're sure?"

"Who better?" Jagged turned to Djor. "Unless *you* would care to enlighten the admiral, Commodore?"

Djor frowned, then said, "I'd be happy to, Head of State—if I had the slightest idea what you're thinking."

Jagged shook his head in mock disappointment. "This is going to be harder than I thought. Imperials clearly have no idea how democracy works." He flicked a hand toward Tahiri. "I'm afraid you'll have to do it, prisoner Veila."

"Very well, Head of State." Tahiri faced Reige and returned the cruel smile he had given her earlier. "Admiral Reige, you're going to be what's known as a spoiler."

Reige frowned. "A spoiler?" He looked to Jagged. "What am I to spoil?"

"Daala's chances of winning the election, of course," Jagged explained. "You're about to become the third candidate in the race to become the Imperial Head of State."

Djor's eyes lit with comprehension. "Of course—an admiral against an admiral," she said. "You intend to split the military vote!"

"Very good," Jagged said. "We *might* make a political adviser of you yet."

Reige scowled, looking none too happy about the prospect of running against his superior officer. "I'm sorry, Head of State. Are you *ordering* me to enter the election against you?"

Jagged turned and leaned away from the admiral. "Do I *need* to?"

"Uh, no?" Reige replied, looking more confused than ever. "I'm happy to serve the Empire in any way I can, sir."

"Good." Jagged smiled and stood, then clapped a hand on Reige's shoulder. "You have no idea how happy I am to hear you say that, Admiral."

Chapter Twenty-one

IF THE KILLIKS OF THE CELESTIAL PALACE TRULY BELIEVED THE End OF Time was upon them, they had a strange way of preparing for it. Upon hearing of Abeloth's escape, the nearly dormant hive had burst into action, preparing the nursery comb to receive new eggs and rushing out to prepare for planting. In just days, they had cleared the scrub from their fields and partitioned them into rock-walled plots, and now they were busy opening a giant web of irrigation ditches already beginning to shine with the silver gleam of sunlight on water.

Even Raynar, who understood the unlimited potential of Killik industry better than anyone, found the progress astounding. They had prepared over five square kilometers for planting, and they were already bringing out seed casks to warm in the sun.

But none of that meant their crops would grow. From what Raynar could see, the land surrounding the Celestial Palace was a dust bowl. The ground was so powdery that even a gentle breeze sent clouds of it dancing across the plain, and if the dirt held any humus, it was not enough to be called soil.

A soft rustle sounded in the corridor behind Raynar, and his Killik guide stepped to the window next to him. She braced her upper hands on the sill and leaned out to study the fields below, then began a conversational rumble.

"Little grows here without the Force to help it," she thrummed. *"Still, the hive must prepare and be ready."*

To Raynar's surprise, he understood every word.

"Because the Force will come again soon," the Killik continued.

Raynar did not answer, for a cold knot had formed in his stomach. Maybe he was just remembering a foreign language, the way anyone might after returning to an alien culture in which they had once lived. But the Killik language was incredibly subtle and complex, with touch- and stress-dependent meanings, and over thirty different vowels that all sounded like the letter *U* to the human ear. So as much as he *wanted* to believe the language was just coming back, it seemed far more likely that he understood Thuruht because he was *becoming* Thuruht—because his pheromone counteragent had worn off and he was becoming a Killik Joiner again.

"That is why you have come, to share the Force with the hive," Thuruht said.

"I see," Raynar said, finally beginning to understand why Thuruht had been so circumspect about sharing the hive's knowledge. "And that's why you have been so slow to tell us about Abeloth. You've been stalling until we become Joiners."

"Thuruht is not stalling!" the guide protested. *"How can Thuruht show the Jedi what the Jedi have not prepared themselves to see?"*

"What does it take to prepare?" Raynar asked, fairly certain that he already knew the answer. "Becoming Joiners?"

Thuruht circled her antennae in a negative gesture. *"You are ready now,"* she said. *"The other Jedi require more time."*

"The Jedi can't wait until we're *all* ready," Raynar said, anticipating the Killik's next excuse for continuing to withhold the hive's knowledge. "Abeloth is free now, and our friends are hunting her now."

"Then you must hope your friends fail, or they will die," Thuruht said. *"You will understand, when the time is right."*

"And the time will be right after I share the Force with the hive?"

Raynar asked, trying to get Thuruht to at least name her terms. "Is that what you're proposing?"

"*Without the Force, the hive cannot grow,*" Thuruht said. "*And the hive must grow, if Thuruht is to be ready when the Ones call us to service.*"

The deal could not have been clearer, at least by Killik standards. Thuruht would share its knowledge of Abeloth, and in exchange Raynar would use the Force to help the Thuruht restore its hive. Unfortunately, there were two big problems with the agreement. First, it would anger the Chiss, who had not forgotten the war they had fought the *last* time Raynar had lived among Killiks. Second, if he stayed with Thuruht much longer, all of the counteragents and filters aboard the *Long Trek* would not prevent him from becoming a Joiner again—and there was only one thing in the galaxy that Raynar feared more than losing his identity to a Killik hive again.

That thing was Abeloth.

After a moment, Raynar nodded. "Done," he said. "If you share all of Thuruht's knowledge of Abeloth with me and my friends *now*, I promise to stay behind and use the Force to help the hive reestablish itself. Agreed?"

Thuruht clacked her mandibles in acceptance. "*Now you are ready to see the Histories,*" Thuruht replied. "*And when you understand Abeloth, you will understand how important Thuruht is to the galaxy. You will want to help Thuruht. Even the* Chiss *will see that Thuruht must be strong!*"

With that, Thuruht turned back toward the palace interior, where Lowbacca, Tekli, and C-3PO were studying the reliefs carved into the corridor wall.

Thuruht pointed to a set of panels that depicted a trio of beings living in isolation on a mountainous forest world. One panel depicted a smiling, pale-haired woman with oval eyes. She was running through a forest in full bloom, followed by clouds of butterflies and swarms of frolicking Killiks. The next panel depicted a powerful-looking man in dark armor, marching through a lifeless forest of bare branches and barren ground. He had a craggy face and two stripes tattooed over his bald pate; the only signs of life in his forest were a toad being crushed beneath his boot and a line of Killiks chained behind him.

A third panel depicted a high mountain peak that loomed over both forests, with the barren forest lying to the left side of a dividing river and the forest in bloom to the right. Looking out over the scene from the balcony of a cliffside monastery was a gaunt old man, his arms spread so that one hand was suspended above the dark aspect of the forest and one over the luminous aspect. On the old fellow's face was such an expression of weariness and sorrow that Raynar felt his own shoulders sag, weighed down by a burden as mysterious as it was ancient.

As Raynar stood contemplating the panels, a long Wookiee groan sounded behind him—Lowbacca, complaining that he was tired of having his time wasted and suggesting that they return to the *Long Trek* immediately. The Wookiee went on: they hadn't seen anything *yet* that concerned Abeloth or the Celestials, and he was beginning to think the only connection between Thuruht and the Celestials was the name of their anthill.

Thuruht asked for a translation, and C-3PO said, "Jedi Lowbacca was wondering about the connection between these fine Bururru religious panels and Abeloth." The droid's tone grew confiding. "I'm sorry to say he has no appreciation of art for its own sake. He seems convinced that everything you show us should have some connection to Abeloth or the Celestials."

Thuruht turned to Raynar and thrummed a sharp reply. *"You see? The other Jedi are not ready. They do not see what is in front of them!"*

Raynar wasn't sure that he saw, either. Maintaining a thoughtful silence, he stepped closer to the panels and contemplated the three scenes. The luminous woman and the craggy warrior were no doubt symbols of life and death. Since Thuruht clearly had an understanding of the Force, perhaps the pair even represented its light and dark aspects. And that would mean that the figure in the third panel—the old man with one hand over each aspect of the forest—was a symbol of the Balance.

But that did nothing to explain Abeloth.

Finally, Raynar turned back to Thuruht. "It's not just Jedi Lowbacca who doesn't see. I don't, either."

"Because you look only for what is in the stone," Thuruht replied. *"To find Abeloth, you must see what is missing."*

The Killik had barely spoken before Raynar understood.

"The mother, of course," he said. "We have a Father, a Son, and a Daughter. But there isn't a Mother."

Thuruht droned approval.

And Lowbacca growled in alarm.

Raynar turned to find both of his companions eyeing him. Lowbacca looked ready to snatch Raynar up and run for the *Long Trek*, while Tekli was watching him with narrowed eyes, clearly pondering whether Raynar was still in control of his own mind.

"Raynar," she said, "it appears that you no longer need See-Threepio to communicate with Thuruht."

There was no use denying the obvious. "I don't," Raynar admitted. "But I still have some time. I'm not in telepathic communication yet."

Lowbacca rumbled the opinion that it was time to go. Thuruht was just stringing them along, trying to make them Joiners, and they weren't learning anything.

"We are *now*, Lowie," Raynar said. "Thuruht has offered to share everything the hive knows about Abeloth."

"In exchange for what?" Tekli demanded.

"Buub," Thuruht replied, and C-3PO translated, "Nothing."

"That's right," Raynar said.

He felt a bit guilty about deceiving his companions, but he did not want to risk undermining Thuruht's willingness to discuss Abeloth by stopping to argue about the sacrifice he was making. Besides, Thuruht had accually *demanded* a promise from Raynar, so the statement was at least technically true.

Raynar turned to Thuruht. "What else do you have to show us?"

Using both left pincers to wave the Jedi after her, the Killik descended the corridor through several archways to another series of reliefs. The first depicted a jungle paradise, with a small clearing in the bottom of a shallow gorge that emptied into a vast swamp. In the center of the clearing was an erupting geyser, and in the vapor cloud above it floated three ghostly figures, so insubstantial it seemed their limbs had not yet finished coalescing. The trio appeared much younger than in the previous panels, but they were still recognizable as the Father, Son, and Daughter from the forest panels.

In the following two scenes, a walled pool had been built to catch the water from the geyser. In one panel, a fiendish-looking beast with the Son's head stood at the edge of the pool, drinking from it as the shocked faces of the Father and Daughter watched from the edge of the clearing. The next panel showed the Daughter swimming in a different pool, one located inside a grotto. The head on her shoulders was that of a luminous bird, and it was looking back toward the cave's pillar-flanked entrance with its beak gaping wide in surprise.

Raynar motioned at the two creatures, first the brutish-looking man-beast, then the luminous bird-woman. "They seem to be changing from one form to another," he said. "*Are* they the same beings?"

"*Do you think the Ones are made of crude matter?*" Thuruht replied. "*The Ones are beings of the Force. The Ones take any form they desire.*"

As Raynar considered this—and whether that meant the Daughter or another figure might be Abeloth—Tekli stepped forward.

She pointed at the pool in the grotto. "Does that remind you of anything?"

"It's the Pool of Knowledge that Master Skywalker described in his report," Raynar said.

Lowbacca pointed at the previous scene and moaned the opinion that it matched the description of the Font of Power that Master Skywalker and Ben had visited on Abeloth's home planet.

"It does." Raynar turned back to Thuruht and asked, "What are these three beings? Celestials?"

Thuruht shivered her antennae. "*Celestials are in the Force,*" she said. "*The Ones are what Celestials* become.*"

"Become?" Raynar asked. He thought back to the scene that showed the Ones coalescing out of the Font of Power. "When they emerge from the Force, you mean?"

"*The Force is all around us, in us . . . the Force is us,*" Thuruht said. "*How can a being emerge from what she is?*"

Raynar fell silent, allowing C-3PO to catch up with the translation while he tried to puzzle through Thuruht's bewildering explanation. He felt sure that she was telling him what she *believed* to be the truth, but it was impossible to know how accurate those beliefs were. A Killik memory could come from any number of sources—their own experience, something that once happened to a Joiner, even a holodrama enjoyed by someone before becoming a member of the hive. It was all the same to the Killik hive-mind. In time, the hive's collective memory became a random jumble of recollections, with fact and fiction and myth all intermingled in a single unreliable "truth." Raynar pointed at the first panel in the series, the one that showed the trio coalescing out of the vapors above the geyser. "This is how the Ones first arrived?"

"That is how they became, *yes,"* Thuruht clarified. *"That is precisely how we remember it."*

Well aware that the Killik's "precise" memory could be nothing more than some species' creation myth, Raynar groaned.

"We are sorry," Thuruht said. *"We do not know how to explain the Celestials any better. They are beyond the understanding of mortals."*

"There's no need to apologize," Raynar said. "But we have seen enough about the Celestials for now. Take us to the panels showing the history of Abeloth."

"But this is *the history of Abeloth,"* Thuruht protested. *"Her story is long and complicated. You will see."*

Waving them to follow, Thuruht ascended the corridor to another set of reliefs. At first, it appeared that Thuruht was showing them more of the same. The first two panels portrayed a horrified Father trying to keep the peace between the Son and the Daughter as they struggled to claim larger parts of the forest for themselves. But the third panel contained a new figure—a young woman who looked barely older than the Daughter, with a wide smile and twinkling eyes.

At first, Raynar took the newcomer to be a servant. The Son and the Daughter were raising their glasses, obviously expecting them to be filled from an ewer in the woman's hands. Meanwhile, the Father was looking on her with obvious warmth, returning her smile as she poured.

Thuruht tapped a pincer against the woman's foot. *"Abeloth."*

Raynar studied the figure more closely, comparing the figure in the relief with the Abeloth in the Skywalkers' report. The twinkling eyes weren't exactly the star-like points they had described, and while her smile was wide, it hardly stretched from ear to ear. It seemed to Raynar that he was looking not at Abeloth, but at the seed that would *become* Abeloth.

"Why didn't we see her emerging from the fountain mists?" Raynar asked. "Isn't she like the rest of the Ones?"

Thuruht spread all four arms. *"A servant appeared in the courtyard one day. We do not remember how she arrived."*

Once C-3PO had translated, Tekli asked, "But this *is* Abeloth? The Servant, not the Mother?"

"Abeloth is the Servant who became the Mother," Thuruht replied. *"You will see."*

With that, Thuruht walked up the corridor.

The next series of reliefs showed Abeloth turning the Ones into something that resembled a happy family. She kept the Son and the Daughter busy with games and chores, and she doted on the Father. She even stepped in to channel the Son's destructive energies into something useful, having him use his Force lightning to blast cozy little rooms into the sides of the gorge. By the third panel, she seemed to be a full member of the family, eating at the Father's side and holding her glass out for the Son to fill.

Once the Jedi had finished there, Thuruht ascended the corridor and paused in front of a scene depicting a much older Abeloth. Now Abeloth seemed old enough to be a wife to the Father—and a Mother to the Son and Daughter. In this panel, she was standing in front of a long arcade that had been carved from the wall of the gorge, leaning on the Son's shoulder in front of a stack of paving stones. Meanwhile, a weary-looking Daughter was working on hands and knees to pave the courtyard. In the background, the Father sat in a contented slumber, his hands resting across his stomach.

In the next scene, Abeloth was elderly. She was standing at one end of the courtyard, apart from the others. In the center, near the Font of Power, the Father was having a heated argument with the Son and the Daughter. All three were gesturing wildly, and in the air around them whirled uprooted tree ferns, boulders, and even a couple of six-legged lizards the size of rancors.

To Raynar's surprise, Thuruht moved on without giving him and the others much time to contemplate the panel. Immediately suspicious, he signaled Tekli and Lowbacca to remain where they were.

"Is there something you don't wish us to see here?" he demanded.

Thuruht stopped and spun around, her antennae erect with irritation. *"Linger if you wish,"* she said. *"It is nothing to the hive. But you are the one who said the Jedi needed to know about Abeloth quickly."*

Lowbacca moaned his agreement, urging Raynar to keep moving—
before he became a full Joiner.

"That is an excellent suggestion," C-3PO said. "I am recording
each panel in full holographic resolution. When we return to Coruscant, the Masters will be able to analyze every detail."

Thuruht gave a smug rumble, then hurried to the next set of images. When Raynar caught up, a chill raced up his spine.

The first panel showed an aged Abeloth sneaking a drink from the
Font of Power, while the Father hurled Force lightning at both the
Son and Daughter. In the second panel, a much younger-looking Abeloth swam in the Pool of Knowledge, looking sly and defiant as she
smiled up at the Father, who stood at the edge of the basin. His hands
were raised and extended toward Abeloth, as though he were using
the Force to pull her from the pool, and his expression was as sorrow-
ful as it was angry. Behind him stood the Daughter, using a Force
shield to prevent the Son's fiend aspect from leaping on the Father's
back.

The third panel depicted the arcade complex again, this time with a
much-changed Abeloth standing in the heart of a stormy courtyard.
Her hair had grown coarse and long, her nose had flattened until it was
practically gone, and her sparkling eyes had grown so sunken and dark
that all that could be seen of them were the twinkles. She was raising
her arms toward a cowering Daughter and a glowering Son, with long
tentacles lashing from where her fingers should have been. Stepping
forward to shield them was a furious Father, one hand pointing toward
the swamp at the open end of the temple, the other reaching out to intercept her tentacled fingers.

"I am beginning to believe Abeloth *can't* be a Celestial," Tekli observed. "She is too different from the others. She grew old when they
did not—and she was being changed by the Font and the Pool, while
the Son and the Daughter were unaffected."

"It is Abeloth's nature to seek what is beyond her grasp," Thuruht said.
"That is why she is the Bringer of Chaos."

"Then Abeloth *is* a Celestial?" Raynar asked. "Is that what you're
saying?"

Thuruht clacked her mandibles in the Killik equivalent of a shrug.
"Is Abeloth the Bringer of Chaos because that is the wish of the Celestials?

Or is she the Bringer of Chaos because she defied *the wish of the Celestials?"* She spread her four arms, then let them drop. *"We can never know the will of those who are beyond us to comprehend."*

With that, Thuruht turned to ascend the corridor again. Leaving C-3PO to translate the exchange for the others, Raynar followed close on her heels. He could feel a fundamental shift in Thuruht's attitude toward him and his companions, a marked confidence that suggested she already considered them members of the hive. And yet he had not noticed any stray thoughts or flashes of unexpected insight that would suggest the Joining was complete.

"Thuruht, I have the feeling that you are no longer concerned about whether we became Joiners," Raynar said.

"That is so."

"Why?"

"Because we feel how frightened you are," she said. *"How determined you are to stop Abeloth. And when you understand how that must be done, we know you will be happy to join us."*

Raynar shook his head. "You shouldn't count on that," he said. "Our mission is to report what we learn here, so the *Jedi* can destroy Abeloth."

An amused trill shot from the breathing spiracles in Thuruht's thorax. *"Destroy Abeloth? Impossible."* She passed through the next archway and stopped. *"Look."*

In these reliefs, Abeloth stood alone in the courtyard, watching the Father depart with the Son and Daughter. Her face was contorted in anger, and the air around her was whirling with fronds and jungle reptiles and lightning. In the panels that followed, she looked even more deranged. The courtyard was overrun with vegetation, and a large winged lizard was struggling to escape her grasp, its eyes wide with terror, it wings straining as it struggled to pull its foot out of her hand.

The third panel made Raynar's blood run cold. It depicted a band of six-tentacled cephalopods entering the bone-littered courtyard. Wearing elaborate robes and headdresses, they were dragging a trio of huge saurian prisoners toward the Font of Power, where Abeloth stood grinning in delight.

"The first time Abeloth escaped her cage," Thuruht explained. The Killik led the way up the corridor, through the next archway. They

passed a series of panels depicting a massive battle between the cephalopods and the saurians. *"The war had been raging only a few centuries when Abeloth was freed. Usually, it takes much longer. Often thousands of years."*

"Wait," Raynar said, stopping beneath the next archway. "You mean every time there is war, Abeloth is freed?"

"Not with every war. But yes, when Abeloth escapes, it is always in a time of great strife." Thuruht started up the corridor again, motioning for Raynar to follow. *"Sometimes, when war grows too powerful, the Bringer of Chaos is released. She shatters the old order, so a new one can rise."*

"Wait," Raynar repeated. He did not want to get so far ahead of the others that C-3PO had trouble recording Thuruht's words. "Are you saying that Abeloth is *part* of the Celestial plan?"

Thuruht spread her hands. *"Who can say if the Celestials are the kind of beings who have a plan?"* Ignoring Raynar's request to stop, she continued up the corridor. *"But that is how the galaxy works. It is how the Force works."*

Raynar glanced back at his companions and motioned for them to hurry, then rushed to catch up. They were bypassing a long series of reliefs, though these seemed to be little more than a history of the war between the cephalopods and the saurians.

When he caught Thuruht, Raynar asked, "But why would Abeloth be freed *now*? The galaxy isn't at war."

Thuruht stopped, then cocked her head and fixed a single bulbous eye on Raynar's face. *"Of course it is,"* she said. *"The Jedi and the Sith have been at war for five thousand years."*

Raynar went cold inside. "You're saying that *we* set Abeloth free?"

Yes. You and the Sith. Together, you released the Bringer of Chaos.

Thuruht started up the corridor again, and Raynar stumbled after her. He did not want to believe the Killik's version of history, but the truth was clear. Centerpoint Station had been destroyed during the war against the Sith Lord Caedus, and its loss had launched a catastrophic chain of events. Sinkhole Station had been crippled, allowing the Lost Tribe to discover Abeloth and her planet. There could be no denying Thuruht's claim. The war between the Jedi and the Sith had led directly to the freeing of Abeloth.

No, Thuruht said, speaking inside Raynar's head. *Qolaraloq's destruction followed, but it did not cause. It was just one link snapping, in a chain full of snapping links.*

Deep within his mind, Raynar knew he should be alarmed by what was happening to him. Terrified, even. Now that he was in telepathic communication with Thuruht, his final transition to Joiner was a foregone conclusion.

But compared with the level of destruction that would soon descend on the galaxy, his own fate seemed unimportant. What mattered to him now was learning about Abeloth—and about the cause of her release, if it had not been the destruction of Centerpoint Station.

You know, Thuruht replied. *Abeloth was freed the same way she is always freed. The Current was turned.*

The current of time? Raynar asked. He thought of Jacen Solo and his flow-walking. Tahiri had told the Masters that she was convinced that Jacen fell to the dark side trying to prevent some tragic event that he had seen in the future, and that he had been fond of using flow-walking to look at both directions in time. *Or do you mean the Force current?*

Is there a difference? It is the Force that guides the future.

After hurrying through two more archways, Thuruht finally stopped before a set of panels depicting three devastated worlds. In the first, an entire city lay in ruins. There were fungi rising from the rubble, and a drove of three-eyed bipeds could be seen fleeing a horde of tentacled felines. The second relief showed scores of dazed woodland creatures struggling through a blast-flattened forest, many fighting in vain to escape the fangvines wrapped around their legs. The third scene was the most gruesome of all. It was an ocean world with flocks of seabirds hovering over floating islands of moldy flesh. Hanging in the sky of each world was a female face with a gaping, fang-filled smile that stretched from one ear to another.

And when the Current turns, Thuruht said, *it is the Force that suffers.*

Raynar felt sick. He and Jacen had become close friends at the first Jedi academy on Yavin 4. In fact, Jacen had been among those who helped Raynar and his father protect a lost arsenal of bioweapons from an anti-human terror group. And when Raynar's father died,

Jacen had been one of the friends who comforted him. So when Jacen fell to the dark side and became Darth Caedus, it had been hard for Raynar to accept. At first, he had refused to believe the betrayal was sincere, and then he had blamed it on the torture Jacen had suffered as a prisoner of the Yuuzhan Vong. But as the Second Civil War had raged on, Caedus's actions had grown steadily more ruthless, and Raynar had finally understood that his old friend had become one of the most murderous of all Sith Lords. Now it seemed even *that* condemnation was not terrible enough. In his drive to change the vision he had seen, Darth Caedus had unleashed Destruction herself.

Chaos, not Destruction, Thuruht corrected. *Chaos brings destruction, but she also brings new energy and change.*

As Lowbacca and the others joined them, Raynar began to speak aloud, both so his companions would understand, and so C-3PO could record him.

"Thuruht believes that a change in the Current caused Abeloth's release," Raynar said, summarizing for his companions. He turned back to Thuruht. "But the Jedi believe the future is always in motion. So I have trouble seeing why a change in the Current would release Abeloth."

"Is a river current not in motion?" Thuruht replied, also speaking aloud. *"And will it not carry a boat to many different places, depending on how the riders paddle?"*

"Yes, that's true," Raynar said, with some impatience. "But wherever they land, they do not usually free Abeloth."

"They do not ever free her, because they have not changed the Current," Thuruht replied. *"They have only ridden it to one of many different destinations. But if they wish to go where the Current cannot carry them, the current must be turned."*

"And to do that, the river itself must be altered," Raynar finished.

"Yes," Thuruht replied. *"The Force guides the Current. It is impossible to turn the Current without also changing the Force."*

"And *that* is what frees Abeloth," Raynar clarified.

"Yes," Thuruht agreed. *"The Force is in the dominion of the Celestials. When their power is usurped, the Bringer of Chaos comes."*

Raynar waited while C-3PO translated the exchange for his companions. He was about to recap his suspicions regarding Jacen when Tekli arrived at the same conclusion.

"Then *Jacen* freed Abeloth?" she asked.

"*Yes.*"

"By changing what he saw in his Force vision?" Tekli clarified.

Thuruht clacked her mandibles in a Killik shrug. "*We do not know what Jacen saw in his Force vision.*"

Tekli's ears flattened in frustration. She looked to Lowbacca, who let out a sad groan and replied that even Tahiri had not known for certain. She believed the vision had to do with a dark man who ruled the galaxy, and that Jacen had been so disturbed by what he saw that he had turned to the dark side to prevent it.

After C-3PO had translated Lowbacca's explanation, Thuruht curled her antennae in the Killik equivalent of a nod.

"*Then, yes,*" Thuruht replied. "*If the dark man was the future Jacen wished to prevent, then it must be the future he changed.*"

With that, Thuruht turned and led the way up the corridor to the next set of reliefs—and Raynar saw why Thuruht was so confident he would remain to help the hive.

The first panel showed a long, tubular space station still under construction. The skeletal structure was teeming with Killiks, all wearing thin suits and bubble helmets. And that was all. There were no jet-packs, no space cranes, not even any tether cables—just millions of Killiks, floating together in banks the size of small asteroids. In front of them, enormous durasteel girders appeared to be drifting into position with no visible means of propulsion.

Raynar understood what he was seeing. Thuruht had used the Force not only to assemble the station itself—which certainly had the shape of Centerpoint—but also to move *themselves* about in space.

When we build, we use the Force for all things, Thuruht confirmed.

She directed Raynar's attention to the next panel. It showed a band of Killiks using Force blasts to extract ore from a stony asteroid. They also seemed to be using telekinesis to move the ore into a smelting furnace, which appeared to be powered by another swarm using a ball form of Force lightning.

To mine, to move, to smelt.

Raynar understood why Thuruht needed to harness the Force. But even if he knew how to share it, he was not strong enough to share it with so *many* beings at once.

Thuruht was amused by his confusion. *By the time we are ready to build, you will be no more,* she said. *The Architects will be the Ones who give us the Force then.*

"The Architects?" Raynar asked aloud. They were once again drifting into an area of conversation the Masters would need to hear. "Who are the Architects, exactly?"

The Brother and the Sister, Thuruht explained, still speaking inside Raynar's head. *Abeloth is the only thing capable of bringing them together. It angers them to see her destroy civilizations they have spent millennia cultivating.*

The Killik stepped to the next panel, where a pair of insects stood looming over a small swarm of Killiks who seemed to be assembling some sort of oversized fusion core. The first overseer was a luminous butterfly with large oval eyes and gossamer wings. Her companion was a powerful-looking beetle with heavy wings and a craggy head adorned by two raised stripes.

Soon, the Architects will form a pact and emerge from hiding, Thuruht continued. *And when they do, the hive must be ready to answer their call.*

"These are the Architects?" Raynar asked. He stepped closer to the panel and pointed at the two supervising insects. "You're saying that the Brother and the Sister are *insects?*"

Thuruht spread her four hands. *They are to us.*

"Ah . . . of course." As Raynar spoke, a torrent of memories flooded into his mind, of the Architects joining with Thuruht and dozens of other hives, of suddenly just *knowing* how to build wonders like the World Puller and Still Curtain and the Chasm of Forever, and he knew that Raynar Thul was no more. He nodded. "Now we understand."

When he turned away from the panel, he found Tekli and Lowbacca looking not at the crucial scene, but at him. Lowbacca's muzzle was hanging half open, baring his fangs less in menace than in shock, and Tekli's eyes had gone wide with alarm.

"Raynar," she said, "it's time to leave."

That cannot be, Thuruht said, her words coming in a flash almost before Tekli had finished speaking. *The hive must be ready when the Ones call—*

—and for that to happen, the hive needs a Jedi to help it grow. The agreement was reached in the time it took a thought to flash from one mind to another, and when Raynar turned to address Tekli, it was so quickly she did not even seem to realize that another, unheard conversation had taken place.

"We agree," he said. "The time has come to report what we have discovered to the Jedi Council." He pointed at the two insects in the panel. "Tell the Masters that the Ones do not look like this to all beings. They take a form that suits their servants."

Lowbacca roared that *he* wasn't going to tell the Masters *anything,* that Raynar was going to be the one doing the talking. He raised a furry claw, reaching for an arm, but stopped when his friend used the Force to gently push it down.

"We are sorry, my friend, but we must stay," ThurThul said. "And you must go. Raynar Thul is no more."

Chapter Twenty-two

ARMED WITH AN IMPERIAL INTELLIGENCE ID COURTESY OF JAGGED FEL, Tahiri had no trouble securing cooperation at the only spaceport on Hagamoor 3. She simply presented herself at the security commander's office and demanded to see the file on the Mandalorian who had arrived a few days earlier. The officer—a grizzled old captain—inserted her identichip into his decryption pad, then his face paled. He snapped to attention and offered a crisp salute.

"Sorry, milady," he said. "I wasn't informed that Head of State Fel had reactivated the Hands."

The captain's anxiety was understandable. Answerable only to the Imperial Head-of-State, the Hands were Force-sensitive operatives whom Palpatine had used as merciless instruments of his will, dealing death and threats to anyone who incurred his wrath. Tahiri knew better than to think Jag would ever employ them in the same ruthless manner—but he was certainly not above trading on the name.

Ten minutes later Tahiri's StealthX was under guard in a sealed hangar, and she was sitting in front of a vid display. On the display was a four-day-old surveillance vid that showed Boba Fett—or someone in identical armor, with a very similar gait—working his way down an inflatable pedtunnel.

Unfortunately, Fett's Mandalorian armor did not seem out of place in the tunnel. Hagamoor 3 was an open-access mining moon where claim jumpers, ore thieves, and every sort of swindler were on the prowl for victims, and it had a flourishing bodyguard industry. Every third person on the display was both armed and armored. To make matters worse, once Fett reached the business district in the main dome, the lanes were choked with riot troops facing off against pro-Daala protestors. Both sides were armored, of course. To track Fett, Tahiri finally had to resort to watching for his battered green helmet. With its T-shaped visor and distinctive rangefinder rising along one side, it was the easiest thing to follow from one vid archive to the next.

Fett was taking care to stay close to other armored figures and avoid some of the security cams, but he couldn't afford to be too obvious. Any conspicuous attempt to avoid surveillance in an Imperial population center—even one as rustic as Hagamoor City—only drew extra scrutiny. As Tahiri watched, the Mandalorian visited a succession of hospitality houses and supply businesses. The Imperial surveillance net did not extend to the interior of most facilities, but on one occasion she did catch a glimpse of Fett through a transparisteel door. A salesclerk was turning a data screen around so the Mandalorian could examine a list of sales.

Fett was clearly hunting someone, and Tahiri was beginning to think he didn't care who knew it. He could have disguised his purpose by buying a few supplies, varying the length of his visits, or emerging with a handful of sales flimsis. Instead he was simply moving from one business to the next as quickly as possible, staying only long enough to bribe or intimidate whoever happened to be behind the counter. It almost seemed as though he *wanted* his prey to know he was coming.

Maybe he did. Hagamoor 3 was in Moff Getelles's sector, and if Daala had anything to say about it, Getelles's days were numbered. He had betrayed her—and played a crucial role in trapping her and her allies at Exodo II. So it stood to reason that Daala would want to make an example of Getelles to keep other would-be defectors in line. And what better way to make her point than by dispatching the infamous Boba Fett to handle the retaliation?

Of course, Tahiri realized that Fett's involvement was no guarantee that Abeloth would also show up on Hagamoor 3. Tahiri was still playing a hunch on that. Since they both had a connection to Daala—Fett had rescued Daala from Coruscant, and Abeloth had run the blockade at Boreleo to visit her—she was hoping that they would eventually end up in the same place. But even if Fett didn't lead her to Abeloth, finding out what the mercenary was doing on Hagamoor 3 would be a good thing for Jag.

Tahiri fast-forwarded through the next three days of surveillance, then finally spotted Fett entering a used-vehicle dealership. A short time later, a sealed landspeeder emerged through the dome's rear air lock and headed off across the moon's dusty surface. A comm call from one of the post's security agents confirmed that the landspeeder had been purchased by someone wearing green Mandalorian armor. It also yielded the activation code for the vehicle's emergency locator.

Hagamoor 3 was in Imperial territory, so the security agent could activate the locator beacon without alerting the driver. Tahiri soon learned that the vehicle had stopped a kilometer short of the Moon Maiden, a subsurface mine that had been advertising heavily for new employees over the last two weeks. A check of the tax records, however, revealed no recent additions to the workforce, only a modestly sized crew that seemed to have a lot more technical staff than was warranted. A rather cryptic remark at the beginning of the tax file noted that the mine was owned and managed by Suarl Getelles, eldest daughter of the Moff. There was no mention in the file—or anywhere else—of what kind of ore the Maiden produced.

The spaceport security commander was happy to arrange transport for Tahiri, and she quickly departed in a Mabartak G7 All-Environment Assault Sled. It took only a few hours to find Fett's vehicle sitting, abandoned, just a couple of kilometers from the Moon Maiden. A few minutes after that, Tahiri was standing in the Mabartak's cramped air lock, sealed tight inside an Imperial Security Special Tactics vac suit. Her best estimate placed her less than half a day behind Boba Fett—or whoever it was wearing his armor, she reminded herself. It seemed unlikely that she was chasing an impostor, but where Fett was concerned, it was unwise to take *anything* for granted.

Which was why Tahiri decided not to use the vac suit's integrated comlink. Fett could certainly detect it, even if he lacked the necessary software to decrypt the transmission. Instead, Tahiri opened her faceplate and depressed the Mabartak's intercom key.

"I'm ready," she said. "Cycle the air lock."

"You're sure you don't want an escort?" asked the vehicle commander—a handsome lieutenant about her own age. "The intelligence team keeps trying to find out what's really happening in there, but they can't get anyone inside. And now we have *Boba Fett* sniffing around the place? He's not someone you want to mess with alone."

Tahiri almost smiled. "You're sweet, but . . . no. I don't need an escort." She picked up the service pack she had assembled from the post's armory. "Just be here when I return, Lieutenant Vangur. Maybe I'll have a reward for you."

Vangur's voice grew hopeful. "A reward, ma'am?"

"Something for the *intelligence* team," Tahiri said. Vangur had spent the whole three-hour journey from Hagamoor City trying to flirt with her, and the truth was that she had been happy to have the distraction. But now it was time to focus on her mission—and to get Vangur focused on *his* mission, too. She put a little edge in her voice. "I hope you don't think I meant something else, Lieutenant."

"No, ma'am. The thought never crossed my mind."

Tahiri slung the bulky service pack onto her shoulders, then asked, "And what thought would that be?"

"Any thought you might find inappropriate." There was a note of amusement—almost mockery—in Vangur's voice that suggested he was not all *that* intimidated by his passenger. "Ma'am."

"Never lie to an Imperial Hand, Lieutenant," Tahiri warned. She actually found Vangur's cockiness attractive, but she didn't need attractive or cocky right now—she needed reliable. "It's bad for your health."

"I understand, ma'am." Vangur's voice remained confident, but this time there was no humor in it. "It won't happen again."

"Good," Tahiri said. "Just be here when I return, and we'll both stay happy."

She closed her faceplate and waited. When the status light on the control panel turned green, she opened the hatch and stepped out onto the dusty surface of Hagamoor 3. Fett's landspeeder sat on its struts a hundred meters away, resting at the base of a curving ridge that looked like the rim of a small impact crater.

Knowing that any attempt to approach the vehicle was likely to set off a remote alarm that would alert Fett to the presence of a pursuer, Tahiri extended her Force awareness in the vehicle's direction. When she didn't sense anyone inside, she traversed up the slope toward a little notch, where Fett's tracks skirted the crest of the ridge. In the moon's weak gravity, the climb was so easy that she did not even trigger the suit's cooling system. But she had to use the Force to avoid kicking up a plume of dust that could have easily risen to thirty meters high. As she neared the top, she dropped to her hands and knees. Being careful to avoid any rocks that might rip her suit, she crawled the rest of the way, then pushed her head up above the crest.

The interior of the crater was packed with hundreds of vehicles, most resting on their struts in neat, orderly rows. Trails of boot-packed dust led toward the mine's entrance, a small permacrete portal with the name MOON MAIDEN across the top. Jutting out of the slope above and behind the portal was a squat durasteel office building with two transparisteel viewing bands. The lack of visible doors—or any hint of a trail ascending the slope beneath—suggested that the only way to enter the building was from inside the mine. Just beyond the crater rim, a cloud of hot yellow fume was boiling away into the void, no doubt rising out of an exhaust shaft not visible from Tahiri's location.

She could almost feel Fett's bewilderment lingering in the Force. The number of vehicles parked in the crater suggested a workforce of thousands. But judging by the size of the portal and office building, the Moon Maiden was a small operation—so small that they hadn't even bothered with a surface perimeter or security post. Nor did Tahiri see any equipment for processing, storing, or hauling ore. And if it didn't handle ore, then the Moon Maiden was no ordinary mine.

Tahiri activated her helmet's reconnaissance kit. The electromag sensors picked up dozens of small emission sources arrayed at even intervals along the inner rim of the crater. They were almost certainly hidden security cams. When she viewed the durasteel "office" building at 20X magnification, it grew obvious that the walls beneath the transparisteel viewing bands were dotted with camouflaged weapons ports—many large enough to serve laser cannons. And the portal itself was sealed not by a standard air lock hatch, but by a blast door capable of withstanding a turbolaser strike.

Most disturbing of all was the mine's thermal readout. Hagamoor 3 was a hunk of metal-rich rock scarcely large enough to generate its own weak gravity. The tiny amount of compression heat that it *did* generate barely lifted the ambient temperature above absolute zero. But the area near the mine read more like the ground around a geyser. Tahiri began to worry that the yellow smoke rising beyond the crater might mean the entire mine was on fire.

Seeing that Fett had not descended directly into the crater from there, she went down the slope until she was below the mine's line of sight and followed his trail a few hundred meters along the exterior of the rim, then returned to the crest. Now she was adjacent to the portal, about fifty meters above it. Fett's trail ended there, where a large blast circle suggested he had activated his jetpack to descend to the portal in a single hop.

Tahiri didn't have a jetpack, but she did have the Force. She took a moment to brush the dust from the emitter nozzle of her blaster pistol. She transferred a couple of thermal detonators from her pack to her belt, then pulled her lightsaber off its hook and took a deep breath. She felt like she ought to be making a situation report before jumping into action, but even if she *had* wanted to break comm silence, there was little to gain from it. If she failed to return, Vangur would report the obvious to Head of State Fel: the Imperial Hand followed Boba Fett into the Moon Maiden and failed to return.

In the weak gravity, Tahiri required only two Force bounds to descend to the crater floor. Her third bound left her standing in front of the Moon Maiden's portal, which was indeed a heavy blast door. Designed to swing outward in two interlocking halves, the door appeared to be made of a reflective duratanium alloy that was practically impervious to laser-based artillery. A faint shimmer in the metal suggested that the area was protected by a nullifier field, typically used in military installations to dampen the triggers of thermal detonators and other handheld explosives. But what *really* riveted Tahiri's attention was the sense of boiling darkness she felt in the Force—an outpouring of fear and grief that seemed to be building somewhere deep inside the mine.

Maybe Fett had led her to Abeloth, after all.

Could I really be that lucky? Tahiri wondered. *Could I really be that* un*lucky?*

She caught a flash of movement in the corner of her faceplate as a security cam descended on its control tether to give her a closer inspection. She extended a hand, using the Force to draw it into her grasp, then pulled the lens close to her faceplate and hit the chin toggle for her comlink.

"Imperial Security." She sent a surge of Force energy into the lens, creating a bright flash that would temporarily blind the cam. "Let me in . . . *now*."

"Sure thing, boss." The reply was so static-scratched that it was impossible to identify the speaker's species, but the voice sounded too thin and chirpy to be human. "If you're sure that's what you want."

Tahiri felt a small ground shudder as one of the blast doors cracked open, creating a gap just wide enough for her to slip through. Half expecting the sentry to swing the door shut as she crossed the threshold, she slipped through the opening in a single quick bound. Inside, she found herself standing in an industrial air lock. It looked like a thousand others she had occupied, save that this one had a set of blaster cannons mounted high in the corners. She waved a finger at each of them, using the Force to push the barrels away—and to wreck the control system's calibration.

"Hey!" came the scratchy voice. "Who do you think you are?"

"I told you," Tahiri said. "Imperial Security."

She stepped over to a man-sized hatch in the rear wall of the air lock and peered through a head-height viewport down a long, well-lit tunnel. It was lined by white plastoid panels far too clean to belong in a working mine. The sentry's post, wherever it was, could not be seen.

"Are you going to open this air lock now?" Tahiri demanded. "Or am I going to blast through this hatch and decompress your whole operation?"

"You didn't say you were in a hurry." The blast door thumped shut behind her, and the voice said, "Just give the pressure a minute to—"

"No."

Tahiri stepped away from the hatch, then used the Force to hit the emergency release and shove it open. A tremendous squealing became a tremendous roaring, and she was nearly swept off her feet as air blasted into the chamber. After a second, the blast faded to a raging wind, and she sprang through the hatchway.

A cold shiver of danger sense raced down Tahiri's spine, and she spun around in time to see a weapons port sliding open in the door of a small sentry booth. With no face visible in the viewport above, she merely extended a hand toward the slot and *shoved* with the Force. In the next instant a line of blaster bolts stitched up the interior side of the viewport and began to traverse the ceiling.

Tahiri ignited her lightsaber and stepped over to the booth, then peered through the carbon-scorched viewport. On the floor lay a furry, meter-high rodent-like being holding a T-21 repeating blaster that was almost as long as he was tall. With oversized ears and big round eyes, he could have been described as cute—if he hadn't been a Squib. Tahiri used the Force to release the door lock, then opened it from the outside and stepped into the cramped compartment.

She raised her faceplate. "You have a death wish?" She jerked the T-21 from his grasp with a Force pull. "I *said* Imperial Security."

"Yeah, right. And I should take your word for it?" the Squib retorted. "Do I look like some sort of fuzzling to you?"

Tahiri studied his spotted fur and oversized ears, and then realized she had a pretty good idea of the Squib's identity. Shortly after she had entered Jagged Fel's service, the Solos had put the Head of State into contact with three Squibs—a female and two males. The trio had volunteered to test an experimental youth serum, which was being developed by none other than Moff Getelles. Test subjects who used the serum tended to develop overly youthful traits—like big ears and spotted fur.

After a moment, she nodded. "Actually, you *do* look like a fuzzling," she said. "Which one are you? You're male, so it has to be Grees or Sligh."

The Squib narrowed his eyes. "Do I *know* you?"

"You know my superior, Jagged Fel," Tahiri said. In truth, she was not quite sure how to describe her half-prisoner, half-Imperial-agent status. "You did an undercover job for him not too long ago—a job that was *supposed* to be over."

"That deal *is* over," the Squib said. He began to crawl backward on the floor—and promptly ran into the wall. "This is a different one."

Tahiri shrugged. "Whatever you say . . ." She paused, as though she were using the Force the way Master Skywalker did—to pick people's names out of their thoughts. Then she simply took a guess. "*Sligh.*"

When the Squib's ears went back in alarm, she knew she had guessed right. "Why don't you tell me about this new deal of yours," she said. "And remember, I'll know if you're lying."

Sligh shook his head. "I don't think so, Blondie."

"Okay, then I'll tell *you*," Tahiri said, deciding to bluff. "You're working for Daala now."

"*Wrong,*" Sligh said smugly. "Some Jedi you are."

"I'm no Jedi—not anymore," Tahiri said. She opened herself to the Force again and sensed the same boiling darkness she had felt from outside the portal—and the same outpouring of grief and anguish. "And you didn't let me finish. You're working for Daala through her agent, an Imperial lieutenant named Lydea Pagorski."

Sligh's gaze shifted away. "I didn't say that."

"You didn't have to," Tahiri replied. "Pagorski is in charge of Daala's election campaign, if you call starting riots a *campaign.*"

Sligh shrugged. "It's how they do things in the Empire. Who are we to judge?"

"You have a point," Tahiri said. Shifting to a friendlier interrogation technique, she shut off her lightsaber and motioned for Sligh to stand. "What I can't figure out is why Pagorski came here, to Hagamoor Three. This is Getelles's territory, and Getelles is on Jag's side."

"What makes you think *we* had anything to do with it?" Sligh demanded. "We're just contract agents."

Even had she not sensed the Squib's alarm in the Force, Tahiri would have known he was lying. "*You* brought Pagorski here—because you've been here before," she said, quickly seeing how the pieces of the puzzle fit together. "The Moon Maiden isn't a mine. It's the lab where Getelles was developing his youth serum—the lab where you were experimented on."

Sligh only blinked and tried to look innocent.

"Pagorski was looking for a secret base of operations, one where no one would think to look for her," Tahiri continued, watching the Squib closely. "And she needed it to be a place where a lot of people could disappear without being noticed. Because she's not Lydea Pagorski anymore, is she? She's something much more deadly. Something you don't understand, and that you probably wish you had never gotten involved with. Right?"

Sligh's quick drop of gaze was all the confirmation Tahiri needed.

"And then things got even worse, didn't they, Sligh? Fett tracked you here—because *he's* looking for the scientists who were experimenting on you." The scientists who had developed the youth serum had also designed a nanokiller specifically attuned to Boba Fett's genetic code—a nanokiller that the Moffs had released into Mandalore's atmosphere, ensuring that Fett would never be able to return to his beloved world. "Fett's not here because Daala sent him. He's here because he wants your scientists. And you couldn't stop him from going inside either. He's already gone down the tunnel to find them—hasn't he, Sligh?"

Sligh's ears went straight back, and his hands flew up so quickly that Tahiri instinctively ignited her lightsaber again. But the Squib's hands only went to the sides of his face, and then he spun away from Tahiri and began to whip his head from side to side so hard she feared he might break his own neck. Suddenly he turned and hurled himself at her feet.

Tahiri brought her lightsaber down, almost lopping off his head before she realized there was no aggression in his Force aura—only panic, terror, and confusion. She deactivated the blade at the last instant, then lifted one leg just in time to avoid being knocked off her feet as the Squib hit the floor beneath her.

He shot out of the sentry booth into the white corridor beyond. Then, still whipping his head from side to side, he looked back and called, "Stay out of my brain, witch!"

Chapter Twenty-three

IF THE MOON MAIDEN HAD EVER BEEN ANYTHING BUT A SECRET LABO-
ratory disguised as a mine, Tahiri saw no hint of it in the primary access tunnel. At just two meters high by three meters wide, the passage
was adequate for speeder traffic but too small for heavy equipment. It
was also incredibly clean. Both the duracrete floor and the white plastoid liner had been carefully sealed to prevent the slightest ground infiltration, and even the glow panels were recessed behind transparisteel
panes to minimize the number of joints where caulking might disintegrate. And every fifty meters, she passed through an ion curtain that
captured any dust particles clinging to her vac suit.

Outside the second ion curtain, Tahiri came to a pair of loaded
hoversleds parked along the wall, as though being held there until the
cargo could be transported. Crates on both hoversleds had been broken into recently—no doubt by a curious Boba Fett—and Tahiri removed a poster flimsi from a crate on the first sled.

The flimsi showed an image of Admiral Daala in profile. Her eye
patch was prominently displayed, and she had a noble, serious expres-

sion on her face. Below the picture were the words: NATASI DAALA. A TRADITION OF SERVICE AND SACRIFICE—FOR *YOUR* EMPIRE.

As Tahiri looked at the image, she experienced a sudden surge of respect and confidence, and she found herself feeling like Daala might make a pretty decent Head of State after all.

Force suggestion.

Tahiri recognized what was happening only because she felt the power of the Force in it, and even then the flimsi's influence was difficult to resist until she crumpled it up and threw it on the floor.

The second sled contained a stack of holosign projector pads. Rather than activate one and risk having a hologram of Daala pop up and start talking, Tahiri concentrated her Force awareness over the sled. There was a dark aura clinging to the projector pads, as though they had been imbued with a tiny amount of Force energy by a very powerful dark side Force-user.

Abeloth.

Tahiri started down the tunnel again, more concerned than ever. After the trouble Abeloth had gone to in running the blockade at Boreleo, it seemed all too likely that she had formed an alliance with Daala and was using her powers to boost Daala's popularity in the Empire—and this discovery certainly supported those suspicions. But it also cast the campaign to elect the admiral in a whole new light. Tahiri could see only one reason for Abeloth to use her powers to guarantee Daala's victory, and that was because she expected the admiral to become her puppet ruler.

Abeloth intended to take the Empire for her own.

And once Abeloth had the Empire, there would be no stopping her. The Empire would be an ideal base from which to expand, and against their combined powers, even the Galactic Alliance would not be able to oppose her for long.

As Tahiri continued to walk, the cleanliness of the tunnel began to fade. Three hundred meters in, dark spots of mildew began to appear along the walls. At four hundred meters, the plastoid had turned dark with growth, and the fungus was starting to form mounds. By five hundred meters, she was picking her way past stalks of meter-high fungi and ducking under dangling curtains of moss. Though she had never visited a world where Abeloth held sway, she had spoken to enough Jedi to know what she was seeing—and how cautious she needed to be around the strange flora.

Tahiri was about six hundred meters down the tunnel when she came to a scene as puzzling as it was gruesome. A secondary passage opened out to the left, where it became a steep ramp ascending toward the surface building that sat above this part of the Moon Maiden.

At the base of the ramp, half a dozen human security guards lay scattered among the fungi stalks. Another half a dozen—probably the first to arrive—had made it into the main tunnel, where the plastoid walls were painted with blood and the floor was littered with bodies and weapons. A pair of guards had lived long enough to fling their blaster rifles aside and flee down the passage. Tahiri could see their corpses lying among the club mosses with huge char holes in their backs.

Probably Fett, Tahiri decided. The handiwork was certainly his style, and she knew from her interrogation of Sligh that the Mandalorian had come down the tunnel ahead of her. Not wanting to risk leaving a ruthless bounty hunter between her and the exit, she started up the ramp toward the surface building—which, given all the dead guards, she was now confident in calling a security bunker.

Tahiri had to travel only about thirty paces before realizing she had no need to worry about Fett. The bounty hunter was hanging in the center of the tunnel, upside down and motionless, trapped in a curtain of ropy moss like a flitnat in a spiderweb. Some of the moss-tendrils had worked their way into the seams of his armor and, presumably, penetrated the neoplas body glove underneath. Never having visited one of Abeloth's strongholds before, Tahiri could only guess at the nature of the moss's attack. Most likely it was some sort of acid or contact poison, though strangulation and allergic reaction were also possibilities. But the one thing she knew for certain was that if Fett had been expecting to be attacked by a plant, he wouldn't have been captured—and perhaps killed—by one.

It was a good lesson to bear in mind.

Having stashed her helmet inside her vac suit cargo pack, Tahiri pulled the mike up from her suit collar and used the Moon Maiden's internal network to link to a surface antenna, then opened a secure channel to Lieutenant Vangur aboard the Mabartak.

"Change your mind about the escort?" Vangur asked, not even

bothering to identify himself—or confirm that he was, indeed, talking to Tahiri. "We can be there in five minutes."

"Tempting, but no," Tahiri said. "I need you to do something for me."

"Yes, ma'am," he said. "What?"

"First, you're to be two kilometers clear of the Moon Maiden in one hour, whether I'm aboard or not," she said. "And that *is* an order. Understood?"

"Absolutely."

Though even Vangur was too much of an Imperial officer to ask for an explanation, Tahiri could hear the curiosity in his voice.

"Trust me," she said. "If I'm not back, you won't want to be anywhere near the Maiden."

"If you say so, ma'am."

"I do," Tahiri replied. "Next, I need you to relay a situation report to Head of State Fel—and to him alone. Do you understand?"

"Of course." Vangur's voice had finally grown serious. "But I don't know if the Head of State is going to accept a direct communiqué from a—"

"Tell him it's from the Imperial Hand," Tahiri interrupted. "You'll get through. You're to give Head of State Fel this location, along with this message: *She's here. Act soonest . . . regardless.*"

"*She's here. Act soonest, regardless,*" Vangur confirmed. "Will the Head of State understand that last part? I mean, regardless of what, exactly?"

"Regardless of *anything*, Lieutenant."

"Ah . . . I see." Vangur went silent a moment, then asked, "Off the record, ma'am?"

"Make it quick."

"Thanks for thinking of my crew," he said. "And I hope you don't mind, but we'll be waiting the *full* hour."

"Mind?" Tahiri replied. "I may be *counting* on it."

She closed the channel, then checked her chrono and saw that it was eleven in the morning, Galactic Standard Time. She had allowed herself one hour. Given that Head of State Fel had assigned a frigate to her, and that she had left that frigate on station about midway between Hagamoor 3 and its planet, there *was* a small possibility that Jag might be able to initiate a turbolaser bombardment in less time. But the order would need to be issued and confirmed, and then the frigate would have to move into position and verify the Moon Maiden's location. Realistically, an hour would be a lightning-fast response.

But this was Abeloth, and therefore Jag would make it happen.

So Tahiri had until midday GST to confirm Abeloth's presence and take down any shield generators hidden inside the facility. She also needed to develop a way to observe and verify the target's destruction, and to arrange something that would hold Abeloth's attention until the barrage began. And while Tahiri was doing all *that*, if she could also think of some way to survive the barrage herself . . . well, that might be nice, too.

The first place to check for shield generators, of course, was the security bunker. Deciding it would be wise to have some idea of what she would find waiting above, Tahiri extended her Force awareness toward the building—and felt only a single groggy presence, a short distance up the ramp.

Fett, of course, hanging trapped but alive.

Using the Force to clear her path of any flora that looked like it might spray, sting, or snare, Tahiri advanced a few paces toward the bounty hunter. Jagged had given her free rein to do whatever it took to stop Abeloth, and he had specifically mentioned killing Fett. That would probably have been the smart thing to do, given how dangerous Fett was—and how rarely anyone encountered him in such a vulnerable state.

Tahiri hesitated for two reasons. First, she was not absolutely confident that it was Fett inside the armor. While impostors had a way of meeting quick ends, con men had been known to collect enormous fees by copying Fett's armor and passing themselves off as the infamous bounty hunter. Second—and most important—if that *was* Fett, he could not be working with Abeloth, or he would have known better than to let himself be captured by her carnivorous plants. So maybe—just *maybe*—Tahiri could steer him into helping her instead. He would certainly be the kind of fodder that might keep Abeloth too busy to notice that a turbolaser barrage was about to descend.

Tahiri stopped five paces short of Fett—and the curtain of flesh-eating moss that was holding him captive. "Boba Fett?" she called. "Is that you?"

The figure hanging before her remained motionless.

"Come on, Fett, I know you're alive," she said. "I can feel it in the aaaah *krrriffff!*"

The assertion changed to a curse when Tahiri noticed Fett swinging his one free arm in her direction. She used the Force to push the limb back as she turned and dived for cover.

She landed a couple of paces from the bottom of the ramp and rolled the rest of the way, coming to a stop face-to-face with a moldering corpse. From behind her came the roaring crackle of a flamethrower.

Tahiri expected to hear the clatter of an armored body crashing to the floor as Fett freed himself from the moss. Instead a helmet-muffled voice began cursing in modern *Mando'a,* and she spun around to find the bounty hunter's situation even worse than before. The moss had melted into a big gob that now covered not only the flamethrower but Fett's entire arm. And the tendrils had contracted as they melted, immobilizing the limb and pulling it back toward the wall.

Tahiri picked herself up and shrugged. "Okay, Fett. Suit yourself." She wiped the mold off her face and turned back toward the main tunnel. "Sorry to bother you."

"That's *it,* Veila?" Fett called. "You're just going to leave me hanging here . . . *alive?*"

Tahiri checked to make certain there were no carnivorous plants snaking her way, then looked back toward Fett.

"What did you expect?" she asked. "You tried to slag me."

"I *expected* you to finish the job," Fett said. "Not that I'm complaining, but I didn't expect you to be squeamish about the wet work. Your reputation must be overblown."

"Fett, let me ask you a question," Tahiri said. She knew he was just trying to draw her in close so he could get the drop on her and force her to help him escape—and it was so unnecessary. "Can you move stuff with your mind?"

"Stupid question," Fett growled. "You know I can't."

"Right. But *I* can. So if I wanted you dead, why would I walk over there and call your name?" Tahiri pulled the pack off her back and opened it, then used the Force to lift a thermal detonator out of the interior. "Why wouldn't I just float one of these bad girls over there next to you?"

Fett's helmet turned until the T-shaped visor was pointed in her direction. "Are you enjoying this?"

"A little bit," Tahiri admitted. She armed the detonator and set the fuse. "And I *will* kill you, if need be."

"And this is where I convince you there's no need?"

"That depends. How much do you want to live?"

"Enough," Fett grunted. "If you're offering a deal, let's hear it."

Tahiri smiled. She could do a lot worse in the hired-scum department. Fett might be a murdering sleemo, but he was a murdering sleemo with his own code of honor and an enormous pride in his work. When he made a deal, he usually honored it.

"My orders are to end your involvement in Imperial politics," she said. "*How* I do that is at my own discretion."

"Sorry, but I'm not leaving here until I get what I came for."

"The scientists who developed the Moffs' nanokiller?"

Fett was normally cool, but Tahiri could feel the heat of his hatred boiling in the Force. "Jessal Yu and Frela Tarm," he confirmed. "They're supposed to be here with a bunch of Squibs."

"I can let you have the two scientists," Tahiri offered. "Unofficially, of course."

"In return for?"

"I told you, staying out of Imperial politics," Tahiri replied. "That means your deal with Daala is over."

"I got her here." Fett was finally beginning to sound interested. "That *was* our deal."

"Good. Then you're free to make a deal with me."

"To do that, I'd have to trust you," Fett said. "And given the company you keep, I don't."

"Caedus was a long time ago," Tahiri said. She knew the biggest obstacle to an arrangement with Fett was her former apprenticeship to Darth Caedus. Caedus was the one who had authorized the Moffs to dump the nanokiller targeting Fett into Mandalore's atmosphere— *after* torturing his daughter, Ailyn Vel, to death in the opening weeks of the Second Civil War. "But if you can't put the past behind you, I'll be happy to end your embarrassment forever—just to make sure my reputation doesn't suffer."

"I wasn't talking about Caedus," Fett said, refusing to be intimidated.

"I'm no Jedi, either," Tahiri said. "At the moment, I'm working for the Empire."

A snort sounded inside Fett's helmet. "Only until Daala takes over."

"Is that any business of yours?"

"I guess not." Fett paused. "What's in it for you?"

"We have a mutual enemy."

"Here?"

Tahiri nodded. "How much do you know about Abeloth?"

"Who?"

"Abeloth is more of a *what*," Tahiri said, certain now that her earlier assumption about Fett working with Abeloth had been mistaken. "And if you want your scientists, you'll have to deal with her first. Let me cut you down, and I'll tell you what we're facing."

"I haven't agreed yet," Fett reminded her.

"You will." Tahiri returned the detonator to her pack and the pack to her shoulders, and then started toward the ramp. "Trust me—you're going to want the help."

Taking care to stand well away from the tendrils, she used her lightsaber to cut Fett free and helped him clean the moss from his armor. He removed a hypo from one of the utility pouches on his belt and gave himself an injection to combat his pain and grogginess, and Tahiri began a quick rundown on Abeloth, explaining that she was an ancient Force entity who had escaped from the Maw. The Jedi were still learning about her, but so far they had established that she could move between bodies and change her appearance at will. And she was proving *very* difficult to kill.

Fett only shrugged. "Maybe the Jedi aren't using the right kind of ammunition."

"Do *not* take her lightly," Tahiri warned. "She has more ways to kill than you do—and you'll never see her coming."

"You think you're scaring me, Veila?" Fett asked. "I *always* see them coming."

Tahiri pointed at the moss they had just cleaned off his armor. "You didn't this time."

"*That* was her doing?" Fett asked, glancing at the sticky pile. "I thought it was my scientists, doing something *else* they need to die for."

"I'm afraid not," Tahiri replied. "This stuff grows wherever Abeloth sets up house. It's how she feeds."

"On fungus and moss?" Fett asked. "What is she, some kind of cave-creeper?"

Tahiri shook her head. "Abeloth is no herbivore, Fett. She feeds on fear. Anguish. On what beings feel as they suffer and die."

Fett's helmet swung back. "You're telling me she feeds on *death?*"

"Not in the way you mean," Tahiri replied. "She feeds on the *feelings* death causes. Fear and pain release a lot of dark side energy. *That's* what Abeloth is after."

Fett fell silent, and Tahiri could tell by the stillness in his Force aura that she was finally making him understand what they were up against—that he needed her help for more than just finding his scientists. He needed her to get him out of the Moon Maiden alive.

Finally, Fett nodded. "Okay, she's a Force-drinker," he said. "I get it."

"Not yet," Tahiri said. "You're still thinking on a mortal scale, like Vader or Palpatine. Think bigger, like a storm or a tide. Like a living *Force volcano.*"

Fett's helmet tipped back. "A living Force volcano?" he echoed. "That's running it pretty far into Wild Space, Veila."

"I don't think so," Tahiri said. "You saw all those speeders out in the crater?"

"They would have been hard to miss," Fett said. "I figured Yu and Tarm needed a bunch of lab rats."

"I guess that's one explanation." Tahiri waved a hand at a clump of fungi. "But they can't be doing much experimenting right now . . . and the Moon Maiden is still advertising heavily for new workers."

"You think Abeloth is running through her feeding stock?"

"That's my guess," Tahiri replied. "It certainly fits the facts *I* see."

Fett looked away, and Tahiri felt his Force aura grow cold and apprehensive. "Okay," he said at last. "We're up against a Force volcano. How do we kill it?"

"I'm still working on that." Grateful that Fett couldn't sense what was in *her* Force aura, she smiled. "I was hoping you might have some ideas."

Fett studied her for a moment, then finally nodded. "Deal," he said. "But you take point."

"Fair enough," Tahiri said.

She started up the ramp toward the security bunker.

"No need," Fett said. "Nothing up there but bodies. Dead ones."

"Nothing?" Tahiri asked. Guessing Fett might be reluctant to stick around if she mentioned there was turbolaser barrage on the way, she was trying to find a subtle way to ask about shield generators. "You cleared it?"

"*No*. They just died of fright when they heard I was coming."

Tahiri rolled her eyes. "I was wondering about surveillance, hatch lockouts, patrol droids . . . that sort of thing?"

"Do I look like an amateur?" Fett demanded. "I said *nothing*. Nothing living, nothing functional."

"Okay . . . thanks," Tahiri said, deciding that Fett's definition of *nothing* meant she could check *destroy shield generators* off her mental to-do list. "That's good to know."

She returned to the primary tunnel and began to follow the darkness in the Force deeper into the Moon Maiden. The passage was clogged with fungi and corpses, and the walls and ceiling were festooned with hanging moss. Using fire and the Force, they cleared the way as they advanced, leaving the tunnel behind them choked with foul-smelling smoke. Twice, Tahiri stopped Fett from spraying flame over still-living beings. The first was an unconscious human female whose red-pocked face was coated in yellow spores. The next was a screaming Twi'lek with a leg exposed to the bone by flesh-eating mold. Fett remarked that Tahiri wasn't doing the Twi'lek any favors by stopping him. She had to admit that he had a point, but she still wouldn't let him burn the poor woman alive.

About eight hundred meters in, they came to a fire bulkhead with a locked hatch. Tahiri felt a large gathering of terrified Force presences on the other side, spread over perhaps a thousand square meters. But she sensed no one lurking just beyond the hatch, so there was no ambush. She looked into Fett's visor until a curiosity came to his presence, then pointed at the hatch controls and made a typing motion. He nodded and pulled a lock slicer from his thigh pocket.

As Fett worked, Tahiri did a Force reconnaissance of the area beyond the hatch, trying to get an idea of what they would find on the other side. There was a boiling mass of fear and anguish about half a kilometer directly ahead, tightly packed and stationary—probably a group of beings trapped in a detention area. Scattered to the left were about fifty presences, also frightened, but not in much pain—probably workers of some sort.

Directly ahead, a dozen beings seemed to be moving back and forth across a space about a hundred meters long and twice as wide as the tunnel. Up and to the right, on what felt like a second story, were a trio of shifty presences that Tahiri instantly recognized as Squibs. And a short distance beyond the Squibs was the target.

Tahiri had no doubt that it was Abeloth. It was a seething orb of darkness larger than any she had felt before, as hot in the Force as a fusion core, and it was reaching into her even as she reached for it.

Tahiri tried to shut down quickly, withdrawing from the Force and making her presence small, but it was not easily done. The thing had already started to sink its tentacles into her, and she could feel them writhing about inside, struggling to keep hold, until she finally closed herself off entirely.

For a moment, Tahiri sat, fighting not to tremble, trying not to wonder whether she was really up to this fight. She had confirmed the target's presence, and, in Fett, she had something likely to hold even Abeloth's attention until the turbolaser barrage began. Now she just needed to arrange a way to verify the enemy's destruction—and to do that, she had to get close enough to see her.

Tahiri felt Fett's gaze on her, then looked over to find his helmet turned in her direction. In his hand, he was holding a tiny black spy droid about the size of her thumb—large by Jedi standards, but small enough for their purposes.

"Ready to take a peek?"

"Not yet," she said. "I have some intelligence."

She told Fett about what she had sensed in the Force, laying out for him as accurately as possible the dimensions of the chamber and the location of the presences she had felt. She paid special attention to Abeloth and the Squibs, describing how the Squibs seemed to be somewhere up high, with Abeloth perhaps thirty meters beyond and at the same level as most of the other beings.

"Impressive," Fett said. He activated his spy droid and reached for the hatch lever. "I still like a vid feed."

"Uh, we might not want to take that long," Tahiri said. "I'm not the only Force-user here, remember? While I was sensing Abeloth in *there*, she was sensing me out *here*."

"Great," Fett said, feigning disgust that Tahiri did not feel in his presence. "Now she's expecting us."

"So?" Tahiri knew Fett's effort to make her feel guilty was just an attempt to pull their center of power in his direction, and she wasn't about to play along. "Did you ever think she *wouldn't* be expecting us?"

"I guess not," he admitted. "But we still go after the Squibs first."

Tahiri checked her chrono and saw that they had about twenty minutes before her projected midday GST bombardment. So time wasn't the problem—and going after the Squibs would give Abeloth something to think about other than why they weren't coming after her.

"Okay," Tahiri said. "Squibs first."

Fett's hand remained poised over the hatch lever. "Okay?"

"Sure," Tahiri said, nodding. "A deal is a deal, and the Squibs aren't going to be a problem for us. After we finish with Abeloth, that might not be true anymore."

Suspicion flooded Fett's presence, and he pulled his hand away from the lever. "That was way too easy, Veila," he said. "What's your plan?"

"It's too late for a plan," Tahiri replied. Determined to get the fight started before Fett had a chance to break their deal, she used the Force to depress the hatch lever. "We need to move fast if we want to catch those Squibs."

The hatch opened with a soft hiss. Before Fett had a chance to ask about how she had forced the issue, Tahiri used the Force to push it halfway open.

A gust of hot, dank air rolled through the narrow opening, and Tahiri nearly gagged. The stench seemed equal parts ammonia and unwashed bodies. Fett used his free hand to tap his sleeve controls—activating his helmet's filter system—then dropped into a fighting crouch and led the way through the hatch.

Through the bulkhead, the tunnel opened into a huge vault. A broad corridor ran from in front of Tahiri and Fett straight ahead to an identical bulkhead more than a hundred meters distant. Along both sides of the chamber ran ten-meter walls of white durasteel, each partitioning off a block of office suites.

The entire space was filled by thickets of knee-high fungi and towering pillars of club moss. Scurrying through this underground forest, Tahiri saw a dozen haggard beings dressed in miner's overalls. Instead of hauling laserdrills and detonite tubes, however, they appeared to be pushing—and in a couple of cases, abandoning—hoversleds piled with meter-high stacks of poster flimsi and holosign projector pads.

The Force was sour with the slaves' fear, and now that she was inside the chamber, she could literally see Force energy gathering in oily, iridescent swirls. In fact, it was flowing through a pair of bantha-sized doors into the largest room on the right—just about where she sensed Abeloth's presence.

No one seemed to notice them, and for a moment Tahiri thought that Abeloth's captives were just too exhausted or terrified to pay any attention to a guy in Mandalorian armor and a tall blond wearing an Imperial Security Special Tactics vac suit.

Then a bearded human pulled a stubby E-11 blaster rifle from inside his overalls and threw himself to the floor, firing as he dropped. A single bolt pinged off the bulkhead before Fett's arm came up and a tongue of crimson flame shot out of a sleeve nozzle to engulf the man.

In the next instant everyone in the chamber was diving for cover and pulling blasters. Tahiri ignited her lightsaber and began to bat bolts toward their sources.

"See? Definitely expected," she said. "Told you it was too late for a plan!"

"These miners are no trouble." Fett tipped his head forward and sent an arm-sized rocket screaming into the center of the chamber. "It's the snarkin' plants that scare me."

The rocket detonated with a deafening blast. Tahiri was thrown against the bulkhead behind her by a shock wave hot enough to singe her hair. But the battle fell suddenly quiet, and when the blast-dazzle cleared from her eyes, she saw that the entire chamber had been more or less cleared of flora.

Fett's gloved hand clamped around her forearm. *"Move."*

He started toward the right side of the chamber, and a tingle of danger sense raced down Tahiri's spine.

Fett continued to pull her toward the chamber wall. "I want those—"

"No!" Tahiri yelled. "Down!"

She dived in one direction and shoved Fett in the opposite. In the weak gravity, they both traveled a good five meters before hitting the floor. A chain of *plinks* sounded next to her as a line of pellets ricocheted off the floor where she had been standing.

Tahiri rolled onto her back and saw two shatter gun barrels protruding through an observation port in the wall. They were located on the second floor, about fifteen meters to the right of the big doors where Abeloth was hiding. One barrel was swinging toward her, the other toward Fett, and peering over the top of each was a pair of beady Squib eyes.

"There!"

Tahiri pointed and used the Force to shove the nearest weapon into the other one.

Fett's method was more direct, simply raising his arm and loosing a tongue of flame. It shot through the center of the observation port— but not before both Squibs dropped their weapons and ducked out of sight.

"Go!" Fett yelled, springing up. "Don't let them hide!"

Tahiri was already on her feet, racing for a small door below the port. It was locked, but these were just sliding doors, not hatches. Her lightsaber required only a few seconds to cut through the thin durasteel.

By then Fett had drawn his blaster pistol and caught up to her. He hit the door at a full sprint, planting a boot sole in the center and kicking the panel down almost before Tahiri had finished cutting it free. She followed him through and found him charging up a pedramp, exchanging blasterfire with three pack-burdened Squibs and yelling at them to stop shooting before he got serious.

They continued to fire, of course.

Tahiri and Fett caught them at the top of the ramp. Tahiri took the lead, using her lightsaber to deflect their attacks as she advanced, trying to force them to the back of a service corridor so they would have no choice except to surrender. Fett took a more direct approach, using his height to fire over Tahiri's head. He downed all three Squibs in barely nine shots—which was *very* good shooting, considering that he was in the middle of a firefight and had to time his bolts to get them past a whirling lightsaber.

Tahiri started to chastise the bounty hunter for killing their best means of finding his scientists—then noticed that the three Squibs were lying on the floor twitching, their eyes bulging as they helplessly watched their attackers approach.

"Those didn't *look* like stun bolts you were firing," she commented.

"Yeah, I'm full of surprises. You live longer that way." Fett stepped past her, then jerked a thumb toward the adjacent wall. "You see what we've got in there. I'll handle the interrogation."

Tahiri did not turn away. "I don't think so," she said. "I can't let you—"

"*You* have a conscience?" Fett interrupted. "Since when?"

"Prison changed me," Tahiri replied, knowing it would be a waste of time to explain to Boba Fett that she was trying to make amends for killing Admiral Pellaeon. "And I can't let you murder helpless captives, Fett. I'm not that person anymore."

A muffled sigh sounded inside Fett's helmet, and then he nodded. "Fine. As long as they tell me what we need to know, I'll let someone else take out the vermin. Good enough?"

One glance at their trembling captives told Tahiri that Fett would have no trouble extracting all the information he wanted from the trio. She nodded and turned toward the door without another word.

The door, of course, had been locked. She used her lightsaber to cut through the durasteel panel, then stepped through the hole.

The room beyond was a basic lab-workroom outfitted with a large table that contained built-in sinks and warming pads at one end. To Tahiri's left was the observation port through which the Squibs had opened fire. To her right, in the back of the room, were several computer stations with chairs. Two of the chairs were occupied by humans in white lab coats, one a redheaded male and the other a brunette female. They sat staring at her with looks of absolute terror on their faces. Considering the firefight that had just taken place outside their office, Tahiri found it difficult to understand why they had not fled— until she noticed the shackles securing their legs to their chairs.

"Yu and Tarm?" she asked from the door.

The woman nodded. "I'm Dr. Frela Tarm," she said. "He's Dr. Jessal Yu."

"Good," Tahiri said. "If there's anything here you need to stop the nanokiller targeting Boba Fett, I suggest you get it together now."

The man—Jessal Yu—scowled and yanked at his ankle chain.

"In case you haven't noticed, we can't exactly move," he said. "Besides which, there *isn't* a way to stop it. You can't deactivate a nanokiller after you've set it loose. You have to design the obsolescence into the original molecules."

"I wouldn't admit that to Fett," Tahiri said. "Because he's here now, and you're only going to live for as long as he continues to believe you *can* stop it."

Tarm's eyes went wide, and the Force shivered with such fear that Tahiri almost felt sorry for the two scientists—until she reminded herself what the pair had done. They hadn't just targeted Fett. They were also the masterminds behind a line of illegal weapons that had wiped out the entire Verpine soldier caste on Nickel One—and killed much of Tenel Ka's family. Whatever punishment Fett meted out to the scientists, it would never be justice enough.

After a moment of wallowing in fear, Yu turned to Tarm and asked, "Perhaps a counteragent, Doctor?"

Tarm considered this for a moment, then nodded. "It sounds believable," she said. "And who knows? There might even be a way to make it work."

"Stranger things have happened," Yu agreed. He turned toward his computer station. "I'll download the old data. You gather the samples."

"Agreed, Doctor." Tarm turned toward Tahiri, then pointed at her shackles. "Could you?"

Tahiri shook her head. "That chair has rollers," she said, knowing how Fett would react if he came in and discovered she had actually freed one of his scientists. "And you can tell *me* where to find a vidcam and an uplink around here—preferably one I can use without Abeloth noticing."

"Who's Abeloth?" Yu asked.

"I think she might be referring to Pagorski," Tarm said. She looked back to Tahiri. "An Imperial lieutenant, tentacles and some *very* strange powers?"

"The tentacles and the powers sound right." Tahiri was not as surprised as she might have been. Pagorski had been acting as Daala's campaign coordinator since the day the election was announced, and she *had* reappeared in the Empire shortly after someone very strong in the Force had used her powers to run the blockade at Boreleo. It was certainly not a stretch to conclude that Pagorski and Abeloth were one and the same—or, more accurately, that Pagorski had been *possessed* by Abeloth. "I think she's in the next room over. Is there a way I can get a look at her without her seeing me?"

"The lieutenant is in the main lab," Tarm replied. Her gaze shifted to the wall opposite Tahiri, then slid down its length and finally came to rest on a transparisteel viewing panel about three quarters of the way to the front of the room. "So you can certainly sneak a peek at *her.*"

"Thanks." Tahiri pulled the pack off her back and began to transfer combat supplies to the utility pockets on the outside of her vac suit. "About that vidcam?"

Wu looked toward a cabinet above his head. "In the cabinet over here. But you're going to have to use a hard wire for the uplink." He pointed to a set of socket receptacles on the side of the big lab table. "We can't, er, *couldn't* have any signal interference in this lab."

Deciding that it might be wise to make a quick situation check before she spent five of those minutes setting up a vidcam and uplink, Tahiri removed her helmet from her cargo pack. She attached it to the convenience carrier on the back of her vac suit shoulder, then tossed the pack aside and checked her chrono. Eight minutes before midday GST. Whatever happened next, she had to keep Abeloth occupied for at least eight minutes. She leaned out the door into the corridor, where Fett was still interrogating the Squibs, and told him to let them go.

"You found my scientists?" he asked.

"Yes," she said. "And Abeloth, too."

Without awaiting his reply, she started toward the viewing panel. As she approached, she could see down into what had clearly been the facility's primary laboratory. Even from a dozen steps away, she could see the tops of several fermentation tanks and what appeared to be a large walk-in freezer. But those were hardly what caught her eye. Floating in the smoky air in the heart of the lab were the heads of eight Imperial Moffs. She saw square-chinned Jowar, flabby-jowled Quillan, long-necked Poliff, and five more—all of them Daala's most ardent public supporters.

At well over a meter in diameter each, the heads were too large to be real, of course. But they looked far more substantial than holograms, and their necks were as thin as tentacles. In fact, as Tahiri drew nearer to the viewing panel, she could see that they *were* tentacles.

The tentacles led down to a pair of stubby arms, which belonged to a thin female human dressed in a tattered uniform. It had originally been an Imperial lieutenant's uniform, but all that remained was a collection of rags with a rank bar. A river of Force energy was rushing in through the big doors at the front of the room and flowing into the woman. Her short yellow hair stuck out straight and stiff, and her face seemed to be dissolving into flakes and smoke. Her wide, full-lipped mouth stretched into a cruel smile, and her narrow blue eyes rose toward Tahiri.

Tahiri Veila. The voice was deep and resonant with Force power, and it sounded inside Tahiri's head. *How nice of you to come for me.*

Chapter Twenty-four

THE NUMBERS ON LUKE'S CHRONO READ 11:52 GST. AT PRECISELY 12:00 GST, a brigade of Void Jumpers would hit the exhaust port. That meant Luke and his team had eight minutes—eight minutes for three Jedi to do the impossible or die.

The Jedi, obviously, were hoping for the impossible.

Their objective was a small deflector shield generator that protected the main exhaust port in this corner of the Temple. It lay 150 meters ahead, at the end of a long run of ventilation ducting. Between Luke's team and the objective were two vertical airshafts, which joined the main duct from below. Technically, the shafts were called stack-heads, but in his exhaustion Luke could no longer remember why the engineers used such an odd term. He knew only that the shafts were a pair of broad, windy chasms spaced roughly fifty meters apart, and that the grit they carried was going to make advancing down the cramped duct feel even more like being caught in a Tatooine dust storm.

But at least the duct's maintenance lighting had been activated, so it was possible to see the biggest problem that Luke and his team faced. At the far end of the run, beyond the second stack-head, four Sith were kneeling behind a tripod-mounted heavy blaster. The deflector shield generator, of course, was *behind* the Sith, floating on a tethered hoversled in the middle of the exhaust port.

If Luke and his team succeeded in destroying the shield generator, several thousand elite Void Jumpers would come crashing through the exhaust port. Along with their Jedi liaisons, they would disperse throughout the Temple and open other breaches in the Sith defenses, and the rest of Bwua'tu's space marine volunteers would flood in to finish the job.

This new assault plan would cost many more Galactic Alliance lives than the admiral's original plan. But the Sith would quickly find themselves cornered and outnumbered, and the Jedi and their allies would, sooner or later, liberate the Jedi Temple.

Liberating the Temple would not win the war against the Sith, or even end the battle for Coruscant. But Luke and his allies were counting on it to be the turning point, when the Sith went from entrenched defenders to hunted quarry, and momentum swung back toward the Jedi.

All Luke's team had to do was take out that shield generator.

On most days, that would have been an easy job for two Jedi Masters and Jaina Solo, who, as the Sword of the Jedi, had proven time and again that she was the combat equal of anyone in the Order.

But Luke and his two companions were not at their "normal" best. They had been fighting and retreating—mostly retreating—for far too long. At this point, they were all suffering from serious wounds. Jaina had a broken arm and probably several broken ribs. Corran had lost two fingers to a stray blaster bolt, and he was limping around on a knee swollen to the size of a hubba gourd. Luke had taken a blow to the head that still had him seeing stars, and he had a painful lightsaber burn along his left side. They were all drawing on the Force so heavily that they were virtually glowing with cell overload. Jaina had already entered a stage of Force euphoria, and it would not be long before she experienced a crash every bit as severe as a spicehead coming down from an overdose.

Corran Horn tapped Luke with a three-fingered hand, then tipped his head and croaked, "Company."

Luke looked in the direction Corran was indicating, down the duct behind them. A lavender-skinned Keshiri woman was rounding a corner about two hundred meters away. The distance was too great to see her features plainly, but Luke had no need. He knew she had dark hair, oval eyes, and a wide, cruel smile. Her name was Korelei, and she was the reason Luke and his companions were on the verge of collapse.

The three Jedi had first encountered Korelei in the corridor outside the computer core, when they had lured the Sith away so Ben and the Horn siblings could get Rowdy inside. Noticing how the other Sith deferred to her, Luke had intentionally waited until she was on top of the first detonite mine before triggering it. Instead of shredding her and every other Sith within three meters, the blast had simply dissipated into some sort of Force shield that she had flung down.

And the situation had deteriorated from there. Korelei and her troops had continued to hound the three Jedi since, never giving them a moment's rest, always finding them when they hid, continually herding them away from the computer core. It was hard to understand how she could be so cunning and powerful and *not* be the Grand Lord of the Lost Tribe, but so far she had kept her quarry too busy for such speculation. She had made it impossible for Luke's team to reunite with Ben and the Horn siblings—or even to discover what had happened to them. Luke and Corran knew only two things about the fate of Ben, Valin, and Jysella. First, they had not succeeded in getting the blast doors open, or the primary shields down. Second, neither he nor Corran had felt anything in the Force to suggest that any of their children had died. Beyond that, the two fathers were left to fear the worst and hope for the best.

Luke drew his blaster pistol. "Time to go."

"*No-we-have-to-wait!*" Jaina's voice was rapid and full of excitement, a symptom of the Force euphoria that was the only thing preventing her collapse. "It's still five minutes before midday."

"I know," Luke said. "But we can't wait."

"But if we blow the generator early," Jaina insisted, "every gunner on this side of the Temple will be taking aim up the assault corridor!"

"Jaina, they are *now*." Corran's voice was gruff and impatient, a sign that he was in such bad shape himself that he didn't seem to recognize what was happening to Jaina. "When have we done *anything* to surprise that she-voork chasing us?"

"We *haven't*." Luke watched Korelei pause in the duct. Perhaps sensing the blaster in his hand, she waved several of her followers ahead of her. "She's the first Sith who actually worries me."

"Thanks," Jaina said. "Didn't need to hear *that*."

"Sorry." Luke winced at his slip; obviously, he was not in top form, either. "I thought you would have noticed. But we can't wait, not with her behind us."

"Better to blow the shields early than not at all," Corran agreed. "I'll take out the generator."

"Good," Luke agreed. "Take Jaina with you. I'll handle rear guard."

"Alone?" Jaina sounded confused. "How can you stop them alone?"

"I only need to slow them, Jaina," Luke said patiently. "Taking out the shield generator is the important thing here—the *only* important thing."

Jaina started to nod—then seemed to realize what he was saying and shook her head vigorously. "No way," she said. "I'm not leaving you to die. Not—"

"Jaina!" Corran grabbed her by the arm. "We're *all* going to die, most likely. Let's just get this done first, okay?"

Jaina's eyes brightened with alarm. Then a sudden calmness came to her face, and Luke knew her Force euphoria was passing. She had only minutes before her body collapsed, literally burned out by the constant flood of Force energy she had been drawing through it. She gently pulled her arm from Corran's grasp and nodded.

"Right." She looked down at her splinted arm, then tried to make a fist and failed. "Looks like I should take the lead."

Corran studied her in silence, no doubt taking the same meaning from her suggestion that Luke did. Jaina was offering to serve as a human shield for Corran, who at least had the use of both hands, and thus would be in the best possible shape to finish the job when he reached the Sith protecting the generator. It was a sound tactic, considering the circumstances, and it broke Luke's heart to nod in agreement.

There could be little doubt that he was sending his own niece to her death—just as he had sent her brother Anakin to *his*. But what else could he do? The Jedi attack plan had failed miserably, and the price of that failure was death—his and Jaina's and Corran's, almost certainly. But if they could take out the shield generator and open a route into the Temple for the Void Jumpers, then at least they would be putting the Sith on the defensive.

And they would be giving Ben and Valin and Jysella a chance to make it out of the Temple alive.

As Jaina unclipped her lightsaber and turned to leave, Luke flooded his presence with feelings of respect and gratitude. He reached out to her in the Force, then said, "Master Solo?"

Jaina stopped, but didn't turn, and for a moment Luke thought he had made a mistake of timing. But after a couple of breaths, he felt her calming and growing stronger in the Force, and she asked, "Yes, Grand Master Skywalker?"

"I just wanted you to hear me say it," Luke said. "May the Force be with you."

Jaina nodded without turning around. "Thanks," she said. "That means a lot right now."

"Glad you feel ready, Master Solo," Corran added. "The Order needs you like it never has before."

Jaina was quiet for a moment. Luke could tell by the sorrow in her Force aura that she was thinking of her loved ones—her parents, Han and Leia; her lost brothers, Anakin and Jacen; her niece, Allana. And most of all Jagged Fel, the man she was probably not going to live to marry. Luke almost told her to wait—that he and Corran could do this alone.

But that was not who Jaina Solo *was*. She was a warrior, and broken or not, she would have cut off her own arm before she allowed him and Corran to attack the Sith without her.

A moment later, Jaina nodded to Corran and said, "You're just saying that because I'm going first."

Without awaiting a reply, she rose into a crouch and took off down the main duct at a sprint, her footfalls booming off the metal like thunder. Corran limped after her, moving surprisingly quick for a man with a damaged knee. A few breaths later the enemy gunner's heavy blaster opened fire, filling the run with a screeching storm of light and heat. It went silent again almost instantly as Jaina raised her broken arm and gestured, using the Force to shove the weapon and its tripod back into the main exhaust port behind it.

The Sith leapt free. For just an instant, the blaster and its tripod hung suspended in the shaft, caught between gravity and the fierce updrafts created by the huge turbocharged circulation jets that drew air through the Temple's ventilation system. Finally, gravity won, and the weapon plummeted out of sight.

By then, Jaina was at the first stack-head, leaping the two-meter pit where it opened into the floor. The Sith unleashed a combined volley of Force lightning and blasterfire. The range was still nearly a hundred meters, so the pistol bolts ricocheted off the duct's metal lining and lost all their energy long before reaching Jaina. But both Force lightning attacks found their target—just as she was in midair over the stack-head.

Jaina caught the first fork on her lightsaber blade. The second seemed to hit her square in the chest. Luke saw her shoulders rock back; then her momentum vanished, and she started to drop.

Corran was in the air half a step behind her, somehow keeping pace despite his swollen knee. He reached down and caught a handful of robe. They both crashed onto the floor just centimeters beyond the stack-head, then went tumbling along the duct until they rolled free of the Force lightning. At the far end of the duct, the Sith started forward toward the second stack-head to stop Jaina and Corran from leaping across.

Unfortunately, Luke couldn't afford to watch what happened next. The time had come for him to leave Corran and Jaina to their objectives and tend to his own. He turned to find Korelei's troop a little more than a hundred meters away, with two more stack-heads between him and them. They were charging down the main duct three abreast, their crackling lightsabers creating a moving bubble of crimson light. Korelei herself was not visible, though somewhere in the second or third rank Luke could feel a menacing presence that could only be her.

Deciding to make the same use of terrain as the Sith defending the shield generator, he stepped to the edge of the nearest stack-head and opened fire across the pit. The three Sith in the front rank began to bat his attacks back toward him, so he dropped to his belly and continued to aim at their chests—until they reached the first stack-head and jumped into the air, when he shifted his pattern and began to switch between leg and head shots.

As he had hoped, the sudden change took the Sith by surprise. One Saber took a leg hit and collapsed into a tumbling heap when he landed on Luke's side of the pit. A second grew careless when trying to block a face shot and ended up removing the head of the woman next to him. A third Sith perished when the tumbling head struck him in the face and he fell short of the edge, then toppled into the shaft.

But the rest made it across, half a dozen of them, now only fifty meters away, with Korelei in the second rank urging them on. Luke continued to fire, switching between their legs and heads and barely slowing them down. Behind him, the screech and crackle of the battle between Jaina and Corran and the four Sith *they* faced was rising to a crescendo—a sure sign that Jaina and Corran were approaching the last stack-head. The impossible mission was beginning to seem more impossible every moment.

Then Jaina yelled at Corran. "Go now!"

With Korelei's band still forty meters away, Luke glanced back in time to see Jaina pulling up short on the near side of the stack-head and using the Force to throw her lightsaber. It went spinning across the pit horizontally. Corran was about a step behind her, his own blade whirling madly as he batted blaster bolts aside.

Jaina's lightsaber reached the far side of the pit and was quickly batted aside by one of the Sith. By then Corran was already leaping across, his blade rising into a high guard and his boot coming up for a thrust kick—which seemed almost certain to cost him a leg, until Jaina extended her hands. She hit the Sith with a Force blast that Luke had not thought she still had the strength to deliver, and all four enemies went tumbling backward.

A heartbeat later Corran was on the far side of the stack-head. Nothing remained between him and the shield generator but four still-tumbling Sith and fifty meters of duct. Luke saw him twist the hilt of his dual-phase lightsaber, then the silver blade turned purple and was suddenly a third longer as the second focusing crystal took over. The first Sith screamed, and Luke began to feel a lot better about their chances.

But on the near side of the stack-head, Jaina was done. She was on her knees, swaying in exhaustion and dangerously close to falling unconscious. Luke used the Force to pull her a safe distance away from the pit's edge, then turned to find his own trouble almost on him. With the first rank of Sith only two steps from the other side of the stack-head, he tossed his blaster behind him and extended a hand, grabbing four Sith ankles in a crushing Force grasp. He pulled them toward the pit.

Three of the Sith found themselves suddenly falling into the stack-head. They screamed and twisted, desperately searching for something they could grab—then plummeted out of sight. The fourth Sith managed to Force hurl himself backward and land on his side of the pit. Before Luke could drag him forward, a glass parang left the scabbard hanging from the man's belt and came flying.

Luke redirected the parang with little more than a thought, but by then Korelei and another Keshiri were in the air over the stack-head, their lightsabers ignited and their eyes fixed on Luke. He lit his own weapon and sprang to his feet, at the same time hitting them both with a Force blast that sent the male Keshiri tumbling back across the pit.

Korelei did not even feel it. She merely swung her lightsaber down to block Luke's slash, then planted a stomp kick square in his chest and sent him sailing down the duct backward.

Luke came down five meters away, a crushing pain in his chest. He struggled to draw breath. Korelei was barely two paces away, her fingers already glowing blue with the Force lightning she was about to hurl. With neither the time nor the strength to leap up, Luke merely reached for her in the Force, then turned his lightsaber toward her midsection and *pulled.*

They came together in a collision that left Luke's head spinning and his bones aching. He knew his lightsaber had struck home because he smelled scorched flesh. The hilt was wobbling against his hand as Korelei struggled to free herself of the searing blade. He felt a palm press itself to his chest, so he brought his free hand up and grabbed her arm . . . too late. His entire body sizzled into the joint-crushing grip of a Force lightning strike.

The agony seemed to last forever. Luke could feel his own flesh charring beneath the palm pressed to his chest; he was paralyzed by the lightning, unable to fight free or attack with a head-butt, or even flick his lightsaber blade and finish Korelei. He simply hung paralyzed, one hand clutching her arm, the other pressing the hilt to her chest, wondering how long it would take her to die.

A lot longer than Luke, apparently. Her free arm rose between them, pushing off to create some space. Then she twisted away, hurling him into the duct wall . . . and sliding off his lightsaber sideways. The act opened a gaping chasm in her torso.

The wound did not even slow her down. Leaving Luke to drop unharassed, she raced down the duct after Corran, who had taken out three of the shield generator's defenders and was using a flashing onslaught of lightsaber attacks to drive the fourth Sith back toward the exhaust port. By the time Luke hit the floor, she was halfway to the next stack-head, her shoulders pivoting awkwardly atop a wound that should have left her lying in a lifeless heap ten steps earlier.

Luke had no time to contemplate the source of her toughness. He could already hear boots pounding on the duct floor as her last two followers rushed to catch up. Still trembling with the aftereffects of her Force lightning, he spun himself around to look the way she had come and saw the pair approaching the nearest stack-head. Because of the duct's low height, their heads and shoulders were hunched over, so they looked more like a pair of baby rancors than Sith.

They must have believed Luke was still incapacitated, becaused they did not even cover each other as they leapt. Such arrogance. He waited until they were over the center of the pit, then waved a hand at the one on the left, using the Force to shove him into the one on the right. Both Sith slammed into the wall of the duct and dropped like stones, their arms flying forward as they tried to snag the edge. Luke flicked his hand in their direction, hitting them with a Force shove that rocked both men backward. They cried out in surprise—or perhaps it was anger—and vanished down the stack.

Relieved that at least *some* Sith died the way they were supposed to, Luke summoned his discarded blaster and turned back toward Jaina—and began to understand why Korelei was so hard to kill. From the back, the Sith she-voork appeared to be floating more than running, and the gruesome wound that Luke had opened did not seem to be bleeding so much as venting a dark, greasy fume that rose into the air and spread along the ceiling of the duct.

Korelei was no more a "normal" Keshiri female than was Luke. She was some *other* kind of creature.

And she was halfway to Jaina, who was kneeling in the middle of the duct, slumped over and so motionless that Luke thought she might be dead.

A cry of anguish echoed down the duct as Corran cut down the last Sith between him and the shield generator.

Korelei—or whoever, whatever she was—raised an arm, and a powerful bolt of Force lightning crackled down the run. Taken by surprise, Corran screamed and went down, then lay on the duct floor convulsing and shaking, swaddled in dancing forks of blue energy and unable to free himself.

Luke opened fire with his blaster, managing to burn several bolts into the Korelei-thing even at a distance of over thirty meters. Of course, they barely slowed her down.

Luke had to stop the Korelei-thing—he could not bring himself to even *think* her true name—or the Jedi's last hope of breaching the Temple would be lost. He opened himself to the Force completely, and the energy came flooding in so fast it seemed to lift him, to carry him down the duct on a raging river of power. When he began to gain on his quarry, he fired again, this time pouring so many bolts into her legs that one actually erupted in flame.

And it made no difference.

This thing—this *entity*—had powers almost beyond comprehension. But he was beginning to comprehend.

"Jaina!" Luke reached out to her and was relieved to feel life in her aura. He put the power of the Force into his voice and focused his words on her. "*Master* Solo! The Jedi need you . . . *now!*"

Jaina did not stir.

Luke switched to fire at his quarry's head. A bolt caught the Korelei-thing just behind the ear and went blasting out the other side, carrying with it a spray of bone and brain.

The Korelei-thing stumbled.

He fired again, but now the creature was pivoting around, throwing her free hand up to deflect the bolt and send it ricocheting back down the duct. He didn't care, because at the other end of the run Corran was free, scrambling on his hands and knees toward the shield generator.

Luke grabbed Jaina in the Force. "Jedi Solo! Stand and fight!"

She remained motionless. Luke fired again.

The entity caught the bolt and held it, still burning, in her hand. There was a gaping scorch hole in her cheek where the earlier bolt had exited. Her lavender skin had faded to a blue-tinted alabaster, and when she locked gazes with Luke, her pupils had contracted to mere points of silver light. She smiled, her mouth stretching so wide that it reached from ear to ear, then her arm whipped forward and sent the blaster bolt sizzling straight at Luke's eyes, and he could deny the truth no longer.

Abeloth was here.

Down in the smoky genetics lab on Hagamoor 3, Tahiri had no time to call for help. Not that Fett could have offered much. A tentacle lashed up toward the workroom where Tahiri stood, and the head floating at the end—the one that looked like flabby Moff Quillan—came flying into the transparisteel viewing panel that separated the two rooms.

Instead of bursting against the panel as Tahiri had expected, the head exploded in a purple flash of Force energy. Tahiri brought her arm up, using the Force to push against the blast wave, and barely managed to keep from being shredded by the spray of metal shards that came flying her way.

Then *Tahiri* was flying, being drawn out through the shattered viewing panel into the searing heat of the genetics laboratory. How much time had passed since she had checked her chrono, she could not say. Two minutes, no more than three—and she needed to keep Abeloth occupied for at least eight. Not good.

Tahiri jammed a hand into one of her vac suit thigh pockets and felt the reassuring smoothness of a thermal detonator—and then she was in Abeloth's grasp, wrapped in a tentacle so tightly she could hardly breathe. A second tentacle wrapped itself around Tahiri's wrist and pulled her hand out of the pocket, still holding the not-yet-armed detonator.

Abeloth spun Tahiri around, and she found herself looking into a monstrous face—a face so consumed by Force energy it barely looked human. What little flesh remained had turned as gray as ash, and it was peeling away in flakes the size of thumbnails. The nose had collapsed into open cavities, and the lips had withered into brown strips that looked like they might fall off any moment.

But the eyes were familiar—and shocking. They were the same icy blue irises that had stared at Tahiri from the witness stand as Pagorski testified—as she *lied* about the death of Admiral Pellaeon. But the pupils weren't Pagorski's. They were huge, and they seemed dark and bottomless, with no light except a pair of tiny silver points that seemed to be receding even as Tahiri looked into them, to be drawing her down into a cold and soulless Void from which there could be no escape.

Inside Tahiri's mind, Abeloth's wispy voice said, *There is no need for explosives, child.*

The tentacle squeezed Tahiri's wrist until her hand opened and the thermal detonator dropped to the floor—still unarmed.

We are going to be together a long time, you and I.

Tahiri jammed the emitter nozzle of her lightsaber into the pit of Abeloth's stomach. "Not if I can help it."

She thumbed the switch and saw the tip of her sapphire lightsaber shoot out through Abeloth's back. Guessing it would take more than a single penetrating wound to kill a Force entity, Tahiri immediately whipped her hand down, dragging the blade down through her captor's body at an angle . . . or so she had intended.

When the blade failed to move, Tahiri looked down and saw that this hand, too, was wrapped in a tentacle. She tried to pull free and found that not only was she unable to move the hand, she could no longer even feel it.

That is the thing, my child, Abeloth said. *You can't help it.*

A tentacle rose between them, then bent forward and began to slither up Tahiri's chin.

"What?" Tahiri gasped. A cold terror was rising inside her, and she had to fight to avoid panicking. "What are you doing?"

Did I not say? Abeloth replied. *We are going to be together. The lieutenant's body is weak. Yours will be strong. Yours has felt the Force—*

The explanation was cut short by the sharp crackle of a mini rocket, its roar rising in pitch as it approached. Tahiri glanced toward the shattered viewing panel and saw Fett standing there, the arm with the launcher still pointed down into the lab.

Then Abeloth twisted away, ripping herself open on Tahiri's lightsaber blade, and was gone. The mini rocket arrived an eyeblink later, striking the floor in front of Tahiri . . . and failing to explode. Fett dipped his helmet—as though to say *you're welcome*—then spun away and disappeared about two breaths ahead of Abeloth. She sprang through the hole after him, an oily dark fume pouring from the wound in her side.

It took a couple of heartbeats for Tahiri to believe she hadn't lost her mind. It seemed impossible, but Fett had just risked his life to save hers. And he was using *himself* as bait, when he could have just taken his scientists and fled. Maybe he wasn't such a bad guy after all—or maybe he just valued his word more than his life.

Either way, Tahiri was not going to waste the time he had just bought her—quite possibly with his life. She pulled two more thermal detonators from her vac suit pockets and armed them both, then set one fuse for twenty seconds and secured this detonator inside a thigh pocket. The other detonator she kept in her hand, setting the fuse for ten seconds.

By the time Tahiri finished her preparations, brilliant bursts of orange and blue were flashing in the workroom as Fett unloaded his full arsenal into Abeloth. Keeping a silent count in her head, Tahiri Force-leapt through the shattered viewing panel and turned toward the far end of the room, where the two nanotech scientists—Tarm and Yu—were still shackled and cowering in their chairs.

Fett was in front of the two scientists, crouching behind the large lab table that filled the middle of the room, firing everything he had at Abeloth. The blasterfire she simply took, her wounded body barely flinching as bolt after bolt burned through. The flames she stopped with a shield of Force energy that sent tongues of crimson fire licking in every direction but toward her. And the mini rockets she simply

Force-nudged off-course, sending them streaking past to explode harmlessly against the wall.

Tahiri's count reached five. Abeloth was facing away from her. She had leapt up on the table and was walking across it toward Fett.

Tahiri raised the thermal detonator so Fett would have at least some chance of grasping her plan, then opened her hand and used the Force to float it gently toward Abeloth.

The detonator had traveled barely half the distance when Abeloth pivoted sideways so that she could see both of her enemies, and extended a tentacle. The orb tore free of Tahiri's Force grasp and went sailing toward Fett.

With only a few seconds left before the first detonator exploded, Tahiri went straight to Plan B, activating her lightsaber and Force-leaping to the attack. She was on Abeloth by the count of eight, hacking through a trio of tentacles—which dropped to the tabletop and promptly slithered around her ankles.

A tremendous roar filled the room as Fett activated his jetpack and came streaking toward them, one hand grasping the detonator Abeloth had sent flying toward him—which he had nabbed from the air. He jammed the detonator into the fume-oozing wound in the same instant Tahiri's count reached nine.

She turned to leap away—then something strong clamped her biceps, and her arm nearly came out of its socket as she was jerked into the air. By the time she realized Fett had politely snagged her on the way past, they were crashing into the front corner of the workroom. Everything went white and loud, and Tahiri feared they had failed to escape the detonator's blast radius.

That fear vanished an instant later as she hit the floor in an aching heap. Fett came down on top of her, all hard metal and sharp edges, and Tahiri realized that she had actually survived.

Had Abeloth?

Tahiri looked back toward the lab table. There was no lab table, only a five-meter hole in the floor. Drs. Frela Tarm and Jessal Yu, both utterly blast-shocked, sat staring into the hole.

Tahiri tried to move, but Fett was still lying atop her, silent and limp.

"Fett?" she called.

When he didn't answer, she checked him in the Force and was actually a bit relieved to sense that he was still alive.

"Fett!"

Tahiri started to roll him off gently—until a little voice in her head reached the number fifteen, and she recalled Plan B.

"Fett!" She shoved him hard, bolstering her own strength with the Force. In Hagamoor 3's weak gravity, the effort sent him flying. "Get off!"

Fett clanged into the ceiling and seemed to awaken. He pushed off hard and dropped back toward the floor, growling in a groggy voice, "Don't move!"

Tahiri ignored him and opened the utility pocket where she had secured the second detonator.

"I've got you, scum!" Fett shouted.

Tahiri looked over to find him standing on wobbly legs—and pointing his flamethrower at her. She used the Force to point his arm in another direction, then held the thermal detonator up for him to see.

"Two seconds," she said.

Fett's grogginess seemed to vanish all at once. He pointed toward the shattered viewing panel that overlooked the main genetics lab.

"Get rid of—"

Tahiri whipped the detonator toward the viewing panel, using the Force to guide it and push it along. Even then, the orb had barely passed through the opening before it activated. There came a tremendous *crack* and a blinding white flash that seemed to eat away much of the wall and the floor in front of them . . . and then there came another *crack*, this one deep and sonorous.

The entire facility shook as though it had been hit by an asteroid, and a tremendous clatter echoed through the room as untold tons of stone rained down on the upper side of the ceiling.

Fett's helmet turned so that the visor was fixed on Tahiri's face. "Those are some pretty nice detonators. Where'd you get them?"

Another boom shook the workroom, and this time a two-meter circle of ceiling simply vanished into smoke. The shrill whistle of escaping atmosphere wailed through the room, and everything that was not secured to a wall or a floor—shards of metal, pieces of flimsi, datachips—began to fly toward the hole.

Tahiri grabbed the helmet off the carrying clip on her shoulder and—praying that her vac suit had not been compromised during the battle—pulled it over her head and seated it with a quick twist. Fett, whose armor included a built-in vac suit, simply started tapping keys on his forearm control pad.

"*Veila!*" he yelled over their suit comm. "Is there something you forgot to tell me?"

Another blast shook the facility, this time striking somewhere farther away from the main lab. Tahiri checked her chrono and saw that the barrage had started two minutes early. She hoped that Vangur had noticed the frigate moving into attack position and retreated to a safe distance.

Tahiri toggled her chin-mike. "I didn't think it would matter," she said. "I thought we'd be dead by now."

"*You* might be," Fett warned.

"They're two minutes early, if it's any consolation," Tahiri said. "Jag must really have lit a fire under his staff."

"*Now* the Imperial Navy moves fast." Fett's helmet turned toward the back of the workroom, where Frela Tarm and Jessal Yu were already in the last stages of decompression sickness, with blue skin and blood oozing out around the rims of their bulging eyes. "Of course."

Fett turned toward the viewport through which the Squibs had attacked earlier, then used a mini rocket to blow the transparisteel out of its frame.

"Ladies first," he said. "And no, I'm not going to blast you in the back. I know what happens when you try that on a Jedi."

"I'm no Jedi."

"Yeah, you are," he said. Another turbolaser strike hit the facility, and a second, larger hole appeared in the workroom ceiling. He waved Tahiri toward the frame. "I'm about done being forgiving."

Tahiri looked back toward the two nanotech scientists, who were both convulsing in their final death throes. "What about your counteragent?"

Fett shrugged, and she could feel his disappointment in the Force. "What about it?" he asked. "The sleemos who invented it are as good as dead. There's no use joining them."

"I suppose not," Tahiri agreed. "But Fett, I've got to ask—"

"I'm not your chat-buddy," he interrupted. "It's time to go."

"I know that." Half expecting a tentacle to appear, Tahiri took one last glance toward the main genetics lab. "So why *did* you save me back there? You could have taken the scientists and been gone."

"Maybe I should have, but a deal's a deal," Fett said. "Besides, you saved me first. I hate owing someone like you."

"Like me?"

"A *Jedi*," Fett growled. "Can we go now?"

"Sure," Tahiri said, "but why did you risk your life to save me a *second* time."

"I like *being* owed." Fett stepped toward the opening. "I'm going now, Veila."

"Hold on." Tahiri caught his arm and turned toward the computer stations at the back of the lab. "There's a datachip in there—and I'd like you to have it."

Another strike landed, this time sending tons of stone tumbling down into the central cavern beyond the empty viewport.

Fett cast a meaningful glance upward, then said, "It better be *some* datachip."

"Probably not, but it's the only shot you have," Tahiri said. "I told Yu to copy all his nanokiller files so you'd have the research when you took him and Tarm."

Fett cocked his helmet to one side. "Why would you do that?"

Tahiri shrugged. "Because I like being owed, too," she said. "And because I was Caedus's apprentice at the time."

"I haven't forgotten." Fett turned and started toward the back of the lab to retrieve the chip. "But that's done between us. Okay?"

"Okay," Tahiri said. And then they were both hurrying toward the exit, Fett ahead and Tahiri following close behind. "And thanks."

"That *still* doesn't make us buddies, Veila," Fett said. "To me, you're just another stinking Jedi."

From where Jaina was kneeling in the center of the ventilation ducting, facing the side wall, she could see many things. She could see that the Keshiri woman, with her torso cut half apart and a blaster bolt exit wound where her left cheek used to be, was no ordinary Sith. She could see that Luke was driving the woman-thing straight into her. And at the far end of the run, she could see Corran Horn limping toward the edge of a giant exhaust port, mere meters from lobbing the team's last thermal detonator into the shield generator. She could see that any second now, the Keshiri would have to turn and attempt to stop him, and Jaina could see that her chrono said it was two and a half minutes before midday, GST.

Two and a half minutes was a very long time for an emplacement gunner to adjust his aim. *Too* long. Jaina knew that as soon as the shield generator went down, the Sith gunnery commander would realize there was a fresh attack coming—and where. He would order all of his gunners to break off their battles with the blastboats and assault cars that had been trying to breach the Temple's impregnable defenses for days now. He would order them to turn their attention to the exhaust port. And he would order them to fill the sky above the port with cannon bolts and missiles. Then, in two and a half minutes, the Void Jumpers would find themselves dropping into hell.

And that was why Jaina continued to ignore Luke's order to stand and fight. Instead, she remained motionless, willing Corran to slow down, touching him through the Force and urging him to hang back. But she could feel his concern, his fear that if he delayed, he would be wasting Luke's sacrifice by allowing the indestructible Keshiri woman to catch up. The instant the woman got past Jaina and had a clear lane to Corran, he would launch himself at the shield generator.

But Jaina also knew she could never last two and a half minutes against the Keshiri woman—not anymore. Her entire body felt like it was burning from the inside out, and she was not at all sure her muscles would obey even when the time came—as Luke kept ordering—to stand and fight. She thought she might last thirty seconds, maybe even a minute if the Force was with her. But two and a half minutes? In two and a half minutes she would be dead.

Jaina's chrono advanced to two minutes before midday, and then a strange thing happened. The Keshiri woman wailed in pain. It was not merely the kind of scream that anyone might let out as a blaster bolt tore through a lung. This was something supernatural, a scream that seemed to echo through the Force and roll around inside Jaina's head without ever actually passing through her ears.

The woman staggered, and when Luke blasted her again, she gathered herself to spring after Corran. Time up. Jaina stretched a hand toward her lightsaber and, summoning it into her grasp, used the Force to lift herself to her feet.

The woman surprised Jaina by stopping between her and Luke, and Jaina found herself looking into the face of death. The mouth, where it had not been blown away by Luke's blaster bolt, was a hideous wide thing that stretched from ear to ear, and the eyes were sunken wells of darkness, at the bottom of which burned two tiny points of light.

Abeloth.

Jaina recalled the description well enough to realize whom she was facing, and she knew that her chances of surviving to see Jag again had just dropped to zero. She ignited her lightsaber and leapt into battle with a powerful mid-body strike that she hoped would drive her foe back onto Luke's blade.

Abeloth's hand flicked, and Jaina found herself tumbling down the duct backward. She saw the dark rectangle of a stack-head flash past beneath her; she slammed down and rolled twice before she could finally use the Force to bring herself to a stop. She came up on her knees, facing back the way she had come, and saw Abeloth leaping across the pit toward her.

Jaina brought her lightsaber across in a high guard—only to see her attacker drop down the stack and vanish from sight.

Too exhausted and confused to rise, Jaina remained kneeling where she was, half expecting a hand to come punching up through the sheet metal to grab her by the ankle and drag her to her death. Instead she saw Luke approaching, his lightsaber in one hand and his blaster in the other. When he reached the edge of the stack-head, he extended his arm and blind-fired a flurry of bolts after Abeloth. Then he peered cautiously over the side . . . and looked confused.

He looked back toward Jaina. "What happened?"

"I was about to ask *you* the same thing," Jaina said. "I thought you—"

"Not me," Luke said, shaking his head. "It was something else—something we don't understand yet, I think."

"Something *else* we don't understand about her?" Jaina replied. "Great."

Then she remembered Corran—and that she had not yet heard the crackle of a thermal detonator. Jaina checked her chronometer. It was still a minute and a half before midday. She spun around and was relieved to see Corran standing at the edge of the exhaust port, looking back toward them—and still holding the detonator in his hand.

"Now?" he called. "My chrono is acting up."

Jaina checked her own chrono again, then shook her head. "Not yet." Guessing that it would take her just about a minute to cover those last fifty meters, she motioned for Luke to join her, then rose and began to hobble down the duct toward the shield generator. "Let's do it together."

"Good thinking," Luke called. "The med-evac team will be faster if we all collapse in one place."

Chapter Twenty-five

THEY HAD FINALLY CLIMBED HIGH ENOUGH INTO THE TEMPLE TO ES-
cape the acid-dripping mold and the fungi with poisonous, razor-sharp
edges. This passage was just a typical undercity corridor, with corrod-
ing durasteel walls, layers of grime, and the reek of decay. And since
there were no more man-eating vegetables, Han was no longer in
fight-or-flight mode. Now he was just angry—furious, even.

During the ambush in the loading dock, he had glimpsed a brown-
haired girl standing in the entrance to the access tunnel. She had been
wearing Jedi combat armor, so at first he had assumed she was a prisoner or was fleeing the enemy. Then he had noticed the thermal detonator in her hand, and he had started to think *spy*. The clincher had
come when she had stepped into the loading bay and tossed the detonator toward the *Falcon*'s boarding ramp, where Allana stood talking
with Bazel and Leia. That was about the same time that he got a good
look at the little scar at the corner of her mouth, and he had recognized her instantly.

Vestara Khai.

The little smooka had been playing Ben all along, using the girl-in-danger ploy to make him fall for her. Then, after she had gotten inside the Jedi Order and learned as much as Luke was going to allow, she had seen an opportunity to take out Allana and had slipped back to the Sith to set up the ambush in the loading dock. That much was clear. She had used Ben and fooled Luke.

The only thing Han did not understand was *how*. How had Vestara learned about the drop-off—and that Allana would be aboard? How had she set up the attack so quickly? She had already been inside the Temple when the *Falcon* arrived on Coruscant, and even if she had had some means of eavesdropping on Bwua'tu's headquarters, there had been less than an hour to get into position.

But at least Han knew why the Jedi had been running into so much trouble inside the Temple. There had been a spy in their ranks. And someday Vestara Khai would pay for what she had done. Han would make sure of that, if it was the last thing he ever did.

"Grandpa!" Allana whispered from behind him. "Be quiet!"

Han glanced down at the grime-caked floor, trying to see what he might have kicked or snapped. In the weak glow-panel light, he could see compressed dust and not much else—no stray fusioncutters or beamdrills, no slashrat skeletons or breemil carapaces. He couldn't even see any dead muxi carcasses, and as bad as the place smelled, there ought to have been a thousand of them.

Still walking, he twisted around enough to look back. Leia and Anji were about ten paces away, bringing up the rear. Allana and R2-D2 were following closer behind, almost on his heels. They were both coated top-to-bottom in dust and grime, and Allana looked every bit the combat veteran she had become in the last few days of running, skulking, and fighting. Her big gray eyes were getting that hard, wary edge that Han had watched develop in his own kids as their Force talents and galactic strife conspired to make them warriors when they were barely into their teens. Now Allana's destiny was coming for her at an even younger age. She was learning to kill at the age of nine—and to watch friends die—and it broke his heart. If he could have changed her fate, he would have done it in an instant. But the choice wasn't Han's, or anyone's. She had been born into her role, and the best he could do was prepare her to shoulder the burden.

Han was still looking behind him when he reached an intersection and triggered a set of motion-activated glow panels a few meters to his left. With a company of Sith still somewhere behind them, he knew better than to let himself cry out in surprise—but he couldn't help whirling around and pointing his blaster pistol down the adjacent hall-way.

"*Grandpa!*" Allana whispered again. "Quiet means no blasting, ei-ther!"

Han stopped and turned to face her. "I didn't pull the trigger," he said. "And I *was* being quiet."

R2-D2 flashed a couple of status lights, using the Jedi blink code to contradict him, and Allana shook her head.

"You were muttering again," she whispered. "And I heard some-one behind us."

Han raised his gaze, looking back down the way they had come. Anji and Leia were still behind them, Anji keeping a wary eye on their backtrail while Leia used the Force to smooth the dust. There was no sign of anyone else.

"Are you sure?" he asked.

"Of course, I'm sure," Allana replied. "You were saying something about the little smooka, and how she was going to pay. What's a smooka?"

"Just another word for bad news," Han said. "I meant, are you sure about *hearing* something?"

"I'm sure," Allana replied. "There was a yell behind us. I think someone was surprised."

"I heard it, too," Leia said, joining them and also whispering. "And I can feel them, maybe a dozen presences about half a kilometer back."

"What about Zekk and Taryn?" Han asked. He glanced down at Allana. "You're sure you activated your tracking beacon?"

She turned her arm over, revealing an orange glow where the sub-cutaneous transmitter had been implanted. "I'm sure."

"Blast," Han said. "They should have caught up to us by now."

"Maybe they have," Leia said. "The Force has started to feel empty behind that first group—maybe a little *too* empty."

"Like Zekk is hiding his Force presence?" Han asked.

"Not quite," Leia said. "If that were the case, he'd just be drawing it in around himself. This feels more like a bubble—like he's trying to hide more than himself—Taryn, perhaps."

"He can do that?"

Leia shrugged. "Luke can," she said. "I'm not sure about Zekk."

"But if *you* can feel the bubble, then so can the Sith. Right?"

"I'm afraid so," Leia said. "They probably know someone is behind them—just not who, or how many."

"Great—so they're probably thinking they need to make a move on us before it's too late." Han looked up the corridor into the darkness beyond the active glow panels, trying to guess how far it continued before reaching someplace mazy enough for them to lose their pursuers. "Looks like we need to make a run for it."

"We can't," Allana said. "We're too close to the Barabels' nest."

"We are?" Han glanced down at her. "*How* close?"

Allana studied the floor. "When was the last time you saw a slashrat or breemil?" she asked. "Or a granite slug or a muxi? Or even any *sign* of one?"

"I don't know," Han said, looking around the corridor again. "About thirty minutes ago, I guess."

"I see what you mean, Allana," Leia said, also looking around. "This area has been hunted out."

"Right," Allana said. "But the way it smells—we've *got* to be close to the nest."

"Good," Han said, starting up the corridor again. He wasn't sure how the smell fit in, but he *did* know that Barabels were voracious hunters, so being close to the nest would explain why they weren't seeing any vermin. "We can use some reinforcements."

Allana caught hold of his trouser leg. "Are you crazy, Grandpa? If we lead those Sith any closer to the Barabels' nest, *we're* the ones they'll eat."

"I thought you had to warn them about your vision? That's what got . . ." Han caught himself, realizing that if he was not careful about what he said, Allana would end up blaming herself for Bazel's death. "That's what we're doing here, isn't it?"

Fortunately, Allana didn't seem to catch his near slip. "I need to *warn* them about what I saw, not make it come true."

"Yeah, well I've been having visions about Sith and little girls,"

Han said. "So I say we take our chances and team up with the Barabels while we still can. We'll *all* stand a better chance."

"Han, this isn't a decision we can make for Allana," Leia said gently. "It's *her* vision. *She* has to decide what path the Force wants her to follow."

"Since when did the Force become the parent around here?" Han demanded, struggling to keep to a whisper. When Leia only looked at him, he took a couple of breaths and turned to Allana. "Fine. Maybe I can stay here and hold them off while you and your grandmother go find the Barabels."

"Hold off a dozen Sith—alone?" Leia shook her head. "I don't think so."

Han scowled. "I thought you said it was Allana's decision."

"It is, and Grandma's right," Allana said. "We have to stick together."

"And do what?" Han demanded.

Allana frowned in thought, then finally turned to look back along the wall. "Something crazy," she said. "That's what you would do if I weren't here, isn't it?"

Han followed her gaze to the intersection they had just passed. "An ambush?" He rubbed his chin, then looked toward Leia. "That's not a bad idea—not if Zekk and Taryn are coming up behind them."

"That's a big *if*," Leia said. She thought for a moment, then laid a hand on Allana's shoulder. "But it's the last thing they would expect."

"Good." Allana started back toward the intersecting hallway. "We'll set a trip line about five meters in. That way, if something goes wrong, we'll have a chance to run off and draw them away from the nest."

Han rushed to catch up with her. "Not bad," he said. "Mind if I add a couple of things?"

"Not at all, Grandpa," Allana said. She flashed him a little smile. "Han Solo's ideas are always welcome."

Han shared his suggestions, and the two of them went to work. By the time Leia had used the Force to spread a fresh layer of dust over the main corridor, he and Allana had strung the trip wire, disabled the overhead glow panels, and lodged a durasteel door across the hallway, forming a makeshift breastwork that ran between two rooms located across the corridor from each other. Leia joined them, Allana summoned Anji with a hand command, then the three Solos checked their blasters and knelt down to await the Sith.

After half a minute or so, the glow panels in the main corridor flickered off automatically and they were plunged into total darkness. Han knew that this would be the hardest part for Allana, since it was always the moments before a battle when most people's thoughts turned to the possibility of death—and to the friends they had lost in previous battles. And he was right. They had been kneeling in the darkness only a short time before he began to hear sniffles, and he knew she had to be thinking of Bazel Warv's incredible last stand. It was a sacrifice Allana would remember forever, and he knew she would spend the rest of her life trying to be worthy of her friend's heroism.

With the Sith coming any moment, he could not risk trying to comfort her with words. Instead, Han just wrapped an arm around her, wishing that he could use the Force to reassure her that it would get better—that in time she would start to focus more on the good times with Barv than how he died. And maybe Han *did* have the Force, at least with her—because the sniffles stopped, and Allana leaned into him for a moment, just long enough to acknowledge the hug and let him know she was doing better.

Then a glow panel flickered to life out in the main corridor, and Han felt Allana tense for battle. Normally, he would have slipped over to one side of the hall to avoid becoming a target cluster for the enemy, but he wanted to stay within arm's reach of his granddaughter. She had done pretty well in the ambush back at the *Falcon*—great, in fact—but that had happened with no warning. This time, there had been a chance to think, and in situations like these, too much thinking was usually a bad thing.

A dozen heartbeats later, a pair of Sith scouts reached the intersection and cautiously poked their heads around the corner. When the leader narrowed her eyes and leaned close to whisper something in her partner's ear, Han knew they had sensed the trap. He wasn't surprised. Even if the Lost Tribe wasn't quite up to Jedi combat standards, most of them used the Force a lot more naturally than their light-side counterparts—and that was their weakness, to Han's way of thinking. Members of the Lost Tribe had a habit of relying on the Force instead of themselves in a fight, so when they ran into someone who could *really* fight, they usually found themselves in trouble.

Han felt Allana tense as she prepared to open fire, and he quickly placed a restraining hand on her arm. Had he been able to speak to her through the Force, he would have told her to be patient and wait for her grandmother to do her thing—because Leia Solo always had one more trick up her Jedi sleeve.

And sure enough, a gentle *clang* came down the main corridor. The gazes of both Sith swung toward the sound and rose toward the ceiling, and they quickly backed out of sight and vanished down the corridor.

"They got away!" Allana complained.

"Never shoot the scouts," Han explained. "They're expecting it."

"So?"

"They'll deflect your shot," Leia said. Judging by the sound of her voice, she had already slipped into the room on her side of the hallway. "You'll just reveal your position,"

"But they have the Force," Allana said. "They can already *feel* our positions."

"Yeah—*that's* what we're counting on." Han took Allana by the arm and pulled her through the dark doorway on their side of the hallway, where he had already stowed R2-D2.

"Hand me your blaster."

Allana's voice grew suspicious. "What for?"

"Because you're going to need both hands." He pulled her into the far corner, where R2-D2 stood faintly illuminated by his status lights. "Now hand me your blaster, call Anji over and lie down over her head, then cover your ears and close your eyes."

"*What?*" Allana demanded. "Grandpa, I'm not a Jedi yet. I can't sense anyone in the Force *that* well."

"Trust me. You won't need to." Han thought about telling her what he expected to happen next, but decided against it. In his experience, it was better not to know some things were coming. He nudged her shoulder, then said, "Blaster . . . *now*."

With a heavy sigh, Allana handed over her weapon—a petite Q2 that they had lifted from a dead Sith woman a little smaller than Leia— then did as she was instructed. Han tucked the pistol into his belt, holstered his own weapon, then did as he had instructed his granddaughter and pressed his own torso down over Allana and Anji.

Han had barely gotten his hands over his ears before he saw an orange flash through his eyelids and heard the crackling bang of an incendiary grenade. He peeked down and saw Allana staring up with a gaping jaw and eyes wide open. Anji was pressed flat to the floor, squeezed as tight to the wall as possible for a nexu her size.

"Keep your eyes closed!" he said.

She obeyed immediately, and a second later came the deafening crack and blinding white flash of a thermal detonator. Han counted to two, then opened his eyes to see a four-meter circle of corroded durasteel missing from the chamber's front wall. Flashing up the corridor outside was a steady stream of blaster bolts.

Han pulled Allana's blaster pistol from his belt and passed it back to her. "*Don't* leave my side."

"Not if a rancor tries to drag me off!" she assured him. "Grandpa, how did you know—"

"Experience." Han pulled his own blaster. "Lots and lots of experience."

Pulling Allana along, he stepped to within a couple of meters of the hole. On the opposite side of the hallway, he saw Leia looking through an identical hole, her face flashing green in the light of passing blaster bolts. She gave them a smile, then slid out of view behind the remnants of the wall.

It was a smile that said volumes to Han. He quickly had Allana command Anji to stay with R2-D2. He wouldn't normally have given the command much chance of sticking when things got wild, but Allana and the nexu seemed to have some sort of Force connection that might help. After Anji was in place, he positioned Allana in one of the room's front corners and told her what he was planning. He explained what he needed her to do—including hiding her presence in the Force, like her grandmother had taught her—then crawled on his hands and knees past the hole in the room's front wall to the corner opposite Allana.

Over the din of screeching blasters, Han began to hear Sith boots pounding up the hallway toward him. He kept his head down, hiding the whites of his eyes and listening to the footfalls grow louder, until they reached the other side of the hole. By then, the steps were beginning to slow, and Han raised his gaze to find a straight-nosed Sith male leaping toward him through the hole in the front wall.

Han ignored this one and opened fire on the *next* Sith in line, who was spinning around to cover Allana's side of the room. The attack took the woman so completely by surprise that she did not even have time to activate her lightsaber. A smoking hole simply appeared in one side of her head, and she went down like a holograph losing power.

In the same instant a trio of blaster bolts sounded from where Allana was hiding, and the first Sith pitched forward, his still-ignited lightsaber falling so close to Han that he nearly lost an arm.

Paying the close call no attention, he continued to fire down the hallway into the line of charging Sith. Having the benefit of the second and a half it had taken their fellows to die, the first three in line ignited their lightsabers and quickly began to bat Han's bolts back toward him. He kept his head down and continued to fire, and a couple of heartbeats later they were coming through the hole into the room.

Which is when Leia leapt out of hiding. Han continued to pour fire down the hallway behind her, occupying the rest of the Sith just long enough for her to cross the hallway. Her lightsaber droned twice, and two Sith heads went flying.

Allana's blaster screeched again—then *Allana* screeched as the third Sith spun on her, batting her bolts aside and lunging for her.

Before Han could switch targets, Anji slammed into the woman's flank, knocking her back toward the corridor—and her head straight into Leia's blade. The woman's knees buckled immediately, and Han shot her through the spine on the way down.

Allana made a retching sound and rolled away from the woman's still-descending lightsaber.

Han switched back to firing down the hallway, and Leia stepped into the hole beside him, using her lightsaber to deflect the steady stream of bolts the Sith sent back at him. When the enemy realized they had lost nearly half their number, the leader—a brown-bearded Keshiri with pale eyes—yelled something in their own language, and the band began to fall back toward the intersection.

And *that* was when Zekk and Taryn arrived, rounding the corner behind a wall of blasterfire so intense that all Han could see was flashing light. Several Sith voices cried out in agony and surprise, then the brown-bearded Keshiri and three other Sith came racing up the hallway. As they drew near, Han saw the brown-bearded one thrust his hand into his pocket, no doubt reaching for a grenade or thermal detonator. The Sith behind him was doing the same.

Han yelled for Leia at the top of his lungs, but he could not make himself heard over the din of screeching blasters. He pointed at the leader and opened fire on the other one. With Zekk and Taryn firing from behind and Han from the front, the Sith never had a chance. He fell with his hand still in his pocket.

Brown-beard fared better. He managed to pull a grenade from his pocket—and even get it armed—before Leia hit him with a Force blast that sent him tumbling back down the hallway.

The grenade, however, remained in the air—and came sailing straight through the hole into the room where the Solos were hiding.

"Grenade!"

Diving past Leia, Han hurled himself on Allana and wrapped her tight in his arms—then felt himself reverse course and go soaring back at an angle. His shoulder banged against the edge of the wall so hard that his arms nearly opened, and then he found himself spinning across the hallway upside down, with Allana on top of him screaming in surprise and fear.

They were airborne the better part of a second before the small of his back struck something that felt like a table and sent him tumbling. Allana flew from his arms, then someone else—someone big and furry—landed on his chest.

Only *then* did the orange flash of an incendiary grenade fill the darkness—and it seemed to be coming from across the hall.

Han rolled Anji free and sat up, at once trying to blink the blast-dazzle from his eyes and see in the dark. "Allana?"

"Over here."

He was too dazed to even recognize the voice, so he turned toward it and put out his hands.

He found a small, trembling form and pulled her close. "Allana!"

"Grandpa." She hugged him close. "Where's Grandma?"

"I'm not sure." Han began to feel around in the darkness, but found only dust. "She's got to be here somewhere."

"Grandma?" When no answer came, Allana's voice grew frightened. *"Grandma?"*

The only answer was the sound of running boots. Realizing he had no idea how much time had passed, Han clamped a hand over Allana's mouth and squeezed it close.

She fell instantly motionless, and together they listened as the sound of the footfalls receded up the hallway.

Finally, Han whispered, "Keep it quiet until we know what's what."

"No kidding," Allana said. "But where's Grandma?"

"Over here," a voice whispered. "With Anji."

The words came clear and distinct from near the hole in the front wall of the room, so loud that Han thought for a moment that Leia's ears must still be ringing from the grenade explosion. But then the beam of a glow rod swept through the hole, illuminating her face, and Zekk's deep voice sounded from a few meters down the hallway.

"Princess Leia, it's good to see you alive."

"Almost as good as it will be to see the Chume'da alive," Taryn added. "Where is she?"

"There's no need to concern yourselves with me," Allana said, sounding as regal as her mother sometimes did. She gently freed herself from Han's grasp and rose. "I've been well guarded. But see to my grandparents at once. They've had quite a fight."

A second glow rod beam appeared in the hole and swung around to illuminate Allana's face.

"You're well, Highness?" Taryn asked. "You're quite sure?"

"Yes—as you must be able to *see*," Allana said, allowing her irritation to show in her voice. "Now shine that thing somewhere else and see to my grandparents as I . . ."

Allana allowed her order to trail off when a trio of anguished screams sounded from down the hallway. Both Taryn and Zekk turned to shine their glow rods toward the sound, and the unmistakable clatter of a squad of armored soldiers shouldering their blaster rifles sounded behind them.

Even before Han realized the cause of the anguished screams, Allana was rushing toward the doorway. "Stand down! *Stand down!*"

Han rose to his feet and—experiencing a whole body of new aches—limped after her. "It's okay," he called. "They're friends."

Taryn looked over at him with wide, wild eyes. "You're sure?"

It was Zekk who answered. "He's sure." He turned and signaled the soldiers behind him to lower their weapons, then looked back up the hallway and said, "It's good to see you again, Tesar."

"This one cannot say the same," a raspy Barabel voice replied. "What are you doing here?"

Han reached the door and, taking Leia's hand, peered up the hallway to find Tesar and two more Barabels—Dordi and Wilyem, he thought—standing about three meters away, under the last active glow panel. Their scaly shoulders filled the hallway from wall to wall, a not-so-subtle hint that no one would be getting past them. With their talons still dripping Sith gore and their heads only a few centimeters beneath the ceiling, it was easy to see why the Hapans had shouldered their weapons.

Zekk smiled and motioned at Allana. "We were following Amelia Solo."

"*Amelia?*" Dordi rasped. "She brought you? *Here?*"

Allana seemed to recognize that it was up to her to defuse the situation, and she was already stepping into the center of the hallway.

"Not on purpose."

Allana walked up to the Barabels, then stopped in front of Tesar, a little figure that barely rose higher than his knees. Taryn quickly moved to follow, but the Chume'da waved her off. Even then, Zekk had to take Taryn by the arm to make her obey.

Allana craned her neck to look up into the Barabel's slit-pupiled eyes. "But I *did* risk my life—and lost Bazel's—to warn you."

A soft hiss filled the hallway as the Barabels ruffled their scales, and Tesar asked, "Bazel is dead?"

"He was going to warn you alone," Han called. "But we got ambushed dropping him off."

Allana nodded. "He died protecting us," she said. "I'm going to miss him."

Tesar considered this, then nodded, "Bazel was a good defender. The pack will be less without him."

"Yes, it will," Allana said. "Thanks."

"It is only the truth." Tesar shifted his gaze toward Han. "But this one does not understand. What is there to warn us about?"

"Ask Amelia," Han said. "It was her vision."

At the word *vision,* the gazes of all three Barabels snapped back to Allana so quickly even Han felt the sudden tension.

"*What* vision?" Wilyem demanded.

Allana shifted her gaze to him. "There were Sith," she said. "Lots of Sith, and they were in your nest."

"*Our* nest?" Tesar asked. "You are certain?"

"Lots of bones and a couple of dozen little black lizards," Allana replied. "It wasn't pretty."

Tesar's eyes widened. "They are coming for the hatchlingz?"

"Not if you let us help you," Allana said. "Why do you think I'm here?"

Tesar glanced over at Wilyem, who reluctantly nodded and said, "A vision is a vision."

Tesar turned to Dordi, who shrugged and also nodded. "This one is growing tired of Sith anyway," she said. "They have such a bitter aftertaste."

Chapter Twenty-six

THE MIRROR IN JAGGED FEL'S DRESSING ROOM HAD AN INSET HOLOPAD permanently tuned to the Imperial News Network, and the network's Election Day coverage had been interrupted for a special report. Instead of the usual talking heads, the hologram now showed a glassy, still-glowing blast basin set into the rim of a dusty moon crater. A silky-voiced reporter was providing off-cam commentary.

". . . location of a small mine known as the Moon Maiden," she was saying. "That was before the Imperial frigate *Consolidator* struck the site with a sustained turbolaser barrage."

Though Jag had been expecting the report for a couple of days now, the timing took him by surprise. By holding the story until just a few minutes before the Election Day Debate, the network executive board was clearly trying to torpedo his campaign. They were ensuring that the news would be seen by the entire Empire—and leaving him no time to mount a response before the citizenry voted. It was Imperial intrigue at its finest, and even if it was one of the aspects of his job that Jag hated most, he had to admire the skill of his opponents.

The image changed to the face of a handsome lieutenant in Imperial Security, and the voice-over continued, "Imperial News has learned that Lieutenant Dorch Vangur, of the Imperial Security detachment on Hagamoor Three, was on assignment near the Moon Maiden shortly before the strike. He has confirmed that the bombardment was ordered by Head of State Jagged Fel on the recommendation of an unidentified female agent. Unfortunately, Lieutenant Vangur refused to reveal the identity of this personal agent. And so far, our investigators here at the Imperial News Network have been unable to find any trace of her arrival on Hagamoor Three—or even to confirm her existence."

"They must have some pretty incompetent researchers," Tahiri said. She was standing behind the makeup artist, looking at Jag's reflection in the mirror. Her face was still battered and bruised, yet remarkably fit for someone who had recently tangled with a Force entity. "The Hagamoor Three spaceport has more security cams than your palace on Bastion. Any decent reporter with an hour and a thousand credits should have been able to score a vid of me."

"And give you a reason to come back?" Jag met her gaze, then shook his head. "No one wants to meet an Imperial Hand *twice*."

A campaign flimsi appeared in the mirror's holographic inset, and Jag shifted his attention back to the news. The poster featured Daala in a white Grand Admiral's uniform, standing in profile with her eye patch prominently displayed. The slogan read, NATASI DAALA. A TRADITION OF SERVICE AND SACRIFICE—FOR *YOUR* EMPIRE. It was an effective poster—so much so that it practically made *Jag* want to vote for her.

"This is one of Admiral Daala's campaign posters," the reporter said helpfully. "Our preliminary investigation confirms that the Moon Maiden was, in fact, being used as Admiral Daala's campaign headquarters."

The poster was replaced by the face of an attractive brunette reporter. "My fellow citizens, on this first Imperial Election Day, I know you must all have the same questions I do. And you are probably drawing some rather obvious conclusions. But it would be premature of me to suggest that there has been an astounding abuse of power here. An assertion like that would require evidence that I simply do not have at this time. Therefore, I can only report what Imperial News Network knows for certain right now."

The hologram returned to the glassy basin. "This used to be Admiral Daala's campaign headquarters, and Head of State Fel *personally* authorized its bombardment. As you can see, the attack was clearly designed to destroy *all* trace of the facility's true nature."

The glassy basin was replaced by an image of the candidates for the Head of State's office—Jagged himself, Natasi Daala, and Vitor Reige.

"For now," continued the reporter, "all we can do is ask questions. What does this have to do with the three-way contest to pick the Empire's next Head of State? Was this devastating assault something more than an attempt by Jagged Fel to undermine the campaign of his challenger, Natasi Daala? Why did the third candidate in the race—Admiral Vitor Reige—dispatch the *Consolidator* to Hagamoor Three in the first place?"

The images of the three candidates were replaced by an image of the reporter, her face slender and beautiful, with a blade-like nose and green oval eyes.

"So many questions remain. This is Shei Harsi, promising that the Imperial News Network will keep digging until the truth comes out."

The hologram changed to the INN Crowned Helmet logo, and a deep male voice said, "Imperial News Network will continue to issue special bulletins as information on this fast-breaking story becomes available. We now resume our scheduled Imperial Election Day coverage with Tozz Relaton and Salia Deradal."

A pair of commentators appeared in the hologram. Wearing flashy white tunics and oversized glasses, they looked more like a pair of gravball announcers than political analysts.

"That's quite a bomb to have drop on today of all days, Salia—with just hours to go before the election begins," said the man, a big-toothed human with a smile as wide as a gorg's. "The big question is, how will the revelations affect Jagged Fel's chances of winning?"

"Well, Tozz, we'll have our answer when polling closes in just eight hours," said Salia, a carefully coiffed blond who managed to smile continuously while speaking. "But a lot will depend on how Head of State Fel responds to those questions during the Great Election Day Debate—which begins here on INN in a few short minutes."

"That's right, Salia. This is one debate that our viewers *really* won't want to miss—especially since they're required by law to watch!" Tozz agreed. "This could be payback day for Admiral Daala, whose power base in the Galactic Alliance suffered a real blow when Head of State Fel withdrew from the Galactic Unification Talks on Coruscant."

The holo dissolved into static as Tahiri clicked the remote, then she stepped to the far end of the makeup counter and turned to face Jag. "That was *terrible* coverage," she said. "Inaccurate, incomplete, and full of insinuation—and it's going to be a problem for you in the debate."

Not wanting an eye full of lash thickener, Jag resisted the urge to nod. "I didn't expect them to drag Reige into the picture," he said. "That part was completely uncalled for."

"Expect?" Tahiri echoed. "You knew *this* was coming?"

"Of course," Jag said. "They asked me for a response. I'm sure they wanted to include a denial in the same clip."

"And you didn't issue it?" Tahiri asked. "Or even better, just kill the story? This *is* the Empire, you know. The Head of State *has* the power to do that."

"I'm aware of that, Tahiri," Jag said. "But I'm trying to teach the Empire to live by new rules. How would it look to the citizens if I killed a story just because it was inaccurate, biased, incomplete, *and* misleading?"

"It wouldn't look like anything—because no one would *know,*" Tahiri replied. "That's the whole point of shutting down a story."

Jag raised a hand, waving off her objections. "The only thing more worthless than a biased, incompetent press is a *muzzled* press," he said. "Imperial citizens are intelligent. They'll recognize the truth when they hear it."

Tahiri rolled her eyes. "Well, I hope you're thinking of a way to explain it to them," she said. "Because the way you timed this debate, you *won't* have a chance later."

Jag merely smiled. As far as Tahiri knew, the sole purpose for holding the debate on the morning of Imperial Election Day was to force Daala out of hiding and prevent her from rejecting the outcome. With all three candidates and the entire Moff Council in the Gilad Pellaeon Auditorium on Bastion, the election committee—overseen by Commodore Selma Djor—believed it would be impossible for the losers to reject the results and renew hostilities. In fact, the committee planned to ask the losing candidates and the entire council of Moffs to swear an oath of loyalty to the winner—live and on cam during the INN's post-election wrap-up. Anyone who refused would be quietly arrested and imprisoned on charges of treason.

The plan still had a faint smell of tyranny to Jag, but he had agreed to it because Djor seemed convinced it was the only way to bring a true and permanent end to Daala's insurrection. But even more important, the debate gave Jag a chance to address the Empire one last time before the election—and spring his trap.

When Jag remained silent too long, Tahiri asked, "Jagged—you *do* have a way to explain the bombardment, right?"

Jag frowned. "Have some faith, Tahiri."

Tahiri began to look worried, but before she could say anything, a quick rap sounded on the door. "We're on in two minutes," a young voice said. "That is, we're on if *you* are ready, Head of State. My apologies."

Jag glanced at his makeup artist, who gave him a quick nod.

"I'll be right there," he said. "Thank you."

The makeup artist put a final touch on Jag's eyebrows, then removed the paper bibs she had stuffed into his collar to protect his uniform. He thanked her and left his dressing room with Tahiri. His assistant, Ashik, and a quartet of bodyguards escorted him exactly fourteen paces up the corridor to the stage entrance, where Tahiri squeezed his arm and wished him good luck—which, of course, he was not going to need.

Both Reige and Daala were already standing behind their podiums in full-dress uniforms. Jag began to wish that he had opted for civilian clothes instead of the black commander in chief's uniform Djor recommended. But wearing something unexpected might well have put Daala on alert, and if his plan was going to work, he needed her to continue believing she had the upper hand.

As Jag stepped onto the stage, the Moffs in the half-filled auditorium rose and gave him a *very* subdued chorus of applause. Clearly, they believed that the INN report had destroyed his chances of winning the election.

Jag stopped at the first podium, where Vitor Reige stood, looking nervous and unhappy.

Jag offered his hand. "Stand proud, Admiral," he ordered. "You're running for the highest office in the Empire. You should look like you want it."

Reige instantly straightened his shoulders. "Of course, Head of State." His eyes dropped to the mike resting in its holder on his podium, no doubt confirming that it was inactive, then he lowered his voice. "About Hagamoor Three—if you want me to take the blame for the bombardment—"

"Not at all. In fact, I forbid it." Jag leaned in close, then said, "I don't need you freelancing on this, Vitor. It would ruin a good battle plan."

Reige's eyes lit with relief. "Very good, sir."

"Admiral Reige, I'm *ordering* you to tell the truth about the *Consolidator*'s actions," Jagged said. "The *whole* truth. Do I make myself clear?"

Reige began to look a bit more worried, but he nodded. "Very clear, sir."

"Glad to hear it." Jag shook his hand, then spoke more loudly. "Good luck, Admiral. Debate well."

"You, too, sir." Reige cast a sideways glance at Daala, who was watching from her podium across the stage, then added, "May the best man win."

Jag could not help cracking a grin. "Well said, Admiral. Very well said."

He crossed to Daala's podium and offered his hand—only to have her glare at it like something diseased.

"I don't think that's necessary, Jag," she said. "Do you?"

Jagged lowered his hand. "Charming to the last, I see," he said. "Very well, Admiral. I trust you intend to honor the terms of the Election Accord we signed?"

"Why wouldn't I?" Daala replied. "After Hagamoor Three, I have no doubt about the outcome of this election."

Jag lowered his hand. "I guess I wouldn't, either, if I were in your position," he said. "That *was* a rather unfortunate mistake. Perhaps our intel was bad."

Daala gave him a tight smile. "You'll have to do better than *that* if you expect to win, Head of State Fel."

Jag gave her a reluctant nod. "Don't I know it."

A voice sounded over the house speakers, announcing that the broadcast would begin in ten seconds. Jag returned to his own podium in the center of the stage and took a couple of deep breaths he really did not need—he felt surprisingly calm—then listened politely as the moderator welcomed the audience and introduced the candidates.

No sooner had the man finished than Daala went off-script and walked over to wish luck to her opponents, going to shake hands first with Reige, then with Jag. With the holocams emitting a barely perceptible whine and floating just out of Jag's sight line, there could be no doubt that they were on live HoloNet.

Jag squeezed her hand and smiled. "Admiral Daala, how nice of you to offer your hand . . . now that the holocams are live."

Daala returned his smile with one even broader. "I only wanted to do it once, Head of State," she said. "I'm sure you understand."

The retort, amplified by her mike, drew a spontaneous chuckle from many of the Moffs. Jag was left with little choice but to dip his head and acknowledge that Daala had drawn the first blood. She returned to her podium, then listened politely as the moderator announced that each candidate would be allowed five minutes for an opening statement.

The mike light on Jag's podium turned green, and a digital readout began to count the five minutes of allotted time for his statement. Jag removed a datapad from the inner pocket of his dress tunic and propped it over the readout. He really didn't care about the debate rules—and he was fairly certain that once he began to speak, only one person in the room would want to silence him.

Jag looked into the audience and located Moff Getelles, who was seated alone in an empty side section, accompanied only by the two armored guards standing behind him. Jag nodded to the old man. When Getelles reluctantly nodded back, Jag smiled and looked directly into the holocam hovering in front of him.

"Esteemed Moffs, Loyal Citizens . . . ," Jag began, "when Grand Master Skywalker and the Moffs asked me to become the Empire's temporary Head of State at the end of the Second Civil War, there were two things I did not expect to happen. First, I never expected to survive nearly four years as the leader of the Moff Council."

This drew a chorus of pointed chuckles from the in-house audience. Jag looked up and smiled as though he, too, found the Moffs' habit of murdering their leaders a laughing matter, then continued.

"Second, I did not expect to come to love the job as much as I have. For both of those things, I am grateful. And because of that gratitude, I have held your interests at heart in every decision I have made as your Head of State."

Jag turned to look into the holocam, now addressing himself directly to the common people of the Empire.

"But you deserve more than that. As citizens of the Empire, you also deserve a government that is open and honest, and I am sorry to say I have not done as well in this. That changes *now*. Early this morning, I signed a new charter for the Imperial News Network, bestowing on it an endowment large enough to operate for centuries to come. Even more important, this charter also grants INN independence from any form of government censorship.

"In exchange," Jag continued, "I have charged the Imperial News Network with the duty to investigate and report on government affairs at every level, including those of the Head of State and the Imperial Moffs. I have done this so that you, the citizens of the Empire, will have the knowledge required to hold your government accountable."

An angry rustle filled the auditorium as the Moffs began to plot and complain among themselves. Jag paused, confident that the sensitive holocam mikes would pick up and relay every whisper to INN's viewing audience. After allowing the murmur to build for a few moments, he looked straight into the holocam again.

"As you can tell, not everyone is happy about that."

Someone behind the stage let out an involuntary snort. Jag allowed himself to smile along, knowing that the billions of people watching on their home planets would also be laughing along. He paused for a few moments, allowing time for his tone to grow serious, then continued.

"Unfortunately, as almost everyone in the Empire must know by now, it appears that Shei Harsi and the INN editorial board took me at my word, and now I find myself in the position of having to give an accounting of recent events on Hagamoor Three."

Jag grabbed the sides of the podium, trying to look as though what he was about to say would be difficult for him.

"I am sorry to inform you that *most* of Shei Harsi's report is correct. I *did* order the *Consolidator* to bombard Admiral Daala's secret campaign headquarters in the Moon Maiden on Hagamoor Three."

He paused. There were no outbursts or rage or disgust or surprise from the Moffs, or even Daala—which said a lot about the Empire. Such tactics were simply how things were done in Imperial politics, and the lack of even *feigned* indignation among the Moffs made him wonder if he might be trying to usher in democracy a little *too* quickly.

"There are two facts that you should know," Jag continued. "First, any speculation that Admiral Reige had any knowledge of those orders is entirely unwarranted. I issued my orders directly to the *Consolidator,* deliberately excluding Admiral Reige from the chain of command. When he learned what I had done, he grew so angry that he accused me of being spacesick."

This drew a chuckle from the moderator and several members of the backstage crew.

"The second thing you should know," Jag continued, "is the *reason* I ordered the bombardment. The Moon Maiden was much more than Admiral Daala's campaign headquarters—it also housed a secret nano-tech laboratory. And that lab was developing an illegal youth serum extracted from *drochs.*"

At last the auditorium reacted. Drochs were the horrific insects responsible for the Death Seed Plague that had claimed billions of lives in two separate sector-spanning pandemics. Literally stealing the life energy from their hosts, drochs were extremely difficult to detect in an infected person, and it was for that reason that experimenting with drochs was well beyond the limits of civilized behavior, even in the empire. Hearing Jag's statement, most of the Moffs cried out in genuine anger and indignation. And Daala's voice was louder and more vehement than all the rest.

"Liar!" Her eyes were wide and mad, and the fury in her voice suggested that, while the accusation had taken her completely by surprise,

she had grasped instantly the damage it would do. "If you think you can divert attention from your own crime by accusing *me* of involvement in another, you are badly mistaken. The citizens of the Empire are much too smart to fall for such an obvious deception."

Once the audience had quieted, Jag merely nodded. "Indeed, they are smart." He looked up into one corner of the audience seating, where Moff Getelles was sitting flanked by his two armed guards, and cocked his brow. "Which is why I won't ask them to take *my* word alone."

Getelles rose on cue. Speaking as loudly as his wavering voice would allow, he called, "Head of State Fel is telling the truth."

This caused another outburst among the Moffs, and a floating holocam went zipping away from the stage area toward Getelles. As it traversed the thirty meters of distance, Daala turned at her podium and glared at Jag with an expression that seemed equal parts hatred and appraisal. It was impossible to say how much she had known about the lair, whether she believed that it was a political fabrication or realized that Abeloth had indeed been working her Force magic from Getelles's secret nanotech lab. But it *was* clear that she understood that even the mere accusation of being involved with drochs was going to cost her the election.

When the holocam reached him, Getelles drew himself up straight and addressed Daala directly. "I'm sorry, Admiral," he said. "But there's no use lying. They have *evidence*."

"Of course they do," Daala said from her podium. She turned back to Jag. "*Manufactured* evidence. Head of State Fel has obviously planned this charade to the last detail."

"I *am* determined to bring the truth out into the open," Jag replied. He waved a hand toward Getelles. "Please continue, Moff Getelles."

"If I must," Getelles said reluctantly. "The truth is that Head of State Fel discovered the existence of these experiments several weeks ago. He ordered me to shut down the project in exchange for leniency, but I couldn't do it. I needed the youth serum, both to use on myself and for the credits it would bring to my treasury, so I struck *another* deal with Admiral Daala's representatives. I agreed to help the admiral win the election, and in exchange, Daala would allow me to develop and sell my youth serum when she took office."

"My congratulations, Head of State," Daala said to Jag. "That's a very convincing lie. What did it cost you?"

"A full pardon," Jag answered honestly. The representatives that Getelles had mentioned were, of course, the Squibs. Like Getelles, they had been determined to have the youth serum for their own family. But Jag saw no need to mention that. Mentioning Squibs rarely inspired confidence in *anyone's* account. He glared up at Getelles. "I hated to grant that pardon—especially a *second* time—but the good of the Empire demanded it."

"You have a rather self-serving definition of what is 'good' for the Empire, Head of State *Fel*," Daala said. She made his surname sound like an insult. "But your story has the feel of desperate convenience to it. There's no reason to believe a word that *either* you or Moff Getelles says. This incredible story is clearly an attempt to transfer *your* guilt onto the victim of your crime—namely, *me*."

"I can think of one very good reason to believe evreything I say," Jag said. "Because I have nothing to gain by lying about it."

Daala openly snorted. "You call being the Imperial Head of State *nothing*?"

"Of course not. But my name is no longer on the ballot." Jag looked directly into the nearest holocam and said, "I have already issued instructions to remove my name from the electronic ballots that our citizens will be using this afternoon."

"What?" Daala nearly screeched the question. "You can't be serious!"

Jag continued to look into the holocam. "I am—very serious. What I have not yet explained is *how* Moff Getelles's illegal droch project was discovered. The truth is that I *did* send an Imperial agent to find—and destroy—Admiral Daala's campaign headquarters."

He didn't mention anything about Abeloth, of course—there were still *some* things that the average citizen was better off not knowing.

"And it was only through the commission of *that* crime that I discovered Admiral Daala's involvement in an even greater crime," Jag said. "Therefore, for the good of the Empire, I have decided to withdraw from the election and endorse the only worthy candidate in the race, Admiral Vitor Reige."

"What?" It was Reige, rather than Daala, who cried out. "You can't be serious!"

"I am *entirely* serious."

Jag had to struggle to keep the elation out of his voice. And it was not just because he had blindsided Daala so completely that she could never win the race. He had never wanted to be the Imperial Head of State in the first place. At the end of the Second Civil War, Luke Skywalker had thrust him into the position as one element of an overarching peace plan, and he had accepted only to help assure an end to hostilities. Now, with him out of the race and Daala tainted by an illegal droch experiment, only one viable candidate remained—the best man for the job, in Jag's opinion.

Jag gave Daala a sly wink, then left his podium and stopped to shake hands with Reige.

"Congratulations, Vitor," he said. "You're going to make an excellent Head of State."

Chapter Twenty-seven

BEN AWOKE. HE FELT THE FAMILIAR SOFTNESS OF SHIP'S GEL-CUSHION floor beneath his aching body, and his temples pounding with the aftereffects of anesthetic gas . . . the same gas that filled the passenger cabin every time he tried to free himself.

As was his practice, he lay motionless, waiting for the fog to clear, trying to take stock of his circumstances. His hands remained behind him, secured by the same pair of stun cuffs that he had been trying to open when the gas had last come hissing from circulation vents. Judging by the numb ache in his shoulders, his arms had been folded under his back without moving for quite some time, and his tongue felt swollen with thirst. Clearly, this time he had been unconscious longer than a normal sleep cycle—for at least twenty-four hours, maybe even forty-eight.

The muffled rumble of a battle was reverberating up through the floor beneath Ship, and occasionally the entire hull would shudder with the force of an explosion that was either very close or very powerful. If Ben listened carefully, he could even hear the distant screech of blasters—though the sound was so faint it might have been nothing more than wishful thinking.

Don't make me use the gas again. The words came to Ben inside his mind, as dark and full of menace as always. *You need to see what is about to happen.*

"I *need* water," Ben croaked. "How long was I out that time?"

Long enough. Ship never gave information to its captives, but Ben always tried anyway. Sometimes he learned more from what Ship attempted to conceal than he would have from a direct answer. *Sit up.*

Ben raised his legs and rocked upright. A tube dropped down from the ceiling of the passenger compartment and stopped in front of his face. He leaned forward and began to drink. The water was so warm and rank that it tasted foul even to someone as thirsty as he was, but he forced himself to continue. Ship could poison him at will by flooding the cabin with noxious gas, so the bad taste was probably no more than a minor cruelty. And if Ben hoped to recover his strength and escape, he needed to drink.

No sooner had the thought flashed through Ben's mind than the tube retracted into the ceiling. *Have you not yet learned that there is no escape?* Ship asked. *Not from Abeloth.*

A section of hull grew transparent, and Ben saw that Ship was sitting in the formal reception hall just off Pinnacle Platform. Designed to impress, the hall was an immense, cavernous chamber with alabaster walls and a white larmalstone floor. With a sweeping view across Fellowship Plaza, it had once been used by the Jedi Council to receive the Temple's most distinguished visitors. At present, however, it was filled with blast rubble, gray fumes, and a small band of weary-looking Sith.

Abeloth was here, too. She was standing in the wreckage of the hall's grand entry, facing out toward the landing deck, between a pair of laser cannon emplacements. At the ends of her upraised arms, her tentacles writhed in the air—as though she were using them to stir the smoke that was swirling over Fellowship Plaza. Even with her back to him, Ben could see that she was looking toward the distant cylinder of the Galactic Justice Center. Her attention did not waver as a trio of blastboats came roaring toward the platform, their nose guns flashing as they strafed the deck.

The cannon emplacements returned fire immediately. The leading blastboat lost an engine mount, then spiraled out of sight behind the balustrade. A couple of seconds later, Ben felt the sudden rip of half a dozen lives being torn from the Force, and a boiling cloud of smoke and flame rose into view.

By then the remaining two blastboats were crossing the balustrade seven meters above the deck and decelerating hard. Streamers of smoke trailed beneath their bellies as they poured rocket fire into the Sith laser cannons. Both emplacements vanished into balls of orange flame, and Ben thought for a moment that the boats would stop and begin to disgorge space marines.

No such luck.

The blastboats decelerated as expected, and both nose gunners began to pour blasterfire directly at Abeloth. She ignored the attacks until a bolt that should have blown off her right shoulder merely spun her around, tearing her gaze from the Galactic Justice Center—and redirecting it toward her attackers.

Abeloth's left arm came up so fast that Ben did not even see it move, and the fire from the blaster cannons began to ricochet back toward her attackers. Still hovering seven meters above the deck, the two blastboats spun around sideways, dipping their flanks so the barrels of heavy laser cannons in their top turrets could depress far enough to open fire. At the same time, Ben knew, the doors on the far side of both craft would be sliding open to drop their space marines.

Abeloth merely flicked her wrist. The rear blastboat tumbled into the leader's exhaust stream, and the plume of superheated ions melted through the nose armor. The Force lurched with a sudden terror, then both craft vanished inside a cloud of detonating ordnance.

Ben thought for an instant that would be the end of the space marines, but they were not so fortunate. Burning bodies began to drop out of the fireball, limbs flailing wildly and voices screaming as they cooked inside their armor. With their propulsion packs either disabled or blowing white flame over their backs, they had no way to slow their descent. A few lucky ones snapped their necks and died quickly. Everyone else broke arms or legs or spines, whatever hit first, then lay writhing in flames as pieces of blastboat crashed down on top of them. Their pain was pure and fiery in the Force, a searing wave that hit Ben like a grenade blast.

Abeloth remained standing in the wrecked entry, one set of tentacles splayed in front of her, using the Force to shield her from the flame and shrapnel blowing in from the platform beyond. The arm beneath her injured shoulder hung limp at her side, but the tentacles at the end were slowly uncurling. They arranged themselves into a rough cone and began to twitch, and the anguish of the dying marines vanished from the Force.

Abeloth was feeding on the dark side energy of their fear, Ben knew. He had seen her do it on Pydyr, when the entire population of the moon believed they were dying from an illusory plague. And now she was doing it on Coruscant, where the anxiety of the inhabitants had to be mounting by the hour as the battle raged ever more fiercely. With trillions of inhabitants on Coruscant, Abeloth's harvest would be limitless. Ben could not help wondering if this had been her plan all along—to set Jedi and Sith against each other, then feast on the fallout.

You Jedi are such small thinkers, Ship said, interrupting his thoughts. *Abeloth wants so much more, Ben . . . especially for you.*

"Yeah? Well, forget it," Ben said, recalling how Abeloth had taken possession of *two* of his father's old girlfriends. "I'd rather die than let her use me to get close to Dad."

Who said that *is her plan?* Ship replied. *Or that you have a choice?*

"I'm a *person,* not some tangled wad of biocircuits like you," Ben countered. "I *always* have a choice."

Ship withdrew in a swirl of dark mockery, leaving Ben alone to contemplate his growing despair. Despite his brave words, he had no illusions about his chances of resisting Abeloth in his current circumstances. Every time he so much as *thought* about escaping, he heard a hiss in the ventilation duct, then awoke later with no real idea how long he had been unconscious. If she wanted to change bodies with him—or steal his, or whatever it was she did when she took possession of someone—there was little he could do to stop her.

And that was the most terrifying aspect of his captivity. Abeloth had not hurt him—had barely even spoken to him. In fact, most of the time she seemed entirely oblivious of him. Yet he could always feel her presence, a cold tendril of fear that had taken root deep inside him, binding him to her in a way that chains could not. Abeloth wanted

Ben for her own. She always had. He had first felt her touch as a two-year-old child, when his parents had hidden him and the other Jedi younglings at Shelter during the war with the Yuuzhan Vong. He had not been there an hour before the tendril had come, a cold aching *need* that had frightened him so badly that he had closed himself off from the Force for years.

Now Abeloth had him for good. He could feel that in how the tendril had knotted up inside him, in the way its cold filaments had anchored themselves into his heart and his entire chest. Even if he couldn't bring himself to accept it, Ben saw the hopelessness of his position. He was Abeloth's, pure and simple, and the only fate that awaited him now was the one she had planned for him. He understood that.

The only thing Ben didn't understand was *why*. There were hundreds of powerful young Jedi in the galaxy, and dozens right there on Coruscant. Yet Abeloth had gone to elaborate lengths to capture *him*, to lure him into a trap and separate him from his companions. There had to be something special about him—something that Abeloth needed from Ben that no other young Jedi could provide.

The obvious answer, of course, was lineage. Ben was the only child of Luke Skywalker, who himself was the only son of the Chosen One, Anakin Skywalker. Of course, Jaina Solo was also a grandchild of the Chosen One—but only one of her parents had the Force. So that had to be what Abeloth needed from him—his bloodline.

But *why?*

Ben was still contemplating this question when a pair of weary-looking Sith walked into view, approaching from the rear of the reception hall. The first was a tall, lavender-skinned Keshiri woman. Though badly tattered, her elaborate robe suggested her status as a Sith Lord. She had probably been beautiful once—a few days ago, in fact—but now her face was so rash-covered and swollen that the skin had actually split in places. The second Sith—a young woman—was every bit as haggard as the first. Had she not been wearing light combat armor under a brown Jedi cloak, it was entirely possible that Ben would not have realized he was looking at Vestara Khai.

Part of his confusion arose from the lightsaber still hanging from Vestara's hip, and from the fact that she seemed to be walking at the

Lord's side. Vestara's hands were not bound in any way that Ben could see, and her escort's hands were not particularly close to her own weapons. Clearly, the Lord did not feel she had anything to fear from Vestara.

Ben went from stunned to confused to angry in the time it took the two women to walk ten meters to Abeloth, who still stood feeding on the fear and anguish of the dying space marines. He could scarcely believe what he was seeing—Vestara walking free among Sith—and it occurred to him this might be a form of Fallanassi illusion, similar to the one that Abeloth had used to deceive him and Vestara on Pydyr. Maybe Vestara was actually in stun cuffs and unarmed, with a Sith Lord at her back pressing a shikkar to her kidney.

Maybe . . . but Ben didn't think so. Her presence with the Keshiri woman explained too much—like the ambush in the water treatment plant, and how the Sith always seemed to be one step ahead in the assault on the Temple.

The conflagration out on the platform abated as the last pieces of blastboat came crashing down on the space marines. Abeloth lowered the arm she had been using to shield herself and turned to greet Vestara and the Keshiri Lord. Like loyal subjects, both women immediately dropped to a knee and dipped their heads.

Abeloth balled the tentacles at the end of her injured arm and held them out toward the Keshiri, who kissed them as though they were a hand, then rose. Abeloth repeated the gesture with Vestara, this time glancing toward Ben with her broad mouth curled into a self-satisfied smirk.

And that was when Ben recalled what Vestara had done on Pydyr. When she had realized that Lord Taalon was falling under Abeloth's sway, she had killed him. And when her own father, Gavar Khai, had turned up in Abeloth's service, she had killed him, too. Maybe Vestara *had* been a Sith spy all along . . . though Ben was once more finding that hard to believe. But he was sure of one thing: Vestara would *never* serve Abeloth willingly. So either Vestara could not see Abeloth's true form, right in front of her . . . or she was merely playing along—because she had no other choice.

Abeloth continued to look toward Ben for a few moments after

Vestara had kissed the knot of tentacles. Finally, she motioned her "subject" to rise, then led both Vestara and the Keshiri Lord toward Ben. As the trio approached, a section of Ship's hull peeled away and became a boarding ramp. Abeloth motioned the Keshiri woman to stay behind, then led Vestara aboard and stopped just inside the cabin.

Vestara did not even make it into the cabin. She stopped at the threshold, clearly stunned. *"Ben?"*

Ben raised his chin and stared at her, trying to look as though he were struggling to control his anger.

"Sorry about leaving you behind, back at the water treatment plant," he said, thinking of Abeloth so he could put some real spite into his voice. "But it looks like you came out okay. Sleemos always do."

Vestara stepped into the cabin and backhanded him across the face . . . hard. "Watch your tongue, Jedi, or it will be wagging from the tip of my parang."

Behind her, Abeloth's tiny silver eyes twinkled with delight, and Ben decided that—if he was right about Vestara—he just might have a chance of surviving this after all. He glared at her for a moment, then hit her with a Force shove . . . which she was braced to accept. Vestara merely rocked back on her heels, then flicked her wrist and sent him flying so hard his head nearly slammed into the cabin wall when he hit it.

"Be careful, child," Abeloth said, speaking in what sounded like six voices at once. She stepped forward and laid her tentacles across Vestara's forearm, eliciting a barely perceptible shiver. It was just enough to suggest to Ben that Vestara knew exactly who had touched her. "He is no good to me dead."

Vestara glared at Ben with what appeared to be true hatred in her eyes. "As you command, my Beloved Queen."

"Good." Abeloth retreated toward the door. "Ship tells me the boy has been thinking of escape again. You will guard him."

"And if he tries to escape?"

"You won't let him," Abeloth replied. She stopped at the top of the boarding ramp. "Perhaps he will be more inclined to remain if you tell him what you did in the escape tunnel."

Vestara's eyes grew wide, and Ben felt a flash of alarm in the Force. Before she could reply, Abeloth turned away and descended the boarding ramp.

Ben waited until Abeloth had turned back toward the reception hall's wrecked entrance, then looked up and met Vestara's gaze. Her eyes were softer than before, but she wisely resisted any urge to comfort or console him. She knew Ship's capabilities as well as Ben did. Ship could not only watch her, it could eavesdrop on the thoughts in the top of her mind.

"So, what happened in the escape tunnel?" Ben demanded.

"I led an ambush." There was a hard edge in her voice that did not match the apology in her watery eyes. "On the *Millennium Falcon*."

"You *what?*" Ben had no need to fake the shock, anger, or confusion in his voice. Her story made no sense, yet he could see in her face—and feel in the Force—that it was true. "What was the *Falcon* doing down there?"

"Dropping off Bazel Warv. He's dead." Vestara paused, doing a fairly good job of pretending to be cruel by making Ben wait for the news that she knew would be closest to his heart. "The Solos managed to escape into the Temple, but they'll be dead soon enough . . . if they aren't already."

Noticing that she hadn't said anything about Allana or more casualties, Ben breathed a silent sigh of relief and said, "You're a lying shevoork. There's no reason the *Falcon* would be down there."

"Your confusion is understandable." Vestara was managing to sound like she was actually enjoying this—and, perhaps, on some level she was. After all, tapping into one's secret emotions was the key to good acting. "The *Falcon* is supposed to be with the academy students, I know. We don't know why it wasn't—only that our signal people intercepted some chatter about infiltrators entering through the evacuation route. Since I was the only one who knew how to find the tunnel, I led the ambush. Imagine my surprise when it turned out to be the *Millennium Falcon*."

Vestara was telling the truth about being surprised—but she was lying about everything else. Ben could see it in her eyes and feel it in the Force, and she was a good enough liar that it shouldn't have been that easy for him. There wasn't any more she could tell him, and she was letting him know it.

Ben nodded to show he understood, then asked, "So you were just playing me all along? You were never serious about becoming a Jedi?"

"Does it *look* like I was serious?" Vestara's voice held so much contempt that she sounded sincere, and something dark began to burn inside Ben. "Yes, Ben, I was playing you. That's what Sith *do*."

Ben glowered at Vestara, thinking of all the times she had betrayed and deceived him in the past, deliberately allowing the dark ember inside to build into full-blown anger. With Ship able to touch the surface of their minds almost at will, it was important to *feel* the emotions appropriate to their words, or Ship would sense the disparity and realize whose side Vestara was really on.

Ben was still glowering when a faint rumble began to reverberate through Ship's landing struts. It was so dull and muffled that he thought he might be imagining it—until Vestara frowned and glanced down at her feet.

"What's that?" she demanded.

Ben shrugged. "I was about to ask you the same thing."

He looked through the viewport that Ship had created earlier and saw that Abeloth had stepped fully out onto Pinnacle Platform. She was standing at the balustrade, leaning slightly over the rail. And once again, her gaze was fixed on the Galactic Justice Center. One set of tentacles seemed to be pointing toward the base of the distant structure, while the other was hanging down toward the plaza, pulsing and shimmering as she drew on the dark side energy of the frightened crowd below.

"Ah—Abeloth is angry," Vestara said, following Ben's gaze. As she studied the scene, the rumble deepened and grew more audible, and Ship began to sway on its struts. She did not speak again for a second or two, then the entire reception hall started to shake and the wrecked entry began to drop rubble. "The people of Coruscant have disappointed the Beloved Queen. Now they will feel her wrath."

Ben began to have a very bad feeling about what was happening. "A groundquake?"

Vestara turned back to him, her mouth twisted into a smile that

seemed more frightened than cruel. "The groundquakes are just the beginning, you fool," she said. "The volcano will be the true punishment."

Ben recalled the giant volcano at Abeloth's home in the Maw, and
the pool of magma on Pydyr, and quickly understood the truth of
what Vestara was saying. Whether the volcanoes somehow fed Abeloth's power or were a mere side effect, it seemed clear that they were
associated with her presence. And on Coruscant, even a small flow of
magma would kill millions. With footings and foundations melting by
the square kilometer, skytowers would fall by the thousands, tumbling
into their neighbors or dissolving into the same pools of molten stone
that had eaten away their bases. The fumes, superheated and filled with
noxious gases, would kill *hundreds* of millions—and if a pyroclastic
flow developed, the death toll would rise to the billions.

And the whole time, Abeloth would be feeding off the fear and anguish of the victims. She would grow into a being beyond mortal comprehension. With the dark side hers to command, she could literally
reshape the galaxy in any manner she wished.

Ben shook his head, not quite able to grasp the enormity of what
was happening before him. He was watching a deity being born—and
she was not a benevolent one. It felt like he was caught in one of those
terrible nightmares from which it was impossible to awaken, except
that if this *was* a nightmare, it had been going on so long that it had
become his life.

Ben looked back to Vestara and found her studying him, watching
him come to the same conclusion she had no doubt reached days before, when she had made the decision to infiltrate the Sith. Abeloth
had to be stopped at any cost, even if it meant sacrificing themselves—
or each other.

After a moment, Ben asked, "The people of Coruscant have disappointed Abeloth *how*, exactly? There's nothing they could have done
that would justify that kind of punishment."

Vestara's smile turned passably cruel. "Who said the Beloved
Queen needs justification for anything she does? And anyway, it's what
the kreetles *didn't* do that has angered her."

"Which is?"

"They didn't defend her," Vestara replied. "When the Jedi and
their space marine galoomps invaded our Beloved Queen's palace

three days ago, only a few brave spirits tried to protect her. Most Coruscanti just went home and hid like the cowards they are—and *that* is why they will suffer."

"Our forces are inside the Temple?" Ben gasped, uncertain whether to be relieved or alarmed. If they had *already* been inside for three days, then clearly the battle was not going well. "How?"

"They came in like flitnats, through an exhaust portal," Vestara answered. "The fools have been trying to clear the palace of Sith ever since—and they have no idea what they are truly facing. When they finally *do* discover the Beloved Queen, they will wish they had died on a Sith shikkar instead."

Ben glared at Vestara with an expression of pure hatred that he hoped would conceal the gratitude he felt for the information she was so subtly relaying. In telling him the location of the initial breach—an exhaust portal—she had also explained why it was taking so long to clear the Temple. The Jedi and their space marine allies were being forced to fight for every meter, and that was going to take time. But even more important was what Vestara had told him about the attackers having no idea who they were truly facing. If the Jedi didn't know that Abeloth was in the Temple, then they wouldn't be pushing to kill her. They would be taken completely by surprise when the magma began to flow—and by then it wouldn't matter what they knew. Abeloth would be too strong to defeat.

Ben locked gazes with Vestara, then looked quickly toward the still-lowered boarding ramp. "And you're just going to let that happen?" He looked back toward Vestara. "You're just going to let Abeloth annihilate the jewel of the galaxy?"

"As long as it destroys the Jedi, yes." Vestara kept her gaze on Ben. "Why shouldn't I?"

"You're right. I don't know why you wouldn't." Ben looked back toward the boarding ramp, then back to Vestara, then back to the boarding ramp. "It just seems like an awful waste, destroying that much wealth."

He looked back to Vestara and tipped his head toward the boarding ramp. She held his gaze for a moment, then her eyes went soft and she gave a brief nod. She understood. She had to find the Jedi and bring them back to Abeloth.

"Coruscant's wealth is nothing to me." Vestara reached down and unclipped the safety clip on her lightsaber hook. "It belongs to the Beloved Queen, and it is hers to do with as she pleases."

"The Beloved Queen is a sick sack of tentacles." As Ben spoke, he was rising to his feet and spinning around to present his back to her. "I've seen starving Hutts who aren't as crazy as she is."

"Sweat-licking skarg!" A hissing crackle sounded behind Ben as Vestara ignited her lightsaber. "For that, you lose your hand!"

Ben spread his arms as far as he was able, trying to stretch his stun cuffs wide. A searing heat warmed the heels of both palms as the blade sizzled through the armored cable, and his hands came free.

A familiar hiss sounded from the ventilation duct as anesthetic gas began to pour into the cabin, and Ship sank on one side of its struts as it started to raise the boarding ramp to prevent their escape. Ben spun around and grabbed the blaster pistol from Vestara's holster.

"Gas!" He shoved her toward the ramp. "Go! I'll take care of Ship."

Vestara did not need to be told twice. She simply nodded and leapt for the exit. Ben took the blaster off safety and spun away from her, aiming toward a small control nodule in Ship's rear wall. Then Vestara cried out in surprise behind him, and the sizzle of her lightsaber faded into silence.

Resisting the temptation to look, Ben raised the blaster and pulled the trigger—and sent a single bolt burning into the floor as the weapon was Force-jerked from his hand.

In the same instant, Vestara came flying in at his flank, hitting so hard it felt like she had been launched from a missile tube. They flew across the cabin together and slammed into an interior wall, then dropped onto the floor in a tangled heap.

The anesthetic gas was already filling Ben's head with fog, and he could feel a knot rising on his brow where he and Vestara had banged skulls. Still, he managed to fight off the rising tide of darkness long enough to look back toward the exit, where the lavender-skinned Lord was standing on the half-raised ramp, watching Ben and sneering.

"Jedi fool!" the Keshiri said. "If she will betray *us*, she will betray you, too."

Chapter Twenty-eight

IN HER DREAM, JAINA LONGED TO REDIRECT THE KHAI GIRL'S SHIKKAR before it lodged in Ben's eye, but those were not the rules. The fate of the galaxy hung on this fight, and if Jaina wanted the galaxy of the future to be a fair one, then she could not interfere—not even if it meant Ben losing an eye, or his life.

Whose rules, Jaina could not recall. She knew only that she had arrived at the rim of the gorge to find the pair locked in battle, their lightsabers sparking and popping as they drove each other back and forth across the stone courtyard. She had snatched her own lightsaber from her belt and sprang down into the yellow fog that was rising from the Font of Power—and immediately found herself back where she had started, with her lightsaber hanging back on her belt.

A voice that was neither male nor female had said *"No!"* and Jaina had understood that she could not help her young cousin. The Balance itself hung on the fight between Ben and his Sith girlfriend—not on its outcome, but on the combat itself.

At the last second, Ben leaned away from the flying shikkar, but the blade passed so close to his head that Jaina saw a spray of blood and the tumbling crescent of an ear tip.

Then the yellow fog lifted again, and Jaina felt herself rising through the viscous warmth of a bactabath. How long it had been since the med-evac team had extracted her—and Luke and Corran—from the Jedi Temple, she had no idea. Her injuries no longer ached, but she could tell she was being pulled from the cylinder early. Her arm felt a bit weak in the area of the break, and when she tried to expand her lungs, she experienced a momentary hesitation that suggested her body still expected it to hurt.

Once her head had cleared the top of the tank, Jaina found herself looking out on the utilitarian interior of the Galactic Justice Center infirmary. Like most prison infirmaries, it was little more than a long hall, with a row of opaque bath cylinders along one side and a row of security stalls along the other. Gavin Darklighter—the admiral in command of the Galactic Alliance Space Marines—had commandereed it for use as a field hospital, and groaning space marines lay everywhere—strapped onto hovergurneys parked in the central aisle, stretched out on exam tables in security stalls, even lying on the floor curled into fetal positions. At least a dozen Emdee droids were performing surgery out in the open, and there were probably thirty sentient nurses performing triage or emergency life support. Clearly, the battle for the Jedi Temple was still raging—and it was not going well.

When Jaina was clear of the cylinder, the hoist swung her over to the side and lowered her to the floor, where a weary-looking Duros female in blood-smeared scrubs stood with one finger pressed to the control panel. In her other hand, the Duros held Jaina's lightsaber and equipment belt, and there was a set of clean clothing folded over her arm.

"You look busy," Jaina said, reaching for the clothes. "I can handle dressing by myself."

The Duros pulled her arm away. "You were supposed to be in the tank for another twelve hours." She offered Jaina some underclothes. "So I need to stay to make sure you're not going to faint."

"Jedi don't faint," Jaina said, slipping into the underclothes. "And you have a lot of other patients who really need you."

"And the sooner you stop arguing with me and finish dressing, the sooner I can tend to them," the Duros said. "Besides, I have a message, Master Solo. You're to join the rest of the Jedi Council as soon as possible. They're meeting in Senator Wuul's office in the Senate Building."

Under other circumstances, Jaina might have experienced a thrill at being addressed as a Master and asked to sit on the Jedi Council. Instead she felt the weight of her new responsibilities. The future of Coruscant itself was at stake, and an entity that no one quite understood had holed up inside the Jedi Temple. Jaina knew she would soon be asked to do the impossible again—and this time, she wondered if she would be up to the job. She glanced down the long row of opaque bacta tanks, checking for Luke and Corran. When she sensed through the Force that none of the occupants were Jedi—or even Force-sensitive—she nodded to the Duros.

"I understand—and I'm *not* going to faint. How long ago did the Masters Skywalker and Horn leave?"

"After his knee surgery was finished, Master Horn only needed the tank for a few hours," the Duros replied. "But Master Skywalker extracted himself early, less than an hour ago."

"Early?" Jaina grabbed her chrono and saw that she and the others had been recuperating almost four days. "That must have been some concussion he had."

"The concussion was not the problem," the Duros replied. "The burn on his chest has been slow to heal. *Very* slow. He's still not a hundred percent."

"Could it be the Force lightning?" Jaina asked, frowning in concern.

The Duros shrugged. "You would know better than I."

A sudden shudder shook the entire room—hard enough that Jaina heard the bacta slosh in the tanks.

"What was that?" she asked, closing her robe.

"I was hoping you could tell *me*," the Duros said. "The shaking seems to be growing stronger and more frequent. It must be something to do with the battle, yes?"

"That would make sense," Jaina agreed. "But I'm not sure what it is. Maybe they're using baradium bombs down in the sub-basements or something."

The Duros' complexion faded to pale blue. "It had better be 'or something.' There aren't enough medcenters on Coruscant to handle that much baradium poisoning." She studied Jaina for a moment, then handed over her lightsaber and equipment belt. "You might want to check your comlink. Someone has been trying to raise you all morning."

With that, the Duros turned and left. Jaina quickly clipped on her equipment belt and lightsaber, then checked her comlink and saw that there were several unanswered HoloNet relays from Tahiri Veila.

Jaina's heart climbed into her throat. Immediately worried that Tahiri was trying to reach her to tell her something had happened to Jag, she left the infirmary and headed for the nearest turbolift. Only after she was safely inside, dropping toward the Galactic Justice Center's local-transit level, did she dare retrieve the most recent message. It was Jag's voice, filled with concern—and perhaps just a little irritation.

"Where are you? I'm starting to worry." There was a short pause, then he said, "Listen, we're about to jump. We should be coming in system at eleven seventeen Galactic Standard. If you get this message before then, leave one on Tahiri's comlink letting me know how you are. We've heard that the Temple was breached and that you were taken to a medcenter, but not much else . . . See you soon—and you had better be well."

Jaina checked her chrono again and saw that she had only three minutes before Jag was due to enter the system. By the time she stepped out of the turbolift into the transit level, she had listened to half a dozen earlier messages from Jag, announcing that he and Tahiri were on their way to Coruscant without explaining the reason. Jaina assumed by his tone of voice that he was bringing good news, but that was really all she could determine from the cryptic dispatches.

Luckily, with the battle for the Temple raging across Fellowship Plaza and the Galactic Justice Center shuddering and shaking, the transit platform was deserted. Jaina barely had time to delete the messages from her comlink before she was seated alone in a four-person capsule, shooting through the transit tubes.

"How long will it take to reach the Senate Building?" Jaina asked the empty capsule.

"Approximately three min*utes* and ten *sec*onds." The reply came from the tiny speaker in the ceiling, the voice stilted and awkward because capsule droids were not given a lot of extra processing power. "You *have* been *pre*-cleared through security, so there *will* be no *delay*."

Jaina's chrono showed eleven sixteen, a minute before Jag and Tahiri were due to emerge from hyperspace—and become accessible via HoloNet relay. She opened the channel anyway. It seemed like forever since she had heard Jag's voice, and with so little time available before she would have to sign off again, she wanted to listen to it every second she could.

After a short delay, a connection chime surprised her by sounding in her earpiece, and Jag's voice asked, "Jaina?"

"Yes, Jag. It's me."

There followed a moment of silent relief as they paused to savor the sound of each other's voices.

Then Jag seemed to gather his wits and asked, "How are you? I've been worried."

"I know. Sorry about that," Jaina said. "I've been in a bacta tank, and the medics have too much going on right now to take messages."

"But you're all right?" Jag pressed.

"I got a little beat up during the assault, but I'm fine now." Jaina checked her chrono. "Listen Jag, we don't have much time. I'm on my way to a Council meeting."

"In that case, I need to pass you over to Tahiri," Jag replied. "I have big news, but she has intelligence the Masters will need to hear when you see them."

"Jag, *what* news?"

"It can wait . . . I love you, Jaina." His voice grew faint as he passed the comlink over, but not so faint that she could not hear him say, "I have the ship."

"You have the ship," Tahiri confirmed, obviously passing control of whatever vessel they were in over to Jag. Her voice grew louder and more distinct in Jaina's earpiece. "Good to hear your voice, Jaina."

"Thanks, Tahiri—yours, too." With all that was going on in the galaxy right now, Jaina was glad to have a friend and former Jedi at Jag's side—especially since it sounded like he didn't have much other protection. "You and Jag are flying your own ship?"

"Afraid so," Tahiri replied. "The *Pellaeon* went with the Head of State's job."

"Jag *lost* the election?" Jaina gasped.

"Not exactly," Tahiri replied. "He—"

"We only have two minutes," Jag's voice interrupted in the background. "Tell her what happened on Hagamoor Three."

"Okay . . . what happened on Hagamoor Three?" Jaina asked, reluctantly accepting that she would have to wait for Jag's news. "And exactly where *is* Hagamoor Three?"

"It orbits Antemeridias," Tahiri said. "And it's where Boba Fett and I killed Abeloth."

"Really?" Jaina asked. Between Jag's eagerness to get off the channel and Tahiri's claim to have been aided by the same bounty hunter who had broken Daala out of detention, she was starting to wonder whether the people on the channel were impostors. "You've been working with Boba Fett?"

"Long story," Tahiri replied. "You *did* hear the part where I said we killed Abeloth—right?"

"I heard," Jaina said cautiously. "But I'm having a little trouble with that part. Abeloth almost killed *us* inside the Jedi Temple."

There was a short silence, then Tahiri asked, "Didn't Master Skywalker have to kill her twice on Pydyr?"

"Right. In two different bodies." Jaina began to have the sinking feeling that she was talking to the real Tahiri after all. "I *had* been assuming that Abeloth just moved from one dying body into a living one."

"But if we were both fighting Abeloth, and we were thousands of light-years apart at the time . . ." Tahiri let the sentence drift off incomplete, then sighed deeply. "So now we know. Force entities *can* be in two places at once."

"Let's hope it's *only* two." Jaina checked her chrono again, then said, "Why don't you give me the highlights?"

"I'll try," Tahiri said. "But two minutes isn't much time . . ."

Tahiri recounted the basic facts of her encounter with Abeloth, starting with the powerful Force presence she had felt slipping through the blockade at Exodo II and quickly proceeding to her suspicions about Abeloth's role in the election. She believed it had been

Abeloth behind Daala's proposal to avoid a bloody civil war by holding a vote instead. When it became obvious that Abeloth was using the
Force to assure a victory for Daala, Tahiri had tracked the entity to
Hagamoor 3 and—finding Boba Fett on the moon pursuing an objective of his own—she had struck a deal to work together.

Without explaining how Abeloth had come to select this facility as
her lair, Tahiri gave a quick account of how she and Fett had tracked
her into a secret laboratory owned by Tol Getelles. They had found
their quarry inhabiting the rapidly decaying body of Lydea Pagorski—
the same Imperial lieutenant who had perjured herself at Tahiri's trial
on Coruscant. A vicious battle with Abeloth had followed, and Tahiri
and Fett had barely survived.

"The only reason you're talking to me now," Tahiri explained, "is
that Abeloth didn't kill me outright. She needed *my* body next, because Pagorski's was burning out. Apparently, the bodies of Force-
users last longer."

The transit capsule began to slow as it approached the Senate
Building boarding station.

"You're *sure* you killed her?" Jaina asked.

"That depends on how you define *kill*, I guess," Tahiri said.
"Pagorski's body was destroyed by a thermal detonator; then an Imperial frigate blasted the entire lab until the only thing left was a glass
crater. So, I'm pretty sure *that* Abeloth was destroyed. Until I heard
about the one in the Jedi Temple, I thought we might have gotten her.
Now I'm just scared."

"Yeah, I'm not too happy about having more than one Abeloth-
thing running around the galaxy, either." Jaina paused, recalling how
the Abeloth in the Temple had suddenly grown weak and fled. "You
wouldn't happen to know what time you killed the Pagorski avatar,
would you?"

"As a matter of fact, I remember exactly," Tahiri said. "It was two
minutes before midday—"

"Four days ago," Jaina finished. The capsule came to a stop, and
the top half slid back to allow Jaina to exit. "Right?"

Tahiri was silent for a moment, then said, "How did you know?"

"I'll tell you when I see you," Jaina replied, finally feeling like she
was beginning to make a little progress in understanding how to de-

stroy Abeloth. "The Masters will want to debrief you in person. We're using the Senate Building as a temporary headquarters."

"We're still a few hours out," Tahiri replied. "We'll be in touch as soon as we land."

"Good." The capsule began to ping, telling Jaina that it was time to debark. She stepped onto the platform and started toward the turbolift bank at the back of the station. "Now let me talk to Jag."

There was a brief pause as Tahiri passed the comlink back to Jag and took the controls. Then Jag asked, "Did I hear that right? You were hurt fighting Abeloth?"

"Later," Jaina said. "It's my turn to ask the questions. What happened with the election?"

"It's a long story," Jag said. "But basically, I had to withdraw."

"So Daala won?"

"Jaina, you should know me better than that," Jag said, genuinely shocked. "I withdrew so she would lose."

Jaina stepped into a turbolift but did not yet select a floor. Antigravity technology did not mix well with comlink transmissions, and she was likely to lose her connection as soon as she engaged the repulsor drive.

"Then who's the Imperial Head of State?" she asked.

"An actual Imperial," Jag replied. "Vitor Reige."

"Pellaeon's former adjutant?"

"Vitor was one of my best admirals," Jag said, sounding a bit defensive. "He'll make an excellent Head of State."

"I know that," Jaina said. "It's just that—well, I wasn't expecting this. I'm very sorry, Jag."

Jag's voice grew puzzled. "What for?"

"That you had to withdraw, of course."

Jag actually laughed. "Well, *I'm* not."

The turbolift began to chime, pestering Jaina to select a destination or step off. She ignored it.

"Really?" she asked. "You're not going to miss running your own interstellar Empire?"

"Dodging assassination attempts and analyzing tax-stream reports? Not as much fun as you might think." For the first time in ages, Jag's voice actually sounded happy. "Right now, my greatest fear is that once Reige realizes how simultaneously mind numbing and nerve-racking it is to be Head of State, he'll find a way to drag me back."

Jaina laughed, too. "In that case . . . congratulations." The turbolift's chiming became a constant, irritating ring. "Listen—"

"You've got to go," Jag finished. "I love you, Jaina Solo. We'll be together soon—and we're going to stay that way."

"Count on it," Jaina said. "And I love you, too, Jagged—even if you can't hold a job."

Jag burst out laughing. Reluctant to click off, Jaina simply selected Wuul's floor and left the channel open, listening to the sound of her future husband's mirth until the signal dissolved into static.

Chapter Twenty-nine

On Jaina's first visit to the offices of Senator Luewet Wuul, she had sat in the plush chairs and enjoyed a snifter of rare burtalle. Now the mugs resting on the handsome borlestone conference table contained cold caf and warm water. The air had gone stale with the smell of nervous sweat and half-eaten sandwiches, and the ventilation system was struggling to remove the heat of all the bodies packed into the meeting room. But it was what lay outside the room, visible through the floor-to-ceiling viewport, that troubled Jaina.

The gleaming cylinder of the Galactic Justice Center, which had been shuddering gently as she left, was now swaying. She knew that Coruscant's skytowers were designed to withstand tremors far more violent than what she was seeing, but she still didn't like it. Had the cause been a simple groundquake, the rest of Fellowship Plaza would have been shaking, too. This looked like something far more sinister—something involving Abeloth.

Jaina felt a gentle pull in the Force. She looked over to see Corran Horn nodding toward an empty seat on the near side of the table, where most of the Jedi Council sat in a semicircle to either side of Luke. With Kyp Durron, Kyle Katarn, Cilghal, Saba Sebatyne, Octa Ramis, and Barratk'l also present, only Kam and Tionne Solusar—who were supervising the students on Shedu Maad—were absent. Seated along the far side of the table, more or less across from the Jedi Masters, were an equal number of military and civilian dignitaries, including Admiral Nek Bwua'tu, his dapper uncle Eramuth, Senator Luewet Wuul, Admiral Gavin Darklighter, and a haggard, sunken-eyed Wynn Dorvan.

Still, it did not occur to Jaina that the empty seat had been saved for her until she began to make her way toward it and found herself squeezing past a long line of assistants forced to stand along the wall. There were military adjutants, bureaucratic assistants, and—much to her delight and surprise—four Jedi Knights whom she would have loved to pepper with questions.

Instead, Jaina had to content herself with a quick smile and a pair of arm squeezes as she slipped past Lowbacca and Tekli, who responded with whispered words of congratulations on her promotion. She was dying to ask where Raynar was, of course. But, with the meeting already in progress, it would have been unthinkably rude to start a conversation on the side.

Standing directly behind the chair that had been saved for Jaina were two Jedi whom she was even *more* relieved to see—Valin and Jysella Horn. Like her, they looked like they had been pulled from the bacta tank early, with bruises and half-healed lacerations still visible on their faces and necks. She had heard during one of her rare breaks from the bacta tank that they had made contact with the space marines, but this was her first confirmation that they had actually escaped the Temple alive. Clearly, the pair had had a hard time after the strike team split, and the absence of the third member of their squad gave Jaina a sinking feeling. She raised her brow and mouthed a one-word question: *Ben?*

Valin shook his head, then shrugged to indicate that they didn't know. Jaina nodded and reached out to the pair in the Force, trying to let them feel how happy she was to see them in one piece. They responded with a smile, and, as she turned to take her seat, she sneaked a quick glance at Luke. There were purple circles beneath his eyes, and his face was clouded by fear and uncertainty—no doubt on behalf of both Ben and the Jedi Order itself. But there was no hint of anguish or grief—and Jaina would have sensed both, had Luke been unable to feel his son's living presence in the Force.

Jaina slipped into her seat, assuming her place on the Jedi Council with no pomp or ceremony, just a couple of nods from across the table and a whispered *"Welcome, Master Solo"* from the Master next to her, Octa Ramis. And it seemed to Jaina that was exactly how the role *should* be assumed, not in celebration or pride, but with a humble willingness to serve.

All eyes were fixed directly opposite Jaina, where Mirax Horn was standing in a gap between Master Barratk'l and Eramuth Bwua'tu. Dressed in the gray uniform of a brigadier general, she was holding a datapad in one hand, but speaking without any need to consult her notes.

". . . who have escaped the Temple are spreading out across Coruscant and launching soft-target terrorist attacks," Mirax said. "Of course, BAMR News is blaming the violence on 'Jedi spice cartels,' and they're urging their viewers to take arms against the Jedi and any 'corrupt' security personnel aiding the 'spice smugglers.' "

Eramuth Bwua'tu twisted his muzzle into a snarl, then tilted his gray-furred head so that he was looking up at Mirax out of one eye.

"And how effective are these lies, my dear?" the Bothan asked.

"There have been a few civilian attacks against Jedi," Mirax replied. "But most of the other news outlets are taking a more balanced approach, attributing the violence to a rogue sect of Force-users."

"They're not even using the term *Sith*?" Kyle Katarn asked.

"There has been some speculation," Mirax said. "But most of the public doesn't really understand what Sith *are*, and those who do are accustomed to thinking of them as loners—either Jedi gone bad, or sinister geniuses hiding in plain sight."

"So the population isn't doing anything to help *us*, either?" Kyp Durron asked.

Mirax shook her head. "Not much," she said. "We've been getting a little cooperation through the security forces—primarily reports of suspicious behavior. But most Coruscanti don't seem to know *what* to believe. They're just keeping their heads down and trying to stay clear of any trouble at all."

"Which is difficult, now that our fight with the Sith has spread beyond the Temple," Luke said. "How bad is the violence getting? Are we starting to contain it at all?"

Mirax pretended to consult her datapad, but Jaina could feel in her Force aura that she was simply gathering the strength to deliver bad news. Finally, she lowered the datapad and gazed around the table.

"Not even close," she said. "When the space marine volunteers entered through the exhaust shaft, the Sith had far too much time to react. We think at least three hundred escaped and spread into the rest of the city, and their only objective seems to be to create as much chaos and destruction as possible. So far, they've launched over three *thousand* attacks, and they've completely destroyed seven hundred skytowers. We're already estimating civilian casualties at over three million."

"And how many Sith have we taken out?" Corran asked.

"Twenty-two," Mirax replied. "But we've lost fifteen Jedi doing it. Security force casualties are running into the thousands—even the Special Weapons Teams are no match for Sith Sabers."

An unhappy silence fell over the table, for the conclusion was clear: so far, the enemy was winning this part of the fight, and there was little hope of turning the tide of battle anytime soon.

After a moment, Luke said, "We all know you're doing everything possible under the circumstances." He glanced out the window at the Galactic Justice Center—which was beginning to sway so wildly now that the deck of Fellowship Plaza could be seen buckling around it—then asked, "What do the reports say about *how* the skytowers collapse?"

"It's usually a well-placed explosion or a hot-burning fire," she said, following his gaze. "We don't have any reports of buildings being *shaken* down, if that's what you're thinking."

"It is, but I still don't like what we're seeing over there," Luke said. He turned toward the government side of the table. "It might be wise to evacuate the Galactic Justice Center."

Both Bwua'tus and Senator Wuul nodded, and Dorvan said, "Would you please give the order, General Horn?"

"Of course," Mirax said. She glanced back to Luke. "Before I see to it, there is one more thing I'd like to mention."

"Yes?" Luke asked.

"We've received several reports of . . . well, of an *observer*," she said. "A tall man with a rugged, tattooed face showed up at hand-to-hand combat near Fellowship Plaza. So far, he's done nothing but watch, but when Jedi Saav'etu noticed a dark side aura and tried to take him into custody, he disarmed her. Then he said something very odd: *'Not yet, Jedi. Abeloth first.'*"

"These tattoos," Luke asked, "did they radiate from around his eyes?"

"Jedi Saav'etu described it as a spray pattern with the eyes at the center," Mirax replied. "Then you know who he is?"

Luke shook his head. "Not at all," he said. "But I caught a glimpse of him during the trouble we had leaving the spaceport. He certainly didn't appear to be a member of the Lost Tribe."

"Then I'll put out a 'report location only' bulletin on him," she said. "We certainly have no need to go out *looking* for a fight right now."

"I think that's best," Luke agreed.

"Thank you." Mirax glanced around the table, then said, "If I'm not needed here, I'll see to the Justice Center evacuation."

Luke dipped his chin and said, "Thank you, Mirax. We'll send you some additional Jedi support as soon as we're able." As she stepped away from the table, he turned his attention to Gavin Darklighter. "How soon can we start withdrawing our combination teams from the Temple?"

Gavin stared at the table a moment, gathering his thoughts, then looked up. "We're making progess." Judging by the dark circles beneath his eyes, he had not slept since the assault on the Temple had begun. "We control everything above Level Three-seventy and below the Pinnacle."

"Above Three-seventy?" Dorvan asked. "Then you haven't captured the computer core?"

Darklighter shook his head. "Not yet."

"Then you have captured *nothing*." Dorvan's voice was pitched high, and his eyes were bulging. He glanced around the table. "Does no one understand? The Beloved Queen is living in the computer, too. She *is* the computer!"

Gavin nodded wearily. "You *did* mention that—several times—in the post-rescue debriefing, Chief Dorvan. And we'll deal with the computer core just as soon as we're able to attack it." He shifted his attention back to the others. "In the meantime, we're splitting the Sith forces that remain in the Temple, driving them down into the sublevels and up into the Pinnacle. We've encountered a lot of resistance in the upper levels, and frankly, if Chief Dorvan hadn't told us that Abeloth was in the computer core, we would be inclined to believe that she is somewhere near Pinnacle Platform."

The message was clear—whatever Dorvan believed, the space marines were pretty sure that they had located Abeloth on Pinnacle Platform. Of course, after her conversation with Tahiri, Jaina realized that it was all too likely that both Dorvan and the space marines were right.

"And why would you believe that she is at the Pinnacle, Admiral?" Luke asked.

A look of pain came over Gavin's face. "Because we just lost three blastboats of Void Jumpers there, and even Sith gunners aren't that good."

Luke nodded. Jaina was relieved to see him turn his gaze toward the Galactic Justice Center. Obviously, he could see what was happening to the skytower, and he had made the same connection as Jaina— that the center was in a direct line of sight from Pinnacle Platform.

"We have to make another run at the platform," he said. "But this time, we'll send an all-Jedi unit. We'll select a team after the meeting. Until then, would you task someone to prepare a squadron of blastboats for us?"

"Of course," Gavin replied. He sat down, then looked over his shoulder and motioned an aide forward.

Even before Gavin had begun to issue the orders, Dorvan complained, "I see what you're doing, you know. But it's a mistake to ignore me. I've been closer to the Beloved Queen than any of you. I *know* what she can do."

"Nobody is ignoring you, Chief Dorvan," Jaina said, leaning forward so she could look Dorvan in the eye. "At least *I'm* not. If you say she's living in the computer core, I absolutely believe you."

"So do I," Luke assured him. "We know for a fact that she had contact with Callista Ming, a former Jedi who once merged her Force presence with a computer. So we have every reason to believe you."

Their reassurances seemed to calm Dorvan.

"Thank you," he said. "I'm glad to hear that. Abeloth may be on Pinnacle Platform, but that doesn't mean that she's not—"

"In the computer core, too," Jaina finished, realizing that Dorvan already knew what she had only recently surmised. She looked around the table at the other Masters. "Unfortunately, Abeloth can inhabit more than one body at a time."

An uneasy hush fell over the room, and all eyes swung to Jaina.

"On the way over here, I spoke with Tahiri Veila." Jaina focused her attention on Corran and Luke. "It turns out that, at the same time we were fighting our *Sith* Abeloth in the Temple ventilation ducts, Tahiri and Boba Fett were fighting *another* Abeloth on Hagamoor Three. They destroyed theirs with a thermal detonator . . . at exactly two minutes before midday GST."

The eyes of both Masters lit with comprehension, and Luke said, "The same time *ours* suddenly lost her strength and fled the fight."

"So the two bodies were linked," Corran said. "Kill one, weaken the other?"

Jaina nodded. "I think so," she said. "Tahiri knew the exact time because she was expecting a turbolaser strike at midday, and we knew the exact time because we had to blow the shield generator at midday. *Our* Abeloth was winning—until the precise moment they killed *theirs.*"

"That would explain what happened to Dyon Stadd in the Maw," Luke said. "I *knew* I was killing Abeloth when I fought her there—"

"But you were killing just *one* part," Saba said. "The part that was in the body of Dyon Stadd."

Luke nodded. "Exactly. And when that part died, the part in Abeloth's *other* body was weakened, too—the same way that the Abeloth here in the Temple was weakened when Fett and Tahiri killed the one on Hagamoor Three."

"Then I fear we may be running out of time," Cilghal said, looking out the viewport. The Galactic Justice Center was swaying more wildly than ever now, and pieces of debris could be seen falling from its balconies into a series of dark, smoking chasms that had opened in Fellowship Plaza around its base. "Each time we have killed one of Abeloth's bodies, the other part has fled to hide and recuperate."

"That's right," Kyp Durron agreed, addressing himself to Luke. "When you killed the part in Dyon's body, the other part left the Maw and went to Pydyr to recover. When you killed another body on Pydyr, the second Abeloth fled to Nam Chorios to recuperate. If she stays true to form, she'll be leaving Coruscant any minute now—if she's not already gone."

"A good observation," Kyle Katarn said. "But the pattern is rather different now."

"Different *how*?" asked Nek Bwua'tu. "Because there are three parts this time?"

"For starters, yes," Kyle said. "First, we have the part that Tahiri and Fett killed on Hagamoor Three. Second, we have the part that Luke and his team fought in the ventilation system. Presumably, she is the part that's now on Pinnacle Platform. Third, we have the part that Chief Dorvan reports is living inside the computer core."

"And if there can be three parts, why not four?" asked Nek. "Why not five, or a hundred, scattered across the entire galaxy?"

"Because all of Abeloth's bodies are part of one Force entity, yes?" Barratk'l asked in her gravelly voice. "She has grown much in power since we discovered her, but each time we kill a part, she is weakened. So there are limits. As she grows stronger, those limits rise. And now she has three bodies."

"That we *know* of," Kyle reminded her.

"Yes, but there is a correlation, or she would not need to hide from us when a part of her has been killed," Barratk'l said. "So we must ask ourselves this: what, exactly, are we harming when we kill a body she has taken?"

She turned an expectant eye toward Cilghal, who—as the Jedi Order's most knowledgeable healer—was the most likely source for an answer. The Mon Calamari nodded and raised a finger to indicate that she was contemplating the question. When she finally looked up, her bulbous eyes looked uncertain.

"The answer must lie in the Force," she said. "But it is difficult to grasp without knowing how she takes control of her victims. If it was just Force telepathy, or a simple exertion of will, she wouldn't be harmed when one of her bodies is killed. She would simply withdraw and find another."

"I saw her take Lydea Pagorski," Dorvan said tentatively. "Would it help if I tried to describe the process?"

All eyes swung toward him, and Cilghal said, "Very much, Chief Dorvan."

Dorvan's face went pale and blank, the way torture victims' faces did when they relived their torment. But he swallowed hard and said, "I'll do my best."

"Just take your time and tell us everything you can remember," Cilghal said. "No detail is too small."

Dorvan nodded. "It seemed very fast," he said. "Abeloth was using Roki Kem's body at the time, but it wasn't holding up well. The skin was starting to peel, and her eyes were starting to bulge."

Jaina saw Luke exchange glances with Saba and Corran. No doubt they were all thinking the same thing that she was—that Abeloth had been hiding in plain sight the whole time they were searching for her.

"Those are very helpful details, Chief Dorvan," Cilghal assured him. "Please continue."

Dorvan closed his eyes, then said, "First, Roki Kem told Pagorski that she was simply going to erase her memory of what she had seen inside the Temple. Pagorski believed her, so she didn't resist. Then Kem grabbed Pagorski's head and locked gazes with her. For a moment, nothing happened. Then the air started to shimmer between them. Pagorski's eyes opened, and she looked terrified."

Dorvan paused and began to shake as he recalled what happened next. "Kem's fingers started to grow, then her arms suddenly dissolved into tentacles, and she . . . well, she became Abeloth. I mean, she always *was* Abeloth, but now I could see her real nature."

"Can you describe her?" Cilghal asked.

"She had coarse yellow hair and eyes that weren't really eyes—just silver points of light set deep in the sockets," he said. "Her mouth was more like a deep gash. It stretched most of the way across her face."

"No doubt about it, that's Abeloth," Luke said. "What happened next?"

"Well, Pagorski started to scream, then Abeloth's tentacles shot down her throat," Dorvan said, still keeping his eyes closed. "And into her ears and nostrils. Pagorski made very horrible sounds, like she was gagging and choking, and the tentacles started to pulse. After a few seconds, Pagorski just collapsed and hung from the tentacles, looking terrified."

Dorvan fell silent, no doubt lost in a memory more terrifying than any nightmare.

After a few moments, Cilghal prompted gently, "And that was the end of it?"

Dorvan shook his head. "That was just the beginning," he said. "After a while, the terror finally drained from Pagorski's face. I thought maybe she had died. But then her face turned so pale that I could see the tentacles writhing around under her skin, pumping something dark and viscous through her nose—up into her sinuses— and down into her throat. I didn't think there was any way she could live through that, but she did. I could see her chest rising and falling as she breathed, and she never—well, she never went slack, the way dead people do. Finally, she seemed to get stronger, and she sort of looked at me and smiled. But it wasn't just Pagorski looking. She was still in there, and I could see in her eyes that she was going crazy with fear. But Abeloth was in there, too—and she was enjoying it."

"As though she were feeding on it?" Luke asked.

Dorvan opened his eyes and thought for a moment, then nodded. "Yes," he said. "Exactly like that. She was feeding on the fear."

"We've seen that before," Luke said. "On Pydyr, Abeloth seemed to be creating an aura of fear so she could draw on the dark side energies it released. We're fairly certain it's how she rejuvenates herself."

"A Force being that feeds on fear?" Dorvan looked through the viewport, out over the battle havoc that filled Fellowship Plaza, and shook his head in open despair. "In that case, Master Skywalker, you had better kill her soon—while it is still possible."

"That's what we're doing here, Chief—trying to figure out how," Kyp said. "What else can you tell us?"

"Nothing more about taking Pagorski's body," Dorvan said. "I'm afraid my memory after that is . . . well, muddled. But I think you should hear what happened when I killed her."

A dozen brows rose, and Saba Sebatyne sissed and slapped her palm on the arm of her chair. "Thank you, Chief. This one needed a joke!"

Barratk'l shot a furry glower across the table at the Barabel. "I think the Chief is serious, Master Sebatyne." She turned to Dorvan. "Yes?"

Dorvan nodded, but shot a self-deprecating smile in Saba's direction. "Master Sebatyne has every right to laugh," he said. "You see, Abeloth *wanted* me to kill her."

Most of the beings at the table once again began to look at Dorvan as though he were having a breakdown, but Kyle Katarn merely cocked his head in curiosity.

"I'm afraid we're not really following you, Chief," he said. "Why would Abeloth *want* you to kill one of her bodies?"

Dorvan shrugged. "Maybe because it was wearing out, or maybe because she was going to enter the computer core anyway," he said. "All I can tell you is that I stole a hold-out blaster and put a couple of bolts through her head. The next thing I know, I'm flying into a wall—and I discover that she has manifested herself out in the computer core. I realized later that the whole thing was just a trap for Ben."

Luke shifted forward in his chair. "For *Ben?*" he asked. "What makes you think it was just for Ben?"

"Because Ben is the one they took." Dorvan looked over at the Horns, then said, "But maybe you should ask Valin or Jysella. They were in a better state of mind than I to make that judgment."

"There's no doubt about it," Valin said, stepping forward. "Looking back, Abeloth was trying to isolate Ben from the moment we started down the corridor. She could have taken us all out along the way, but she wanted Ben alive."

"I'd even say that she might have been driving us toward the computer core just to set up Ben's capture," Jysella agreed. "Everything was timed to the millisecond, then once she had Ben, she left the rest of us alone."

"Which isn't to say she actually let us go, in case anyone's wondering," Valin said. "She just left us to the Sith and didn't expend any more of her own effort on us."

Jaina understood the need for the clarification. Valin and Jysella Horn had been among the first Jedi Knights to become infected with the Force psychosis when Abeloth began to reach out from her prison in the Maw, and they had actually become her spies for a time. Fortunately, they had been cured after Abeloth's defeat on Nam Chorios, and everyone assumed the cure was complete. Still, had the Masters known where Abeloth was hiding when they were preparing to storm the Temple, the Horn siblings were the last two Jedi Knights they would have sent in with the initial wave.

"And Abeloth didn't reach out to you at all while you were inside the Temple?" Cilghal asked. "You had no episodes of paranoia or confusion?"

"We didn't say that," Valin replied with a grin. "We're *still* trying to figure out why she took Ben and ignored us. It seems kind of suspicious."

"I think I may know the answer," Jaina said. She turned to Dorvan. "You said the body you killed in the computer core was wearing out?"

"That's right," Dorvan replied. "She was pretty emaciated by then."

"And this was Roki Kem's body, correct?"

"That's right," Dorvan replied. "Didn't I say that?"

"I just wanted to be sure." Jaina looked back to the rest of the table. "When I spoke to Tahiri Veila, she mentioned that Pagorski's body was deteriorating, too. In fact, Tahiri said the only reason she and Fett survived was because Abeloth didn't *want* to kill Tahiri. She wanted to trade Pagorski's body for Tahiri's."

"Of course," Cilghal said. "Pagorski and Kem weren't Force-users. Their bodies would not tolerate so much Force energy."

"That doesn't explain the focus on Ben," Kyle said. "If it was just a matter of being a Force-user, Abeloth could have taken Valin or Jysella—or one of her Sith servants—just as easily. It's something else . . . something that makes Ben special."

"Well, he *is* a Skywalker," Kyp Durron pointed out. "The grandson of the Chosen One."

"And Jaina is a grand*daughter* of the Chosen One," Luke countered. "I'm more inclined to think it has something to do with Shelter. Maybe Abeloth just wants him because he withdrew from her touch when he was a toddler."

Kyp shook his head. "Sorry, but no," he said. "Jaina is Han's daughter just as much as Leia's, and that means only one parent is a Force-user. Ben is the son of *two* parents who were both *very* strong in the Force. No offense to Jaina, but Ben has Special Destiny written all over him."

Luke's face fell, and Jaina could tell by the silence that followed that he saw the wisdom of Kyp's suggestion—as did everyone else at the table. Abeloth had gone after Ben because of what Ben was . . . and that meant she had something special in mind for him.

"Okay," Luke said at last. "Abeloth wants Ben for a reason. Any ideas what that might be?"

A chirrupy voice spoke out from the wall behind Jaina. "No specific ideas," Tekli said. "But the time has come to discuss what we learned about Abeloth from the Killiks."

"By all means, if you think it will help." Luke waved Tekli and Low-bacca toward the open space on the other side of the table, then turned to the rest of the attendees and explained, "Jedi Lowbacca and Tekli have *just* returned from a mission to learn what the Killiks know about Abeloth. I understand that Jedi Thul was forced to remain behind in exchange for the information, but from the little I've heard about it, they have uncovered some very interesting history."

As Tekli stepped to the table, a sudden jolt shook the room, then quickly diminished into a series of sporadic shudders. Dorvan and several of the non-military personnel began to eye the floor with uncertainty and fear. Nek Bwua'tu merely cleared his throat and muttered something about a blasted groundquake, but Jaina—and no doubt the other Jedi in the room—felt the wave of fear that came from the Galactic Justice Center. When she looked out the viewport, she saw that fissures had begun to appear in Fellowship Plaza's undulating deck, and now there were long columns of smoke rising through the cracks.

"Maybe we'd better rush that strike on Pinnacle Platform," Kyp suggested, "before the Galactic Justice Center collapses into the undercity."

"Don't you mean before we finish a proper evaluation of the battlefield?" Nek Bwua'tu countered. "Rushing into a fight half blind has never saved a blasted thing, son. We'll *all* be better off if the Masters stay here and do their jobs. You're leaders. And leaders are supposed to plan and think—not rush into an ambush every time the enemy does something unexpected."

Kyp's eyes widened at the admiral's harsh tone, but he accepted the admonition with a graceful nod. "Valid points, Admiral. I yield to your wisdom . . . and Master Skywalker's orders."

"I agree with Admiral Bwua'tu," Luke said. "I've had my fill of walking into Abeloth's traps. We need to finish this briefing and come up with a plan."

Luke nodded to Tekli, who was standing at the table, barely tall enough for her short-snouted face to appear above the edge. Behind her, Lowbacca loomed over the entire group like the furred giant he was, holding an oversized datapad in his hands.

Tekli cleared her throat, then said, "Given the time constraints, this will be a brief summary of what we have learned. See-Threepio is currently loading a full videographic account of everything we discovered into the Jedi Archives."

"Thank you," Luke said. "I'm sure that will be helpful if we need to explore Abeloth's history in more detail."

Tekli looked up at him out of a single eye. "Trust me, Master Skywalker, you *will* need to explore it."

She snapped her fingers, and a panel of carved stone, done in low relief, appeared on the display. The image depicted a jungle paradise, with a steep valley wall in the background and a swamp in the foreground. In the middle ground was a clearing with an erupting geyser. Three ghostly figures were floating in the vapor cloud: a luminous-looking woman, a craggy warrior type, and a gaunt, bearded man with a fatherly bearing.

"This is a panel from the Histories of Thuruht," Tekli explained. "The Histories detail—among many other things—the birth of a family of Force entities whom the Killiks call the Ones. The young woman, they call the Daughter."

As Tekli spoke, Lowbacca changed the image to another panel. This one depicted a pale-haired woman running through a forest in full bloom, followed by clouds of butterflies and swarms of Killiks.

"The Daughter seems to be associated with the light side of the Force," Tekli explained. "The Killiks could not explain the exact nature of the association, but my best guess is that she is an embodiment of its nature."

Lowbacca changed the image again, this time to a panel depicting a powerful-looking man in dark armor, marching through a dead forest.

"The Son is associated with the dark side of the Force," Tekli continued. "Again, the Killiks were unable to explain exactly what this means. But it seems obvious that he embodies its devouring, deadly nature."

Lowbacca tapped a key, and the datapad showed a panel with a river meandering down its center, dividing the luminous forest on one bank from the dark forest on the other. In the back of the image, a gaunt man was standing on the balcony of a cliffside monastery. He was looking out over both forests, his arms spread so that one hand was suspended above the dark aspect and one over the luminous.

"The Father is the Keeper of the Balance," Tekli said. "There were several other panels showing him trying to keep the peace between the Son and the Daughter."

"I see," Luke said. "And these beings—the Ones—are they the Celestials the Killiks claim to have served in the past?"

Tekli shook her head. "I don't believe so, at least not the way you mean," she said. "Thuruht says they are what the Celestials *become*."

"And what does Thuruht say the Celestials *are*?" Corran asked.

"They don't, really," Tekli replied. "They claim it's impossible to explain the Celestials, because no mortal mind can grasp their true nature."

With a long groan, Lowbacca noted that the Killiks believed the Celestials were *in* the Force. But they were adamant about saying that the Ones didn't *emerge* from the Force, because the Force was all around us, in us, and *was* us—and any being with two brains could clearly see that it was impossible to emerge from what one *was*. Tekli translated for those who didn't understand Shryiiwook.

"Soooo . . ." Kyp sighed. "The usual Killik mugwump."

"Well, it did make some sense at the time," Tekli replied. "Perhaps it will seem more logical in the video record."

"No doubt," Kyle said. "But you said this would help explain Abeloth. Are we to take it that she is this Daughter? That the Son was able to draw her over to the dark side?"

"Not at all," Tekli replied. "To understand Abeloth, you need to think about what's missing from the family."

"You mean the Mother, of course," Luke said. "Abeloth is the other parent?"

Tekli snapped her fingers again, and Lowbacca changed the image on the datapad. This time, the panel contained a new figure, a young woman barely older than the Daughter, with long flowing hair, a wide smile, and twinkling eyes. She was obviously supposed to be some sort of servant, for the Son and the Daughter were looking away while they held glasses up to be filled from an ewer in her hands. But the Father was looking at her with obvious warmth, returning her smile as she poured for him.

"Abeloth is the servant who *became* the Mother," Tekli said. "At first, she seemed to bring joy and harmony to the family."

As Tekli spoke, Lowbacca ran through a series of images depicting Abeloth keeping the Son and the Daughter busy with games and chores, doting on the Father, even stepping in to channel the Son's destructive energies into useful tasks. Before long, she seemed to be a full member of the family, eating at the Father's side and holding her glass for the *Son* to fill.

"But as time passed, Abeloth seemed to age while the rest of the family stayed young," Tekli explained.

The image on Lowbacca's datapad showed a much older Abeloth, one who appeared old enough to be a proper wife to the Father. The next panel portrayed an aged and wrinkled Abeloth, standing at one end of a small temple complex—a complex that resembled *exactly* the one in Jaina's dream of Ben and Vestara fighting.

The Force roiled beneath a powerful wave of astonishment and shock, and Jaina looked over to find Luke and all of the other Masters studying first the image, then one another, and she realized that she was not the only one who had experienced the dream. Whether they had all seen the same fight was impossible to say, but it was very clear that every Master present recognized the temple complex.

Jaina felt Luke reaching out in the Force, radiating a sense of calmness and patience, and she quickly understood the message. *Say nothing until the meaning grows clear.*

The images on Lowbacca's datapad continued to advance, now showing the Father arguing with the Son and the Daughter, gesturing wildly while boulders and six-legged lizards whirled through the air around them.

"As Abeloth aged, she appears to have become a disruptive influence," Tekli said. "We think she may have been growing resentful of her mortality, since the rest of the family never seems to age."

Lowbacca changed the image on the datapad, to a panel that showed an elderly Abeloth sneaking a drink from the Font of Power while the Father hurled Force lightning at both the Son and Daughter. In the next image, a much younger-looking Abeloth was swimming in the Pool of Knowledge, looking sly and defiant as the Father used the Force to pull her from the water.

"In her desire to remain with her immortal family, she did the Forbidden—and paid a terrible price."

Lowbacca tapped a key, and a new panel appeared on the datapad. In the heart of the temple's courtyard stood a much-changed Abeloth, her hair now coarse and long, her nose flattened, and her once sparkling eyes so sunken and dark that all that could be seen of them were two pinpoints of light. She was raising her arms toward a cowering Daughter and a glowering Son, with long tentacles lashing out from where her fingers should have been. A furious Father was stepping forward to shield them, one hand pointing toward the open end of the temple and the other reaching out to intercept her tentacled fingers.

"The Killiks call Abeloth the Bringer of Chaos," Tekli said, motioning for Lowbacca to lower the datapad. "They seem to view her as the counterpart to the Father's role as Keeper of the Balance, and associate her with strife and violence."

"Am I understanding you correctly?" Eramuth Bwua'tu asked. "Are you saying that Abeloth is some sort of war goddess?"

"That would be a great oversimplification," Tekli replied. "The Killiks claim that war is part of the galaxy's cycle of change. As they explain it, sometimes war grows *too* powerful, and that's when Abeloth comes—to destroy the old order and make room for a new one."

"So you're saying Coruscant's destruction is part of some Celestial Plan?" Dorvan asked. He looked pointedly out the viewport. The smoke rising through the crevices around the Galactic Justice Center had grown so thick that it was starting to drift across Fellowship Plaza, obscuring even the majestic pyramid of the Jedi Temple. Then he glared back across the table at Luke. "That the Galactic Alliance has no choice but to accept its destruction?"

"There's *always* a choice," Luke said. "Remember, this is the Killiks' view of the galaxy. And we know that Abeloth has been imprisoned before." He looked back to Tekli. "Why don't we move ahead to what we know about stopping her."

Tekli's tiny ears pivoted slightly outward. "Unfortunately, Master Skywalker, I don't believe the Killiks are going to be much help in that regard," she said. "At least not to *us*."

Lowbacca contributed a long rumble, explaining that while Thuruht's entire purpose of existence seemed to be imprisoning Abeloth, they needed the Ones to guide their efforts. From what he and Tekli had surmised, the Son and the Daughter agreed on only one thing— that it angered them to see Abeloth destroy civilizations they had spent millennia cultivating in their own image. Eventually, the pair would form a pact and emerge from seclusion to stop her, and Thuruht expected to spend the next century or so building up its numbers so the hive would be ready when it was called into service.

"So it's really the Ones who imprisoned Abeloth the last time?" Kyle asked. "And also created Centerpoint Station?"

"That is how the Killiks remember it," Tekli said. "But only the Son and the Daughter are involved. They seem to take more of an interest in the state of the galaxy than the Father."

"*Took,* I'm afraid," Luke said. "If Thuruht can't imprison Abeloth without the Son and the Daughter, the hive will be waiting a lot longer than a century for a call to service."

Tekli's nose twitched in confusion. "Then you have heard of the Ones, Master Skywalker?"

"Not by that name," Luke replied. "But when Yoda was training me in the swamps of Dagobah, he told me about a strange mission that Obi-Wan and my father had undertaken during the Clone Wars. Apparently, they were drawn to a free-floating artifact called the Mortis monolith and transported to a world very much like the one depicted in the Histories of Thuruht."

"You're saying that *they* met the Ones?" Kyp asked. "Are you *sure?*"

Luke shot him an impatient look. "It's very hard to be sure of *anything* involving the Celestials, Master Durron," he said. "But yes, I do believe the trio Yoda described were the Ones."

"*And?*" Kyp demanded.

"At the time, I thought he was just making up a story, trying to make a point about not refusing my destiny." Luke paused, then said, "But now . . ."

"You think he may have glimpsed something in your future," Kyle said. "Something to do with Abeloth?"

Luke shrugged. "That might be a stretch," he said. "But Yoda must have sensed that I would need to know about Mortis someday."

"So are you going to tell us what Master Yoda said?" Jaina asked. She couldn't contain herself, and she wasn't the only one—every Jedi in the room was leaning toward Luke. "I mean, that *is* the reason you mentioned it, isn't it?"

Luke nodded. "Of course," he said. "But there isn't a lot to tell. In Yoda's story, Obi-Wan and Anakin Skywalker encountered the Father when he was dying. The Son and the Daughter were at odds because the Son wanted to take the Father's place. The Father told Anakin that *he* had been chosen to assume the Father's place—and keep the balance between the two siblings. When Anakin refused, matters came to a head. The Ones fought, all three were slain, and their world died with them."

"And you didn't think *that* was important?" Corran asked.

"I didn't know Yoda was talking about the Ones," Luke said, a bit defensively. "Or even what the Ones *were*."

"It *does* sound more like a parable than an action report," Kyle agreed. "I'm sure I would have assumed the same thing."

"Are we sure it *isn't* just a parable?" Kyp asked. He looked to Tekli and Lowbacca. "No offense, but we all know how muddled the Killik sense of history is."

Saba slapped both palms on the table. "*This* one is certain. It explainz too much—why there is so much darknesz and change in the galaxy, why war comes so often and nothing stayz certain." She glanced around the table, meeting the gaze of each Master in turn, then said, "The Force has no Balance."

Jaina nodded, then said, "And it also explains what Abeloth wants with Ben."

An uneasy silence fell over the table, and she realized that many of the other Jedi had not yet made the connection between the loss of the only family Abeloth had ever known—the Ones—and the terrible longing and loneliness that had made an imprisoned Force entity reach out to Ben and the other younglings who had been hidden at Shelter.

But Luke understood. That much was clear in the way his face had paled—and in the care he was taking to keep his Force presence damped down, lest his fear reverberate through the room like a thunderclap.

When the faces of most of the other Masters remained puzzled, he nodded to Jaina. "You said it first," he said. "You explain."

"It's still just a guess," she said. "I could be wrong."

"*Are* you?" Luke asked.

Jaina thought for a moment, then shook her head. "No, I'm not." She took a deep breath and addressed the others at the table. "Abeloth took Ben because she intends to re-create the . . . well, the Family of the Ones, for lack of a better name . . . on her own terms."

An astonished rustle filled the room as beings shifted in their seats and stepped closer to the table.

Jaina gave the idea a moment to sink in, then continued, "Look, it doesn't matter whether the Killiks are right about the Ones—or even whether Yoda is. The only thing that matters is what *Abeloth* believes. She's trying to rebuild the family she lost."

"*I'm* convinced," Luke said, nodding. "It explains everything *I've* seen her do."

"But with herself taking the Father's place," Kyle observed. "Though she may have wanted *you* to take the role for a time. That would explain why she tried to keep you and Ben from leaving Sinkhole Station."

"Yeah, but then Luke kept killing Abeloth's bodies," Kyp observed. "After a while, she finally took the hint and decided she'd have the family on her own."

"Probably," Kyle agreed. "And it's safe to assume that Abeloth would be a force of constant change in the galaxy, rather than stability."

"She certainly wouldn't bring much Balance to the Force," Jaina agreed. "And Ben, obviously, will be the embodiment of the light side."

"Clearly," Corran said. "And Vestara Khai will embody the dark side."

It was stated as a fact rather than a guess, and none of the Masters questioned his conclusion—no doubt because they had all felt the astonishment of the others when they saw the image on Lowbacca's datapad. The hand of the Force was moving in this, and Jaina knew that all of the Masters felt it—even if they had not yet learned what it was doing.

When all of the Masters simply looked at one another and nodded, Luewet Wuul spoke from the other side of the table. "I hope you will forgive the foolish questions of one of the uninitiated, but . . . *how*? I know Jedi can use the Force to extend their lives, but isn't this Abeloth supposed to be twenty-five *thousand* years old?"

"She is far older than that, Senator," Tekli said. "The Histories of Thuruht have panels suggesting that Abeloth is at least a hundred thousand years old . . . but she started as a mortal."

"We have already seen the answer," Barratk'l said. "Abeloth was a mortal woman, yes? Then she drank from the Font of Power, and she swam in the Pool of Knowledge."

Wuul's cheek folds flattened in alarm. "Those are real?"

"Unfortunately, yes," Luke said. "And if Ben and Vestara drink from them . . ."

He let the sentence trail off, but Barratk'l finished it. "Then Ben and Vestara would become like *her*, yes? A family of Abeloths—with the Bringer of Chaos in charge."

"Something like that," Jaina agreed.

For a moment, no one said anything.

Then another groundquake hit, this one much more powerful than the first. The entire room began to shake violently, rattling caf cups and sending a decanter of fine burtalle crashing to the floor at the far end of the room. All eyes turned toward the Galactic Justice Center, where a two-hundred-meter fountain of white magma could be seen spraying up next to the gleaming cylinder, speckling its silvery skin with droplets of molten stone.

Saba braced her knuckles on the table, then rose and leaned forward to address her fellow Masters. "If the Ones are dead, then it seemz to this one we must all swear on our blood to destroy Abeloth."

As she spoke, a gaping melt hole appeared in the side of the Justice

Center, and the cylinder began to lean toward the interior of Fellow-ship Plaza.

"Because that egg eater is as mad as a blind shenbit," she contin-ued. "And the galaxy will not last a year with her on the loose."

"I quite agree, Master Sebatyne," Nek Bwua'tu said. He looked across the table, directly at Luke. "How would you feel about order-ing a baradium strike on the Temple?"

Gavin Darklighter was the first to object. "While I still have space marines inside?"

"Withdrawing them *would* alert Abeloth to our plan, General," Bwua'tu said. "And certainly, were *I* inside with an enemy like this, I would want my commander to do whatever it takes to destroy her."

"As would their Jedi companions," Luke said. "But I'm afraid that a baradium strike isn't an option."

"May I ask why not?" Eramuth inquired. "I realize that there's a certain element of betrayal—"

"That's not the problem," Luke said. "I doubt *any* of us have a being inside who wouldn't make the same sacrifice willingly, but there are other considerations." He glanced quickly in Jaina's direction. "The Solos are also inside."

Jaina's brow rose. "They *are?*" As surprised as she was, she didn't understand why Luke was making her parents' presence the critical factor in ruling out the baradium strike. Under the circumstances, they would have been the first to call it in on themselves—well, her mother would have been. Her father would have opted for a blaster duel at high noon. "I didn't even know they were on the planet."

"I'm afraid so," Luke replied. "It's a long story, but apparently they volunteered to drop Bazel Warv off at the entrance to the escape tun-nel, and the *Falcon* was disabled in an ambush. Han and Leia escaped into the Temple . . . with Amelia."

Now Jaina understood. Luke wasn't about to sacrifice Allana Solo, not after he had seen her sitting on the Throne of Balance in a Force vision. Unfortunately, not everyone present was privy to the secret of the young girl's destiny, so there were a lot of puzzled scowls along the non-Jedi side of the table.

Finally, Luew Wuul asked the question outright. "I don't understand, Master Skywalker. I know the Solos quite well, and I can't imagine either of them hesitating to make such a—"

"It doesn't matter, because it wouldn't work," Dorvan said, interrupting. "Abeloth would see it coming."

Nek Bwua'tu turned in his seat to face Dorvan. "I don't see how, Wynn," he said. "I can have a baradium barrage on the Temple in sixty seconds."

"And if you did, she would have seen it coming and *already* be gone." Dorvan glanced over at the puzzled faces flanking him, then seemed to realize the source of his problem. "You *do* realize she can look into the future, right?"

Admiral Bwua'tu's shoulders sank in despair, but any reply he intended to make was cut short by another bone-rattling *boom* from the Galactic Justice Center. All eyes turned toward the sound—just in time to see the gleaming cylinder vanish behind a kilometer-high pillar of boiling magma and billowing ash.

Jaina was as shocked as everyone else in the room, and she would probably have continued to watch as the conflagration melted the Justice Center into a river of molten durasteel—had she not felt a familiar presence tugging at her from the other side of Fellowship Plaza. Realizing that the eruption made a very effective diversion, she slid her gaze back toward the Jedi Temple. Amid the cloud of speck-sized blastboats still circling its gleaming pyramid, she caught a glimpse of a single-winged orb streaking away from Pinnacle Platform, ascending through the smoke on its way out of the Coruscanti gravity well.

Ship.

Jaina spun back toward Luke and found him already moving toward the door, motioning for her to follow.

Abeloth had Ben . . . and they had just departed for the Maw.

Chapter Thirty

SAGGING GIRDERS AND DANGLING PEDWALKS KEPT EMERGING FROM THE smoke, ghostly silhouettes that turned dark and solid so fast Jag had little time to react. Again and again, he jerked the yoke and sent the *Parting Gift* banking away from a collision, only to find new danger looming ahead. Bits of jagged durasteel plate fluttered through the air like confetti, riding updrafts from volcanic rifts more than a kilometer below. Pillars of flame—usually burning buildings, but sometimes geysers of magma—brightened the ash-filled gloom. And to top it off, an endless stream of cannon bolts was streaming out of the Temple to pound the little yacht's forward shields.

And yet no one seemed nervous. Tahiri sat calmly in the copilot's seat, monitoring—and cursing—BAMR newscasts as she adjusted shield loads and jammed the enemy's target acquisition bands. Behind and between their seats stood Saba Sebatyne, hissing what sounded like a Barabel nursery rhyme as the *Parting Gift* juked and dived and rolled. Strapped into the seat behind Tahiri was Sergeant Major Gef Olazon, a lanky Void Jumper with a bushy gray mustache and an armored vac suit that had more battle patches than his face had wrinkles. His chin was on his chest, and he was actually snoring.

Who did they think was flying this mission—Han Solo?

The blue blossom of a turbolaser strike erupted ahead, hitting the *Parting Gift* with a blast of heat and a shock wave that felt like they had flown into a cliff. Jag and Tahiri slammed against their crash harnesses and Saba dropped to her knees. Then the space yacht was spiraling out of control, its powerful repulsorlift engines driving it down through the smoke and ash toward the crooked white line of a magma rift less than a thousand meters below.

Jag cut the power to the ion engines immediately, and the *Gift* began to buck and spin as it was buffeted by thermal updrafts. He used the attitude thrusters to roll the vessel upright again, then peered into the boiling ash cloud until the waypoint marker on the heads-up display indicated he was pointed toward the Jedi Temple again, *then* he hit the ion drives and shot forward.

"We must be getting close," Olazon said from behind Tahiri. His gravelly voice was still thick with sleep. "They're bringing out the big guns."

"*Turbolasers?*" Jag asked. "When did the Jedi put those in the Temple?"

"The *Jedi* didn't," Saba replied, as though that were the only explanation needed.

"I see," Jag said. Cannon bolts started to stream into the *Parting Gift*'s forward shields again, and he began to jerk the yoke around, trying to cover their approach with buildings or dangling girders or anything else that might prevent the turbolaser crew from resolving a good target. "Just tell me I'm going to live long enough to see Jaina."

"This one does not look into the future," Saba replied. "It is more fun to be surprised."

"I'd say things are looking pretty good from this end," Olazon said. "You're not a half-bad combat pilot—even in this overarmored tub."

"Thanks," Jag said. He activated a mirrored panel in the canopy, then looked at Olazon's reflection. "What do you mean 'from this end'?"

Olazon's eyes went directly to Saba. "You didn't tell him?"

A thud reverberated through the deck as Saba thumped her tail. "There was no time," the Barabel said. "By the time the *Parting Gift* was strutz-down, we were only five minutes to rendezvous."

Olazon scowled. "You should have told him," the Void Jumper said. "When a guy leaves on a mission like this, he has a right to know."

"This one *said* there was no time." Saba glanced back, baring her fangs at Olazon. "He will be told after the rescue."

The Void Jumper scowled back at Saba, so obviously unintimidated that Jag would have been impressed—had he not been worried about Jaina. "Tell me *what?*"

When Saba did not immediately respond, Olazon said, "Your girl had to take off with Master Skywalker about an hour before you landed," he said. "She left a vid message for you."

Olazon's tone was grave, and Jag had spent enough time in the military to understand what the sergeant major was telling him. Jaina had left one of those in-case-I-don't-return messages—the kind soldiers had been leaving for their loved ones since the time of rocks and spears.

"Why would she leave a message like that?" Jag demanded. A building to their starboard took a turbolaser hit and exploded into an orange fireball. Jag ignored it and shifted his gaze to Saba's reflection. "And no more dodging the question."

A soft clatter sounded as Saba ruffled her scales. "Abeloth has taken Ben and Vestara," she said. "Master Solo is with Master Skywalker, trying to stop . . . whatever it is Abeloth intendz for them."

"Wait . . . Jaina is a Master now?" Jag smiled, despite the alarm he felt at the rest of Saba's news. "It's about time."

Saba tipped her scaly head. "Perhapz you did not hear the part about hunting Abeloth?"

"I heard," Jag said. He was terribly disappointed to have missed Jaina, and even more alarmed to learn she was off chasing Abeloth. But he had fallen in love with a courageous, dedicated, stubborn woman, and he had accepted long ago that there would be times like this in their relationship—and, soon, their marriage. He wouldn't have wanted it any other way. "What I don't understand is why you thought it would make any difference?"

"Because the message is eight minutes long, and we had only five minutes to make our rendezvous," Saba replied. "It will still be waiting *after* you drop us at the Temple and rescue Master Solo's sister and parentz."

Saba said this last part casually, as though it were no big deal, but Jag suddenly understood why Saba had been in such a hurry when she commandeered him and his ship. Jag was not "officially" in the know about Allana Solo's true identity, but he had spent a lot of time with the Solos, and he had eventually guessed who "Amelia" really was—and why she was so important to the Jedi.

"So *they're* at the Temple, too. How did *that* happen?" Jag asked.

"Something went wrong," Saba replied. "Let us hope the Solos live long enough to explain what."

"Agreed," Jagged said. "But why wait for *me* to pick them up?"

"You were already in the atmosphere when the Solos asked for extraction," Saba replied. "And Jaina is alwayz saying that you fly as well as her father."

Jag's heart swelled. "Really?" he asked. "Jaina says *that?*"

"Don't let it go to your head," Olazon said. "We're running short on transport, and this overarmored space palace of yours was the best available ship."

"*This?*" Tahiri asked. "A Sandalso twelve-being personal LuxiCruiser was the best thing the Jedi could scrape up for a rescue mission?"

"It has military shieldz and countermeasures?" Saba asked.

"Of course," Jag replied. "When Head of State Reige gave it to me, he made it very clear he didn't want me getting killed anytime soon."

"Then yes, a Sandalso LuxiCruiser is the best we could do," Olazon said. "Roomy enough to hold a squad of Void Jumpers, tough enough to deliver them."

"The situation is that bad?" Tahiri pressed. "You couldn't find a spare blastboat to mount this operation?"

"All out hunting Sith saboteurz, along with most of our Jedi Knightz," Saba said. "So you will be coming along when this one and the sergeant major debark into the Temple."

"Don't I have a choice in the matter?" Despite the question, Tahiri actually sounded a bit pleased by the request. "I'm not even a Jedi."

"Welcome back," Saba replied.

A metallic bang rang through the hull as a piece of durasteel flot-sam crashed down on the *Gift*'s unshielded stern. A damage alarm began to scream, and the yacht nosed up.

"Stuck vector plate," Tahiri said, reaching for her control console. "Shutting down thrust nozzle four."

"Affirmative," Jag replied.

The *Parting Gift* began to fly normally again, even if the yoke was a bit sluggish. Jag swung the yacht around a shrinking column of flame that was either a collapsing building or a subsiding magma fountain. Finally, through a thin veil of smoke and rising ash, he spotted the Temple—a vast silver incline sloping up toward the sky. Saba's arm shot forward between the seats, pointing toward a tiny gray circle that was perhaps a hundred meters above the level of the *Parting Gift*.

"There," she said. "The utility hatch."

"I see it," Jag replied.

A turbolaser strike blossomed between them and the hatch, distant enough this time that the shock wave merely sent the *Gift* barrel-rolling deeper into the gloom. The rain of cannon bolts they had been facing became a flashing storm that lit up the ash cloud like the interior of a Ryloth dancecaf. The yacht's interior lights dimmed as all available power was transferred to the shield generators. Jag shoved the throttles forward, covering the last two kilometers in a wild helix that lasted no more than five seconds before the silvery, inclined slope of the Temple wall filled the entire canopy.

Finally, the laser cannons could no longer depress their barrels far enough to hit the *Parting Gift,* and the steady stream of bolts began to fly past well beyond their stern. Jag pulled back on the throttles and swung the yacht up in the direction of the access hatch that Saba had pointed out.

"Balance the shields," he instructed, "and get me a bearing to our rendezvous point."

"You mean the utility hatch?" Saba asked.

"Unless we're making the pickup somewhere else," Jag said. From so close, going so fast, the Temple's exterior skin was just a sheet of polished durasteel flecked with geometric bumps, pits, and spires. The details flashed past so quickly that it was impossible to recognize their function. "I'll need a four-second warning to stop."

Saba pointed up the Temple wall, toward a dull oval a bit to their starboard, then said, "Stop *now*!"

Jag swung the nose around and hauled back on the throttles, decelerating hard. The oval rapidly became a gray circle as they drew nearer. Saba and the sergeant major turned and raced from the flight deck back toward the boarding ramp. Tahiri unbuckled her crash harness and looked over at Jag.

"You going to be okay without me here?"

A line appeared down the center of the gray circle—the hatch starting to open.

"Go . . . be a Jedi," Jag said, waving her toward the back. "You weren't cutthroat enough to be an Imperial Hand anyway."

Tahiri cocked a brow. "Only because you were too incorruptible to make much of an Emperor."

Jag managed to keep from smiling until after Tahiri had left the flight deck. By then, Han Solo could be seen leaning out the open utility hatch, frantically waving at him to hurry. Jag eased to within two meters of the Temple wall and moved his thumb over the attitude control pad, but held off activating the thrusters.

The ramp alarm on the copilot's control panel began to chime as Saba and the Void Jumpers opened the *Gift*'s boarding door. Jag ignored the chime and kept both hands steady on the yoke. As the vessel slipped closer to the utility hatch, he began to glimpse the action inside the Temple—the flickering colors and sudden flashes of a fairly intense firefight. He activated the attitude thrusters and turned their nozzles forward, but waited until the yacht's nose reached the edge of the hatch before calling for maximum power.

The *Parting Gift* lurched to a crawl. As the flight deck slid past the open hatchway, Jag craned his neck to see inside. About five meters into a gloomy chamber, a line of Hapan commandos stood fighting someone deeper in the Temple. They were supported by the flashing lightsabers of half a dozen Jedi Knights—four Barabels, along with Leia Solo and Zekk. On the floor behind the battle line, he glimpsed a a swarm of small dark reptiles. Allana Solo stood in the hatchway with her pet nexu, protected by Han and a tall red-headed woman.

Then the flight deck slid past the hatchway, and Jag was left staring at the Temple wall. He continued to reverse the attitude thrusters until the *Gift* stopped completely, then eased backward until he felt the jolt of the boarding ramp slamming down inside the hatchway. He killed the thrusters and tried to hold the vessel steady as the Void Jumpers debarked. It wasn't easy. The ship rocked and lurched—then rocked and lurched some more as new passengers boarded.

A flurry of explosions sounded deep inside the Temple, then the battle quickly began to calm as Saba and the Void Jumpers established a perimeter. Leia's voice rang out from the passenger salon, ordering Allana to keep Anji off the flight couches, and a strange chittering began to roll forward—along with a stench so foul that Jag pulled his facemask from its holder and activated his emergency oxygen feed.

A moment later, twenty hand-sized lizards came boiling onto the flight deck, most of them dragging dead, half-eaten rodents and—in a couple of cases—what looked like human fingers. They were immediately everywhere, in the copilot's seat, on the navigation computer, hanging upside down from the canopy—a couple even jumped into Jag's lap and sat staring up at him. One was holding a blue Keshiri thumb, and the other had what looked like a hawk-bat wing. They bared their tiny fangs and began to blink at him with their tiny eyes.

From behind Jag came a young girl's voice. "No . . . *friend*!"

"Amelia?" Jag asked.

"Uh . . . right," came the reply. Allana Solo stepped onto the flight deck and began to pluck the little lizards off the seats and equipment. "Don't be afraid."

"I'm not," Jag said from behind his face mask. "Just a little surprised."

"Surprised is better than afraid," Allana said. She tossed an armful of lizards back into the main salon. "They might bite to establish dominance, but at least they won't try to eat you."

"Thanks for the tip," Jag said.

He stared down at the two lizards in his lap and reminded himself that he was the pilot of this ship. The two lizards blinked at him a few more times, then suddenly curled up in his lap and began to gnaw on their prizes.

Before Jag could ask Allana what he should do next, a raspy Barabel voice spoke from behind him. "They like you."

Jag glanced up and, over his shoulder, saw Tesar Sebatyne peering down on the two lizards. "Not as an appetizer, I hope."

Tesar sissed almost uncontrollably. "Silly human," he said. "Hatchlingz don't need appetizerz. They are alwayz hungry."

A soft *clunk* reverberated through the *Parting Gift* as the boarding ramp was raised, then Han came rushing onto the flight deck and stepped toward the copilot's seat.

"Okay, we're good to . . . *Jag?*" Han stopped halfway to sitting. "What the blazes are *you* doing here?"

"Rescuing *you.*" Jag glanced down at the two hatchlings making a mess of his lap. "And a bunch of baby Barabels, apparently."

"They're called a clutch," Han said. "And whatever you do, don't be—"

"Afraid of them—I've heard." Jag activated the ion engines. "Is everyone aboard?"

"Everyone who wants to be, anyway." Han craned his neck to look back toward the Temple. "The last I saw of Tahiri and Saba and her Void Jumpers, they were chasing a dozen Sith deeper into the Temple."

Jag's brow went up. "They *stayed?*"

"Of course they stayed," Tesar said, sounding a bit wistful. "They are going on the hunt of a lifetime!"

Chapter Thirty-one

SWELTERING AND DARK AND FILLED WITH THE SMELL OF FRESH DEATH, the corridor felt like one of the old burrows where Saba and her pack-mates used to wait out Barab I's deadly sixty-hour day. A couple dozen bodies lay strung along thirty meters of floor, mostly Hapan comman-dos, but also a few Sith—and even a handful of hatchlings who had proven too slow or too unlucky to escape the carnage. Many of the Sith were missing fingers and ears and other parts that a hungry hatch-ling could chomp off as it ran past, but Saba was impressed to see that none of the Hapans had been bitten. Teaching young Barabels to leave their dead friends uneaten was no easy thing.

A few things in the corridor reminded Saba that she was not in the old day-burrows, of course. The first was blowing ash. Barab I had been a humid world where it rained twenty hours every night, so the ash turned to mud long before it had a chance to clog nasal passages or inflame throats. The second was the river of Force energy rushing past Saba and her packmates. It was being drawn down into the heart of the Jedi Temple, where in the computer core on Level 351, Abeloth

was feeding on the dark side power being released by billions of terrified Coruscanti.

The third thing that reminded Saba she was not in a day-burrow
was the band of Sith advancing down the corridor toward her. Back
when Barab I had still existed, the Jedi had believed that Sith only
came in pairs, a Master and a servant. Saba had always found that dis-
appointing, because it had meant that she would probably never have
a chance to hunt Sith herself—and even if she did, by the time she became good at it, the prey would be extinct. But now, after the emer-
gence of the Lost Tribe, there would be an almost limitless supply of
Sith to stalk—and there were several *hundred* of them between her and
the quarry she had come to claim.

Truly, this was going to be a fine hunt.

Saba assumed an exaggerated fighting stance, then ignited her
lightsaber and began to twirl the blade through a showy and complicated defensive pattern. Her intent was not to intimidate the Sith, but
rather to convince them that she was a combat novice who believed
such a display might actually have an effect on seasoned enemies. Next
to her, Tahiri activated her own weapon and held the blade in front of
her body, upright in salute.

The Force rippled with scorn, and the Sith abandoned their cautious approach and broke into a run. Saba adjusted her stance, in the
process backing two steps down the corridor. Tahiri glanced over.
Finding herself suddenly alone in front, she also retreated two steps.
Then she made her Force aura shudder with fear—a nice touch that
launched the Sith into a full charge.

A pair of sharp cracks rang off the durasteel walls and two forks of
Force lightning came sizzling down the corridor. Tahiri stepped forward, catching both bolts on her blade in a standard defensive maneuver that left her partner free to counterattack. Saba extended a clawed
finger, pointing down the first fork, and Force-hurled the first caster
into the second. The Force lightning crackled out, but the charge continued, the remainder of the Sith warriors either leaping or trampling
their prone companions.

Olazon's voice sounded over Saba's comlink earbud, calm and almost banal. "Raising trip wire."

Even though she knew where to look, the nanoedge filament was so thin that Saba did not see it rising across the corridor. She simply felt the Sith's sudden puzzlement as shivers of danger sense began to race down their backs, then saw their leaders attempt to pull up short—only to be pushed onto the deadly fiber when their companions behind them failed to stop running.

One Sith was cut completely in two, the top half of her body tumbling forward to hit the floor while the bottom half was still on its feet. The midsections of her two companions simply began to spray fans of blood as they Force-hurled themselves backward into their charging fellows.

Olazon's voice sounded again in Saba's ear. "Jedi, *down*."

Saba and Tahiri hurled themselves to the floor facedown. By the time they hit, a steady *phuutt-phuutt* was sounding behind them as the Void Jumper sniper team opened fire with their silenced slugthrowers. Red circles blossomed in three Sith heads, and the targets crumpled to the floor, dead before they knew they were hit.

Reacting quickly, the survivors extended their arms and used the Force to jerk the weapons from the snipers' hands.

"Legloppers," Olazon ordered.

A loud *pop* sounded from the magpackets—Olazon's demolition team had slapped two of them on the corridor walls after the scouts had reported the enemy approach—and then a pair of fan-shaped cutting lasers flashed across the passage at about knee height. All six Sith screamed in anguish and surprise as their legs were severed, and they tumbled to the floor writhing in pain.

"Stompers."

A deafening clang shook the corridor as a four-meter section of wall peeled open adjacent to the killing zone, and then a pair of Void Jumpers in full-power armor came hissing and whirring through the breach. The first turned up the passage to provide defensive cover in case there were more Sith rushing to aid the ambushed band. The second Stomper stopped at the edge and covered the floor with a spray of flechettes, killing everything that was not already dead.

Less than sixty seconds after the initial warning, Stomper Two stopped firing and announced, "Kill zone clear."

"Clear forward," Stomper One said.

"Approach clear, two hundred meters," Scout One reported.

"Backtrail clear," Sniper One reported. "Thirty meters."

"All clear," Olazon said. "Good work, everyone. Good ambush."

"Good pack," Saba added, returning to her feet. "Their longtailz will not be so eager next time, this one thinkz. Now we start *our* hunt."

"*Our* hunt?" Tahiri asked, rising next to Saba. "So you always *meant* to let the *Parting Gift* leave without us and the Void Jumpers?"

"It was overloaded," Saba said. "And there is quarry for us here . . . very great quarry."

As they spoke, Olazon and his Void Jumpers began to emerge from their hiding places. One of the technical sergeants began to collect comlinks, while the second clamped on a pair of knee magnets and began to climb the corridor wall.

Tahiri watched the preparations for a moment, then her eyes grew narrow. "You wanted the *Gift* because *I* was aboard, didn't you?" she asked. "You want me to go after another of Abeloth's manifestions with you."

Saba shrugged. "It was Master Horn'z idea," she said. "But you have already killed *one* Abeloth. When the time comes, this one expectz you to let the Master take first strike."

Before Tahiri could agree, Tech One stepped between them and held out a hand. "We need your comlinks," he said. "And chronos, too, if they have an autocheck function."

Seeing that Tech Two was magclamping a small silver orb in front of the vidcam that covered this section of corridor, Saba quickly passed over the requested equipment, then asked, "What about lightsaberz and blasterz?"

"Not this time," the tech replied. "This is just a small blinder. It's only going to take out RF and a bit of optical."

Tahiri passed her equipment over. "You're disabling the surveillance system?"

"Everything within three hundred meters, anyway," the tech said. "We can't do the whole thing at once without crashing every speeder and blastboat within fifty kilometers."

Tahiri turned to Saba. "No one put a backdoor in the Temple's surveillance system?"

"Of course," Saba replied. "But Abeloth entered the computer core and removed it—along with all our other backdoorz. She controlz all systemz in the Temple now."

Tahiri's eyes widened in alarm—or perhaps it was excitement. With humans, Saba could never tell.

"When you say *entered*," Tahiri said, "do you mean Abeloth actually moved her Force presence into the circuits, like Callista did aboard the *Eye of Palpatine*'s computer?"

"Yes . . . that is why we must destroy the surveillance system," Saba said, forcing herself to be patient. "Before one can kill the kranbak, one must put out the eyes of the kranbak."

"But that means setting off a blinder every six hundred meters." Tahiri stopped to do the calculations, then her face sagged with disappointment. "We're going to be here for *days*."

"The time will pass faster than you think, Jedi Veila," Saba said. "We have much to prepare before Master Skywalker signalz the attack."

They had been given nothing to drink since departing Coruscant, and the dark waters of the Font of Power were starting to tempt even Ben. The journey had taken days, and Abeloth had refused to allow her captives either water or food, urging them instead to throw off the shackles of mortality and claim their destiny. Ben, she insisted, was to become the eternal Prince of Light, and he would keep burning the twin flames of justice and forgiveness. Vestara was to become the irresistible Daughter of the Night. She would guard the forbidden mysteries of the Force—and she would bring life to the galaxy by filling dreams with images of beauty and desire. Together, the three of them would become the Ones, and they would live forever and remake the galaxy however it suited them.

Ben and Vestara had made the mistake of telling Abeloth they would rather die than become part of her insanity, and now they were standing back-to-back in the yellow fog that surrounded the Font of Power. Their noses and throats were raw from its caustic steam, and their eyes were burning, but they were so dehydrated that their bodies were imploring them to drink—and it did not matter that the water was so tainted with dark side energy that it made them shudder inside. Their heads were pounding and their vision was blurring, and their thoughts were coming slow and muddled. They had to drink or die—and when faced with those choices, the body always chose to drink.

Vestara's shoulder shifted against Ben's, and he could tell that she was looking toward the Font . . . no doubt wondering the same thing he was, what would happen if they drank, whether there was any way they could risk even a sip.

"Don't do it, Ves." Ben's throat was so dry and swollen that words came out as a croak. "That has to be what she wants, why she didn't let us drink on the trip. So we'd drink from the Font."

Vestara's shoulder did not shift back. "That might be better than dying, Ben."

"Think so?" Ben asked. "You remember what happened to Taalon, right?"

"That was the Pool of Knowledge," Vestara pointed out. "And he *fell* in."

"And this is the Font of Power," Ben replied. "I can feel the dark side gushing out. Do you really think you can touch that and not turn into the kind of freak he became?"

"That might be better than dying," Vestara repeated.

A swirl appeared in the fog a few meters ahead, and Abeloth spoke in her multiple voices. "You see, Ben? She cannot be trusted to resist temptation." The swirl approached closer and resolved into a ghostly face. The face had tiny silver eyes and a too-wide mouth, full of pointed fangs. "*That* is why I brought you here—so that you would learn whom you can truly trust."

Vestara pivoted around to stand at Ben's side. "And that would be you?"

"I am not the one hiding my betrayal from him," Abeloth replied.

"If you're talking about the attack on the *Falcon*," Ben said, "I know all about it. Vestara told me what happened."

"Yes, but did she tell you *everything*?" Abeloth asked. "Did she tell you about—"

"Of course I did." Vestara looked over and caught Ben's eye. "You can't listen to her, Ben. She's just trying to drive a wedge between us."

"No worries, Ves, it's not going to work," Ben said. "All we've got is each other—and no way am I letting that go on *her* word."

"Good, Ben," Vestara said. "We just have to remember who's holding us captive."

"You are holding *yourself* captive, Vestara," Abeloth said. She raised an arm, and four fluttering tentacles pointed toward the churning fountain next to them. "The power you crave is there. It is *Ben* holding you back—not I."

Vestara glanced past Ben toward the pillar of dark waters, then shook her head. "No, Ben's right," she said. "Drinking from the Font would destroy us, not save us."

Abeloth lowered her arm. "The choice is yours to live with." She withdrew into the fog. "Or to die from."

Ben waited until even the swirl of her retreat had vanished, then said, "Good job, Ves. We can get through this as long as we stand firm—and stand together."

"Don't take this the wrong way, Ben, but that's a load of poodoo." Vestara pivoted to stand back-to-back again. "In case you didn't notice the last hundred times we tried to leave the courtyard, we're kind of outclassed here. No way are we getting past Abeloth to safe water."

"Probably not." Ben tipped his head as far as he could toward Vestara, then whispered, "But we just have to hold on. Dad's on his way—I can feel him reaching out to me in the Force."

Vestara whispered, "Are you sure?"

"Would I lie about something like that?" Ben asked. "Trust me. He'll be here."

"When?"

"As soon as he can," Ben said. "I tried to let him know we're desperate."

"Well, that's something, I guess."

"It's hope," Ben replied quickly. "And hope is enough to get us through this . . . as long as we stick together."

Vestara fell silent for a moment, then said, "I'm with you, Ben. That's not going to chaaa . . . aaaigh!"

Vestara screamed as she stumbled back into Ben. He spun around instantly and found Abeloth already on Vestara, tentacles probing for her mouth and nose. Lacking a lightsaber or any other sort of weapon, Ben stepped into the melee and slammed a palm-heel into the center of Abeloth's chest, at the same time hitting her with a panic-fueled blast of Force energy.

Abeloth went flying, doubled over, trailing a spray of bloody bile. Vestara recovered her footing and stepped forward into a fighting crouch, her arms raised and ready to attack, either hand-to-hand or with the Force. Ben found himself staring in amazement at the cone of red mist that Abeloth had left behind, surprised by the power of the Force blast he had just unleashed. He felt cold and queasy from the effects of so much dark-side energy, and had he not been so thoroughly dehydrated already, he probably would have vomited.

"Ben?" Vestara grabbed his arm and stepped in close, propping him up. "Are you okay?"

"I will be, as soon as I get rid of this rot inside," he said.

"Rot?"

Ben jerked a thumb toward the Font of Power. "The Force is corrupt this close to the fountain," he said. "All dark side."

Vestara turned toward the pillar of dark water. "We may have to use it anyway, Ben. The Force is all we have to protect ourselves with."

"No—it's like poison," Ben said. "We can't use the Force until we get out of this fog."

Vestara shook her head. "You know that isn't going to happen," she said. "That's why Abeloth is keeping us here. She's trying to corrupt us."

"We won't let her," Ben said. "We won't use the Force."

"Ben, we're going to *have* to," Vestara said. "It's the only way to hold her off until your father arrives."

Ben fell silent. Just a small taste of the Font's dark side energies had convinced him that it would be better to die than to let himself be corrupted by its power. But of course, they *wouldn't* die. Abeloth would take them as her avatars, just as she had done with Callista and Akanah and countless others, and they would learn the literal meaning of a fate worse than death.

"Then we're going to have to make a run for it," Ben said. "She can't be in two places at once, so at least one of us should be able to get clear."

"And then what?" Vestara asked.

"And then we make sure that she doesn't make an avatar out of the one who falls behind," Ben said. "We've used the Force here before, so we know that the fountain's corruption doesn't extend for more than a few meters. Once we're both clear, we can fight with the Force again."

"So one of us is almost sure to die?" Vestara asked. "And the other one is going to have to do the killing?"

"Probably," Ben said. "But it has to be better than the alternative."

Vestara turned toward the Font. "That's *one* way to look at it, I guess."

Ben frowned, unsure of what Vestara was suggesting. "If you have another way, I'm all ears."

"Maybe dying *isn't* the best thing." Vestara turned back to Ben and touched her hand to his chest. "Maybe there's a reason we're here . . . a reason that we were brought together in the first place."

Ben's frown grew deeper. "Like what?"

Vestara stepped back, as though his stern tone had pushed her away. "We need to follow the will of the Force, Ben."

"And you know what that will *is*?"

Vestara nodded, turned toward the Font of Power. "I think I do, Ben."

"I don't like where this is headed," Ben said, following her gaze. "Ves, you can't be serious."

Vestara continued to gaze into the Font's dark waters. "But I am, Ben. If we *both* drank, together we would be stronger than Abeloth—probably strong enough to destroy her." She reached out and took Ben's hand. "And wouldn't *that* be the best thing for the galaxy?"

It had been three days since the frigate *Redstar* had dropped Luke and Jaina at the entrance to the Maw, and that meant it had been three days since Luke had first been handed the crumpled flimsy he now held in his hands. On the flimsy was the text of a short S-thread message from Corran Horn, which the *Redstar*'s communications officer had retrieved as soon as the frigate emerged from hyperspace outside the Maw.

Solos out safe with Amelia. Jedi Warv killed in Sith ambush led by Vestara Khai. *Falcon* crippled, but target healthy for now.

The message was only three short lines, but it had done more to incapacitate Luke than any of the wounds he had suffered fighting Abeloth. He had *trusted* Vestara—had even been the one to persuade the other Masters she would be a valuable asset inside the Temple during the battle against the Sith.

He could not have been more wrong.

His mistake had cost Bazel Warv his life and—assuming he was correctly interpreting Corran's conspicuous use of the word "target"—nearly gotten Allana killed. Now, after three days of meditation, he continued to find himself mired in doubt, wondering what else he might be wrong about, and reluctant to trust his own judgment.

And he was running out of time.

The *Rude Awakening*, a sleek little pinnace infiltrator manufactured for the space marines' elite Void Jumper units, was already approaching the choke point where Sinkhole Station had once hung suspended in a binary black-hole system. Luke could see the accretion whorls of the two black holes with his naked eye, a pair of fire-rimmed disks centered in the forward viewport, and he could feel Ben ahead, on Abeloth's hidden planet, reaching out to him in the Force, urging him to hurry.

And *still* Luke didn't know what to do, whether he was following the will of the Force by following Ben—or defying it.

The Histories of Thuruht had convinced him and the rest of the Jedi Council that the galaxy went through a regular cycle of destruction and renewal, and that Abeloth—as mad and deadly as she was—played a crucial role in that cycle. But the cycle had been disrupted by the death of the Ones, and without the Son and the Daughter, there was no one capable of ending Abeloth's chaos and supervising Thuruht's construction of a new prison. Unless the Jedi could stop her themselves—and that seemed to Luke a very big *if* indeed—she would go on sowing disorder and chaos until civilization itself vanished from the galaxy.

"A little advice from the junior Master on the Council?" Jaina asked from the other side of the cockpit. Even smaller than her mother, she looked almost child-like sitting in a pilot's seat designed for a two-meter Void Jumper in full combat armor. "Not that I want to rush your planning or anything, but a mind divided against itself cannot win."

Luke cocked a brow. "You interrupted my meditations to quote a training aphorism that the Banthas learn in their second week?"

"Yes," Jaina said. "That, and we're about to get jumped."

"You've sensed Ship?"

"Not yet," Jaina replied. "But we're entering a choke point, and it's where *I* would mount an ambush."

Luke nodded. "And Abeloth is trying to draw us in," he said. "Ben has been reaching out to me, trying to let me know their situation is desperate."

Jaina shoved the throttles to their overload stops. "And you didn't tell the pilot?"

"You're not the only one expecting an ambush."

Luke started to tell her to pull the throttles back. Then he decided Jaina was as aware of Ship as he was and that it was better to let her fly her own vessel, and then he almost decided to tell her to slow down anyway, so they could develop a plan. That was the trouble with being so emotionally involved in a mission. It made you indecisive, clouded your thinking. He wanted nothing more than to rush to Ben's side and rescue him. It was killing him not to do it—but he knew just how foolish that course of action would be. Abeloth was baiting him, trying to *make* him race in unprepared, because that was the surest way to a kill.

Then, too, there was the other thing—the thing that had been consuming Luke's thoughts since departing Coruscant. "And, I'm still trying to decide whether we're doing the right thing."

Jaina's astonishment quivered through the Force, and she took her eyes off the fiery whorls ahead long enough to look over in open shock. "You mean by going after the Sith Abeloth?"

"Sort of," Luke said. "I mean by going after Ben and Vestara."

"It's all part of the same problem." Jaina's reply came a little too quickly. She was arguing for what she wanted to believe, not for what she knew to be true. "To recover Ben and capture Vestara, we have to take out Abeloth. Take out Abeloth, and we recover Ben and capture Vestara."

"That's one way of looking at it," Luke said. "But I went back and checked the Archives for anything on the Mortis monolith."

"And?"

"I found confirmation in a report from Obi-Wan," Luke said. "It was just as Yoda told me. Obi-Wan seemed to think that he and Anakin had been drawn to Mortis because the Father was dying and wanted Anakin Skywalker to take his place as the Keeper of the Balance."

Jaina's jaw dropped. "*Chosen One* indeed," she said. "What happened?"

"Obviously Anakin didn't accept," Luke said. "The Son ended up murdering the Daughter with a special Force-imbued dagger, and the Father tricked the Son by sacrificing himself with the same dagger—so that Anakin could kill the Son."

Jaina nodded. "I see what you're thinking. It was your father's refusal that resulted in the death of the Ones. So maybe it's your *son's* destiny to become the new Keeper of the Balance?"

"Close," Luke said. "I'm wondering if it's Ben's destiny to take the Daughter's place and become the embodiment of the light side."

"And Vestara's to become the embodiment of the dark side?"

"After the way she played us, you have to admit she fits that role," Luke said. "And since the two of them are in love . . ."

"You think it has the will of the Force written all over it," Jaina said. "The two lovers, opposites bound together."

"Something like that," Luke admitted. "And you know it's not just the Archives. I have other reasons for thinking this might be the will of the Force—all the Masters do."

Jaina sighed. "The dream," she said. "Ben and Vestara fighting for the Balance in the courtyard of the Font of Power."

"That would be the reason," Luke said. "If I had been the only one to see that, maybe it could be dismissed as a dream. But when all of the Masters have the same dream . . ."

"Okay, that's hard to ignore," Jaina agreed. "But the will of the Force? It's pretty arrogant to claim the Force is telling you what it wants. That's the kind of thinking that led Jacen to . . . to do what *he* did."

As Jaina spoke, the fire-rimmed orbs of the two black holes ahead began to swell and rapidly drift apart. The two Masters were approaching the point of no return, and Luke still didn't know whether going after Ben was the right thing. Perhaps Luke was being just as selfish as his own father had been when he refused to become the Keeper of the Balance. Perhaps all that had followed—his own birth and Leia's, then Ben's birth and Mara's death and Ben's short journey into darkness—had been destiny. Maybe it was simply a way for a new trio to restore Balance to the Force.

Luke shook his head. "Jaina, I want to agree with you, to say that we have to do the obvious thing and rescue Ben. But—"

"But that's the trouble," Jaina finished. "You *want* to agree, and that's why you can't be certain it's the right choice."

"There is no emotion, there is peace," Luke agreed. "But I'm *filled* with emotion. I'm terrified for Ben, and it's clouding my judgment."

"Of course it is," Jaina said. "You're Ben's father—and that's part of the Force, too."

Luke frowned. "I'm not sure how that fact helps."

"I'm saying that you can't ignore who *you* are in this," she said. "If the hand of the Force is at play in Ben's fate, then it's at play in yours, too. You can't hold yourself above the will of the Force, or you make the same mistake Jacen did."

"So I should just do what I want to?" Luke shook his head. "Sorry, life is never—"

"No—I'm saying you should do what you know is right," Jaina corrected. "And you *do* know what is right. It's simple—it's *always* simple."

"So, act on principle," Luke said, boiling her argument down to three words. "Don't worry about the results."

"Mortals can't always *know* the results," Jaina replied. "Not for certain. We can only act according to our true natures, and leave the rest to the Force."

"And we just ignore the visions the Force sends us?"

"Of course not," Jaina said. "But we don't take them literally, either. The Force doesn't send comm messages, right?"

Luke half smiled. "I suppose not," he said. "When dreams speak, they do it in symbols."

"Exactly," Jaina said. "So, who's Ben? The ideal Jedi, right?"

"And Vestara is pure Sith," Luke agreed. "It's the Jedi and the Sith who must take the place of the Son and the Daughter . . . and deal with Abeloth."

"That's *my* guess," Jaina said. "The only thing I don't see is, if the Father is dead, who keeps the Balance?"

Luke thought for a moment, then said, "Us, I think—the Jedi and the Sith. Thuruht said the galaxy enters a new age whenever Abeloth is freed—and the dream means that in this age, it's the Jedi and Sith—each following our own natures—who will keep the Balance."

"So, Jedi and Sith, at war forever?" Jaina asked.

"Not forever," Luke said. "Just until the next time Abeloth is freed."

"*If* we can stop her this time," Jaina said. "And that's a very big—"

Jaina's voice was suddenly drowned out by the screeching of proximity alarms and target-lock alerts. She started to put the *Rude Awakening* into an evasive spiral, then glanced at the gravity readings and seemed to realize that they were already too deep into the choke point to risk maneuvering. She simply activated the automatic laser cannons and brought up the shields, then watched wide-eyed as lines of color began to fly back and forth between the little pinnace and a dust-sized propulsion halo hanging dead center between the two black holes, blocking their only approach to Abeloth's hidden world.

"Ship?" Luke asked.

"Could it be anything else?" Jaina replied, the tension already thick in her voice.

"Not really." Luke clicked out of his crash harness, then rose and turned to go aft. "Don't get vaped, but try to get past him. Make it look good."

"Wait, *look* good?" Jaina glanced over at his departing form. "Where are you going?"

"To strap into a medbay bunk," Luke replied. "I don't know how long this is going to take, so I should probably make sure my body is lying down when I leave it."

Chapter Thirty-two

As the *Rude Awakening* sped onward, the fire-rimmed orbs ahead rapidly began to swell and drift apart, leaving the area between them webbed with blazing whorls of accretion gas. Against this brilliant backdrop, Ship also began to swell, growing from a propulsion halo the size of a dust mote to a dark sphere as large as Jaina's thumb.

A constant stream of fire streaked back and forth between the two vessels, cannon bolts from the *Awakening* and plasma bulbs from Ship. Both vessels were taking the attacks dead center in the forward shields, making no attempt to evade. With the grasping hand of a black hole reaching from both sides of an ever-narrowing safe corridor, there was no room to maneuver, or even to flee. Flying skill did not matter, nor even combat training. Pilots had one choice and one choice only: punch it out head-on.

And in that kind of fight, it was usually the pilot who attacked quickest and hardest who survived. Jaina checked the range and, seeing that the two vessels were closing in even faster than she thought, armed the *Rude Awakening*'s first missile.

Jaina had chosen the *Rude Awakening* for good reason: it was a
Void Jumper assault pinnace. That meant it could get in fast, evade de-
tection, take a beating, and deliver a devastating attack. In fact, it was
one of the most fearsome tactical combat vessels in the galaxy, designed to go head-to-head with a Mandalorian *Bes'uliik* and be the
craft that emerged from the fireball. Jaina could not imagine any better combat transport to fly head-on against Ship—especially not after
she had fitted the entire missile magazine with baradium warheads.
Talk about a *rude awakening*.

The targeting computer chimed once, announcing that the two
crafts had closed to effective missile range. Jaina did not bother to try
for a target-lock—Ship would defeat it anyway, and in this fight a quick
attack was everything. She simply launched, then pulled the throttles
back so the *Awakening* would not be inside the lethal radius when the
baradium detonated. The blazing white disk of a thrust ring appeared
in front of the cockpit then, as the missile streaked away, quickly
shrank to a white dot.

In the next instant a tiny gray dot appeared in front of the *Awakening*. In an eyeblink, it expanded into the gray, oblong lump of one
of Ship's Force-hurled stones. Fighting the urge to dodge—a mistake
that might well have carried them across a nearby event horizon—
Jaina held the pinnace steady and thumbed the intercom pad on her
control yoke.

"Brace for impact back there," she said. "This one is going to take
down our shields."

Luke rose out of his body with a jolt, then hung floating above it, staring at the underside of the bunk above. A week passed, or maybe it was
a second—he had no idea. Time had no existence outside the body. A
heartbeat lasted a week, a lifetime flashed by in an instant. But *Luke
Skywalker* remained, a manifestation of Force essence that embodied
mind and form, more real than the material husk he had left strapped
in the bunk below.

He exhaled, or imagined himself exhaling, and his connection to
his body grew more tenuous. *There is no life, there is only the Force.* It
was the code of the Mind Walkers, an assertion that the corporeal was

illusion, that a living being was nothing but a luminous swirl in the Force. And perhaps they were right.

Luke exhaled again, and a purple radiance appeared above, shining down through the crude matter of the upper bunk as though it were a hologram. He reached, and the light came flooding in, filling him with a calm as deep as space. He became the Force, and the Force became him, and he knew only the pure, eternal joy of existence.

Luke called to mind a lake he had once visited, a narrow mountain lake nestled between a granite dome and a boulder-strewn meadow with hummocks of knee-high moss, and he started to walk. Whether the journey took a week or an instant was impossible to say. But then he was *there,* standing on the shore of the Lake of Apparitions, looking across its still, black waters toward the silver mists that concealed the far end.

There was no silhouette floating in the fog, no half–hidden woman beckoning him onward. Abeloth was nowhere to be seen.

Of course she wasn't. Luke was the one looking for a fight, not Abeloth. She was too busy trying to create her divine family, to transform Ben and Vestara into a twisted version of the Son and the Daughter who had once kept the Balance in the Force. The last thing Abeloth wanted now was to face Luke in a final combat that she just might lose.

But the choice wasn't hers.

Luke stepped into the water and began to wade forward. He did not make any sloshing sounds or disturb the dark surface as he moved. Soon, the hummocks and boulders along the shore began to cast reflections not of themselves, but of the faces of the dead—Wookiees, Barabels, humans, a hundred other species. Their eyes all seemed to be watching Luke as he passed, sometimes showing disappointment when his features did not turn out to be those of a loved one, often lighting in recognition and curiosity as they realized they were looking on the Grand Master of the new Jedi Order.

Many of the faces Luke saw belonged to old friends—Ganner Rhysode, Numa Rar, Tresina Lobi, and a dozen others—but he continued by them without pause. During his four decades as a Jedi, Luke had lost a hundred good friends and more acquaintances than he could count, and he was certain they would understand if he did not have time to stop and greet them all.

Finally, he came to the face he had been looking for—a slender female face framed by auburn hair, with high cheekbones, full lips, and large green eyes. It watched Luke approach with longing, and with growing concern. He stopped beside her and squatted on his heels, waiting for her face to float to the surface, wishing that he were not in such desperate need of the help he was about to request.

As soon as her face broke the surface, she raised her brow and said, "We can't keep meeting like this, Skywalker."

Luke smiled despite himself. "Last time, I promise," he said. "Mara, I need your help."

"There's not much I can do for you anymore," Mara said, looking more disappointed than sorry. "You know that."

"Can you help me draw Abeloth out?"

Mara studied him in silence for a moment, then shook her head. "You can't kill her, Luke. She's one of the Old Ones."

"It doesn't matter what she is," Luke said, more sternly than he had intended. "She's taken Ben."

Mara's eyes went wide, but she said nothing.

Instead it was a scornful voice to Luke's left that spoke. "How did you let *that* happen?"

Luke turned to find Jacen Solo's gaunt face peering out of the dark waters. "We were trying to stop the cataclysm *you* caused."

Jacen's lip curled into a sneer. "You Jedi never tire of blaming the Dark Lord for your own failings, do you?"

"My failings have nothing to do with this," Luke said. "You're the one who set Abeloth free."

"*Me?*" Jacen scoffed. "I was dead."

"Thuruht says you did it when you changed the future," Luke explained. "They say that's how Abeloth is *always* freed."

Jacen began to look less certain of himself. "Who's Thuruht?"

"The oldest Killik hive," Luke explained. "The one that helped build Centerpoint Station and imprisoned Abeloth the *last* time she escaped."

"Then you should be talking to Thuruht, not Mara and me," Jacen replied, growing haughty again. "There's nothing we can do. We're dead."

Luke turned back to Mara. "I just need to know her weak points, or how to find her in the Mists of Forgetfulness," he said. "Anything that will help me stop her before she . . . before she does something terrible to Ben."

Mara's eyes grew glassy with sorrow. "Luke . . . Jacen is telling the truth this time," she said. "We can't help you."

I can. It was a voice that Luke felt rather than heard, a darkness that pulled at him from behind. *And I will.*

Luke turned to find the form of a shadow-wrapped human approaching from the shore by which Luke had entered the water, the same shore by which all mortals came to the Lake of Apparitions. The silhouette was tall and broad-shouldered, with a head hooded in darkness and glowing eyes that never seemed to match colors, that went from brown to orange and yellow to blue, that sometimes grew dark as ebony and seemed to be not there at all. As the silhouette drew nearer, it began to resemble a man Luke had seen many years before, a man who had appeared only in his dreams—and always shortly before he awoke feeling uneasy and frightened.

Luke glanced back at Mara, then said, "It's *him.*"

"Who?"

"The man I kept seeing in my dreams, before Jacen turned Sith."

Mara looked confused. "But the man in your dreams *was* Jacen."

"I thought so," Luke replied. "Who else *could* it have been?"

He turned back to the figure and saw that the cloaking shadows had coalesced into a suit of dark, spiked armor. The newcomer's right arm seemed a mere ghost, as though he had only a holographic projection where there should have been a limb. And his left eye had become an empty white circle that looked more like a window into another universe than an actual organ. His face was weathered and chiseled, though—with a web of tattoos radiating outward from an angry gaze and deeply etched scowl—he could not be considered handsome. He stopped three paces away and stood staring, as though trying to decide whether to attack Luke or speak to him.

"*You,*" Luke said. It was the man with the tattooed face—the one who had been behind Luke's team in the Manarai Heights Spaceport, and who had later disarmed Yaqeel Saav'etu near Fellowship Plaza. "Who are you?"

"No one whose help you want," Jacen said. "That's the dark man I saw on the Throne of Balance."

"And the only one who can help you," the stranger said. "With the Ones gone, there is only one way to stop Abeloth . . . Jedi and Sith together."

Luke studied the stranger without answering for a moment, trying to imagine him without the scowl. The man was hardly ugly, but he certainly did not share the Lost Tribe's usual obsession with careful grooming and good looks. And the tattoos were unusual, too. Vestara had claimed that while the Lost Tribe enjoyed painting their bodies with decorative vor'shandi markings, they would never defile themselves with permanent ink. Of course, she might have been lying—it certainly wouldn't have been the only time—but Luke couldn't see how that would have benefited her.

At last, Luke said, "I recognize your face. You've been watching the fight on Coruscant."

"And that surprises you?" the stranger asked. "What happens on Coruscant shapes the fate of the entire galaxy. Of course we are watching. We are *always* watching."

"Which is how you know so much about Abeloth," Luke surmised. "You have a spy."

"What makes you think there is only one?" the stranger said. "We Sith are legion . . . as you now know."

Luke shook his head. "If you were Lost Tribe, your appearance would be more refined. And you wouldn't have tattoos."

"Too much talk, Master Skywalker," the stranger said, stepping past Luke. "I came to fight. Let us find her."

Luke turned to follow—and there she was, a gray silhouette just emerging from the Mists of Forgetfulness, her long saffron hair cascading almost down to the water, her tiny pinpoint eyes shining out of sockets as deep as wells.

Luke's hand dropped to his hip, automatically reaching for a lightsaber that did not exist beyond shadows. He tried to continue the motion and bring it up to deliver a blast of Force energy, but Abeloth had already launched her own attack by then, delivering a bolt of Force lightning that blasted straight through the stranger into Luke. He felt himself fly backward, consumed by pain, his entire being a column of blue, crackling Force flame.

*   *   *

What Saba felt in the Force was not exactly a go-command. It was a blast of fiery anguish so intense that it lifted her scales and made her fear for Master Skywalker. Still, the message was clear. The hunt was over and the kill was at hand—even if the prey had drawn first blood. Saba leaned forward and peered around the corner, looking up a dark, dead-end corridor toward the computer core. To her Barabel eyes, which could see well into the infrared spectrum, the passage was a long rectangular tube of cool blue walls ending in the orange glow of the computer core air lock. A couple dozen green lumps lay scattered along the floor, Sith bodies that had been dead long enough to start cooling.

Satisfied that nothing had changed since their initial assault here, Saba pulled her head back and turned to look at the survivors of her own pack. Tahiri had obviously sensed the change in Saba's disposition and alerted the four Void Jumpers. They had all pulled their thermal imaging goggles over their eyes, and they were looking in Saba's direction.

Five survivors, out of an original pack of fifteen. The battle to blind Abeloth and cut her power feeds had been as bloody as it was long. The Void Jumpers had lost all of their infiltrators, both snipers and tech sergeants, and one of the demolition men. But Olazon was still leading the Void Jumpers and in good health, as were both of the power-armor Stompers. The surviving demolition man had lost one leg below the knee, but he had still been able to rig enough chain explosives—and instruct others in strategic placement on adjacent levels—to prevent Sith reinforcements from reaching the final staging area.

It was still a good pack.

Saba dipped her chin in a curt nod. Her companions—save for Braan, the injured demolition man—rose to their feet and brought their weapons to the ready. Olazon spoke into his throat-mike, and Stomper One stepped into the middle of the formation. In his suit-mandibles, he held an oblong orb that was about a meter in length. On top was a covered activation pad, with a digital counter that read 0:05:000.

Saba bared her fangs in approval. "It is time to deliver our egg to itz nest," she said. "May the Force be with you."

"Thanks." Olazon disengaged the firing safety on his shatter gun. "You, too."

He started to step forward to lead the way around the corner, but stopped when Tahiri used the Force to pull him back and wagged a finger in his direction.

"Where are your manners, Sergeant Major?" She ignited her lightsaber and stepped to Saba's side. "Ladies first!"

Saba sissed at the joke and ignited her own blade, then charged around the corner . . . into a corridor filled with the red eyes of Sith shadow-ghouls.

If anything, the steam had grown thicker. Ben was only five meters from the Font of Power, and he could tell its location only by the sound of its gurgling waters. Even Vestara, standing halfway between him and the fountain, looked more like a gray Force shadow than the woman he loved.

"Ves, we're *not* drinking," Ben said. "You saw what happened to Taalon after he fell into the pool. The same thing—or something even worse—will happen to us if we drink from the Font. You *know* that!"

"Maybe we're *meant* to change," Vestara said. "Abeloth is the *Destroyer* of Keshiri legend, and we're the *Protectors*, Ben—you and me. That's why the Force brought us together in the first place. We're the only ones who *can* stop her."

Ben shook his head. "Not by drinking from the font." He stepped closer to Vestara and pointed toward the fountain behind her. "That thing is a dark side nexus—probably the most potent one in the entire galaxy. You don't use something that powerful. It uses *you*."

"So instead we let Abeloth just *take* us?" Vestara countered. "Use our bodies to raze the galaxy?"

"No, Ves—we fight back," Ben said. "But we do it without drawing on the font—without touching the dark side at all. That's the only way we don't become the thing we're trying to destroy."

Vestara studied Ben with a look that was equal parts pity and admiration, then finally said, "You're a noble fool, Ben." She turned away and started toward the fountain. "But I'm through discussing this. We can't beat Abeloth *without* the font's power."

Ben remained where he was. "And you can't beat her alone, Ves."

He waited for her to glance back, or at least to hesitate. When she didn't, he turned away . . . straight into Abeloth.

Her tentacles were on him before he could cry out, entwining his body and pulling him close, slithering over his eyes and probing at his ears, sliding past his lips and into his mouth.

Ben bit down hard and felt a gristly tip about the size of his small finger come off. Immediately, his mouth was filled with a thin, foul-tasting oil. He exhaled fiercely, spewing both the tentacle tip and the rancid blood into Abeloth's bottomless eye sockets.

She only pulled him closer. A tentacle curled around the back of his neck, then slithered into his nose and started to ascend. He punched and kicked, slamming fists and elbows into her body and stomping at her legs, driving knees into her thighs and abdomen. But he was still too close to the font to use the Force, and without the Force his blows were nothing to her. Abeloth took them all without flinching or groaning—with no reaction save a smile. The tentacle wormed its way up Ben's nose into his sinuses, and his face flared with unbearable pressure and pain.

"You will drink, young Skywalker, or you will serve me another way," Abeloth said, speaking in her multitude of voices. "That choice is the only—"

The threat came to a crashing end, and Abeloth's tentacle tore free as she went flying backward on a bolt of Force lightning as thick as Ben's leg. He dropped to his knees, his agony fading quickly. Blood poured from his nose.

Abeloth dropped to the ground about three meters ahead, limned in blue and still pinned against the cobblestones by the Force lightning. As she writhed, her tentacles were twining around themselves, coalescing back into arms. Her long golden hair grew silky and dark, her eyes became oblong and normal, and her skin darkened into the lavender tones of a Keshiri Sith.

Vestara came up beside Ben. Her hands were still extended toward Abeloth, pouring Force lightning into the fallen Keshiri.

"Ben?" Vestara asked. "Are you hurt?"

Instead of replying, Ben continued to kneel on the cobblestones, looking up at Vestara. Her hair and clothes remained relatively dry, and he saw no redness in her face or hands to suggest she had actually put them into the steaming waters and drunk. But as she continued to pour Force lightning into the Keshiri, he could feel the font's dark energy flowing across the courtyard, swirling over him and through him, filling him with the cold queasy ache of its corrupting power.

"Ben?" Vestara asked again. "Answer me!"

"I'm fine," he said.

"Then get up!" Vestara said. There was a glow in her face, and Ben kept telling himself that it was not joy, that it had to reflect something other than the usual Sith thirst for power. "Together, we can *kill* Abeloth."

Ben spun on his knees and wrapped one arm around Vestara's legs. He rose to his feet, throwing her over his shoulders and using his free hand to catch her far arm and hold her in place.

"No." He started across the courtyard, away from the Font of Power. "Not like this, we can't."

The white points at the bottom of Abeloth's eyes flared into nests of blue lightning, which kept growing larger and flashing brighter until they finally spilled out of the sockets to engulf her whole head. Luke hurled another blast of Force energy in her direction, then braced himself to take the most devastating counterattack yet.

The counterattack never came.

Instead, the Force blast rocked Abeloth up on one leg, where she hung teetering over the Lake of Apparitions for a thousand heartbeats. Luke's chest was a searing ache around a fist-sized scorch hole, and his Force essence was bleeding out from a dozen smaller wounds, leaving a crescent of twinkling light spread across the dark water. He sprang anyway.

Abeloth only seemed to sag, and it appeared that she might tumble into the water in the eternity it was taking to reach her. But that would have been too easy. Luke and the Sith stranger had been hurling Force attacks at her for a lifetime—or perhaps it was a mere eyeblink—and this was the first time she had shown any reaction.

Then Luke was there at Abeloth's side, stomp-kicking her legs, knife-handing her throat, grabbing for her head. It was like cotton striking gauze—no popping ligaments or crunching cartilage, just Force essence pushing into Force essence. But the damage was done. Luke's foot went through Abeloth's knee; her leg buckled. His hand sank into her larynx, and she drew back wheezing.

He pivoted around behind her, swinging one arm around her shoulder and grabbing for her chin, slipping the other arm up under hers and pressing his wrist into her neck. But grappling was different beyond shadows. There were no pressure points or joint locks or choke holds, only his presence merging with hers, binding him to her in a writhing knot of energy.

Tentacles began to lash at his face, probing for his nose and ears and mouth. A pair of gray tips shot into view, blurring and growing large. Luke closed both eyes and turned away, but not quickly enough. The right eye socket exploded in pain, and everything went dark on that side of his head.

The tattooed stranger stepped in from the left, then slid to the front and drove his stiffened fingers deep into the pit of Abeloth's stomach. A black spray erupted from the wound, and she writhed in pain as the stranger probed for something to grab.

Abeloth loosed a Force blast, trying to drive the stranger off. He held tight. So did Luke, and all three went tumbling across the lake in a snarled mass of limbs and tentacles.

Then Luke felt an icy twinge between his shoulder blades. The twinge became a sting, and he began to feel something cold flowing down the center of his back. His first thought was Abeloth, that she had sunk a tentacle into his spine—until the lashing of her tentacles slowed and she began to shudder.

Luke did not understand until an eternity later, when the stranger rolled up on his feet and jerked them all to a halt. The Sith seemed to be growing stronger as Abeloth grew weaker, and there were wisps of dark fume swirling off his shoulders and head. It did not take a Jedi Grand Master to understand that Luke was being betrayed by a Force-draining technique.

Still holding Abeloth tight, Luke shifted his hips, rolling them both onto their sides, and kicked a foot through the stranger's knee. The joint buckled, and the Sith dropped onto the surface of the dark water, still on the opposite side of Abeloth from Luke.

"I'll release her!" Luke warned.

"Abeloth?" The stranger shook his head. "Never."

Despite the Sith's words, the cold stinging inside began to subside, and Luke realized the stranger was not pulling as hard. Abeloth continued to struggle, slipping a pair of tentacles around Luke's throat and trying to tear herself free. But she was growing weak faster than Luke.

The draining seemed to continue for days; then the stranger threw back his head and screamed in anguish, and it suddenly seemed that only a breath had passed. Shiny black Force energy began to pour from the Sith's wounds into the lake, spreading outward around them in an oily slick so hot the water began to steam and hiss. Still, the stranger continued to drain Abeloth, and Luke realized that he was not being betrayed—the Sith was suffering as much damage from the attack as was Luke.

Abeloth whipped her chin free of Luke's hand, ripping the energy knot where they had joined and sending a sparkling line of both of their Force essences splattering across the surface of the lake. She began to roll her head around, gnashing and spitting, trying to sink her fangs into Luke's arm or the stranger's—anything she could reach.

Luke slipped his arm down around her throat and pulled hard, merging his form into hers, doing his best to keep her under control.

"Keep going," Luke urged the stranger. "Pull harder!"

The red glow in the eyes of the shadow-ghouls faded suddenly to pink, and openings began to appear in their staggered-gauntlet formation. Saba sprang into the first gap, holding her ignited lightsaber between her and the nearest ghoul, trying to reach the body to which it was attached by a long writhing tail. The thing kept trying to slip around the blade's purple-white glow to slash at a head or shoulder or hip.

Saba advanced behind a whirling shield of blocks and slashes, cutting through a shadowy arm here, a leg there, even a neck or body. The pieces dropped away, withering into nothingness before they hit the floor, and the ghoul instantly grew a replacement. Still, the constant hacking was enough to keep the thing from touching Saba, and at last she reached the body itself. She cut the tail free of the corpse's chest, at the same time kneeling down and reaching for its face.

As quick as she was, the ghoul had already reemerged from the corpse. It came diving in at her, sinking two shadowy hands into her thigh. Saba's entire leg went numb, then erupted in icy anguish as the thing's shadowy claws began to slide through her muscle.

Saba used two fingers to close the corpse's eyes, then rose hissing and cursing and limped away. Olazon was at her side instantly, hitting the corpse with a blast from his flamegun and incinerating it. As he worked, Tahiri was already leaping past them to wave back the next shadow-ghoul. They had tried incinerating the bodies from a distance—before closing the eyes—but that had only complicated matters. The shadow-ghouls had stayed attached to the scorched remains, and it was impossible to make them go away as long as the eye sockets were uncovered.

Once Olazon had finished, his voice came over the reception bud in Saba's ear. "You're getting quicker," he said. "And only one hit that time. You okay?"

Saba put her weight on her aching leg and, when the muscle merely clinched with cold agony and did not collapse, nodded.

"Yesss, but this one is not growing quicker," she said. "They are growing slower. Keep going."

"You sure, Master Sebatyne?" This from Stomper Two, also speaking over the comm net. "I don't like the changes in their eyes—or how their formation has opened up. This feels like a trap."

The Void Jumper's caution was understandable. The pack had advanced only fifteen meters, and already they were down to four hunters. A shadow-ghoul had gotten inside Stomper One's power armor and caused it to self-destruct, which was why Stomper Two was now at the rear of the pack, carrying a badly dented EMP bomb. And no one was quite certain what had become of Braan, the wounded demolition man. A wave of terror had simply rolled through the Force from his direction, and then a thermal detonator had gone off.

But Saba suspected the change was a good sign. During their strategy meeting on Coruscant, the Jedi had realized it was possible to temporarily weaken at least one of Abeloth's avatars by killing another.

Kill one, weaken the others. The theory was that Abeloth had only a single Force presence, shared by her avatars, so harming *any* of her
avatars would make it easier to defeat all of them. Assuming that the
shadow-ghouls were being animated by Abeloth—and Saba saw no
other possibility—then they were growing weaker because Luke was
succeeding in the Maw.

And *that* made it even more important to succeed here—and to
succeed quickly. It would do the galaxy no good to kill Abeloth in the
Maw if she survived here.

Tahiri dropped to a knee, reaching over to close a corpse's eyes, and
a second ghoul drifted over, reaching for her from behind. Saba sprang
to her defense, slashing off the thing's shadowy arms, then slipping in
to drive it back with a flurry of lightsaber strikes and sweeps.

As she fought, Saba sneaked a glance up the corridor. Between the
flashing of their lightsabers and the fiery glow of Olazon's flamegun,
her infrared vision was completely washed out, and it was impossible
to tell how far they still had to go. But the eyes of the ghouls were still
visible, and there were at least a dozen pairs glaring out of the darkness
ahead.

Too many, too long.

Saba cut the next shadow-ghoul down the center, then leapt
through its coalescing body toward the body to which it was con-
nected. She landed astride its chest, aching and chilled to the bone,
and quickly closed its eyelids—then popped a thermal grenade off her
harness, armed the fuse, and rolled the corpse over on top of it.

"Grenade!" she yelled, and leapt at the next set of glowing eyes.

The Keshiri was trembling in agony. Greasy dark smoke was rising
from a shoulder that had been so badly scorched it looked like a
burned nerf roast. Her cheeks were hollow, her complexion was so
wan it was pale blue, and her sunken eyes were rimmed in red.

But she was still standing, coming at them across the courtyard's
mossy cobblestones.

Even knowing what the woman was, Ben could barely believe his
eyes. Vestara had hit her with a bolt of Force lightning powerful
enough to take out a *Canderous*-class hovertank. Still, the avatar had

returned to her feet the instant Vestara had been carried too far away from the Font of Power to continue drawing on its power. And now Vestara was standing at his side, shaking even worse than the Keshiri, her complexion still shadowed by its dark energy, her eyes dulled by Force overload.

When the Keshiri snatched her lightsaber off its belt hook and ignited its crimson blade, Ben was almost relieved. It was such a mundane threat that it made him think perhaps Vestara's attack had driven out Abeloth after all—perhaps all they had to fight now was a simple Sith Lord.

Then the Keshiri spoke, and his hope evaporated. "We are done with patience," she said in a thousand voices. "Drink together—or die together."

Ben opened himself to the Force completely, shielding himself from the Font of Power's darkness by drawing its energies through the power of all he loved in the galaxy, through his faith in the Jedi purpose and the promise of the future—through his confidence in Vestara and the sure knowledge that she would soon join him in the ranks of the Jedi Knights. The Force came pouring into Ben from all sides, irresistible and pure, a flood of light and purpose that no being in the galaxy could deny. He felt himself *become* the Force, a swirl of power and energy, and he focused all that he was on the approaching Keshiri, hitting her with a Force blast that would have knocked a frigate out of orbit.

The blast caught the avatar square in the chest and rocked her shoulders back *at least* a couple of centimeters. She paused almost noticeably before she took her next step.

Ben staggered back, exhausted, and nearly fell before Vestara's hand clamped around his biceps. She pulled him to his feet and began to retreat, pulling him toward the cloud of steam still enveloping the Font of Power.

"So, Ben, what was *that* supposed to be?" she asked. "The power of the light side?"

"You didn't do much better," Ben replied. He pulled his arm free and stopped a few meters outside the steam. "And *you* were drawing on the font."

"Yeah . . . because I'd kind of like to survive this," Vestara replied, reluctantly stopping with him. "What's your point?"

"That we don't have to surrender to her," Ben whispered. He glanced across the courtyard toward the ruined arcade, then used the Force to lift a section of broken pillar and bring it spinning toward the back of the avatar's head. "We just have to work together."

There was no time for Vestara to waste with a witty reply. She simply raised her hands and unleashed another fork of Force lightning, this one far less powerful than when she had been drawing on the font's power. The Keshiri's hand rose so fast that Ben barely even saw it move, and he realized their ploy could actually work—that even an avatar could fall prey to a tactical diversion.

The Keshiri caught the lightning bolt in the palm of her hand, and its white-hot energy dwindled to a spark. But the pillar kept coming, striking the back of her head with a sickening thud and sending a bloody spray of skull and brain all the way across the courtyard to splatter Ben and Vestara's legs.

The avatar did not instantly drop dead. She staggered a few steps forward, carried by the momentum of the impact, then raised her smashed head to reveal that one eye had been knocked free of the socket and was now dangling on her cheek.

The other eye fixed its gaze on Ben.

"*Sheeka*, Ben!" Vestara took a step away from him—not because she was abandoning him, Ben felt sure, but because it was the smart tactical move. "I think you really made her mad."

"Let's make her even madder," Ben said, reaching out for another section of pillar. "Hit her agai . . . rrgh!"

The order came to a strangled end as he felt himself flying back into the arcade. His shoulders hit a pillar dead-center, folding so far backward that both shoulder blades touched stone. Then a tremendous *crack* sounded inside his skull, and his head exploded into dark pain. He felt himself sliding down the pillar toward the cobblestones below, and the last thing he saw was Vestara retreating toward the Font of Power, disappearing into the yellow steam with the avatar close behind.

Abeloth lay tangled in Luke's arms, a writhing mass of Force energy that had suddenly gone limp a second or a day ago, only to explode an hour or a nanosecond later into a flailing tempest that had sent them all rolling and bouncing across the Lake of Apparition's dark waters. The stranger was tumbling with them, his hand still buried in Abeloth's chest, now wailing in agony as gleaming black Force energy steamed from his wounds.

They bounced so close to the shore, Luke grew worried that Abeloth was trying to carry them away from the lake into some new place beyond shadows. And *then* what? His back hit the water again, and he spun them all around so that his feet were toward the shore. He planted his feet against a moss hummock and kicked off—and sent them all somersaulting back toward the center of the lake. Abeloth stopped struggling and seemed to shrink in his arms, and Luke dared to think that maybe, just *maybe* she had finally lost hope, that they had exhausted her to the point that she was no longer capable of fighting.

Then she was gone, leaving the stranger and Luke with nothing between them but twenty centimeters of space and the stump of the Sith's hand, now pointed at Luke's chest and still drawing Force energy, draining it not from Abeloth now, but directly from Luke.

They stayed like that for an eternity, a void of cold nothingness growing inside Luke as the stranger continued to hang in the air above, draining him. It seemed to Luke that the Sith's betrayal was premature, that they at least ought to make certain Abeloth was truly dead before they turned to fighting each other . . . but that was not the way Sith did things.

Luke started to bring his hand up, intending to hit the stranger with a Force blast. But before he could loose it, the Sith's feet dropped to the water's surface, and he raised his stump and pointed toward the far end of the lake.

"There!"

Luke craned his neck and saw Abeloth's silhouette backing into the Mists of Forgetfulness—with the stranger's wrist still protruding from her chest.

"Stop her!" Luke yelled. "If she disappears into that fog . . ."

Luke left the sentence unfinished as a fountain of oily black Force energy erupted from the protruding wrist. Abeloth's mouth gaped open, and her piercing shriek broke over the lake, reverberating across the water like a clap of thunder. Luke glanced over and saw the stranger standing beside him, pointing in her direction, using the Force to draw his missing hand back toward its stump.

Abeloth did not come dancing in to counterattack, did not even try to stand off defensively and weaken them with a blast of Force lightning. She did not have time for such tactics. Luke doubted she would have fled the battle in the first place if she were not *already* dying, and with her Force essence gushing out of her like a geyser, she had to attack *now*.

And she did.

In the next thought Abeloth was simply there in front of the stranger, driving a ball of tentacles deep into *him*. Luke sprang forward to help—and felt a blistering iciness slide deep into his own chest. His entire right side flared into cold anguish, and the tentacles began to dig and grab, tearing him apart inside in a way no lightsaber or blaster ever could.

Luke attacked anyway, driving an elbow strike into the side of her head. As before, there was no crunching, no physical sense of impact, only Force energy plowing through Force energy, sending waves of pain and damage rolling through them both. Luke sensed his elbow come free as it pushed out the other side of Abeloth's head. Then she simply fell away, her still-balled tentacles tearing free of both Luke and the stranger . . . each clutching a handful of dripping, pulsing Force essence.

The stranger collapsed with a gaping hole in his chest. Luke felt his own form grow limp and weak, and he sensed his mouth falling open to scream, then his whole body was falling, weak and aching for breath.

Jaina had heard death screams many times before, on battlefields from Anthus to Zelaba, and they had one thing in common: death screams always contained as much surprise as pain, as much anger and disbelief as sorrow. It was as though men meeting a violent end could never quite believe what was happening, that they had finally met a fighter who was better and luckier than they were. Or maybe it was death itself they were cursing, angry at how it preferred to cheat great warriors of their lives rather than take them in a fair fight. Jaina couldn't be sure of the feelings behind the scream, but she knew one thing for certain—a death scream was always raw and loud.

And that was the kind of scream she had just heard from the *Rude Awakening*'s medbay, where Luke had strapped in his body before he went beyond shadows.

But with black holes reaching out from both sides and Ship still holding the choke point with a steady assault of boulders and plasma, leaving the pilot's seat to go check on him was out of the question. The *Awakening*'s shields had long ago failed, and she had so many weak spots in her bow armor that Jaina was seriously considering spinning the ship around to start taking damage in the stern.

She had been fighting back, of course—using a steady onslaught of baradium missiles against Ship. Her goal was to hold on long enough so Luke could return from beyond shadows. By then, she hoped the *Awakening* would be far enough through the choke point to force its way through with one last shot. But Luke's scream had shown her the folly of her patient approach. She needed to finish this fast and get to Abeloth's planet.

Jaina checked the missile magazine. Three left.

She launched two, a single second apart, then hit the throttles and accelerated after them. This time, it would be Ship who had to decide how crazy the other pilot was.

By the time Saba reached the air lock at the entrance to the computer core, the shadow-ghouls were barely shadows anymore. Their eyes had paled to white, and they moved so slowly that it was easy to dance past and close the eyes of their corpses. And even when one of them did make contact, there was no life draining or pain, just a sudden cold ache that passed as quickly as the ghoul was destroyed.

Clearly, Master Skywalker had robbed Abeloth of much of her strength. But Saba feared that *he* had also been greatly weakened, for she had not sensed him reaching out to let her know of his success— to warn her that Abeloth would now be desperate and looking to escape. Saba paused in front of the air lock and reached for him in the Force, but there was nothing . . . no hint of whether he was relieved or in pain, whether he had destroyed Abeloth or not.

Tahiri came up behind her and said, "That was almost *too* easy." Her voice was trembling with exhaustion, but there was no pain in it, only the joy of returning to the hunt with her true pack. "Are you thinking trap?"

"This one is *alwayz* thinking trap," Saba said. "It is the best way to hunt."

"Not what I meant," Tahiri replied. "I don't like how that fight suddenly got easier. Abeloth is up to something."

"So are we," Olazon said, limping up to join them—and wisely cutting short any discussion of tactics. The pack had planned this part of the attack before drafting Tahiri to join them, and it would not be wise to explain their intentions where Abeloth could be eavesdropping. "And if you call *that* easy, we could use a few Jedi in the Void Jumpers."

As Olazon spoke, he pulled a bell-shaped explosive from his gear bag and affixed it to the center of the air lock's outer hatch. Saba could see dozens of dark splotches on his arms and body—areas of dead tissue where the ghouls had touched him and his flesh was no longer emitting normal heat. She knew that if he lived, he would spend the next few weeks inside a bacta tank, trying to replace the flesh the med droids were going to have to cut away.

Once he had set the timer, Olazon asked, "Anyone have a detonator left?"

Saba pulled one off her combat harness and passed it to Tahiri. "Jedi Veila has one."

"I do *now*." Tahiri frowned up at Saba, then turned to Olazon. "Set a one-second fuse and float it in?"

Olazon smiled. "Done this before, I see."

"A few times," Tahiri said, clearly understating the case.

Olazon nodded, then turned to Stomper Two, who was still carrying the shiny, badly dented orb of the EMP bomb. "You ready?"

"Big Blinder armed, safeties off," the Void Jumper reported. "I'll start the detonation timer when Jedi Veila blows the inner hatch."

"Good." Olazon flipped the fuse toggle on the first charge, then spun away from the hatch and pressed himself flat against the wall at the end of the corridor. "Fire in the hole!"

Everyone else did the same, Stomper Two going to Olazon's side of the corridor, and Saba and Tahiri to the opposite side.

"Master Sebatyne," Tahiri asked, "what's the rest of our—"

The word *plan* vanished into a deafening bang. A slender cone of blowback flame shot five meters down the corridor, but most of the blast's power was focused in the opposite direction. The entire hatch buckled inward, filling the interior of the air lock with a cloud of durasteel shrapnel.

The flames had barely died away before Tahiri rolled away from the wall and used the Force to send the thermal detonator floating toward the inner hatch. A second later a white flash flared from inside the air lock.

Saba was around Tahiri and through the hatchway even before the baradium glow had faded. Leaping across a three-meter hole that the detonator had left in the floor, she landed on a transparisteel service balcony inside the computer core. The balcony protruded about a dozen meters into a vast, spherical cavity filled with the faint pink striations of energy-starved circuits. Scattered around the chamber were a handful of drifting, radiant clouds—the tiniest amount of memory that an energy-starved computer needed to keep active to avoid shutting down.

Flying toward Saba from the depths of the chamber was a cloud of white-hot radiance, shaped like a woman's face, but with a hugely broad mouth and eyes so sunken they looked like wells. As the cloud approached, tendrils of light began to reach out in front of it, stretching toward Saba.

Tahiri alighted at Saba's side. "Stomper Two!" she yelled. "Big Blinder *now*!"

"Stay here," Saba ordered, stepping away from Tahiri toward the banks of display screens and interface consoles at the front end of the balcony. "Protect Big Blinder."

"Master Sebatyne, wait!" Tahiri called. "She's just energy—you need the pulse bomb to kill her."

Holding her lightsaber at waist height, inactivated and out of position, Saba ignored the warning and continued forward. What Tahiri *didn't* know was that Abeloth could see the future, and that meant

they had to use the future to defeat her. That was why Olazon had sacrificed so much to bring the pulse bomb along—so that Abeloth
would foresee it destroying the computer core with her inside.

What the prey *hadn't* seen was how Saba intended to react when
Abeloth tried to change the future—or at least Saba *hoped* Abeloth
hadn't seen that. By the time the cloud of radiance reached the front
edge of the service balcony, the tendrils of light had solidified into
fleshy tentacles, and Abeloth's face had lost its luminous quality and
started to grow opaque.

Still holding her lightsaber down by her waist, Saba Force-sprang
into the air. The tentacles immediately stretched toward her, already
pulsing with the dark Force essence that Abeloth intended to pump
into Saba—that she *needed* to pump into Saba if she was to take a new
avatar and escape to recover from the wounds that she had already suffered in the Maw.

They were still two meters apart when the first tentacle touched
Saba's face, then her entire head was webbed in tentacles. They were
trying to push in everywhere, into her nostrils and her eyes and her
mouth, tapping against the tympanic membranes that covered her ear
canals, even trying to slip up beneath her scales.

Saba ignited her lightsaber and brought it sweeping up, cutting all
of the tentacles away at Abeloth's shoulder. Expecting a geyser of Abeloth's Force essence to come spraying out of the wounds, she immediately sealed the membranes that protected her eyes and nostrils. But
the heat of her blade seemed to cauterize the wounds, and all that happened was that the tentacles flew off in every direction. There was an
instant of stunned silence, then Abeloth released an ear-piercing shriek
of pain and rage.

In the next millisecond they both slammed down atop an interface
console. Saba felt metal buckling and clearplas shattering, then they
tumbled off on opposite sides, Saba hitting the deck near Tahiri and
Abeloth landing on her feet by the balcony's edge. Fearing that her
prey would attempt to retreat into the computer core, Saba grabbed at
Abeloth in the Force, at the same time slashing her lightsaber through
the console that separated them.

The blade suddenly died. For an instant Saba thought the pulse
bomb had detonated early. She cursed her pack's lack of faith in her

skill, but then Abeloth was racing toward her, coming in faster than she was being pulled, and Saba realized that her prey had extinguished the blade.

Even with no arms left to fight with, Abeloth remained determined to take Saba's body. Her huge mouth gaped open, revealing two rows of fangs—fangs sharp enough to shred blast armor, set in jaws wide enough to bite through a rancor neck.

That was no way to fight a Barabel.

Saba brought both fists up together, jamming them into Abeloth's mouth in a Force-enhanced double punch. The blow knocked a ten-centimeter hole through both sets of fangs, and when Abeloth bit down there was nothing but toothless gum clamping Saba's scaly forearms.

Still, the pain was excruciating, and Saba came close to stopping before she felt her forearms snapping. Hissing in pain, she balled her fists anyway, locking her talons deep into the back of Abeloth's throat. In one smooth jerk, she pulled her prey's head down sideways and exposed the neck.

Then Saba sank *her* fangs in deep. They sliced through skin and gristle and just kept sinking, cutting through muscle and bone and spinal cord. Abeloth's body went limp with shock. Saba used her broken arms to jerk the head down farther, exposing even more neck. She ripped flesh. She gnashed sinew. She crushed vertebrae. She whipped her muzzle back and forth, and she felt the prey's head pop loose.

Only then did Abeloth's jaws open and release Saba's broken arms. She let her hands open, and her claws slipped free. The head went flying across the balcony and landed at the feet of Tahiri and the two Void Jumpers. All three stared at the gruesome thing in open shock, until Tahiri finally seemed to recover her wits and look toward Saba.

"Master Sebatyne?" she gasped. "Is she . . . did you get her?"

"Yes, Jedi Veila," Saba said, struggling to her feet. "Now we have *both* killed an Abeloth."

Ben's brain was so muddled—and his vision so blurry—that at first he took the flickering blue ball to be a sun about to go nova. Next, he thought it might be the efflux nozzle of a departing starship. Then he noticed the arch of a stone arcade before him, and the cobblestone courtyard all around him, and he recalled that he was on a planet somewhere in the Maw. He had been taken there by a Sith meditation sphere named Ship, at the command of a being called . . .

Abeloth.

His eyes went back to the column of yellow fog at the heart of the courtyard. *That* was the source of the flashing. There was a ball of blue energy dancing inside it, crackling and drifting back and forth. And there was a voice, too, a familiar female voice . . . calling his name.

"Ben?"

Vestara Khai's voice.

"Ben!"

His girlfriend's voice.

"Ben, where *are* you?"

She sounded terrified.

"*BEN!* I need you!"

Her voice began to quaver . . .

"Ben, don't give . . . up . . . on . . . me."

She was panting for breath.

"Please, not . . . don't let this . . ."

Ben sprang to his feet. His head began to throb so hard he thought it would split, and he felt warm blood cascading down the back of his neck. He staggered forward anyway—and nearly vomited when he entered the yellow cloud and took his first breath of acrid steam.

The blue ball was dancing toward him now. As it drew closer, he could see that the glow was being caused by a crackling cage of Force lightning. Inside the cage, two figures were locked in hand-to-tentacle combat, one a beautiful young woman with brown eyes, the other a hideously battered thing with a mass of smashed skull and spilled brains. It looked as though a Keshiri had grown tentacles and stepped into a threshing machine.

The beautiful young woman—Vestara—was blasting away with a constant stream of Force lightning, trying to use it to hold her attacker at bay. The Keshiri mess was grasping at her with two sets of arm-tentacles, using one set to keep them bound together while the other set probed at her mouth and nostrils. Protruding from a small scabbard on the Keshiri's belt was the handle of a glass dagger. Ben recognized it as one of the favorite weapons of the Lost Tribe of Sith, a thin glass stiletto known as a shikkar.

Ben did not even hesitate. He used the Force to pluck the shikkar from its scabbard, then drove the tip up through the center of the Keshiri's back, angling the blade so that it passed through her spinal cord, straight into her heart.

A spray of dark blood erupted around the shikkar's handle, and the Keshiri collapsed to her knees, then threw her smashed head back and let loose with an eerie wail. Her tentacles slid free of Vestara and started to swing around toward her back.

Ben used the Force to snap off the shikkar's handle.

Vestara hit the Keshiri in the face with a blast of Force lightning.

The Keshiri toppled over backward and lay writhing, apparently helpless, but somehow still alive. Ben used the Force to drag her out of the yellow fog, away from the Font of Power and out into the light of the planet's bright blue sun.

The Keshiri stopped struggling, and her eyes grew vacant and glassy. Her tentacles fused back into arms, then her entire body went slack. Ben used the Force to summon the pillar fragment that he had used to smash her skull earlier and dropped it across her chest. He heard bones snapping and air fluttering from her lungs, but no screams or groans or half-heard wails to suggest the woman was anything but dead.

Then Vestara stepped out of the yellow fog. Her face was wild, and the font's dark power was swirling around her legs so thickly that it looked as though she were floating on a black cloud. She raised her hands and pointed them at the corpse. Clearly, she intended to hit it with another blast of Force lightning—to burn it to a crisp and destroy every last trace of the thing that had tried to take them.

"No, Vestara." Ben quickly stepped to her side and placed a hand across her wrists, then gently forced her arms down. "There's no need for that. We're done with her now."

Ship hung in the exit to the choke point, a small dark spot silhouetted against a blue giant sun. Jaina knew her opponent had to be as battered as the *Rude Awakening*. It had stopped returning fire after she

had hit it with the double baradium strike and driven it out of the nar-
rows. But it had refused to give up entirely, always remaining just close
enough to remain a threat, to make one last suicide run and take them
both out.

Unfortunately, the shock waves had taken a toll on the *Awakening*
herself. She had at least three hull breaches, and Jaina had been forced
to close her helmet and seal the medbay cabin where Luke lay strapped
into a bunk. Now she truly had only one way to save him—assuming
that was still possible. She had to set down on a planet with an
atmosphere—and this deep in the Maw, that meant Abeloth's own
world.

Jaina fired the last baradium missile. Then, praying that the *Awakening* could take one more battering, she accelerated after it . . . and
watched in disbelief as the distant dot suddenly began to shrink and
vanished into nothingness.

Finally, Ship had turned and run.

Chapter Thirty-three

THE LAKE OF APPARITIONS WAS NEITHER WARM NOR COLD, STILL NOR roiling. It simply *was,* beyond time and sensation, beyond fear or desire or duty. It embodied surrender and attainment, death and immortality, and Luke had never felt more ready to slip below its dark surface and join his beloved Mara, to wrap himself in her liquid embrace and let the Depths of Eternity wash away the anguish of his wounds, the ache of his lonely despair.

But something would not let him sink.

He lay on the water for a year or a minute, hurt and exhausted, watching Abeloth's pale form vanish. Her eyes were empty and dark, her tentacles curled into loose balls. Her golden hair was fanned about her head in a floating halo, and she did not seem to be sinking so much as merely shrinking. Luke continued to watch as she dwindled to the size of a thigh, a foot, a finger, then a mere sliver that seemed to hang below him, wavering and flickering, before it finally slipped from sight.

And still Luke did not sink. He was too weak to rise, and he could feel nothing of himself except the aching void Abeloth had torn in his chest. It occurred to him that he might well be dying, and it was not a thought that brought him any fear. Even if his life had not been as long as Yoda's, it had been a good one filled with close friends and much-loved family. He had been of some small service, at least, to his fellow sentient beings. And in the new Jedi Order, he had rekindled a light that had once gone out in the galaxy. He had few regrets for anything he had done, and if the time had come to let another Jedi carry the torch, he was ready.

"Not yet, Skywalker."

The voice was warm and familiar, and it came from beside Luke. He turned to find Mara's face breaking the surface of the water. Then he saw a hand gripping the back of his biceps and realized that she was floating beneath him, preventing him from sinking.

"Mara, it's okay," Luke said. "I'm ready. I want to be with you."

"Too bad." He felt his upper body rising as she tried to push him upward. "I don't want to be with you—not here, not yet."

"*What?*" Luke asked, feeling more confused than resentful. "Mara, I'm wounded . . . badly. Abeloth took something out of me."

"She wounded *him*, too." Mara's other hand rose out of the water and pointed past Luke's head, toward the tattooed Sith who had helped Luke kill Abeloth. The stranger was on his feet, limping toward the far shore with both hands clutched to his chest. "If he can do it, so can you."

Luke forced himself to sit upright. The effort made his head spin and his whole being ache, but he refused to collapse back into the water. He had no idea of the Sith's true identity, but it did not seem wise to let him return to the physical galaxy alone.

"That's ridiculous. Their injuries may be different." This voice came from Luke's other side, sinister and cajoling . . . and *also* familiar. "Besides, Sith are stronger. They have the dark side."

"Who *is* he?" Luke asked, turning to find Jacen looking up from the water on his other side. "You know, don't you?"

"I told you," Jacen replied. "He's the one I saw sitting on the Throne of Balance."

"The dark man of your vision?" Luke asked. This was the best opportunity he would ever have to learn for certain why Jacen had turned to the dark side, and he was determined to take advantage of it. "The one you sacrificed yourself to stop?"

"I saw only one," Jacen replied. "And you're letting him win."

Luke shook his head. "He *can't* win, Jacen. Whatever damage you caused to the Force, you accomplished that much. The Sith will never rule the galaxy . . . not now."

The tattooed man stopped and whirled, and Luke found himself preparing to dodge a fork of Force lightning. But the stranger was in no better shape to fight than Luke. He had a gaping wound in his chest, just like Luke, and Luke could see that his entire form was shuddering. Instead of attacking, the Sith just stood staring at them, one eye shining yellow and the other an empty socket, his right arm a useless ghost of a limb.

Then, after an eternity that might have been a mere second, he said, "You must not be so certain of yourself, Master Skywalker. You may think you have stopped the Sith, but you know nothing of us . . . nothing at all."

"I know that Jacen changed the future," Luke retorted. "And you know it, too—or you wouldn't have been here to help me fight Abeloth."

The stranger dipped his chin in acknowledgment. "There is *that*," he said. "But can you be sure the change will last? Perhaps Caedus did not *change* the future. Perhaps he only *delayed* it."

Luke felt his energy and his determination come rushing back. "I guess that remains to be seen, doesn't it?"

A slow grin crept across the stranger's mouth. "Indeed it does." He turned and began to limp away. "And we *shall* see, Master Skywalker. I promise you that."

Luke returned to his feet and stood watching, until the stranger finally stepped onto the shore and vanished. The man was barely gone before Jacen spoke again, this time from the water in front of Luke.

"What does Abeloth have to do with this?" Jacen asked. "She wasn't part of my vision."

Luke studied his nephew's bitter face, debating how much he should reveal about what Raynar had learned from Thuruht—whether it would be justice or cruelty to let Jacen know that he bore personal responsibility for an apocalypse.

"As I thought," Jacen sneered. "You're as much a liar as I am."

Luke shook his head. "I'm not a liar, Jacen. You are the one who released Abeloth."

"*Me?*" Jacen's tone was snide, but Luke could see the shock in his eyes. He truly did not understand what he had done. "How?"

Luke shook his head. "I'm not sure I should tell you," he said. "It would do no good."

"You expect me to believe you're *protecting* me?" Jacen scoffed. "*Truly?* Because, I assure you, I can handle the truth."

"All right," Luke said. Jacen had *already* guessed what had happened, and it would only be cruel to leave him wondering if he had guessed right. "But first, you must answer a question that's been bothering me."

"I might," Jacen said. "It doesn't hurt to ask."

"Sometimes it does," Luke said. He squatted down, then looked straight into Jacen's dead eyes. "I want to know why you didn't come to me."

"About my vision?" Jacen asked.

"About *any* of it. For a while, I thought it was because *I* was the dark man you saw on the Throne of Balance—that you were trying to take my place." Luke gestured toward the shore where the stranger had disappeared. "But if the *Sith* is the one you saw, that makes no sense. You didn't have to confront this alone. We could have done it together—"

"No, we couldn't," Jacen said, shaking his head. "Because the dark man had nothing to do with my decision."

Luke frowned. "Then what did?"

"It was who I saw standing *with* the dark man." Jacen's gaze shifted away, and his expression grew at once very determined and very sad. "I saw Allana."

Chapter Thirty-four

THE ASSAULT PINNACE *RUDE AWAKENING* SAT AT THE FAR END OF THE courtyard, hissing and popping as the heat of its fiery descent dissipated into the humid jungle air. Its hull was carbon-scorched and dented, and several deep pits went down through the thick battle armor all the way to the orange circle of an emergency hull patch. The assault vessel had obviously been through a terrible battle—no doubt with Ship, which Abeloth had sent back into space the instant she had debarked with her two prisoners. Ben could only hope that the ancient meditation sphere had suffered as much damage as the *Awakening*, because otherwise they would be an easy target when they tried to leave the planet.

"What's taking so long?" Vestara asked. She was standing at Ben's side, one hand tight on his biceps and holding him steady. "Can't your people see that you need medical attention?"

Ben glanced over. His vision was still a bit blurry, but with a purple bruise around her throat and a face covered in welts and cuts, she didn't look much better than he felt.

"We *both* need medical attention," Ben said. "You look like you stepped on a Hutt's tail."

"Thanks a lot," Vestara said. "Next time, I won't mess my hair saving you."

Ben cocked his brow. "Didn't I save *you*?" he asked. "That's the way I remember it."

Vestara filled her voice with mock concern. "Poor Ben—you must have hit your head harder than I thought." Pulling him along by the arm, she started across the courtyard. "We need to get you into a medbay *now*."

They had covered about half the distance when a dark rectangle separated from the pinnace's battered hull and began to descend, slowly folding out into a boarding ramp. A slender female figure appeared in the opening at the top. Her brown hair was pulled into a tight bun, her eyes were sunken with exhaustion, and she had furrow lines as deep as canyons in her brow. So it took Ben a moment to even recognize her as his cousin, Jaina Solo. She was dressed in a combat vac suit and holding her deactivated lightsaber in one hand, and the entire front panel of her suit was smeared in red, frothy blood.

"Jaina!" Ben rushed forward, weaving slightly as he pulled Vestara along. "Are you okay?"

"I'm fine." Jaina's gaze shifted toward Vestara, and her entire body grew tense and alert. "How about you, Ben?"

"Ben took a blow to the head," Vestara said, steadying Ben as he stumbled. "He's lost a lot of blood and is having a few balance problems."

Jaina's eyes returned to Ben, and this time there was as much concern in them as wariness. "You'd better come aboard then."

Ben and Vestara crossed the last few steps to the pinnace, then Jaina raised a palm to stop Vestara from stepping onto the boarding ramp.

"Just Ben for now," she said. "Please."

The Force grew cool and still with the tension between the two women, and Ben and Vestara stopped at the base of the ramp. Ben frowned and looked from Jaina to Vestara, trying to figure out why the pair had suddenly grown so wary of each other. Then Vestara lowered the hand she had been using to support him, creating a chain of eddies in the dark aura that continued to cling to her, and he understood. He took Vestara's hand and started to pull her up the boarding ramp with him.

"You don't need to worry about that dark stuff, Jaina," Ben said. "It's just an aftereffect."

Jaina moved the hand holding her lightsaber to the waist-high ready positon. "Of *what*, exactly?"

"I was standing too close to the font when I used the Force," Vestara explained. "I knew it would taint me, but we needed its power. It was the only way to kill Abeloth."

"But the taint will fade," Ben said. "It's already faded a *lot*."

"I'm glad to hear it." Jaina did not take her eyes off Vestara. "But it's actually your father I'm thinking of, Ben."

"Dad?" Ben started up the ramp, so shocked that he was still holding Vestara's hand. "What happened?"

"I don't really know," Jaina said, placing herself squarely in the center of the boarding hatch. "It happened beyond shadows."

Ben's heart sank. "That's bad," he said. Physical injuries could usually be repaired in any decent medcenter, but beyond shadows was the realm of the spirit. No amount of surgery or bacta immersion was going to heal a wound suffered there. "Is he awake?"

"Not yet." Jaina switched her gaze to Vestara, then said, "I've got some repairs to make and my sensors are gone, so I need you to keep watch. Ship could be around somewhere."

Jaina's request made sense—and even if it had not, Ben was too worried to protest. He hadn't felt anything to suggest that his father had died, but he couldn't sense his father's presence, either. It was as though Luke Skywalker had gone missing from the Force.

Vestara pulled her hand free, then gently placed her palm on his chest. "Go on, Ben. Check on your father."

She rose onto her toes and kissed Ben on the lips. It was long and deep and filled with love, and under normal circumstances it would have made his heart skip beats. But with his father lying wounded inside the pinnace, Ben took it as a gesture of support—Vestara's way of being there for him even though she had to stand watch outside. He allowed the kiss to continue until it finally began to feel a little sad and frightened, then placed his hands on her shoulders and looked into her brown eyes.

"There's nothing to worry about, Ves," he said. "If Abeloth couldn't kill us, Ship doesn't stand a chance."

Vestara nodded and forced a smile. "I know that." She stepped back, then flicked her fingers toward the hatchway. "Go on, now. I hope your father is going to be okay."

"Thanks," Ben said. "I'll see you in a few minutes."

He turned away and, once Jaina had stepped aside, boarded the pinnace. It was a typical elite-forces strike craft, compact and loaded with specialized equipment—much of it cratered, scorched, and shattered by the hits that had breached the hull. The flight deck lay to the right, behind a durasteel bulkhead and an open iris hatch.

Jaina pointed down a narrow corridor that led toward the stern of the craft. "The medbay is aft." She pressed a couple of buttons on a control pad mounted on the inner hull, and the boarding ramp began to retract. "I'll be back in a minute."

Ben frowned. "What are you doing?" he asked. "I keep telling you—"

"I can't check hull integrity with an open hatch," Jaina interrupted, giving him a look that seemed equal parts sympathy and impatience. "And your girlfriend is fine. It's Luke Skywalker you should be worrying about."

Ben could tell by Jaina's abrupt manner that she wasn't being entirely honest with him, but it was hard to argue against the need for a hull-integrity test. He studied her a moment, trying to figure out why she was acting so strange—and what she *wasn't* saying. Finally, he decided that whatever she was hiding, it could wait until after he had seen his father.

"Okay, but don't even think about leaving without Vestara," he said, going down the corridor. "If not for her—"

"Ben, don't worry," Jaina interrupted. "The last thing I intend to do is leave Vestara Khai on this planet."

Ben ignored the sharpness of her tone and continued on toward the medbay. He could tell by the heavy odor of antiseptic and bacta salve that his father was in bad shape. He reached out in the Force, trying to find some hint of his father's condition, and felt the lukewarm presence of a non-sentient being—or a Jedi so deep in a healing trance that he appeared to be in a coma.

Ben took a calming breath, then stepped through the hatch into a ten-bunk medical bay. As a Void Jumper assault vessel, the pinnace was outfitted for both combat *and* the aftereffects. His father lay secured in a bunk along the cabin's back wall, with a breathing tube down his throat and half a dozen IV catheters secured to his arms, neck, and legs. A huge bandage covered the right side of his chest, and while his skin was not dry or flaky, it had turned the color of ash. Whatever Jaina was thinking about Vestara, she was telling the truth about Ben's father. Luke Skywalker was close to death.

A hollow ache started to build inside, and Ben's vision suddenly narrowed and went completely black. He thought for a minute that he might be passing out, but there was no dizziness or nausea to suggest that the vision change was the result of a concussion. He braced a hand on the hatch jamb and stood waiting for his sight to return.

Instead, stars and nebulae began to appear in the darkness, rushing toward him at extreme velocity, but with no noticeable red-shift and without spreading apart as they drew closer. He began to feel apprehensive and disoriented, as though he were traveling through a galaxy far different from the one his parents had known. He saw Coruscant's scintillating golden orb mottled by patches of flickering red flame and black banks of drifting smoke, and beyond it there was a legion of dark silhouettes rising from a shadow-cloaked world, fanning out across the galaxy to meet a much smaller force of luminous shapes.

He saw a pair of tiny disembodied eyes floating through the darkness, collecting wisps of drifting gas and specks of loose dust, in its endless patience swaddling itself in the stuff of cold matter.

And Ben saw his cousin Allana, a young girl sitting cross-legged in front of a white throne, playing with her pet nexu while a small circle of Jedi fought a desperate battle at the foot of the dais, holding off an endless onslaught of beings. There were dark silhouettes and bejeweled women and horned aliens, and every so often a gray tentacle, which would appear on the steps to the dais and attempt to slip past unnoticed before a lightsaber descended to send it skittering back into the darkness.

What Ben did not see was his father, and it was an absence that frightened him more than anything he had seen. With the Jedi facing a future more perilous than he could imagine, the Order was going to

need the leadership of its Grand Master more than ever. But Luke Skywalker was only mortal. Even if it was not today, there would soon
come a time when he and the other elder Masters were no longer there
to guide the Jedi, when the burden of leadership would start to fall on
Jaina Solo and her generation. It was an inevitable change, and—
considering the new threats the Jedi now faced—probably even
healthy to introduce a new way of thinking.

But that did not mean Ben was ready to become an orphan. Jedi
Knight or not, he still needed his father, and regardless of what the
Force was showing him, he was going to fight to keep Luke Skywalker
alive for as long as possible. He let go of the hatch jamb and stepped
into the darkness of his vision, and he found himself abruptly back in
the medbay cabin, looking at the skull-like visage of an Emdee droid
that had just moved into his path.

The droid extended a hand holding a surgical mask.

"Mask yourself," it said. Its brisk, no-nonsense tone was probably
standard issue for Void Jumper droids, for Ben had spent enough time
in the company of elite soldiers to know that short and crisp was their
preferred mode of communication. "Then lie down on the examination table, on your side facing the back wall."

"I want to see the other patient first." Ben hooked the mask's re-
tainer loops over his ears, then asked, "What's his condition?"

"Grave," the droid replied. "Unexplained coma, unclassified rapid-
onset infection, and massive chest trauma—due to loss of second tho-
racic rib and superior lobe of the right lung."

Ben frowned. "Trauma *due* to the loss of a rib and a lung lobe?" he
asked. "Isn't the loss of parts usually the *result* of trauma, not the
cause?"

The droid fixed its beady photoreceptors on Ben. "Are you a physi-
cian, soldier?"

"I'm trained in field medicine," Ben replied.

"And *that* qualifies you to question an EmDee's diagnosis?"

"Not at all," Ben said. He was unaccustomed to dealing with this
kind of droid, but he knew enough about elite-force protocol to realize he would learn nothing by backing down. "But I *am* qualified to
know when something doesn't make sense."

"I didn't say the injury made sense." The droid stepped back, giving Ben a clear path to his father's side. "The cause of the injury appears to be the spontaneous ejection of the superior lobe. I found nothing to suggest the primary cause."

"No shrapnel wounds or internal burns?" Ben asked.

"Had I found either, I wouldn't have said 'spontaneous ejection.' " The droid stepped aside. "You may speak to the patient, but keep it short. You are in need of attention, too."

Ben went over to the bunk and grew even more alarmed. Even with the tape over the lids, it was clear that his father's eyes were sunken—in fact, the sockets looked empty. And his chest bandage was stained with circles of yellow and green ichor, which suggested an infection far nastier than any normal complication. Most worrisome of all, however, was the fist-sized basin in the center of the bandage. It looked like his father had taken a bolt from a blaster cannon, and Ben had trouble understanding what could have happened beyond shadows to cause such an injury to a physical body. He grasped the curled fingers of his father's hand, at the same time reaching out to him in the Force.

"Hey, Dad, thanks for coming after us," Ben said. It was well established that many coma patients could hear someone speaking, so Ben tried to keep the fear out of his voice. "I don't know what happened beyond shadows, but it probably saved us. Vestara and . . ."

Suddenly his father's hand clamped down so hard Ben thought his fingers might break.

"Dad?"

His father's grasp weakened, but it did not go entirely slack.

"Dad, are you awake?"

The Emdee droid stepped to the foot of the bunk and plugged into the data socket.

"I'm sorry, soldier. The patient's brain activity is still minimal."

"He squeezed my hand," Ben said. "In fact, he's still squeezing it."

"It's just motor response," the droid said. "With this level of brain inactivity—"

"I don't care what your scanner says," Ben interrupted. "This man is a Jedi Grand Master. He has capabilities you can't begin to understand."

The Emdee fixed beady photoreceptors on Ben and pushed its head forward. "Alternative medicine is the folly of the weak-minded, soldier."

"Jedi Knights are not weak-minded," Jaina said, stepping into the cabin. "And the Force is hardly 'alternative medicine.' Clear?"

She pointed a finger, and the droid went floating back toward its primary interface socket at the front of the cabin. A steady stream of static spilled from its vocabulator, but Jaina ignored both the sputtering and the insincere apology that the droid offered once its feet were on the deck again.

Instead she came to stand next to Ben. "Luke squeezed your hand?"

"That's right," Ben said. "He's not squeezing it right now, but he definitely squeezed. It started when I was talking to him."

"When you mentioned Vestara?"

As soon as she said Vestara's name, his father's hand clamped down on Ben's again.

Ben turned to study Jaina. "What's going on?"

"I imagine he's trying to tell you something."

"Like *what*?" Ben asked. "If you're going to tell me she can't be trusted, forget it."

Jaina's eyes remained hard. "I don't think I need to tell you *anything,* Ben. I think you already know."

Ben shook his head. "What I *know* is that Vestara risked her life to save me from Abeloth." Despite his words, he could not help recalling how willing she had been to drink from the Font of Power, how she had justified it by claiming it was the only way to defeat Abeloth. "She *can't* still be Sith. They turned her over to Abeloth . . . with *me*."

Jaina spread her hands. "I can't explain that," she said. "But there's something you need to know about the battle in the Temple."

Ben's heart fell, but he continued to shake his head. "No . . . you can't possibly blame the ambush in the treatment plant on her," he said. "She didn't even know the plan until *after* our capsule was in the line."

"That's a very good point," Jaina admitted. "And she *wasn't* the one who told the Sith where we would be entering. Abeloth did that."

"Abeloth?"

Jaina nodded. "Wynn Dorvan clued us in," she explained. "He was Abeloth's prisoner for a while, and he said she could look into the future. We think she was probably flow-walking."

Ben began to feel a glimmer of hope. "You see? If Vestara didn't—"

He was interrupted by a horrible gagging noise from the bunk beside him, and his father's grasp grew so tight that Ben's knuckles popped. He looked down to see his father's eyelids fluttering and his mouth moving as he tried to speak around the breathing tube.

"He's awake!"

Ben looked for the EmDee droid and found him racing foward, interface arm already reaching for the bunk's data socket. His father made another gagging sound, and this time it grew apparent that he was trying to say a single word. The initial sounds were too wet and guttural to make out, but the final syllable sounded like *ih.*

Ben leaned over the bunk and said, "Hold on, Dad. The EmDee will take the breathing tube out in a second, and then you can talk all day."

"That wouldn't be possible with bruised vocal cords, even if he *were* returning to consciousness." Leaving his interface arm in the data socket, the droid's head rotated to face Ben. "The brain activity is still minimal. I'm afraid he was just trying to swallow."

"Nonsense—watch this," Ben said, not looking away from his father. *"Vestara."*

Again, his father tightened his grasp and made a horrible gagging sound.

"I've never seen this before," the droid said. "The patient isn't coming out of the coma, but the name seems to trigger a primitive fear response."

Ben frowned. "Fear response?"

"He's afraid for *you*, Ben," Jaina said. "I think I know what he's trying to say."

Ben turned to glare at her. "Okay, Jaina. You've been treating Vestara like the spawn of Palpatine ever since you landed. Whatever your problem with her is, it's time to lay it out."

Jaina's expression softened, and that was when Ben knew he was in trouble. His cousin wasn't known for her compassion, so this had to be bad.

Jaina looked him directly in the eye and spoke in a quiet, almost apologetic voice. "After you were captured, Vestara was seen inside the Temple with a band of Sith."

"Of course. She was a Sith prisoner," Ben said carefully.

"She wasn't a prisoner," Jaina said gently. "It was an ambush, and Vestara was leading the attack."

Now Ben understood why Jaina was being so careful. She was telling him something that *couldn't* be true. He wanted to say that someone had misinterpreted what they had seen, but his father's grasp had tightened to the point that Ben feared a bone in his hand would break. He was beginning to have a sick feeling . . . and it was growing hard to ignore.

"And you're *sure* it was Vestara?" Ben asked. "That she was actually *with* the Sith?"

Jaina gave a reluctant nod. "My parents are the ones who told me," she said. "They contacted us via the HoloNet, just before we entered the Maw."

Ben's heart fell. With everything Jaina said, the accusation kept seeming more likely to be true. "How were Aunt Leia and Uncle Han involved?"

"They're the ones the Sith ambushed—and they both saw Vestara leading the attack," Jaina explained. "The *Falcon* was making a drop at the loading bay where the evacuation tunnel comes out. Vestara was there, waiting with a couple dozen Sith. She used a thermal detonator to disable the *Falcon* while the rest of her team attacked. Dad is positive it was her."

Ben was too shocked to ask himself how Vestara could have known where the Solos would be and when, or why the *Falcon* had been on Coruscant when it was supposed to be ferrying students to Shedu Maad. The Solos were too fair-minded to make such an accusation without being absolutely certain of what they had seen, and he knew better than to think they might be lying about it. The simple truth was that Vestara Khai had led an attack on the Solos. The *ugly* truth was that Ben had allowed that to happen by letting Vestara play him for a fool.

After a moment, Ben pulled his hand free of his father's crushing grasp and squeezed his forearm. "Thanks for the warning, Dad. I understand." He turned away and fought to keep the tears from his eyes. "Vestara Khai is a Sith. She always has been."

"I'm afraid so," Jaina said. "I'm sorry, Ben."

"Don't be," Ben said, almost resentfully. He didn't deserve her sympathy—not after he'd given Vestara so much access to the Jedi Order. "Is everyone okay?"

Jaina's voice grew somber. "Mom and Dad are fine," she said. "But Bazel Warv died in the ambush."

Ben's shock began to turn cold and bitter. He did not understand how he could have been so blind to Vestara's deceit, how he could have believed for so long that there was a hope of redeeming her—that *any* child raised by the Sith could ever turn her back on the dark side.

Ben let his chin drop to his chest. "It's my fault," he said. "I can't believe I let her fool me—or that I was ever stupid enough to think she really loved me."

Jaina put a hand on his shoulder. "Don't be so hard on yourself. I'm pretty sure that Vestara *does* love you. It's the only way she could have tricked you long enough to pull this off."

Ben looked up, confused. "How so?"

"Ben, you're a fairly sensitive young man and as strong in the Force as your father," Jaina said. "Don't you think you would have noticed if she were lying about her feelings?"

Ben considered the question for a moment, then finally began to understand the true depth of Vestara's treachery. "You're right," he said. "She *did* love me. It just didn't matter."

"That's what Sith *do*—they draw on the power of their emotions to get what they want."

Jaina took her hand off Ben's shoulder, and he could feel her gathering the strength to tell him something else—something that she thought would devastate him.

"Go on," Ben said. "Tell me the rest."

"I wish I didn't have to, but you need to know," Jaina said. "That ambush Vestara was leading? They were after Allana. The Sith know who she is."

* * *

Vestara sat hiding in the jungle, looking out over the courtyard and feeling worried and useless and alone, silently calling for Ship. Whether Ship had been destroyed or somehow remained under Abeloth's sway, he wasn't answering, and his silence left Vestara struggling to see some way her current situation did not end with her dead, imprisoned, or marooned.

Jaina Solo knew what had happened in the bowels of the Jedi Temple. That would explain why she had worked so hard to get Ben alone on the pinnace—and refused to let Vestara aboard. She probably thought that Vestara was a Sith assassin, with Luke Skywalker as her next target. By now, Ben believed the same thing.

It tore Vestara apart to imagine how Ben must be reacting to the accusation—the anger and the hatred for her that he must be feeling—but she knew better than to think she could deny it, or attempt to talk her way out of trouble. Even were the two Jedi willing to listen, there was no excuse in the galaxy that would make them forgive an attack on Allana Solo. Their Order was founded on foolish idealism and the nobility of sacrifice, so even a truthful explanation—that Vestara had only revealed Allana's true identity to save herself—would merely deepen their contempt.

And that left Vestara with only three choices: flee into the jungle and spend her life marooned here alone; surrender and hope to escape from the Jedi sometime in the next decade; or attempt to steal the battered pinnace. All three options could only be described as desperate, but she was leaning toward the third. After the battle against Abeloth, she was hardly in prime fighting condition, and stealing the pinnace would not be accomplished without killing both Ben and his Sword of the Jedi cousin. But after Jaina had raised the pinnace's boarding ramp, the first thing Vestara had done was return to the Font of Power to recover the lightsaber and parang from the Keshiri body that Abeloth had been using, so at least she was armed.

And besides, Sith do not surrender. The voice was raspy and weak and familiar, and it came to Vestara only inside her mind. *Sith fight, and if they find they must die, they never die alone.*

Vestara's heart suddenly began to grow lighter. "Ship?" She looked skyward and saw only the green-tinted clouds of this strange world, then spoke only in her mind. *Is that you?*

Such as I am, Ship responded. *And entirely at your command, my master.*

Then Abeloth is truly dead? Vestara asked.

As much as that is possible, yes.

"As much as that's possible?" Vestara asked, in her alarm speaking aloud. "What does that mean?"

Only that there are some things the Force does not reveal to us, Lady Khai. A dark speck appeared beneath the distant clouds and began to descend toward her. *And that we are finally free to return to our own kind.*

A muffled *thud* sounded from the battered pinnace below, and the boarding ramp began to descend. A terrible pang of loss shot through Vestara, and for the first time in her life, she began to feel utterly without hope. Not only had she lost Ben's love, but she had lost her home, her people, and her identity. Wherever her future carried her now, she did not see how she would ever be a Sith again. She stood and retreated deeper into the jungle, stopping only when it began to grow difficult to see the vessel through the vegetation.

I'll take the ride, Vestara replied. *But I'm not sure my own kind will have me. I've killed too many of them.*

Lady Khai, do you really believe the Lost Tribe to be the only Sith in the galaxy? Ship asked. *There are others—and they have need of you.*

"Other *Sith*?" Vestara began to feel a bit more optimistic. "Sith who would welcome me?"

Sith who have need *of you,* Ship repeated. *You have spent time with the Skywalkers—a great deal of time. How can you fail to see the value in that?*

Vestara's optimism swelled into confidence—pride, even. She *had* done something that no other Sith in the galaxy could have managed. She had lived with Luke and Ben Skywalker for nearly a year and—so far—survived to exploit it.

Then you had better hurry, she told Ship. The pinnace's ramp clanged down on the cobblestones again, and she added, *Ben and Jaina are coming for me now.*

I arrive in two minutes ten seconds, Ship said. *Surely, a Sith Lord can stall them that long.*

A Sith Lord? Vestara felt more confused than excited, for she had never heard of a Sith Lord under twenty—not even under thirty. *I'm hardly a Lord. I'm not sure I'm ready.*

You are a Sith Lord if I say you are, Lady Khai, Ship said. *And I say it now. Two minutes.*

Vestara didn't know whether to be thrilled or frightened, for being a Sith Lord carried as many dangers as it did privileges. But there had been no doubt in Ship's pronouncement. And why should there have been? After all, Vestara had deceived the renowned Luke Skywalker for months on end. She had slain a Sith Lord and played the key role in slaying Abeloth herself. And—most important—she had discovered the identity of the Jedi Queen.

Perhaps Vestara *was* ready to be called a Sith Lord. Perhaps she had even *earned* the right.

Ben and Jaina appeared at the top of the pinnace boarding ramp, frowning in suspicion as they scanned the courtyard for Vestara. Ben was still dressed in his blood-soaked robe, and Jaina was in her combat vac suit. Neither appeared to be holding weapons—at least none that Vestara could see through the vegetation.

"Vestara? Where are you?" Ben called. She felt him searching for her in the Force, and almost instantly, he looked in her direction. "Come on out."

Realizing her best chance of lasting two minutes against Ben and Jaina together lay in talking rather than fighting, Vestara hid her weapons inside her robe. Then she stood and stepped closer to the drop-off into the courtyard.

"Up here!" she called. "Sorry!"

The gazes of both Jedi went to the ledge where she was standing. They quickly descended the ramp into the courtyard and stepped away from each other.

Ben studied her for a moment, then asked, "What are you doing up there, Ves?"

His voice was so casual it almost made Vestara doubt the conclusion she had reached earlier. But Jaina was continuing to circle away from the pinnace, trying to put herself in position for a flanking attack, and Vestara could see now that Ben's left hand was slightly curled, as though he had something up his sleeve that would drop into his grasp as soon as he straightened his wrist.

Vestara shrugged. "Hiding, obviously." She shifted her gaze to Jaina, who quickly stopped moving and placed a hand on her hip. "If Ship really *is* around here, I didn't want him seeing me."

"Oh, yeah—good thinking," Ben said. "But we're good to go now. Come on down."

Vestara remained where she was and continued to look at Jaina. "You've done a cranial scan on Ben already?"

Jaina nodded. "He's fine." She remained where she was, and now Ben began to circle in the opposite direction. "But Grand Master Sky-walker not so much. We need to get going."

"You did a cranial scan *and* made repairs already?" Vestara asked, trying to sound in awe. "You're fast."

Jaina's eyes narrowed, and she began to circle toward Vestara's flank again. "The EmDee did the cranial scan. Are you coming or not?"

"Sure." Vestara stole a glance toward the sky and saw a dark circle about the size of a fist approaching over the ridge that loomed up beyond the opposite side of the courtyard, then froze Ben in place by looking back toward him. "As soon as Ben shows me what he has up his sleeve."

Ben's brow arched in surprise. "Nothing to worry about, Ves." He straightened his wrist, and a hypo dropped out of his sleeve into his hand. "It's just a sedative."

"And why would I need a sedative?" Vestara allowed herself to take what she hoped would seem a very natural step back into the jungle, then began to draw on the Force, preparing to fight. "Do I seem agitated to you?"

"My fault, I'm afraid," Jaina said, still circling. She was nearly at the arcade now, in position to launch her attack with a single Force leap. "With Luke in such bad shape, I'm in no mood to take chances—and, well, it hasn't been all that long since you were a Sith."

"It's just until we get out of the Maw, Ves." Ben began to circle in the opposite direction again. "It doesn't mean anything. Trust me."

"Ah, Ben." Vestara felt a ripping ache inside, as though her heart had literally been torn from her chest. "Why did you have to say *that*?"

She brought her hand up and hit him with a blast of Force lightning that sent him tumbling with his robes aflame. By then, of course,

Jaina was already Force-leaping to the attack. Vestara pivoted around, bringing her Force lightning to bear on the most immediate threat.

Jaina caught the bolt on her lightsaber and landed atop the ledge only a few meters away.

Leap. The fiery crackle of a fast-approaching vessel began to reverberate down from the jungle ridge, building quickly as Ship descended toward the courtyard. *Leap high!*

Vestara used the Force to launch herself into a high, cartwheeling arc over the courtyard. Jaina spun to follow, but by then a fiery plume was flashing past beneath Vestara—one of Ship's stony projectiles, moving so fast it was literally setting the air aflame.

The projectile crashed into the ledge with a deafening boom, and Ship came sweeping in to scoop Vestara out of the air. She slammed into the rear wall of the passenger cabin so hard that her breath left her, then remained pinned there by acceleration.

I apologize for the impact, Ship said. *I slowed as much as was possible without missing you.*

"You did . . . well," Vestara gasped, trying to get the air back into her lungs. "But you *could* ease off just a bit now."

As you command, Lady Khai. Ship reduced his acceleration to the point that Vestara could swing her legs down to the passenger cabin's soft deck. *I trust you are not hurt.*

"Uh . . . no."

Vestara stepped to the side of the cabin. A transparent area quickly appeared in front of her, and she found herself looking down on the courtyard where she and Ben had killed Abeloth, a thumb-sized oval of gray stone shrinking into the emerald vastness of the surrounding jungle. To her dismay, she felt a tear start down her cheek. She wiped it away at once.

"Not hurt on the outside, at least."

The Force rippled with Ship's confusion. *You have internal injuries?*

"No, nothing like that," Vestara replied. "It isn't physical."

Ah. You suffer over young Skywalker.

Vestara watched as the gray oval became a gray speck and finally vanished beneath an impenetrable blanket of clouds, then turned away and nodded.

"Yes, that's right," she said. "I was in love with him."

Then you will be fine, Ship assured her. *Even better than fine.*

"What makes you so sure?" Vestara asked.

Because love is pain, Lady Khai, Ship replied. *And pain makes Sith strong.*

Chapter Thirty-five

LUKE OPENED HIS EYES TO A GOLD, SCINTILLATING BLUR—CORUSCANT'S night side, he thought, hanging beyond a medbay viewport.

That the medbay *had* a viewport was a good sign. It meant he was aboard a sizable vessel—most likely the frigate *Redstar,* from which he and Jaina had launched into the Maw. It also meant Jaina had survived to fly him to safety. She had prevailed against Ship and, almost certainly, reached Abeloth's homeworld.

And that meant she had found Ben.

Luke reached out in the Force and was overjoyed to sense his son not too far away, near the front of the ship with many other familiar beings. It felt as though they were deep in discussion, their minds focused and their moods solemn.

After a moment, Ben's Force aura crackled with delight, and the other presences began to ripple with excitement as they realized Luke had awakened. He allowed his own joy to fill his being, then was overwhelmed by the torrent of love and delight that came flooding back to him. He could feel Corran and Saba and many of the other Masters, all of them bursting with relief and elation. The depth of their emotion was so pure and powerful that he did not know quite what to make of it. It left him feeling humbled and grateful and a bit confused, wondering how long he had been unconscious—and what had been happening while he lay healing.

The answer came a moment later, when Luke's vision finally cleared and he began to see what had become of Coruscant. The planet remained a sparkling disk of light, but now there were dark areas hundreds of kilometers across—and patches of flickering crimson adjoined by huge swaths of smoke-dimmed light.

Much of Coruscant was either burning or in ruins—and not just in Fellowship Plaza, but in thousands of places across the planet. Despite the Jedi Order's best efforts to keep the worst of the fighting inside the Temple, the Sith had spread the battle across an entire world. And Abeloth . . . Abeloth had brought the darkness.

Luke deactivated the medical monitors so they wouldn't alert an attendant, then removed the IV catheters from his arm. Slowly and with great effort, he got out of bed and dressed in a clean robe he found folded in a locker near his bed. His entire body ached with fever, and his atrophied legs trembled with weakness. But the greatest anguish was in his chest, where he could still feel Abeloth's balled tentacle—an empty sick heat that he thought might stay with him for the rest of his life.

From behind Luke came the soft rasp of a dilating iris hatch, and a set of boots began to stride across the deck toward him. He turned to see his son approaching, dressed in a short brown robe over trousers and boots. The only signs of his brush with Abeloth were a few fading scars and a self-assured bearing that made him seem suddenly taller, stronger, and far less innocent.

"What are you doing dressed?" Ben demanded, pointing toward the empty bed. "You're supposed to be in bed!"

Luke merely smiled. "It's good to see you, too, son."

He opened his arms, then they embraced and talked for twenty minutes. Luke explained what had happened beyond shadows and how he had been wounded, and Ben reported what had been happening while Luke was in a coma—especially the trouble Leia was having trying to convince Han to replace the *Falcon*'s lost cockpit with updated equipment. He listed casualties and survivors, cataloged the devastation on Coruscant, and apologized for being fooled by a Sith spy.

"What can I say? You were right about Vestara from the start." Ben's voice was filled with self-reproach. "As soon as she realized we knew about the attempt on Allana, she took off in Ship."

Luke clasped his son's shoulder. "Ben, don't be so hard on yourself. By the end, you weren't the only one who trusted her." Having fallen for a Sith spy himself as a young man, Luke understood how betrayed and humiliated his son must be feeling right now. "It's called experience, and the important thing is that you learn from it."

"Thanks, but I should never have let her escape," Ben said. "She knew a lot about the Jedi Order—and now, so do the Sith."

"*We* learned a lot, too, Ben." Luke was thinking less about Sith than about the Ones and the Balance, but he didn't want to worry his son by talking Force philosophy so soon after a brush with death. "Besides, I have a feeling you'll have more than one chance to bring in Vestara Khai."

Ben's face remained resolute. "I hope so," he said. "Because I was a karking fool for believing her. And I *hate* that!"

Luke cocked a brow. "Son, you must have missed the part where I said 'by the end, you weren't the only one who trusted her.' "

Ben looked confused for a moment, then winced as he realized that he had just inadvertently called the Grand Master of the Jedi Order a karking fool. "Uh, I didn't mean you, Dad."

Luke smiled, then realized that, in his excitement to see Ben, he hadn't noticed how weak he was starting to feel. He took a deep breath and forced himself to stand up straight.

"I think I can forgive you *this* time, Jedi Skywalker," Luke said. "Now, I need you to do a few things for me."

Ben squared his shoulders. "Of course."

"First, keep the EmDee droids out of here until I'm ready for them," Luke said. "There are some people I need to see—and I don't have the energy to argue with droids right now."

"Okay, but don't you think you should—"

"I know my limits, Jedi Skywalker," Luke said. "Second, ask Master Sebatyne to dispatch a team to bring Raynar Thul home from Thuruht. Obviously, he'll be reluctant to return. But with Abeloth destroyed and the inhabitants of Mortis dead, the Jedi are not going to antagonize the Chiss by helping the Killiks build up their hives."

Ben nodded. "I'll tell Master Sebatyne as soon as I leave the cabin," he said. "What else?"

"I felt Wynn Dorvan's presence among the Masters," Luke said. "Is he still serving as the Chief of State?"

"As acting Chief, yes. He and the Jedi Council have been meeting to . . ." Ben hesitated and glanced out the viewport toward the battered planet below. "Well, the Senate has concerns about the situation on Coruscant—and the Jedi's role in what happened."

"Then I'm glad they're meeting," Luke said. "Ask Chief Dorvan to join the Masters when they come in. There's something we *all* need to discuss."

"Right away, Grand Master." Ben bowed his head to acknowledge the order, then quickly looked back up. "But don't overdo it, Dad. You look like something a wampa dragged in."

Ben retreated through the hatch without awaiting a reply.

Luke smiled anyway, grateful for his son's concern, then turned to look out on the devastation below. It was hard to know whether Thuruht's history of Abeloth's origin was entirely accurate, but Luke *did* trust the Jedi record of the encounter on Mortis—and he found it troubling. His father's refusal to become the new Keeper of the Balance had set off a terrible chain of events. All three of the Ones had died, and now the Force was out of balance.

Looking back over the last half century, it certainly seemed to Luke that there had been a shift toward chaos. Powerful forces of darkness were rising across the entire galaxy—Jacen Solo had become Darth Caedus, the Sith were returning in hordes, and Daala had emerged from the Maw. Boba Fett was now the leader of an entire world of mercenaries, and the Imperial Moffs had developed and unleashed a horrific nanoweapon.

The galaxy was tipping toward darkness before their eyes, and as far as Luke could see, the Jedi and their allies were the only ones capable of restoring the Balance. If they did not dedicate themselves *completely* to the light, all would be lost.

A gentle rasp sounded as the hatch dilated again, and Luke turned to see his niece leading a long procession of Masters into the cabin.

Completely recovered from her own injuries, Jaina looked both robust and beautiful, and there was an inner calm that Luke had not sensed in her before now.

"It's good to see you on your feet, Grand Master Skywalker," Jaina said, crossing to Luke and wrapping him in her arms. "How are you feeling?"

"Honestly, a bit weak, but it is *very* good to be back among the living."

Jaina glanced toward a chair sitting close to his bedside and said, "Maybe we should sit?"

Luke shook his head, "I'll be fine, and there are some things I would like the Council to consider before I grow tired."

Jaina's eyes flashed with concern, but she nodded. "Just don't overdo it, okay?"

Luke promised to be careful, then quickly greeted the rest of his visitors: Corran Horn, Kyle Katarn, Kyp Durron, the Yuzzem Master Barratk'l, Cilghal, Octa Ramis—the entire Jedi Council except Kam and Tionne Solusar, who were still out of touch on Shedu Maad, and Saba Sebatyne, who was lingering just outside the cabin issuing the orders to recover Raynar Thul.

Wynn Dorvan came last, looking calm, alert, and remarkably recovered from his torment at the hands of the Sith. In fact, the only noticeable aftereffects of the torture sessions were his baggy eyes, which suggested that he was having trouble sleeping, and the near-obsessive stroking of his pet chitlik's furry head, which was poking out of his tunic pocket.

"Chief Dorvan, thanks for joining us," Luke said, offering his hand. "Tell me about the situation on Coruscant."

Dorvan stopped petting his chitlik long enough to shake hands. "It's bad, but it's under control," he said. "The volcanic activity has stopped everywhere on the planet—though it will probably be years before we have even a basic survey of the damage to the undercity. The seismic activity team has identified over a hundred thousand sites that need investigation down there, and it's not always easy to tell whether we're looking for a magma well, a terrorist attack, or a building collapse."

"Tell him about the death clouds," Kyp Durron suggested.

Dorvan's face grew grim. "That's right," he said. "Clouds of ash, poisonous gas, and toxic smoke are still spreading through the undercity. We think underdweller casualties are huge. Luke, they could be in the billions already."

Luke felt a sudden wave of nausea. "I'm sorry," he said. "I wish we could have stopped Abeloth before she reached Coruscant."

"I'm just glad you stopped her when you did," Dorvan replied. "And frankly, I'm surprised you *could*. I only saw some of what she was capable of, and . . ."

Dorvan let his sentence trail off.

"We're *all* glad to be rid of her." Luke felt a shudder of uneasiness roll through the Force. He looked back to Kyp and found him glancing over at Kyle with a worried expression. Heart climbing into his throat, he asked, "We're *not* rid of her?"

"As far as we know, yes," Kyle said, motioning for Luke not to get excited. "But we had an unusual report."

"Who from?" Luke asked.

"Jedi Knights Arelis and Saar," Barratk'l replied. "They have been working in the Outer Rim, helping the slaves build free societies, yes?"

Luke nodded. "Go on."

"Three days ago, they were attacked by a tentacle," Barratk'l explained. "It materialized out of the Force and attempted to choke Jedi Saar. When Jedi Arelis ignited his lightsaber, it released Saar and turned to attack Arelis—then just dissolved."

"Sothais said it looked like it wanted to attack," Octa Ramis added. "But it couldn't hold itself together. It vanished back into the Force."

Luke's semi-healed chest wound began to ache. "Any reports since then?"

"None," Kyle confirmed. "We think it's whatever remains of Abeloth, trying to coalesce around symbols of her hatred."

"I think you're right," Luke said. He could still feel her cold tentacle writhing in the emptiness of his chest wound, a phantom memory reminding him that an entity of the Force could never be truly killed—that in a hundred years, or a hundred thousand years, she would grow strong enough to return. "We're going to need to find a way to keep tabs on her. She may not return in our lifetime, but the Jedi Order will need to be ready."

"To do what?" Kyp asked.

"To kill her," Luke replied. He was thinking of the story of his father's trip to Mortis, of the special Force-imbued dagger that had been used to kill both the Daughter and the Father. "We need to find the Mortis monolith."

"Master Skywalker, I hope you'll forgive me for asking," Dorvan said. "But when you described the story Yoda told you, didn't you say the monolith was free-floating?"

"That's right."

"Won't that make it rather difficult to find?" Dorvan asked. "Even if you know the approximate coordinates—"

"And we don't," Luke interrupted.

Dorvan's face fell as he began to comprehend the truth of what Luke was telling him—that when it came to Abeloth, there were no guarantees. She might be gone for now, but someday she would return—and if the Jedi were not ready, the Destructor would finish what she had begun.

As Luke watched the terror of this realization wash over Dorvan's face, he wanted to reach out in the Force and comfort the tormented man, to tell him that the Jedi would be there to protect him and Coruscant and the entire galaxy.

But that would have been a lie. The truth was that Luke no longer knew what the future held, whether he and the Jedi were equal to the challenges ahead of them. All that he could do—all that any mortal could do—was place his faith in himself and his fellow Jedi and do his best. The rest was up to the Force.

"I wish I could tell you that Abeloth won't be back, Chief," Luke said at last. "But the truth is, I just don't know. If the Jedi could have stopped her from coming to Coruscant the first time, we would have. I'm sorry we failed."

"It's not your fault—or the Jedi Order's," Dorvan said, waving the apology off. "*I* know that, even if the Senate doesn't."

Jaina arrived with a chair he had not asked for—a not-so-subtle hint that Luke was looking tired. Luke motioned for her to put it down in front of the viewport, but chose to remain standing for a few more moments. "So there have been rumblings about our failure to protect Coruscant?"

"More than rumblings, yes?" Barratk'l growled. "They have voted us off the planet!"

Luke turned to Kyle Katarn, no doubt the most politically astute of the Masters present, for clarification. "The Senate has asked the Jedi Order to leave Coruscant?"

Kyle nodded and glanced at Dorvan. "That's what Chief Dorvan was just telling us when you awoke," Kyle replied. "They need someone to blame for the apocalypse, and the Inner Rim Caucus was very successful in pinning it on us."

"With enough votes to override a veto, I might add," Dorvan said. A certain coolness came to his Force presence, not enough to indicate a lie—but enough to suggest that he was withholding part of the truth. "I'm afraid all those BAMR slurs *did* have an effect on the Order's reputation."

"Javis Tyrr has popped up again," Corran explained. "He's on a pirate HoloNet feed, claiming that all the destruction is the result of an out-of-control spice war between the Jedi and their rivals."

"And I'm sorry to say that the story has gotten a lot of traction, especially among the ambitious and unscrupulous," Dorvan said. "There are a lot of hungry politicians out there clamoring for the Jedi to leave Coruscant."

"We should consider the possibility that they're right." Luke sat in the chair Jaina had brought over, then added, "Not about the spice war, of course, but about leaving."

Luke was hardly surprised when the only Force aura that failed to ripple with astonishment belonged to Wynn Dorvan. The Chief studied Luke for a few moments, then finally raised his brow in an expression that seemed more curiosity than anything else.

"You would actually be willing to consider it?"

"More than willing." As Luke spoke, Saba entered the cabin and came to stand with the other Masters, dipping her head to indicate she had sent someone after Raynar. Luke nodded, then ran his gaze around the circle of Masters. "In fact, I think it's probably best for everyone to have the Jedi withdraw from Coruscant."

"*Why?*" Corran blurted. "The Sith came here because they wanted Coruscant—not because they were looking for a fight with us."

"That's true." Cilghal's tone was low and thoughtful. "But we all

know that the fight between the Jedi and the Sith is going to
continue—perhaps for centuries."

"And as long as the Jedi remain here, Coruscant will be a battlefield," Luke agreed. "If we leave, the Sith can't hurt *us* by hurting Coruscant."

"That doesn't mean they'll leave Coruscant alone," Kyp objected.
"It's still the capital of the Galactic Alliance. They'll keep coming after
it."

"But not with everything they have," Kyle said, also warming to
Luke's point. "As long as the Jedi are somewhere else, the Sith need to
worry about a flank attack. It will change their tactics—and it will divert their attention *away* from Coruscant."

"The Galactic Alliance isn't exactly defenseless without us," Jaina
said, placing a hand on the back of Luke's chair. "They have the largest
military force in the galaxy. Chief Dorvan could propose a resolution
that *any* attempt to infiltrate the Galactic Alliance would be taken as an
act of open war. The Sith would be very reluctant to come after Coruscant again."

"I think I can arrange that." Dorvan's voice was not quite smug,
but it *was* relieved, and Luke knew that the Chief was getting exactly
what he wanted: the best thing for the Galactic Alliance. He caught
Luke's eye, then raised a questioning brow. "Especially if I can sell it as
the price of the Jedi leaving Coruscant?"

Luke nodded. "Of course," he said. "As long as you don't mind
placing a couple of Jedi in your office to keep watch for Sith infiltrators."

"They wouldn't need to be obvious, would they?"

"It would probably work better if they *weren't*," Kyle said.

Dorvan actually smiled. "Then I think we have an agreement."

"Not quite yet." Luke raised a hand to hold Dorvan at bay, then
glanced around the circle of Masters. "Are we agreed?"

The Masters gave their consent one after the other, some with more
certainty than others, but all in honest agreement. When Luke came to
the newest Master, Jaina turned and looked out over the planet for a
long time, then finally nodded.

"Agreed," she said. "It will be hard living somewhere other than

Coruscant—but not as hard as seeing it torn apart in battle after battle."

Dorvan exhaled in relief, then stepped over to Luke's chair. "Thank you for not making this difficult," he said. "It's not that we're ungrateful for all the Jedi have done and sacrificed, but with a whole world of Sith out there . . ."

He let the sentence trail off, no doubt struggling to find the words to say what everyone in the room knew—that Coruscant had suffered enough.

"There's no need to explain." Luke rose and took Dorvan's hand with genuine affection. "You're going to be one of history's great Chiefs of State. Go with the Force, my friend."

Chapter Thirty-six

IN THE END, LANDO SUGGESTED A COMPROMISE AND ARRANGED TO RE-
place the *Falcon*'s missing cockpit with a customized replica. For Han,
it still had the same seating arrangement and control configuration
that had come to feel like an extension of his own body. For Leia, the
yokes were mounted on telescoping shafts, so she wouldn't need to
hold her arms at shoulder height whenever she took the helm. And the
slave throttles had been moved closer to the copilot's station, to accommodate her shorter reach.

But the best features by far were the new seats. While they looked
like the same basic models that had come stock on the old YT-1300,
they were fitted with the latest in crew-comfort systems—body-
molding flow-foam, built-in heaters and massagers, integrated pilot-
alertness sensors that shook, buzzed, or even shocked at the first sign
of slackening posture. In short, a pilot could spend an entire duty shift
behind the yoke without growing sore or inattentive—and Han was
beginning to think that was a very good thing.

The *Falcon* was sitting on the flight deck of the Super Star Destroyer *Megador*'s executive hangar, looking out upon an entire brigade of Void Jumpers in full-dress uniform. They had been standing at parade rest for an hour, and, judging by the alternating bursts of tense murmurings and nervous laughter rolling up the access corridor, they were going to be standing there for another hour.

Han shrugged and tried not to feel guilty. The elite honor guard had been Gavin Darklighter's idea, a farewell salute and thank-you gift for all the Solos had done for the cause of galactic freedom over the last five decades. It was also a subtle reminder that just because the Solo family would be living in another part of the galaxy, they still had friends in the Galactic Alliance—and Coruscant would always be their home.

But Han had reasons of his own for wishing Leia would speed things up back there. First, it had been a long time since he had decked himself out in high boots and full first-class Bloodstripes, and he had forgotten how hot and itchy his formal pants got when he sat around waiting too long. Second, his wife and daughter weren't the only ones who were nervous, and the longer they took getting ready, the more likely it became that he would need to change his shirt.

And a lot of people were waiting on them. That *always* made Han edgy.

A flight of StealthXs flashed past the hangar mouth, their cruciform profiles silhouetted against Coruscant's pearly brightness for only an instant before they broke formation. They peeled off in ten different directions, moving so fast that Han would not have been able to count their number had he not already known who they were: the Ten Knights, heading out to find the Mortis monolith and the Force-imbued dagger that had killed the Ones. It was a lonely mission that Han did not envy the young Jedi. What little they knew about the monolith was the stuff of legend, and if Luke was right about Abeloth continuing to linger in the Force, one day the future of the galaxy would hang on their success.

Once the last starfighter had vanished from sight, Han wished them a heavy dose of his Corellian luck, then tried to sneak a peek at the control panel chrono.

Of course, Allana caught him.

"Just be patient, Grandpa." Dressed in an elegant white gown and wearing a gem-studded tiara in her golden-red hair, she looked like the beautiful young princess she was. "They can't start without us, you know."

"I know." Han turned to face his granddaughter. "Allana, are you going to be okay with this? I mean, everyone knowing who you really are?"

Allana cocked her head, and Han thought he saw a flash of hope in her eyes—a flash that vanished as quickly as it had appeared. "Do I have a choice?" she asked.

"Not really," Han admitted. "Now that the Sith know, it's only a matter of time until *everyone* knows."

"That's what I thought," she said. "It doesn't take a genius to figure out they won't keep the secret for long. And when your secret is about to be exposed, Mom says it's better to reveal everything yourself."

"That's right," Han agreed. "So it looks like it's your idea."

Allana smiled. "Bluffing rule number one: Always *look* like you're in control—"

"—and you'll *be* in control," Han finished. He paused, sighed, and then spoke in a quiet voice. "I guess it's official."

"What?" Allana asked.

"I've taught you everything I know."

Allana frowned. *"Everything?"* she asked. "That's pretty hard to believe."

"Well, everything that matters," Han confirmed. He let his tone grow serious. "Those are the two secrets to life, Allana. Keeping it simple, and looking like you're in control."

Allana considered this for a moment. "And it took you *how* long to teach those to me?"

Han shrugged, then smiled. "Keeping it simple is harder than you think." He reached down to scratch behind the ears of Allana's pet nexu and was rewarded with a raspy rumble of contentment. "You're *sure* Anji's not going to have a problem with this?"

"Anji's smarter than you think, Grandpa. She understands that this is a big deal."

"That's what I'm worried about," Han said. "She might take the excitement the wrong way."

Allana let out a weary sigh. "Is anyone going to be shooting blaster bolts at her?"

"Let's hope not," Han said. "What about the lightsabers?"

"Is anyone going to swing one at her?"

"I doubt it," Han said.

"Then everything's going to be fine," Allana said. "Trust me."

Han felt a sudden pang of joy and pride. "Well, if you're going to put it that way, I guess I have no choice."

Allana shot him one of her lopsided smiles, then said, "I was *wondering* if you were ever going to figure that out!"

Before Han could protest, Anji's head popped up and turned toward the rear of the flight deck, then C-3PO came clumping out of the access corridor.

"Master Solo asked me to tell you that she's ready."

"About time!" Han fired up the repulsorlift drives. "I was beginning to think she was changing her mind."

Out on the flight deck, Gavin Darklighter barked an order, and the Void Jumper brigade came to attention and saluted. Han flashed the *Falcon*'s landing lights in reply, then engaged the repulsorlifts and eased out of the executive hangar. He swung around beneath the *Megador*'s bow and commed for permission to depart the Super Star Destroyer's vicinity.

To his surprise, it was Admiral Bwua'tu himself who replied. "Permission granted, with our greatest reluctance and gratitude," he said. "Safe journeys, *Millennium Falcon*."

As the *Falcon* sped across the handful of kilometers that separated the *Megador* from the *Dragon Queen II*, Jaina was surprised to sense herself growing utterly calm. With the entire Jedi Order relocating to its secret base on Shedu Maad and the Balance itself tipping ever deeper into darkness, she had expected to experience some amount of doubt today—or at least a little tingle of uncertainty.

But she didn't. The closer the *Falcon* drew to the *Dragon Queen II*, the more confident Jaina grew that she had made the right choice, that she was following the will of the Force in what she was preparing to do.

It was a wonderful feeling.

Her stomach fluttered as the *Falcon* decelerated on final approach. A moment later a series of loud thumps sounded from the lower hull, and the old transport groaned and hissed as it spun around and settled onto its landing struts inside the Queen Mother's Privy Hangar.

Jaina's mother reached over and squeezed her hand. "Ready?"

"I've never been readier for anything in my life." Jaina straightened her dress—she had gone with a traditional white gown with a long train—then took the bouquet her mother was holding. "And I've kept him waiting long enough, don't you think?"

Her mother cracked a smile. "It never hurts to be sure."

Allana and Anji came running out of the access tunnel, Allana holding up her skirts so she didn't trip, Anji freshly shampooed and looking about as cuddly as a four-eyed feline with a mouthful of fangs *could* look. Allana took one look at the bouquet in Jaina's hand and smiled. She retrieved the basket of rozal petals she would be carrying, then took her place in front of Jaina.

"Anji, on my left," Allana ordered.

Anji pounced instantly to her master's left side and stood motionless, now nearly as tall as Allana herself.

Jaina's father emerged from the access corridor next, looking roguishly handsome in his high boots and Bloodstripes. He went to her mother and kissed her on the cheek, then stepped back and flicked a tear from beneath his eye.

"I guess you couldn't talk her out of it?"

Her mother's eyes grew wide. *"Han!"*

He laughed, then turned to Jaina and offered his arm. "You know I'm only sore because he used to be the Emperor, right?"

"He was a Head of State, Dad, not the Emperor," Jaina said, taking his arm. "And he's over that."

"He better be," he said, smiling wider than ever now. "I won't have any daughter of mine raising little Imperials."

"Not that it's *your* choice," Jaina replied wryly. "But don't you think you're getting ahead of yourself?"

"Yeah, Grandpa—stop rushing them," Allana said, turning to look up at her grandfather. "They're not even married yet."

His brow shot up. "They *aren't?*" He turned to R2-D2, who was standing next to the boarding ramp control panel, and pointed a finger at the little astromech droid. "Maybe it's time to do something about that."

R2-D2 let out a joyful tweedle, then plugged into the droid socket and lowered the boarding ramp.

"Wait!" C-3PO objected, rushing past the procession toward the ramp. "I'm not in position!"

R2-D2 responded with a chastening whistle, causing C-3PO to stop at the top of the ramp and turn toward him.

"Well, it certainly isn't *my* fault!" he objected. "You lowered the ramp—"

The rest of the objection was drowned out by the fanfare of a hundred Hapan long-horns. Realizing that he was about to miss his cue, C-3PO turned and plunked to the bottom of the boarding ramp. From her vantage point inside the passenger cabin, Jaina could not see much more than the deck upon which he emerged. But she could sense through the Force that there were hundreds of people gathered just out of sight, all looking expectantly toward the *Falcon.*

C-3PO turned away from the ship, then spoke in a loud, regal voice that echoed across a cavernous space.

"Your Royal Majesty, ladies and gentlemen, may I present the mother of the bride, Jedi Knight, former Chief of State of the New Republic, and Princess of Alderaan, Leia Organa Solo."

Again there came a loud fanfare, this time accompanied by the applause of hundreds. Jaina's mother raised her chin and descended the boarding ramp, looking both elegant and beautiful in the plain white Jedi robe she had chosen for the ceremony.

When she reached the landing deck, her brother stepped into view and offered his arm to her, lingering long enough to peek up the ramp. Even three months after awakening from his coma—or healing trance, or whatever it had been—Luke still looked pale and weak, and his pain was a constant dull ache in the Force. But his suffering did not diminish from the warmth of his smile, and Jaina could feel how happy he was for her.

Once Luke and Leia had turned away and started up the aisle,

C-3PO announced, "The first heir to the Hapan Throne, the Chume'da Allana Djo Solo."

The long-horns sounded again, this time almost deafening in their volume, and the hangar erupted in thunderous applause.

Allana cringed, then let out a heavy sigh. "I guess I'm going to have to get used to that."

"Looks like it, kid," her grandfather said. "But there *is* a bright side."

Allana craned her neck to look back up at him. "Really?"

"Sure," he said. "You'll get to spend more time with your mother. And when you're on Shedu Maad training, nobody's going to applaud. They'll just yell."

Allana smiled. "Thanks, Grandpa," she said. "That's going to be a relief."

With that, she clicked at Anji to follow, then started down the ramp sprinkling rozal petals in Jaina's path.

Once she had vanished from view, C-3PO announced, "Your Royal Majesty, ladies and gentleman, may I present the bride, Jedi Master Jaina Solo, and her father, a former general—"

The rest of the introduction was drowned out by the fanfare of the long-horns and applause. Jaina could feel her father's pride warm in the Force, glowing almost golden in his aura, and not for the first time she wondered if his legendary luck might not be due to just a touch of Force sensitivity. He squeezed her hand and smiled down at her, then cocked a brow.

"What do you say, *Master* Solo?" he asked. "Is it time to make Jagged Fel the happiest man in the galaxy?"

Jaina nodded, and together they descended to the landing deck, where Kyp Durron was waiting at the end of a long double row of Jedi. Across from him, standing in a place of honor reserved for close friends who risked their necks ferrying Jedi into the Maw and who found ways to make impossible repairs to the *Falcon,* were Lando Calrissian and his family.

Jaina felt Kyp reach out in the Force. The two rows of Jedi raised their lightsabers and ignited them, forming a tent of crackling color over the aisle through which Jaina and her father were to pass.

At the other end stood Jagged Fel, dressed in a dark civilian tunic and trousers, looking back toward Jaina with a smile as wide as his face. She returned his smile and, almost dragging her father along, started up the aisle to marry the man she loved.

The darkness was eternal, all-powerful, unchangeable.

She had stared into it for too many years, alone and unblinking, determined that it would not take her.

Now it never would.

Now she was lighting a candle.

About the Author

TROY DENNING is the *New York Times* bestselling author of the *Star Wars: Fate of the Jedi* novels *Abyss, Vortex,* and *Apocalypse; Star Wars: Tatooine Ghost; Star Wars: The New Jedi Order: Star by Star;* the *Star Wars: Dark Next* trilogy: *The Joiner King, The Unseen Queen,* and *The Swarm War;* and *Star Wars: Legacy of the Force: Tempest, Inferno,* and *Invincible*—as well as *Pages of Pain, Beyond the High Road, The Summoning,* and many other novels. A former game designer and editor, he lives in western Wisconsin with his wife, Andria.

Read on for an excerpt from
Star Wars®: X-Wing: Mercy Kill
by Aaron Allston
Coming soon from Del Rey Books

RYVESTER, MERIDIAN SECTOR
13 ABY (31 YEARS AGO)

IMPERIAL ADMIRAL KOSH TERADOC PAUSED—IRRITATED AND SELF-
conscious—just outside the entryway into the club. His garment, a
tradesman's jumpsuit, was authentic, bought at a used-clothes stall in
a poverty-stricken neighborhood. And the wig that covered his
military-cut blond hair with a mop of lank, disarrayed brown hair was
perfect. But his *posture*—he couldn't seem to shake off his upright military bearing, no matter how hard he tried. Loosening his shoulders,
slumping, slouching . . . nothing worked for more than a few seconds.

"You're doing fine, Admiral." That was one of his bodyguards,
whispering. "Try . . . try *smiling*."

Teradoc forced his mouth into a smile and held it that way. He took
the final step up to the doors; they slid aside, emitting a wash of
warmer air and the sounds of voices, music, clinking glasses.

He and his guards moved into the club's waiting area. Its dark walls were decorated with holos advertising various brands of drinks; the moving images promised romance, social success, and wealth to patrons wise enough to choose the correct beverage. And they promised these things to nonhumans as well as humans.

One of Teradoc's guards, taller and more fit than he was, but dressed like him, kept close. The other three held back as though they constituted a different party of patrons.

The seater approached. A brown Chadra-Fan woman who stood only as tall as Teradoc's waist, she wore a gold hostess' gown, floor-length but exposing quite a lot of glossy fur.

Teradoc held up three fingers. He enunciated slowly so she would understand. "Another will be coming. Another man, joining us. You understand?"

Her mouth turned up in the faintest of smiles. "I do." Her voice was light, sweet, and perhaps just a touch mocking. "Are you the party joining Captain Hachat?"

"Um . . . yes."

"He's already here. This way, please." She turned and led them through broad, open double doors into the main room.

Teradoc followed. He felt heat in his cheeks. The little Chadra-Fan—had she actually *condescended* to him? He wondered if he should arrange an appropriate punishment for her.

The main room was cavernous, most of its innumerable tables occupied even at this late hour. As they worked their way across, everything became worse for Teradoc. The music and the din of conversation were louder. And the smells—less than a quarter of the patrons were human. Teradoc saw horned Devaronians, furry Bothans, diminutive Sullustans, enormous, green-skinned Gamorreans, and more, and he fancied he could smell every one of them. And their alcohol.

"You're upright again, sir. You might try slouching."

Teradoc growled at his guard but complied.

There was one last blast of music from the upraised stage, and then the band, most of them nonhuman, rose to the crowd's applause. They retreated behind the stage curtain.

Moments later, the noise of the audience, hundreds of voices, changed—lowered, became expectant in tone. A new act filed out onstage. Six Gamorrean men, dressed in nothing but loincloths, their skin oiled and gleaming, moved out and arrayed themselves in a chevron-shaped formation. Recorded dance music, heavy on drums and wood-winds, blasted out from the stage's sound system.

The Gamorreans began moving to the music. They flexed, shim-mied, strutted in unison. A shrill cry of appreciation rose from Gamor-rean women in the audience, and from others, as well.

Teradoc shuddered and vowed to sit with his back to the stage.

Then they were at their table, only a few meters from the stage. A human man sat there already. Of medium height and muscular, he was young, with waist-length red hair in a braid. Costume jewelry, pol-ished copper inset with black stones, was woven into the braid. He wore a long-sleeved tunic decorated with blobs of color of every hue, mismatched and discordant; it clashed with his military-style black pants and boots. He stood as Teradoc and his guard arrived.

"Captain Hachat?"

"The one and only." Hachat sat again and indicated the guard. "Who's your friend? He looks like a hundred kilos of preserved meat."

The Chadra-Fan seater, satisfied that she had discharged her duty, offered a little bow. "Your server will be here in a few moments." She turned and headed back to her station.

Teradoc glared after her and seated himself, facing away from the stage. He waited until his guard was in a chair before continuing. "Your messenger hinted at names. I want to hear them now . . . and to see proof."

Hachat nodded. "Of course. But, first—would it help you to stop smiling? It looks like it's hurting your face."

"Um . . . yes." Teradoc relaxed, realized that his cheek muscles were indeed aching. He glanced around, noted the postures of many of the patrons around him, and slid down a little in his chair to match their slouches.

"Much better." Hachat sipped his drink, a poisonous-looking yel-low concoction that glowed from within. There were two glasses, mostly empty but with a similar-looking residue at the bottom on the table. "All right. I run a private space naval operation specializing in covert operations, especially retrievals."

Teradoc suppressed a sigh. *Why can't they ever just say, "I'm a pirate, a smuggler, a low-life piece of scum with something to sell?" Honesty would be so refreshing.*

"We recently found a prize vessel . . . one whose value could enable us to retire in luxury."

Teradoc shrugged. "Go on."

"The Palace of Piethet Brighteyes."

"I *thought* that was what your messenger was hinting at. But it's preposterous. In the centuries since it disappeared, the Palace has never been sighted, never reported. It will never be found."

Hachat grinned at him. "But it has been. Abandoned, intact, unplundered, in an area of your sector well away from settlements or trade routes."

"If you'd found it, you'd be selling off its jewels, its furnishings, all those paintings. Through a fence. Yet you come to me. You're lying."

"Here's the truth, Admiral. The vessel's antipersonnel defenses are still active. I lost a dozen men just getting into a secondary vehicle bay, where I retrieved one artifact and some lesser gems. Oh, yes, I could fire missiles at the palace until it cracked . . . but I would prefer to lose half its contents to a worthwhile partner than to explosions and hard vacuum. At least I'd get a partner and some good will out of it."

Teradoc rubbed at his temple. The *boom-boom-boom* from the sound system on stage behind him was giving him a headache. He returned his attention to Hachat. "Don't use my rank. Don't speak my name here."

"Whatever you want." Hachat took another sip of his drink. "You have access to Imperial Intelligence resources, the best slicers and intrusion experts in the galaxy. They could get past those defenses . . . and make us both rich."

"In your original message and tonight, you mentioned an artifact."

"I have it with me. A show of faith, just as you proposed."

"Show me."

"Tell your bruiser not to panic; I'm only reaching for a comlink."

Teradoc glanced at his guard, gave a slight nod.

Hachat pulled free a small device clipped to his shirt collar and pressed a button on the side. "All right. It's coming."

They didn't have to wait long. A meter-tall Sullustan male in the blue-and-cream livery of the club's servers approached, awkwardly carrying a gray flimsiplast box nearly as tall as himself and half as wide and deep. He set it on the table beside Hachat's empty glasses. Hachat tipped him with a credcoin and the Sullustan withdrew.

Teradoc glanced at his guard. The man stood, pulled open the box's top flaps, and reached in. He lifted out a glittering, gleaming, translucent statuette, nearly the full height of the box, and set it down in the center of the table. Hachat took the empty box and set it on the floor behind his chair.

The statuette was in the form of a human male standing atop a short pedestal. He was young, with aristocratic features, wearing a knee-length robe of classical design. And it was all made of gemstones cunningly fitted together like jigsaw puzzle pieces, the joins so artful that Teradoc could barely detect them.

All the color in the piece came from the stones used to make it. Cloudy diamond-like gems provided the white skin of the face, neck, arms, and legs. Ruby-like stones gave the eyes a red gleam. The robe was sapphire-blue, and the man's golden-yellow hair, unless Teradoc guessed incorrectly, was inlaid rows of multicolored crystals. The pedestal was the only portion not translucent; it was made up of glossy black stones.

The piece was exquisite. Teradoc felt his heart begin to race.

There were *oohs* and *aahs* from surrounding tables. Teradoc noted belatedly that he and Hachat were now the object of much attention from patrons around them.

Hachat grinned at the onlookers and raised his voice to be heard over the music. "I have a cargo bay full of these. They go on sale tomorrow in Statz Market. Twelve Imperial credits for a little one, thirty for a big one like this. Stop by tomorrow." Then he turned his attention back to Teradoc.

The admiral gave him a little smile, a real one. "Thus you convince them that this piece is valueless, so no one will attack us outside in an attempt to steal it."

"Thus I do. Now, are *you* convinced?"

"Almost." Teradoc reached up for his own comlink, activated it, and spoke into it. "Send Cheems."

Hachat frowned at him. "Who's Cheems?"

"Someone who can make this arrangement come true. Without him, there is no deal."

A moment later, two men approached. One was another of Teradoc's artificially scruffy guards. The other was human, his skin fair, his hair and beard dark with some signs of graying. He was lean, well-dressed in a suit. Despite the formality of his garments, the man seemed far more comfortable in this environment than Teradoc or the guards.

His duty done, the escort turned and moved to a distant table. At Teradoc's gesture, the man in the suit seated himself between the admiral and Hachat.

A server arrived. She was a dark-skinned human woman, dressed, like the Sullustan man had been, in a loose-fitting pantsuit of blue and cream. Her fitness and her broad smile were very much to Teradoc's taste.

She played that smile across each of them in turn. "Drinks, gentlemen?"

Hachat shook his head. The man in the suit and the guard did likewise. But Teradoc gave the server a smile in return. "A salty gaffer, please."

"You want a real bug in that or a candy bug?"

"Candy, please."

Once the server was gone, Hachat gave the new arrival a look. "Who is this?"

The man spoke, his voice dry and thin. "I am Mulus Cheems. I am a scientist specializing in crystalline materials . . . and a historian in the field of jewelry."

Teradoc cleared his throat. "Less talk, more action."

Cheems sighed. Then from a coat pocket, he retrieved a small device. It was a gray square, six centimeters on a side, one centimeter thick. He pressed a small button on one side.

A square lens popped out from within the device. A bright light shone from the base of the lens. Words began scrolling in red across a small black screen inset just above the button.

Cheems leaned over to peer at the statuette, holding the lens before his right eye. He spoke as if to an apprentice. "The jewels used to fabricate this piece are valuable but not unusual. These could have been acquired on a variety of worlds at any time in the last several centuries. But the technique . . . definitely Vilivian. His workshop, maybe his own hand."

Teradoc frowned. "Who?"

"Vilivian. A Hapan gemwright whose intricately fitted gems enjoyed a brief but influential vogue a few centuries back. His financial records indicated several sales to Piethet Brighteyes." Cheems moved the lens up from the statuette's chest to his face. "Interesting. Adegan crystals for the red eyes. And the coating that maintains the piece's structural integrity . . . not a polymer. Microfused diamond dust. No longer employed because of costs compared to polymers. Beautiful, absolutely beautiful." He sat back and, with a press of the button, snapped the lens back into its casing.

Teradoc felt a flash of impatience. "Well?"

"Well? Oh—is it authentic? Yes. Absolutely. I believe it's the piece titled *Light and Dark*. Worth a Moff's ransom."

Teradoc sat back and stared at the statuette. The Palace of Piethet Brighteyes—with that fortune in hand, he could resign his commission, buy an entire planetary system, and settle into a life of luxury, far away from the struggles between the Empire and the New Republic. A warmth began to suffuse his body, a realization that his future had just become very, very pleasant.

The dark-skinned server returned and set Teradoc's drink before him. He smiled at her and paid with a credcoin worth twenty times the cost of the drink. He could afford to be generous. "Keep it."

"Thank you, sir." She swept the coin away to some unknown pocket and withdrew—but not too far. It was clear to Teradoc that she was hovering in case he needed special attention.

Teradoc glanced back at Hachat. "I'm convinced."

"Excellent." Hachat extended a hand. "Partners."

"Well . . . we need to negotiate our percentages. I was thinking that I'd take a hundred percent."

Hachat withdrew his hand. Far from looking surprised or offended, he smiled. "Do you Imperial officer types study the same 'How to Backstab' manual? You are definitely doing it by the book."

"Captain, you're going to experience quite a lot of enhanced interrogation in the near future. You'll endure a lot of pain before cracking and telling me where the palace is. If you choose to antagonize me, I might just double that pain."

"What I don't get . . ." Hatchat said, shaking his head wonderingly, ". . . is this whole Grand Admiral Thrawn thing. Every hopped-up junior naval officer tries to be like him. Elegant, inscrutable . . . and an art lover. Being an art lover doesn't make you a genius, you know."

"That's an extra week of torture right there."

"Plus, unlike Thrawn, you're about as impressive as a Gungan with his underwear full of stinging insects."

"Three weeks. And at this moment, my guard has a blaster leveled at your gut under the table."

"Oh, my." Hachat glanced at the guard. He raised his hands to either side of his face, indicating surrender. "*Pleeeeease* don't shoot me, foul-smelling man. Please, oh please, oh pleasepleaseplease."

Teradoc stared at him, perplexed.

On stage, the porcine Gamorrean dancers moved through a new rotation, which brought the slenderest of them up to the forward position. He was slender only by Gamorrean standards, weighing in at a touch under 150 kilos, but he moved well and there were good muscles to be glimpsed under his body fat.

With the rest of the troupe, he executed a half-turn, which left them facing the rear of the stage, and followed up with a series of fanny shakes, each accompanied by a lateral hop. Then they began a slow turn back toward the crowd, the movement accentuated by a series of belly rolls that had the Gamorrean women in the crowd yelling.

As, with a final belly roll, he once again faced forward, the slenderest dancer could see Hachat's table . . . and Hachat with his hands up.

He felt a touch of lightheadedness as adrenaline hit his system. Things were a go.

Near Hachat's table, the dark-skinned server moved unobtrusively toward Teradoc.

The Gamorrean dancer, whose name was Piggy, stopped his dance, threw back his head, and shrilled a few words in the Gamorrean tongue: "It's a raid! Run!"

From elsewhere in the room, the cry was repeated in Basic and other languages. Piggy noted approvingly that the fidelity of those shouts was so good that few people, if any, would realize they were recordings.

Alarm rippled in an instant through the crowd, through the dancers.

Suddenly all the Gamorreans in the place were heaving themselves to their feet, sometimes knocking their table over in panicky haste, and the non-Gamorrean patrons followed suit. Confused, Teradoc took his attention from Hachat for a moment and turned to look across the sea of tables.

There were *booms* from the room's two side exits. Both doors blew in, blasted off their rails by what had to have been shaped charges. Tall men in Imperial Navy special forces armor charged in through those doors.

A flash of motion to Teradoc's right drew his attention. He saw the dark-skinned server approach and lash out in a perfectly executed side kick. Her sandaled foot snaked in just beneath the tabletop. Even over the tumult in the room, Teradoc heard the *crack* that had to be his guard's hand or wrist breaking. The guard's blaster pistol flew from his hand, thumped into Teradoc's side, and fell to the floor.

The server stayed balanced on her planted foot, cocked her kicking leg again, and lashed out once more, this time connecting with the guard's jaw as he turned to look at her. The guard wobbled and slid from his chair.

Then the server dived in the opposite direction, rolling as she hit the floor, vanishing out of Teradoc's sight under the next table.

Teradoc grabbed for the blaster on the floor. He got it in his hand.

Hachat hadn't lost his smile. He turned to face the glasses on the table and shouted directly at them: "Boom boy!"

One of the drink glasses, mostly empty, erupted in thick yellow smoke. Teradoc, as he straightened and brought the blaster up, found himself engulfed in a haze that smelled of alcohol and more bitter chemicals. It stung his eyes. Now he could not see as far as the other side of the table.

He stood and warily circled the table . . . and, by touch, found only empty chairs. Hachat was gone. Cheems was gone.

The statuette was still there. Teradoc grabbed it, then stumbled away from the table, out from within the choking smoke.

While the dancers and patrons ran, Piggy stood motionless on stage and narrated. He subvocalized into his throat implant, which rendered his squealy, grunty Gamorrean pronunciation into comprehensible Basic. The implant also transmitted his words over a specific comm frequency. "Guards at tables twelve and forty maintaining discipline and scanning for targets. But they've got none. Shalla, stay low, table forty's looking in your direction."

Small voices buzzed in the tiny comm receiver in his ear. "Heard that, Piggy." "Got twelve, twelve is down." "Forty's in my sights."

Now the guard who had brought Cheems to Teradoc approached that table once more. This time he had a blaster pistol in one hand. With his free hand, he shoved patrons out of his way. He reached the verge of the yellow smoke, then began circling around it, looking for targets.

He found some. His head snapped over to the right. Piggy glanced in that direction and saw Hachat and Cheems almost at the ruined doorway in the wall. The guard raised his pistol, waiting for a clear shot.

Well, it was time to go anyway. Piggy ran the three steps to the stage's edge and hurled himself forward. He cleared the nearest table and came down on Teradoc's guard, smashing him to the floor, breaking the man's bones. The guard's blaster skidded across the floor and was lost, masked by yellow smoke and patrons' fast-moving legs.

Piggy stood. He'd felt the impact, too, but had been prepared for it; and he was well padded by muscle and fat. Nothing in him had broken. He looked at the guard and was satisfied that the unconscious man posed no more danger.

Now he heard Hachat's voice across the comm. "We have the package. Extract. Call in when you get to the exit."

Most of the bar patrons, those who weren't running in blind panic, were surging toward and through the bar's main entrance, which inexplicably had no Imperial Navy troopers near it. Piggy turned toward the exit Hachat and Cheems had used. That doorway did have a forbidding-looking Imperial trooper standing beside it. Heedless of the danger posed by the soldier, Piggy shoved his way through toppled furniture and scrambling patrons. He made it to the door.

The armored trooper merely nodded at him. "Nice moves, Dancer Boy."

Piggy growled at him, then passed through the door, which still smoked from the charge that had breached it.

Once in the dimly lit service corridor beyond, Piggy headed toward the building's rear service exit. "Piggy exiting." He reached the door at the end of the corridor. It slid open for him and he stepped outside into cooler night air.

"Freeze or I'll shoot!" The bellow came from just beside his right ear. It was deep, male, ferocious.

Piggy winced, held up his hands. Unarmed and nearly naked, his eyes not yet adjusted to the nighttime darkness, he didn't stand a chance.

Then his assailant chuckled. "Got you again."

Piggy turned, glaring.

Situated by the door, armed not with a blaster but with a bandolier of grenades, stood a humanoid, tall as but not nearly as hairy as a Wookiee. The individual was lean for his two-meters-plus height, brown-furred, his face long, his big square teeth bared in a triumphant smile. He wore a black traveler's robe; it gapped to show the brown jumpsuit and bandolier beneath.

Piggy reached up to grab and tug at the speaker's whiskers. "Not funny, Runt."

"Plenty funny."

"I'll get you for that."

"You keep saying that. It never happens."

Piggy sighed and released his friend. His eyes were now more adjusted. In the gloom, decorated with distant lights like a continuation of the starfield above, he could make out the start of the marina's dock, the glowrods outlining old-fashioned watercraft in their berths, not far away.

Much nearer was the team's extraction vehicle, an old airspeeder—

a flat-bed model with oversized repulsors and motivators. It was active, floating a meter above the ground on motivator thrust. Signs on the sides of its cab proclaimed it to be a tug, the sort sent out to rescue the watercraft of the rich and hapless when their own motivators conked out. There were sturdy winches affixed in the bed.

In the cab, a Devaronian man sat at the pilot's controls. He turned his horned head and flashed Piggy a sharp-toothed smile through the rear viewport. Cheems and Hachat were already situated in the cab beside him.

Piggy moved up to the speeder and clambered into the cargo bed. The vehicle rocked a little under his weight. He looked around for the bundle that should have been waiting for him, but it was nowhere to be seen. He sighed and sat facing the rear, his back to the cab. Then he stared at the club's back door, at Runt situated beside it. "Come on, come on."

The door slid open long enough to admit the dark-skinned server. Unmolested by Runt, she ran to the airspeeder, vaulted into the bed, and settled down beside Piggy. "Shalla exited." She glanced at Piggy. "Weren't you supposed to have a robe here?"

He knew his reply sounded long-suffering. "Yes. And who took it? Who decided to leave me almost naked here as I wait? I'm betting I'll never know."

Shalla nodded, clearly used to the ways of her comrades. "You made yourself a lot of fans tonight. Those Gamorrean ladies were screaming their brains out. And not just the Gamorreans. You could have had so much action this evening."

Piggy rolled his eyes. As far as he was concerned, those Gamorrean women had no brains to scream out. Augmented by biological experiments when he was a child, Piggy was the only genius of his kind. And unlike some, he could not bear the thought of pairing up with someone whose intelligence was far, far below his.

So he was alone.

Hachat turned to glare back through the cab's rear viewport. "Kell . . ."

Piggy heard the man's response in his ear. "Busy, Boss."

"Kell, do I have to come in there after you?"

"Busy." Then the door slid open for Kell, the armored trooper who had let Piggy pass. He fell through the doorway, slamming to the ground on his back, one of Teradoc's guards on top of him.

Runt reached down, grabbed the guard by the shoulder and neck, and pulled, peeling the man off as though he were the unresisting rind of a fruit. Hent shook the guard, and kept shaking him as Kell rose and trotted to the speeder.

By the time Kell was settling in beside Shalla, the guard was completely limp. Runt dropped him and regarded him quizzically for a second. Then he pulled two grenades free from his bandolier. He twisted a dial on each, then stepped over to stand in front of the door. When it slid open for him, he lobbed them through the doorway. He waited there as they detonated, making little noise but filling the corridor entirely with thick black smoke. Then he joined the others, settling in at the rear of the speeder bed, facing Piggy. "Runt exited. Team One complete."

Cheems expected them to blast their way as far as possible from the Imperial Navy base and the city that surrounded it. But they flew only a few hundred meters along the marina boundary. Then they abandoned their speeder in a dark, grassy field just outside the marina gates and hurried on foot along old-fashioned wooden docks. Soon afterward, they boarded a long, elegant water yacht in gleaming Imperial-style white.

Within a few minutes, they had backed the yacht out of its berth, maneuvered it into the broad waters of the bay, and set a course for the open sea beyond.

Eight in all, they assembled on the stern deck, which was decorated with comfortable, weather-resistant furnishings, a bar, and a grill. Cheems sat on a puffy chair and watched, bewildered, as his rescuers continued their high-energy preparations.

The Devaronian, whom the others called Elassar, broke top-grade bantha steaks out of a cold locker and began arraying them on the grill. Piggy the Gamorrean located and donned a white robe, then began mixing drinks. Kell shed his armor, dumping it and his Imperial weapons over the side. Hachat disappeared below decks for two minutes and reemerged, his hair now short and brown, his clothes innocuous. Runt shed his traveler's robe and set up a small but expensive-looking portable computer array on an end table. A yellow-skinned human man who had not been on the speeder joined Kell and stripped off his own Imperial armor, throwing it overboard. Shalla merely stretched out on a lounge chair and smiled as she watched the men work.

Cheems finally worked up the courage to speak. "Um . . . excuse me . . . not that I'm complaining . . . but could I get some sort of summary on what just happened?"

Hachat grinned and settled onto a couch beside Cheems's chair. "My name isn't Hachat. It's Garik Loran. Captain Loran, New Republic Intelligence. Runt, do you have the tracker signal yet?"

"Working on it."

"Put it up on the main monitor, superimpose the local map."

No less confused, Cheems interrupted. "Garik Loran? *Face* Loran, the boy actor?"

Face did not quite suppress a wince. "That was a long time ago. But yes."

"I love *The Life Day Murders*. I have a copy on my datapad."

"Yeah . . . Anyway, what do you think this was all about?"

"Getting me out of the Admiral's hands, I suppose." Cheems frowned, reconstructing the sequence of events in his mind. "Two days ago, as I was being led from my laboratory to my prison quarters, I felt a nasty sting in my back. I assume you shot me with some sort of communications device. Little buzzy voices vibrating in my shoulder blade."

Face nodded. He gestured toward the man with yellow skin. "That's Bettin. He's our sniper and exotic-weapons expert. He tagged you from a distance of nearly a kilometer, which was as close as we could get to you."

Bettin waved, cheerful. "Damned hard shot, too. Cross-wind, low-mass package. Piggy was my spotter. I had to rely pretty heavily on his skills at calculation."

"Yes, yes." Face sounded impatient. "So, anyway, that was step one. Getting in contact with you."

Cheems considered. "And step two was telling me that I was going to be called on to authenticate an artifact, and that I absolutely had to do that, regardless of what I was looking at."

Face nodded.

"What *was* I looking at? The material had a crystalline structure, definitely, but it wasn't diamond or any other precious stone. In fact, it looked a bit like crystallized anthracite."

Kell, standing at the bar, grinned at Cheems. No longer concealed by his helmet, his features were fair, very handsome. His blond hair was worn in a buzz cut, retreating from a widow's peak. "Very good. It's a modified form of anthracite in a crystallized form."

"So I was within centimeters of ten kilos of high explosive?" Cheems thought he could feel the blood draining from his head.

"Nearer fifteen. Plus a transceiver, power unit, and some control chips in the base." Kell shrugged, accepted a drink from Piggy.

Cheems shook his head. "And I was passing it off as a work of art!"

Kell stared at him, clearly miffed. "It *was* a work of art."

Face caught Cheems's attention again. "Teradoc's habits and methods are well known to Intelligence. We had to have bait that required a gem expert to authenticate; we had to have a sneaky profit motive so Teradoc would bring you off-base to do the authentication; and we had to have the bait be very valuable so when trouble erupted he'd grab it and run."

"Back to his base." Cheems felt a chill grip him. "Back to his most secure area, where his treasures are stored. His personal vault."

Face gave him a now-you-get-it smile. "Which is where, exactly?"

"Directly beneath his secure research-and-development laboratories."

"Where, if Intelligence is right, his people are experimenting with plague viruses, self-replicating nonbiological toxins, and the project for which Teradoc kidnapped *you*, Doctor Cheems."

"A sonic device. The idea was that sound waves pitched and cycling correctly could resonate with lightsaber crystals, shattering them."

For once, Face looked concerned. "Could it actually work?"

Cheems shook his head. "Not in a practical way. Against exposed crystals, yes. But lightsaber hilts insulate the crystals too effectively. I couldn't tell the admiral that, though. To tell him 'This can't work' would basically be to say, 'Kill me now, please, I'm of no more use to you.' " Belatedly Cheems realized that he'd said too much. If this miracle rescue was itself a scam, if he was currently surrounded by *Imperial* Intelligence operatives, he'd just signed his own execution order. He gulped.

Runt turned to Face. "I have it." He repositioned the main monitor at his table so others could see.

The monitor showed an overhead map view of the planet's capital city, its Imperial Navy base, the huge bay that bordered both to the east. A blinking yellow light was stationary deep within the base. Then, as they watched, the light faded to nothingness.

Cheems glanced at Face. "Did your device just fail?"

Face shook his head. "No. It was taken into a secure area where comm signals can't penetrate. Its internal circuitry, some of which is a planetary positioning system, knows where it is—the research-and-development labs. Atmospheric pressure meters are telling it how deep in the ground it is. At the depth of Teradoc's personal vault, well . . ."

There was a distant rumble from the west, not even a *boom*. Everyone looked in that direction. There was nothing to see other than the city lights for a moment, then spotlights sprang to life all across the naval base, sweeping across the nighttime sky.

Faraway alarms began to howl.

Face settled back into the couch, comfortable. "Right now, the lower portions of the labs have been vaporized. Pathogen vaults and viral reactors have been breached. Sensors are detecting dangerous pathogens escaping into the air. Vents are slamming shut and sealing, automated decontamination measures are activating. Before the decontamination safety measures are done, everything in that site will be burned to ash and chemically sterilized. Sadly, I suspect Teradoc isn't experiencing any of that, as he was doubtless admiring his new prize when it went off. But we owe him a debt of gratitude. He saved us months' worth of work by smuggling our bomb past his own base security all by himself."

Cheems looked at Piggy. "I could use something very tall and very potent to drink."

Piggy flashed his tusks in a Gamorrean smile. "Coming up."

Face turned to Piggy. "I'll have a salty gaffer. In Teradoc's honor. Candy bug, please." He returned his attention to Cheems. "We'd like you to do one more thing before we get you off-world and into New

Republic space. I'd appreciate it if you'd go below and appraise any gemstone items you find. We'll be turning this yacht and everything on it over to a resistance cell; I'd like to be able to point them at the more valuable items."

Cheems frowned. "This isn't your yacht?"

"Oh, no. It's Teradoc's. We stole it."

Read on for an excerpt from
Star Wars®: Scourge
By Jeff Grubb
Coming soon from Del Rey Books

A Mystery on Makem Te

MANDER ZUMA PURSED HIS LIPS AS HE MOVED THROUGH THE BACK alleys of Makem Te. He was far from the Tract, far from the necropolis that dominated this world, far from the site of Toro Irana's death.

And far from satisfied with what he had discovered so far about the death of his former apprentice.

Word had reached Yavin 4 and the new Jedi Order in the form of a complaint from the Congress of Caliphs that ruled Makem Te, of a blue-skinned Jedi who had killed a Caliph's nephew. Apologies were made through the New Republic's diplomatic channels, but Mander was pulled from his regular duties in the Archives and dispatched to find out what had really happened.

It made perfect sense to Mander. He had taught Toro in the ways of the Force, and had monitored the young Jedi's own reports back to the Order. His own skill set dovetailed nicely with Toro's assigned mission. Yet the older Jedi was still reluctant to leave behind the Archives, to leave Yavin 4 after years of diligent and productive research.

What Mander found on this planet surprised him. Not that Toro had gotten into a fight—the young man had been headstrong and easily riled even when he had been his apprentice, and the Swokes Swokes were by all reports a prickly species to deal with. But the idea that Toro had gotten into an argument so easily, or that he that he had made such a fatal mistake in combat, troubled Mander deeply as he made the long trip from Yavin to Makem Te. As he stepped off the shuttle and breathed the dusty air of this world, the questions swirled within him. What had gone wrong? Had it been his training that had been at fault? Had Mander prepared him insufficiently? Or were there other factors at work?

As a student, Toro had been a superb warrior—limber and smooth, a blue-fleshed blur in combat. More important, he bonded with his lightsaber, treating the blade as an extension of his self. Even in training, Mander was impressed with the young Pantoran's skill and confidence.

Mander himself had none of that easiness in combat. The Force was strong in the older Jedi, but it was directed elsewhere. He could feel the energy moving through him, but his own lightsaber often felt like an alien thing, a lump in his hand. He had come to the Force late in life, as did many in the later years of the Empire, and it showed.

Toro was better with a lightsaber, and Mander was sure that he would have become a fine Jedi Knight. A better Jedi Knight than he. But now Toro was dead and Mander was not sure why.

Mander's first stop was to claim the body and examine it, a rented medical droid at his side burbling commentary. The dried flecks of blood on his apprentice's lips and the broken bones along one side of his body spoke of a sudden, violent end. But there was also a darkening of the young man's veins and arteries—violet against the sea-blue of his flesh—that had not be present in life, and pointed to an external agent at work.

Further, purple crystals budded at the corner of Toro's eyes. Mander was not sure if this was natural to the Pantorans in death, but he assumed it was not, and took a sample of the material. It had a pungent aroma, more cloying than the acrid dust of Makem Te's air. There were similar crystals in the dead Jedi's darkened veins, now stilled of pulsing life. Something had been injected or ingested, he decided.

Toro was under the influence of something else before the fight, Mander thought, and possibly the two events were tied. The older Jedi double-checked his evaluation before consigning Toro's body to the funeral pyre. The Swokes Swokes, regardless of their official indignation, were extremely helpful with funeral arrangements. It was a point of pride for them.

Mander Zuma visited the scene of Toro's death, the restaurant. It had been closed for a period of mourning for the Caliph's nephew, but already the smashed furniture had been stacked to one side for recycling and a new sheet of plate glass installed, replacing the one shattered by Toro's exit. The wait staff was initially unhelpful, but Mander's modest knowledge of Swoken, the native language—combined with a bit of the Force in the voice—helped smooth out the questions. By the end of the interview the staff was positively chatty about the incident.

Yes, the blue-skinned Jedi had been there. He was waiting for someone, he had said. He had been drinking. A lot. Local stuff, but a Rodian came in with another bottle. A gift. The Jedi had insulted the staff. Insulted the other diners. He had gotten into an argument with the Choka Chok, the Caliph's nephew. The Jedi pulled his lightsaber and killed the Choka Chok. Killed five more regulars as well, and had left a dozen regenerating. Screaming in that weird, liquid-sounding, offworlder Basic. Not a proper language at all. Foaming at the mouth. Then he had smashed his way through the window. The wait staff thought he was trying to escape, but had forgotten he was forty floors up. The joke was on him. No, no one had found the Jedi's energy blade, or at least reported that they had found it. Yes, yes, they had the bottle the Rodian brought somewhere around. They were still cleaning up the mess.

The Swokes Swokes provided the bottle and Mander calibrated his medical datapad. A few simple tests on the dregs in the bottle confirmed his hunch—there was something unusual in the scentwine. Potent, unknown, and similar in composition to the crystalline tears at the corners of the corpse's eyes. Distilled out, it had the same cloying smell. The wine's bouquet covered the smell.

Poison, then. The Rodian brought the wine. Was the poison what clouded his judgment at the end?

The possibility left Mander concerned. Why was Toro unwary enough to drink the wine in the first place? A Jedi in the field had to be aware of his surroundings and potential attacks. Had he trusted the Rodian, or whoever the Rodian represented? And what, if anything, did this have to do with his assigned task, to acquire the navigation co-ordinates for the Indrexu Spiral? Was someone trying to stop the New Republic from gaining those codes? Or had Toro stumbled onto something else?

Indeed, scanning the last communications from Toro to the new Jedi Order had been troubling as well. They had been brief, even terse. He had made initial contacts. He had begun negotiations. He was pleased with the progress. Nothing to indicate that there was a problem. Even so, there was a brusqueness in his communiqués that gave Mander pause. Details were missing.

Now the trail led to this warehouse, made of ancient wood, reinforced with the cold iron that was so much a part of Swokes Swokes architecture. There were few Rodians on Makem Te, and it was relatively easy to track Toro's deadly wine steward back here. A Rodian family cartel ran a small trade out of these warehouses, trafficking in ornate funeral plaques and reliquaries and other offworld items.

The darkness of the alley cloaked him more effectively than any mind trick, but the lock was old and stubborn, and at last Mander used the Force to snap the hasp. So much for getting in and getting out without leaving any trace, he thought. Carefully, he slid the door open, but was met only with a hollow echo of the sliding metal. He slipped inside, leaving enough of a gap that he could leave quickly if things went bad.

Mander moved quietly at first, but, it was quickly clear that no one seemed to be present. Moonlight from the frosted skylights overhead shone on a bare floor. Mander reached into a vest pocket and pulled out a set of magnaspecs—two pinkish lenses set in hexagonal frames. He unfolded the lenses and placed them on the bridge of his nose; magnets in the frame held them there, pinching his flesh slightly. When he tapped the side of the lenses they issued a soft, pale red glow, heightening the available light in the dim warehouse.

Large wooden racks stood in neat ordered rows from floor to ceiling along the length of the structure. Empty cargo containers were lined along one wall, and a trio of manual loadlifters—great walker engines with huge spatulate hands—along the other. These Rodians were too poor, or too cheap, for droid-operated versions. The shelves were heavily laden with blank epitaph plates and bolts of funeral shrouds, all covered in a thin coating of dust. Scraps and more dust were heaped in the corners as well. Whatever business was being done out of this warehouse had precious little to do with mortuary arrangements.

In the center of the room was a pile of broken crates, damaged and abandoned in a rush to clear out. Clear spots showed where other crates once stood, and the dust was disturbed by the broad feet of the loadlifters. Somewhere far off, in some connecting warehouse, there was a soft thunder of people moving crates, but this place was devoid of workers.

Mander frowned. Whoever poisoned Toro expected someone to come after them, and had probably decided to put a few planets between them and their pursuers. No doubt the warehouse was under an assumed name and behind three shell companies. Tracking them down would not be easy.

Mander poked through the trash with his toe—funeral robes and tapestries, metal plates with Swokes Swokes memorials—about three or four containers' worth that had been breached and abandoned. And there, glittering in the moonlight, something dark and crystalline.

The Jedi knelt down next to the pile and examined the crystals. They were purplish, dark almost to the point of being black. He sniffed it, and it gave off a rich, pungent aroma. Spice, but unlike any he had seen before. He pulled out a plasticlear envelope and scooped a handful of crystals into it.

That was when he knew he was not alone. It could have been a shadow against the moonlight or a footstep landing too heavily, but at once he knew that someone else was in the warehouse with him. He rose slowly from his examination, trying to move naturally, his hand fumbling with the strap of the lightsaber. Still, he engaged it and brought the ignited blade up, glowing green, before the first blaster bolt erupted.

Mander parried the energy discharge, trying to send it back to his

attacker but succeeding only in deflecting it among the racks of epitaph markers. Inwardly he cursed at his lack of skill. Another shot unleashed, again from near the warehouse's entrance, and again Mander
turned the energy pulse aside, but only just, and it scorched the wall
behind him. Mander reminded himself that he was in a wooden building containing flammable funeral shrouds. Too many such stray shots
would be a bad thing.

"I can do this all day," he lied to the darkness. "Why don't you
come out and we can talk?"

There was a shadow against the doorway, and for a moment Mander was sure that his assailant would try to flee. Instead, a lone figure
walked into a rectangular square of moonlight. Smoke swirled from
the barrel of her DL-22 heavy blaster. She was almost Mander's
height, and even in the pale radiance Mander could see that her flesh
was a rich blue, marked with yellow swirls on each cheek. Long hair—
a deeper blue in shade, almost to the color of night—was worn short
in the front, woven in a thick braid down the back. A Pantoran, then,
like Toro. Her lips were a thin, grim line and her eyes flashed with
anger.

"Why are you shooting at me?" said Mander calmly, as if being shot
at in a warehouse were a common occurrence for him.

"I'm here for justice," she said, and the barrel came up. Despite
himself, Mander brought up his lightsaber in defense, but she did not
fire.

"Justice is good," said Mander, trying to keep his voice casual. "I'm
seeking justice as well. Perhaps you'd like to help me find some." He
paused and added, "You know, I once trained a Pantoran in the ways
of the Force."

This time she did shoot, and Mander almost toppled back onto the
pile of trash bringing his blade up. Almost too late, and as it was he deflected the bolt upward instead of back. There was the distant crash of
a shattered skylight.

"You're the one responsible for Toro's death, then," said the Pantoran, her words as sharp as a vibroblade's edge.

"Relative?" asked Mander, willing himself to be ready for another
shot. It did not come.

"Sister."

Mander forced himself to relax, or at least give the impression of relaxing. He deactivated his lightsaber, even though he wasn't sure he could reignite it fast enough should she choose to fire. "You're Reen Irana, then," he said. "Toro spoke to me of you."

The blaster jerked toward him for a moment, but the Pantoran did not fire. Mander added quickly, "I was not here when Toro died. I was back at the academy on Yavin Four. I came here when we heard the news. To find out what happened. And to finish Toro's assignment."

The blaster wavered, just a bit, but at last she pointed it away from the Jedi. Even in the moonlight, he could see a wetness glistening at the corner of her eyes. "It's your fault," she managed at last, her voice throaty with grief. Mander waited, giving her time to gather her thoughts. When she spoke again, the iron had returned to her words. "Toro was a dreamer, and you took him to become a Jedi and now he's dead. You're responsible."

Mander held his palms out and said simply, "Yes."

Reen was startled at the admission, and the barrel of her weapon wavered. She had apparently expected the Jedi to say many things, but not this.

Mander looked hard at the young Pantoran—he could see the resemblance to Toro in her face. He continued, "Yes I am responsible. Every man's journey is his own, but I did train your brother, and he was here on Makem Te on Jedi business. So yes, we . . . I . . . put him in harm's way. And . . . I failed to prepare him for what he faced here. That is why I am here. I want to find out who poisoned your brother, to see justice brought against them."

For the first time, the Pantoran seemed confused. "Poison?" she managed.

"I believe so," said Mander. "I found something strange in his blood. And now there is this." He held up the clear envelope with the crystals. "I found it here in the warehouse."

The Pantoran kept her blaster aimed at the Jedi, but reached out with the other hand. Mander held the envelope out to her, and she took it, taking a few steps back immediately in case this was a trick.

Reen stared at the purplish crystals, then shook her head. She holstered her blaster, and for his part Mander returned his now-inert lightsaber to his belt.

"I think it is the poison that was used," said Mander. "A Rodian administered it with some wine he brought to your brother in the restaurant. That was why Toro was unable to defend himself at his full abilities. Why he made such a mistake in combat and plunged out the window."

Another noise in the darkness around them. Mander's head came up. It was not from outside the warehouse this time. Inside. Someone familiar with the area, who knew where to step. "Hold on," he said. "Others are here."

Reen began to say, "Don't worry. That's just—" But her words were cut off as Mander grabbed her and pulled her down. Blaster bolts erupted from three sides, firing into the pile of abandoned crates.

Reen had her own blaster out in a flash, and for a wild moment Mander was afraid she was going to use it on him. But instead she returned fire against the assault, using the discarded shipping containers as cover.

Mander rose to a crouch, his lightsaber ignited and at the ready. The shots were heavy but not well placed, and he managed to bounce a few of them back. There was a shout of pain, and a string of curses in Swoken. Mander thought he must have gotten one of them.

"I'd say a dozen," shouted Reen. "Some of them up on the racks. Swokes Swokes. Some Rodians, too."

"Must be the Rodians that use the warehouse," responded Mander.

"I know the clan." said Reen, bringing down a pair. "Bomu family. I recognize the facial tattoos. We're pinned down!"

"Hang on," said Mander, "I'm going to level the playing field."

Reen may have said something but Mander didn't pay attention. Instead he leapt forward, somersaulting toward one of the racks the Rodians were using as a perch. Blaster bolts fell around him, but he didn't use his blade to block. Rather, he pulled it effortlessly through the rack's iron supports, slicing the metal easily. The entire set of racks shuddered, and then began to collapse in on itself, the shriek of the metal matched by the surprised shouts of the ambushers.

Reen was at his side. "What did you do?"

"I made a new pile of trash to hide behind," said Mander as one of the surviving Swokes Swokes rose from the debris, a thick-barreled blaster in his hand. One swipe with the blade cut the weapon in two, and then the Swokes Swokes fell backward as Reen discharged a bolt square in the attacker's face.

There was a short pause in the battle, and then the blasterfire started again, heavier than before. Looking back, Mander saw that their previous hiding place was on fire, and the flames were already spreading through the bolts of funeral cloth and to the room's supports. The Rodians had climbed down to the ground, trying to surround the pair. They were now clear in the firelight.

"They're trying to burn us out. Can you make it to the door?" asked Mander, but Reen just shook her head and brought down a Rodian from across the room.

Mander looked across the open floor between him and the entrance. Alone, on his best day, he might be able to make it. Carrying the Pantoran, he doubted he could get halfway before the crossfire caught him. He was about the chance it anyway when something extremely large shifted in the background.

It was one of the manual loadlifters, wading into a squad of Swokes Swokes. The huge flat feet smashed one, while the others broke and ran as it spun and slammed into another set of racks, toppling them against their neighbors in a chain of collapsing shelves. The Rodians and Swokes Swokes started pulling back, firing behind them to deter pursuit. Perched in the control pit of the lifter, limned by sparking control screens, was a Bothan—long-faced and furry.

Reen put a hand on Mander's shoulder. "Don't worry. He's with me."

The Bothan was having trouble handling the loadlifter, and as he tried to get the walker under control it grazed one of the already-burning roof supports. The support groaned menacingly, and parts of the roof and skylight started to cascade down around them.

"About time you showed up!" bellowed Reen at the pilot of the stumbling walker. "Now get us out of here before this place comes down around us."

The Bothan got the loadlifter under something like control, and brought one of the large pallet-hands level to the floor. Reen grabbed on, and Mander leapt ahead of her, turning to help her up. Then the pair gripped the sides of the lifter as the Bothan maneuvered it toward the doors through a tunnel of the now-flaming warehouse. The large door was still almost completely shut, but at the last moment the Bothan spun the lifter around and slammed through it backward, smashing the door off its hinges.

Then they were outside, tromping though the alleys. The loadlifter got clear of the worst of the fire, and set the pair down. The Bothan himself slid down from the side of the now-smoking control pit. Whatever the Bothan had done to get it working had set its internal electronics on fire.

"I thought you Jedi were never supposed to be surprised," said Reen.

"I was distracted," said Mander, trying to keep the irritation within himself out of his voice. She was right. Despite her presence, he should have noticed their assailants creeping into their positions.

In the distance there were shouts and klaxons. The local authorities were responding to the fire, and the flames were clear along the roofline now.

"We need to be elsewhere," said Reen. "A pity we didn't get one of the Rodians alive."

"We found the poison that they used on your brother," said Mander. "And we know that they're willing to kill to cover their tracks. For the moment, that's enough."

About the Type

This book was set in Galliard, a typeface designed by Matthew Carter for the Mergenthaler Linotype Company in 1978. Galliard is based on the sixteenth-century typefaces of Robert Granjon.